REIFFEN'S
CHOICE

Jack,

   Keep those
creative thoughts
flowing!

   —S. C. Butler

REIFFEN'S CHOICE

Book One
of the
Stoneways Trilogy

S. C. BUTLER

A TOM DOHERTY ASSOCIATES BOOK
NEW YORK

REIFFEN'S CHOICE

A Tor Book
Published by Tom Doherty Associates, LLC
175 Fifth Avenue
New York, NY 10010

www.tor.com

Tor® is a registered trademark of Tom Doherty Associates, LLC.

Library of Congress Cataloging-in-Publication Data

Butler, S. C. (Sam C.)
Reiffen's choice / S.C. Butler.—1st ed.
    p. cm. — (The Stoneways trilogy ; bk. 1)
"A Tom Doherty Associates book."
ISBN-13: 978-0-765-31477-2 (acid-free paper)
ISBN-10: 0-765-31477-0
1. Kings and rulers—Succession—Fiction.   2. Wizards—Fiction.   I. Title.
    PS3602.U884R45   2006
    813'.6—dc22

                                                          2006005063

First Edition: September 2006

Printed in the United States of America

0   9   8   7   6   5   4   3   2   1

For my parents and my daughters

Contents

USSENE

"For down within the caverns blind
The mansions of the Dwarves are mined;
The lamps of Uhle glow undefined
From deep within cut hearts of stone . . ."

Darkflood

The Great Forest

The Whitewing

FIRRON

VALING   Lugger

The High Bavadars

Far Mouthing

The Inner Sea

CUSPOR

The Toes

The Birdings

100

100 Miles

To The Pearl Islands

SIMMAS

VALING

Twelve years since Dwarves broke the rule
of dark below and, led by Uhle,
emerged to moon and sun.

Twelve years since the Wizards fled
and left behind so many dead
beside the torrent's run.

Twelve years since a princess fair
brought forth in joy wed with despair,
from widow's weeds, a son.

Twelve years since, in one boy's life.
Now Wizards rise with fire and knife.
The Three shall seek the one.

–MINDRELL THE BARD

1

Bear and Boy

ne warm spring day in Valing, a large, fat bear sunned himself on the gray stone of the Neck. His russet coat gleamed, sleek as a nokken's: the long mountain winter didn't seem to have bothered him at all. Half-asleep or half-awake, he lay comfortably between the orchard and the top of the cliff, where the scent of the apple blossoms was almost as lovely as the hum of the bees. Behind him the lake glistened a deep and sparkling blue. Except for a long plume of spray from the falls to the west, there wasn't a cloud in the sky.

Beyond the orchard, however, the Manor was much more active. It was First Feast that night and everyone was busy with three more tasks than usual. The kitchen was filled with the bustle of crockery and cooking; men and women darted like bats on a summer evening across the long porches that looked out over the orchard. In the schoolroom, the children squirmed hopefully as tantalizing smells drifted in through the open windows from the scullery below.

Avender watched from his seat at the window as one of the undercooks rolled a barrel of slops into the yard. The pigs in the pen next door poked eager snouts through the fence and grunted at the fresh stains on the undercook's apron. But, when Tinnet returned to the kitchen without feeding the hogs, Avender switched his attention back to the front of the schoolroom. Nolo was seated on the desk before the class that morning, instead of their regular teacher, and Avender was paying complete attention. He always listened when Nolo spoke, no matter how many times he had heard the story. That was because Nolo was a Dwarf, and Avender, along with everyone else in Valing, was always interested in anything having to do with Dwarves.

Sunshine streamed through the windows, brightening even the dull iron circlet Nolo used to hold back his wild gray hair. The younger children in the front row, not used to seeing the Dwarf so closely, stared at his broad, bare feet. Each toe looked like a knob of gnarled stone. But they were still quite clearly toes because every once in a while Nolo wiggled and stretched them or, if he had an itch, scratched between them with his equally stony fingers.

"Then what happened?" asked little Atty Peaks from the front row: Avender knew the younger boy was very much in awe of the Dwarf's toes, because that was how he had felt at Atty's age. Probably Atty had heard that Nolo could squeeze pebbles to dust between them, and was desperate to see him do it.

Nolo glowered good-naturedly at the small boy. "If you'd pay attention, lad," he said, "and stop asking so many questions, you might hear what I'm saying."

Half-smothered laughter swept through Atty's classmates. The Dwarf looked up. Raising his heavy eyebrows at the older students in the back of the room, he warned, "None of that, now. Atty's doing the best he can. He's not heard the tale before. What he knows about Mennon or Wizards wouldn't half-fill an ore car."

The younger children, safe in the schoolroom on a beautiful spring day, shivered delightedly at the mention of Wizards. Avender and the older ones pretended not to care.

Away in the orchard the bear lifted his snout to sniff the breeze. Something much more delightful than the scent of apple blossoms was now drifting his way. His black nose wiggled. His small eyes opened. Heaving himself up from his comfortable rock, he began sniffing the air with real interest.

"Of course," Nolo was saying back in the classroom, "Mennon was very interested in Issinlough when he woke. Only we Bryddin had ever seen our shining city before, or the Abyss, for that matter. When Mennon first learned to speak he went with Uhle to the bottom of the lowest tower in the city and pointed at the blackness below. 'What's that?' he asked. 'Why, that's the Abyss,' Uhle answered. 'How far is it to the bottom?' Mennon wanted to know. 'There is no bottom,' said Uhle."

"Is there really no bottom?" asked Atty.

Nolo shook his head. "No, lad, no bottom. Issinlough hangs on the underside of the world, and beyond Issinlough there's nothing. Whatever's left of Brydds himself might lie down there in the deep dark, but there's no bottom to the Abyss."

"And no sky, either?"

"No, no sky, either. We Bryddin never knew about the sky till Mennon told us, nor about the sun and moon. But once Uhle heard about them, nothing could keep him from finding the surface. 'Brighter than the brightest of your lamps,' was the way Mennon described the sun to us. 'Brighter than all your lamps rolled into one.'" Nolo stroked his long beard thoughtfully for a moment before he went on.

"Uhle had always dreamed of such a light. He and I searched for it for years. But once he knew it existed, Uhle knew right away how to reach it. We might not have been able to go up the way Mennon had come down, but we could certainly dig our way to the surface once we knew it was there. As all of you know, we Bryddin are very good at digging." He wiggled his fingers and stubby toes. Atty's eyes widened.

"Was that the Sun Road?" asked a girl Avender's age from the back of the class. Avender rolled his eyes, knowing she already knew the answer as well as he did.

"That's what it is now, Ferris," answered Nolo. "But when we first built it, it was hardly more than a long tunnel. We were in a hurry, at least those of us who took up the work. There are still some in Issinlough who wonder what we need with the sun and moon, let alone trees and flowers."

"Or ale, right, Nolo?" teased a boy who sat to Avender's left. Avender grinned. Teasing their regular teacher would have been unthinkable, but Nolo was a much easier master. The Dwarf himself laughed at the joke, his beard rolling in little waves across his chest.

"That's right, lad. Mennon hadn't told us a thing about ale yet. Perhaps if he had, we'd have dug a lot quicker."

The whole class laughed. While they were laughing, a lumbering shape appeared in the yard below. The bear, following the scent he had sniffed out on the back of the breeze, had found his way from the orchard to the side of the sty. The pigs rushed back to the fence as soon as they saw him to snort and squeal at their old foe. They knew what he was up to as soon as he appeared. The bear, however, ignored the pigs completely.

But their squealing did attract the notice of the students closest to the windows above the yard. There was a quiet rustling among the desks as they shuffled about for better views. Avender poked his neighbor with his foot.

"Reiffen," he whispered, nodding toward the window. "Redburr's at the slops again."

The other boy's eyebrows rose with interest. Carefully he stretched across the desks for a better view.

At the front of the room Nolo continued his tale, completely unaware of the activity at the windows. "Can anyone tell me," he asked, "where we Bryddin were when we finally broke out onto the surface? No, not you, Ferris. You can't answer every question. Let's hear from one of the younger lads or lasses who haven't heard the tale before. All right, Nell, why don't you tell us."

Nell stood up straight and tall at her desk beside Atty, very proud of her opportunity. "Um, was it Grangore?" she asked.

"Absolutely correct!" Nolo slapped his thigh hard, almost causing the legs on the desk to give out below him. Nell beamed.

At the pigsty, the great bear rested his forepaws on the rim of the slops barrel and stuffed his heavy head inside. The barrel wobbled but didn't fall. On the other side of the fence the angry pigs began digging furiously as they tried to get at the thief beyond the railing. Contented grunts echoed from inside the wooden barrel.

"It was a beautiful evening," the Dwarf was saying to the class, "the first evening I ever saw. We came out on the middle slopes of Aloslocin, and the sun was just beginning to set behind Ivismundra. Uhle came out first, but it was a while before he returned for the rest of us. We were afraid of coming up beneath a lake or a river, you see, and had dammed off the upper end of the tunnel. Then we had to take another minute after Uhle pulled down the dam to put on our goggles, just in case the sun was too bright for our eyes. Here, I brought mine in to class today so everyone could have a look. Cut the lenses from a large topaz, I did."

He handed a pair of heavy goggles to Atty, who dropped them, he was so overwhelmed by the honor. Meanwhile the bear had snuffled down all the easy pickings at the top of the barrel and had twisted around on his hind legs to improve his leverage into the tub. Several times he came close to losing his balance, but each time he shifted to the side at the last second and caught himself before the barrel tipped.

"That's real batwing." Nolo pointed out the goggle straps, while those pupils still paying attention to him carefully handed them around the classroom. "Very soft and strong, batwing. No lighter leather to be found, under sun or ground. There's a little stretch in it, too, so they fit tight around your head. Say, what are you all looking at out the window there? Avender? Reiffen?"

Nolo had finally noticed that most of the class was gathered around the windows and no longer even pretending to pay attention to him. Not wanting to miss out on whatever was happening in the yard below, he hopped off the desk and hurried across the room.

"Not again." He groaned when he saw the backside of the bear sticking up out of the barrel. Leaning out over the sill on his tiptoes, he called down to the alley, "Hey there! Redburr! Get out of there, you overgrown raccoon! You know better than that!"

By this time the bear had climbed all the way up onto the top of the barrel, his head and shoulders crammed greedily inside. He was in no position to hear anyone's scolding. The barrel was very strong, but the bear was very heavy. Both rocked back and forth precariously as the bear shoveled through the dainties within. But that balancing act was too delicate to last more than a moment. The tub teetered, then toppled with a crash. Several smaller barrels nearby were also smashed as Redburr was thrown crashing on top of them and through the fence around the sty. A pair of fish heads and half a moldy cabbage flew high into the air. Shining in the sun, they floated for a moment right in front of the schoolroom windows, then splashed back down in the dirty alley below.

Briefly the bear lay stunned in a pile of slops, barrel staves, and fencing. Flecks of broccoli and yesterday's gravy speckled his ruddy coat. Then the pigs were on him. He rose up with half an old cheese in his mouth and clubbed a few of the more vicious sows with a swing from each of his heavy forepaws. Piglets squealed as they streamed through the hole in the fence. The alley was filled with guzzling hogs and slippery bear, all fighting over the same hunks of grease and filthy vegetables. They careened back and forth in the buttery mess, bashing fresh holes in the fence and sending the rain barrel at the corner of the kitchen flying. The water sluiced out across the ground beneath them; everything was soon churned to mud by their scuffling.

The door to the kitchen flew open. Hern herself stormed out, her stoutest broom in hand. Her first shout brought Redburr immediately to his senses. Hastily he scrambled to his feet and shouldered the heaviest sow aside. Then he took off back down the alley toward the orchard with all the speed he could muster, a rotten pumpkin bumping on his backside, his prize cheese still dripping in his mouth.

"That's right!" called Nolo from the window, barely able to contain his laughter. "You run away! As if we haven't all seen you at your work already!"

Hern shook her broom and shouted in turn, "You great fat rug! I've told you a hundred times to keep out of the slops! How're we supposed to get any bacon! I'm going to ban you from the feast tonight, I am!"

She turned and stared at the rest of the kitchen staff, who had come out behind her to enjoy the show.

"And what are you all gaping at?" she demanded. She stood with hands on hips, even though she was still holding her broom. "Get these pigs back in the pen! We're behind as it is! We'll never be ready for tonight! And which one of you put that cheese in with the rest of the garbage? Was that you, Tinnet? You know that fool of a bear can't control himself when he gets a whiff of spoiled cheese! You'd better get to work cleaning up this mess before I really lose my temper!"

Plowing straight into the middle of the hogs, she kicked left and right and batted at them with both ends of her broom. The sows fled in terror, grunting as they scrambled back to the safety of their pen, but a few of the piglets managed to escape. They tore off into the orchard with the kitchen staff chasing behind. The children cheered them on.

Hern looked up at the schoolroom. Her eyes narrowed. Every student in sight ducked back inside before she could light into any of them in turn. Nolo wisely followed their example.

He retrieved his goggles from where they had been dropped on the floor and said, "I guess that's the end of this lesson." The students gave another cheer. "Maybe you should all report downstairs to Hern. I think she's going to need all the help she can get catching those pigs."

Another cheer went up, louder than the first, especially from the younger children. Much as everyone liked hearing the Dwarf tell them stories of the Stoneways, chasing pigs was even better. No one waited to be dismissed; they fled through the desks and out the door in a clatter of shoes and shouts of glee.

Avender, however, wasn't so lucky. Nolo caught his arm as he was on his way out the door. Reiffen and Ferris saw it all, and ducked away before they were stopped as well.

"I need you," said the Dwarf.

"You let everyone else go!" Avender knew what was coming, but Nolo's grip was far too strong for him to twist away. "Reiffen and I are supposed to go get mussels from Longback."

"The mussels can wait." Nolo's eyes twinkled beneath his bushy brows. "The Shaper needs you more. Someone has to help him clean up before the feast, lad. And you're the one to do it."

Avender groaned. Grooming a filthy bear was the last thing he wanted to do.

"I've another job I promised Hern I'd help with," the Dwarf went on, "or I'd take care of him myself. Then I could give him the thumping he needs. Now go on and do as I've asked. There may be something in it for you later, if you do."

Avender shuffled off. There was no use hoping he would not be able to find the bear. He had lived his entire life at the Manor and knew every rambling inch of the place, from the highest garret to the deepest cellar. And there were really only a few places Redburr was likely to go. Once the Shaper started to think straight—and there was every chance he had, now that Hern had shocked some sense back into him—he would probably head down to the lake to bathe. Redburr, with his bottomless appetite, looked forward to First Feast as much as anyone; he knew Hern would never allow him in unless he was completely clean. Otherwise he had a tendency to overexcite the dogs. And the quickest way to the lake was through the cellars and down the long stair to the lower dock at the bottom of the cliff.

From the hall outside the schoolroom Avender could still hear the uproar in the yard. Reluctantly he turned away and headed for the cellars. Redburr's most likely route downstairs would be through the back of the house, on the other side of the Great Hall. There was no way he would have risked going through the kitchen to face Hern and her broom again. Sure enough, the boy began to find bits and pieces from the slop barrel on the floor as he neared the back stair. He picked the fallen garbage up as he found it, knowing he would just be sent back to finish the job if he neglected to take care of it now.

The messy trail continued down to the busy cellars. It looked like everyone in the Manor, and not a few from Eastbay and the nearer farms, were carrying sacks of smoked fish and sides of bacon, or rolling great cheese wheels and casks of ale and cider along the stone floors between bushel baskets of cabbages and carrots.

More than a few of them laughed when they saw the boy. "After the bear, are you?" they called. "Well, you won't miss him, that's sure enough. What a stench!"

Ignoring them, Avender hurried on through the stone storerooms. The stair to the lower dock had been cut from the Neck and spiraled down through the rock to the lake, many fathoms below. Lighting the lamp that stood ready at the top of the steps, the boy peered into the darkness. A faint smell of rotten cheese and sodden fur greeted him, but no sound drifted up from the cold stone. The bear would not have bothered with a lamp and was probably already at the bottom.

Avender started down, light in hand. His long legs threw tramping shadows along the wall beside him. But he didn't have far to go. After the second or third turn he heard the click of the bear's claws on the stone ahead. "Redburr?" he called, cupping his free hand to his mouth. "It's me, Avender. If you're coming up fast you'd better slow down or you'll run me over."

The clicking slowed, then stopped completely. A moment later Redburr's muzzle appeared hesitantly around the curve below, followed by the rest of his shaggy head, now dripping wet. His eyes gleamed in the lamplight. For a moment he looked more like a red-wooled sheep than a bear.

"Nolo sent me," said the boy.

"Nolo? Is he mad at me, too?"

The fancy that Redburr was a sheep disappeared as soon as he spoke. His deep voice rumbled out from his furry chest like a rock slide tumbling out the mouth of a cave.

"What do you think?" answered Avender.

"You think Hern's really going to ban me from the feast?"

"So you heard that?" The boy picked a piece of soggy turnip out of the tangled fur at the top of the bear's massive head. His hand was only a little larger than Redburr's ear. "You should've stayed for your punishment. Now she's just going to brood, and that'll make it worse."

"You think I should go take what's coming to me?"

Avender shook his head. "It's too late. Now you're better off staying out of her way till tonight. Then, if you're lucky, she'll be so busy she'll forget all about you."

Redburr nodded, his great head swinging through a much larger arc than any human's. Then he noticed the water dripping from his fur had begun to pool on the stair. Extending his long red tongue, he began to lap it up. Avender added the turnip to the mix, then turned and started back toward the cellars. Behind him there was a quick gulping sound, followed by the padding of heavy paws and the click of claws on stone.

There were a few snickers as they passed back through the cellars, but not many. The bear was too big, and too honored, to be made fun of for doing what was natural enough for him. He hadn't hibernated since arriving in Valing almost ten years ago and, though he could go without hibernation for a long time, the lack of a good, long sleep sometimes confused him. Occasionally he forgot he was living with humans and not deep in the mountain woods, usually when he was around food. But in the end Redburr, who was always very sorry afterward when he forgot himself, was too important to be sent away. He was, after all, a Shaper. Even King Brannis would put up with him if Redburr ever took it into his head to spend ten years in Rimwich.

Together, bear and boy climbed up through the Manor to Redburr's den. Avender thought it wise to keep to the back of the house, as the bear was still dripping and any extra damage to carpets or polished floors would only be added to both their accounts. When they finally reached the top of the house, Redburr crossed straight through the litter of old logs and empty beehives that filled his room to stand at the window with his front paws on the sill, where the strong breeze could ruffle his wet fur. Avender hurried to find the combs and brushes among the husks of bread and stolen jam pots on the floor. If the bear's fur dried before he got to work, untangling it would be impossible.

He saw clouds in the sky when he joined Redburr at the window. In the distance mountains marched down both sides of the lake. Patches of gray shadow skimmed across the dark blue surface along with puffs of sail. Avender reminded himself that the sooner he was done, the sooner he would be able to go out on the lake with Ferris and Reiffen.

He turned to the bear's shaggy coat. As he had feared, the fur was already matted in great tangles and sticky tufts. Choice reminders of Redburr's foraging remained despite his plunge in the lake. The boy set to work currying the thick fur back into some semblance of respectability. Occasionally Redburr asked for an extra scratch or two on his back or belly, and pointed out every time Avender missed a particularly sticky patch. When he had been smaller, Avender had delighted in plunging his hand and face into the thickets of the bear's pelt, and welcomed any chance to rub him down after a swim. But now that Avender was older, he saw it only for the work it was.

"You could at least have used some soap," he said as he worked the remains of one of that morning's muffins off the bear's hip.

"Old Mortin wouldn't lend me any. He said he wouldn't be able to use it himself once I was through with it." Scratching his stomach with his enormous claws, the bear grumbled as Avender pulled the comb hard through a patch on his shoulder that seemed glued together. "I wish Nolo'd sent Ferris up instead of you. She doesn't pull half my fur out with each pass. Ow!"

He cuffed the boy out of the way, not quite gently, and went to work on the troublesome spot with claws and tongue.

"You know," said Avender as he moved to a safer position, "if you'd stop rooting around in the slops you wouldn't have to go through this."

"Maybe that's why I do it, boy," replied the bear, licking away at his sticky fur. "I like rooting around in slops. I am a bear, you know. Mmm. I think I remember that bit."

"You don't always act like a bear. And other bears can't talk."

"You know better than that. I'm the bear of bears. Even when I change into something else I'm still really a bear." As he spoke, a fly buzzed in through the window. Redburr snapped his great jaws at it without even thinking. Large, sharp teeth that might have bitten Avender's arm in two closed with a loud crunch.

"It'd be a lot easier for the rest of us if you'd just be human for the party tonight." The boy flicked some soggy mushrooms on the floor as the bear turned to let him groom the finer fur at his throat. Redburr eyed the mushrooms for a moment before deciding to leave them for later. "Then you could clean yourself up. And you know how nervous those traders from Lugger get when they see a bear sitting next to them at dinner."

"Let them be nervous." Redburr rubbed a heavy paw across his nose. "I can eat more when I'm a bear. And I've got that trip into the mountains tomorrow with Ranner. If I bothered to change now I'd just have to change back again. You know too much shifting wears me out. It'll do those bead sellers good to rub elbows with Mother Nature for a few hours."

Avender combed on without saying anything more. Had it been Ferris doing the grooming, the conversation would never have lagged for a moment. And Reiffen would have asked questions about history and places in the world he had never been. But Avender worked quietly and steadily untangling this knot and unraveling that. After a while the bear began to hum.

"What song is that?" asked the boy.

"A new one I heard part of the other night." Redburr began peeling long strips of wood off one of the old logs that lay scattered about the room.

"Was that when you and Nolo came home drunk from the Bass and Bull?"

"We weren't drunk. You can't get a Bryddin drunk. And there isn't enough ale at the Bass to get me drunk."

"Ferris said you were drunk."

"How would Ferris know? She didn't see us come home."

"No, but they were talking about it in the kitchen the next day. And there were those broken benches in the front hall." Avender picked some pumpkin seeds off the bear's back. Somehow they had burrowed into his fur and had to be rooted out like rocks from a garden.

"That wasn't me," said the bear. "That was Nolo. He wasn't paying attention when he sat down. He knows those benches aren't strong enough to hold him."

"Who sang it?"

"Who sang what?"

"The song you were humming."

"Oh, that. That was Mindrell. A rhymer from the north."

"Is he going to sing tonight?"

"He's supposed to." Redburr raised his head and growled in his deep, rough voice:

"*Beyond the west, beyond the night;*
Beyond the waning of the light . . ."

He stopped and licked his nose. " 'Mennon's Ride,' he called it. Said he'd give us more tonight if we asked him to the feast."

Avender combed silently through a patch thick with butter and gravy on the bear's flank. Most rhymers who came to Valing tended to sing "The Fall of Ablen" once they saw Giserre and her son. Avender was glad this one was going to be different.

Redburr peered at the boy. Slovenly the Shaper was, and always hungry; but there wasn't much that escaped his notice when he paid attention. And he had known Avender for most of the boy's short life.

"It's a good life we have in Valing, isn't it?" he said.

Avender shrugged and kept brushing.

"What will you do when Reiffen goes away?"

The boy looked up. The bear was watching him carefully, his small, black eyes buttoned close upon him.

"Is Reiffen going away?" Avender asked.

"Giserre's been talking about it more and more lately. He can't live all his life in Valing. He has to go to Malmoret eventually."

Avender stood still for a moment. When he went back to brushing Redburr's coat his touch was harder, though the fur had already grown soft and glossy beneath his hand.

"Don't tell me you and Reiffen haven't talked about it," the bear went on. "But you don't need to worry. Giserre'll take you with them if you ask her."

Avender stopped in mid-stroke and looked hopefully at the bear. "You think so?"

Redburr raised his forepaws in a shrug. "You and Reiffen aren't the only ones who've talked about it," he said. "I've already spoken to Giserre. But convincing Hern'll be much harder."

"Why would she mind?"

"You're her ward, for one thing. And she doesn't particularly like the idea of Giserre and Reiffen going, either. She thinks it's too dangerous. It's only been two years since Brannis last tried to have Reiffen killed."

Avender remembered that day all too well, Giserre raging in cold fury through the Manor and Redburr with dark red stains on his heavy paws. Not that anyone had ever seen fit to tell him or Reiffen the whole story.

"Hern can't stop them if they want to go," Avender said. He and Reiffen had spent many a long night talking about just that possibility. "Their people are in Malmoret and Rimwich. Not Valing."

"No, she can't," the bear agreed. "But she can stop you. Your people are here, not there. And it's one thing to be Reiffen's fast friend in Valing and another altogether in Malmoret."

Avender made no reply. He knew it was true. Whom their fathers had been meant little in Valing, but in Wayland and Banking it would mean much more. He just hoped Hern understood how miserable he would be if she didn't let him go.

"How many times," asked the Shaper, "did you knock Reiffen down the first time you met?"

Avender didn't need to think to answer. Old Mortin and the other wags in the Manor still liked to tease both boys about the time someone had finally stood up to the young prince. "Five," he said.

"And when was the last time you knocked him down?"

"I don't know. A couple days ago, I guess. But that wasn't a real fight. We were just wrestling. We haven't had a real fight in years."

"I didn't say you had. Ahh, that feels good." The bear arched his back as Avender scratched him just below the shoulder. "But if Hern does let you go south with Giserre, you'd better remember not to knock him down anymore, no matter how much he deserves it. You could find a sword at your throat for less, especially in Malmoret."

"Then I'll have to knock the swordsman down, too."

The bear gave the boy a friendlier cuff than the first had been, but Avender was ready for him this time and jumped out of the way. Redburr laughed, his sharp teeth flashing. He was clean and dry now, his ruddy coat glowing after all of Avender's attention.

"Go on," the Shaper said. "Go get those mussels. I can taste the stew already. And tell Nolo when you find him, next time he should send Ferris."

Avender didn't have to be told twice. Without another word he threw down his brushes and bounded out of the den in search of his friends.

2

Skimmer

here you are," said Ferris. She and Reiffen were sitting on the stair one landing below the bear's. "We've been waiting for you forever. Mother's starting to get impatient for her mussels."

"Thanks. You didn't have to wait, you know."

"We knew you'd want to come along."

Avender leaned on the banister beside his friends and wished he had found Reiffen alone. As long as Ferris was with them, he couldn't very well bring up the subject of Malmoret. Hern would never let her only child go off on a journey of which she didn't approve, and talking about it in front of Ferris would only make Ferris angry.

"Looking for you was a lot more interesting than chasing pigs." Reiffen pulled himself up from his seat and stood beside his friend. He was slightly taller than Avender, but Avender was much more sturdy.

"Interesting for you, maybe," said Ferris. "I don't know where you went. But I've been waiting here half an hour and it's been pretty boring. At least I knew where to look for him."

"You could have come up and helped," said Avender. "That wouldn't have been boring."

"And smell like grubby bear?" Ferris shook her head. "No thank you. I already took a bath this morning."

"If I hadn't gone off," said Reiffen, "Nolo wouldn't have given me this." He pulled a small sack from inside his jacket and handed it to Avender, whose face lit up at once. It was just the right size and weight to be one of Mother Spinner's bags of maple candy. But it was also already open.

"How many have you eaten?" His eyes narrowed suspiciously as Avender opened the bag and peered inside. A light, sweet flavor lurked within.

"We only had one," said Reiffen.

"Total," added Ferris. She stood up and led them off down the stair. "We shared it."

"It's only fair, since we waited for you. Now you get to go sailing instead of helping fix the sty."

"Well, you're not getting any more." Avender folded the top of the bag and tucked it carefully inside his shirt. "You didn't spend an hour combing wet bear." The paper scratched his skin, but he didn't mind, knowing what was inside.

"It was barely half an hour," said Ferris.

"And well worth it, if you ask me," Reiffen pointed out, "when you consider the reward. I'd have volunteered if I'd known." He eyed the spot where the bag had disappeared. "Aren't you going to eat even one? There're seven more in there, you know."

"Oh, you counted them, did you? Are you sure you only took one?"

Reiffen shrugged. "Well, if you're going to be greedy about it," he said.

"Oh, come on. There'll be plenty for everyone tonight." Ferris pushed both boys ahead of her toward the kitchen as they reached the ground floor. "Mother may not let us even go to the feast if we don't bring her the mussels soon."

They met Giserre in the hall, where she and several other women were on their way to the spare bedrooms with fresh bedding. She gave her son a stern glance as he hurried past with Ferris and Avender. "Are you helping?" she asked. Her dark hair was pulled back behind her head and the sleeves of her plain dress pushed up above her elbows. Even making beds she looked like a princess.

"We're off to get mussels for Hern," Reiffen replied.

Satisfied her son was doing his part, Giserre allowed him to go. In the kitchen, Hern handed him the bag of salt they would swap for mussels with the nokken. Savory smells steamed from every pot. Cooks and undercooks scurried back and forth as Hern hopped from stove to stove around them, a pair of large wooden spoons gripped menacingly in either hand.

From the kitchen the children followed the same route Avender had taken while looking for the bear. Only this time they continued all the way down the long stair to the dock at the bottom. Ferris led the way with the lamp, her shadow dancing along the curving walls. There were many caves beneath the Manor, some natural and others carved by human hands. A few ran deeper than the water at the bottom of the cliff outside, wormed from the rock for ancient purposes and off-limits to even the most curious children. But this particular stair led only as far as the lower dock, where the stewards kept a few catboats and canoes for quick runs into the lake without having to hike all the way to the main docks in Eastbay.

At the bottom they came out in a low cave. The air was damp and cold and smelled of smoke. Dark water lapped against the stone. Enough gray light filtered in from the low opening to the lake for the children to see a row of boats moored to a floating dock beside the quay. At the far end an old man muffled in several layers of sweaters and scarves sat puffing a pipe on a wooden chair, fishing in the dim gloom. Sometimes Old Mortin caught a fish, but more often he caught whoever came down from the Manor above: everyone who passed his dock had to pay a toll in talk and time. Rarely did the lakeman trouble his old bones with climbing all those stairs.

"Well, there," he said to the children as soon as they arrived, "it's about time you were off on your chores. Been up there sneaking round the ovens, I suppose. Can't say I blame you. It's what I used to do when I was your age." He chuckled to himself and took a sip from the mug he kept close beside his chair.

"Are you coming to the feast?" asked Ferris politely. Behind her Avender and Reiffen ignored the ladders set into the side of the little pier and jumped down to the floating platform. Pale patterns danced across the rough ceiling as the light from outside reflected off the rippling water.

"Well, in the usual way I wouldn't." Old Mortin carefully slipped his fishing pole through a hole in his chair's wooden arm. "My knees don't like all them stairs. But I hear that new rhymer's coming to sing, so I thought I might as well row on over to Eastbay and hitch a ride back up the Neck."

"Redburr's been talking about him, too," said Avender from inside the catboat he and Reiffen had picked out. Beside him Reiffen heaved the bag of salt into the bottom of the craft.

"Aye. Redburr and Nolo were both with us over to the Bass the other night when we heard him sing." The old lakeman nodded appreciatively. "Sang 'Pickles and Ale,' he did, and 'The Fisherman's Boil.' It's a beautiful voice he has. Not as good as old Froggy Thicken had when I was a lad, maybe. But fine enough all the same."

Avender and Reiffen worked the boat out from the tangle of other craft while Ferris apologized to the lakeman for being in such a hurry. "Hern needs those mussels as soon as possible," she explained.

Old Mortin brightened at the mention of mussels and tried to steer the conversation toward the best way to make mussel stew, but the children were biting no more than the fish. The lakeman gave a last short wave as Avender sculled the catboat out under the iron gate at the entrance to the little harbor and into the bright sunshine beyond. The children blinked at the sudden glare.

"I'm not sure I'm going to like that new rhymer as much as Old Mortin does," said Reiffen. He dropped the centerboard and unlashed the mast from the side of the boat.

"Why not?" Ferris held her hair away from her face as the brisk wind whipped into them.

"I didn't like the way he was looking at me when I was in the Great Hall."

Ferris frowned. "So that's where you were when I was waiting for Avender." She brought out the gaff and boom while Avender sculled harder to keep the catboat off the sheer cliff behind them. "You know, if you weren't always nicking extra treats from the kitchen you wouldn't have that problem. I'm sure Mother Spinner was watching you, too. And my mother, and everyone else in the hall."

"It's not like I'm the only one who does it." Reiffen glanced at Avender as he helped Ferris unwrap the sail. "But this was different. It was like the rhymer didn't care whether he caught me or not, as long as he knew what I was doing. Like he was a spy. That's why I asked your father who he was."

Avender recalled Redburr's recent reminder about the last attempt on Reiffen's life. Could it be possible this fellow Mindrell was working for the king?

"I guess he just reminded you of yourself," said Ferris primly.

"You'll think the same when you see him," said Reiffen.

The girl made no reply. They were at the bottom of the small bay formed by the Pinch, where the Neck was joined to the eastern shore by a thin rib of rock. The high stone walls loomed like broad battlements far above. A perching gull squawked at them from a scraggly bush close to the water's edge, then took off in a flapping of gray and white feathers out over the lake. Beneath their boat the water was dark and deep, as deep below as the walls above were high, with perhaps a few great pike lurking at the bottom. Pike so big that not even the largest nokken cared to hunt them.

Ferris and Reiffen stepped the mast while Avender continued to hold the boat off the cliff with the oars. The breeze was blowing straight down the lake from the south and he would have to paddle them out into more open water before they could raise the sail. As it was, they were going to have to start with a long tack toward East-bay; even if the wind had been favorable they would never have been able to set their course straight for the island. At that time of year the lake was swollen with snowmelt from the mountains, and the current toward the gorge at the west end of the Neck was the strongest it would ever be.

When his friends were ready Avender brought the bow up into the wind, then switched to the tiller as Ferris and Reiffen hoisted the sail. The canvas filled, and off they sailed, the cold wind stinging their faces. Other boats and canoes speckled the lake around them.

They pulled their collars tight around their necks: the wind was colder on the water than up on the cliff above. Winter ice still choked the western shore, where there was little sunshine in the afternoon. Loose floes dotted the rest of the lake, chilling the wind as it scooped across the waves. But it was still a gorgeous day to be out in a boat, despite the cold. The water hissed and foamed beneath the bow, cutting a sharp white wedge through the water. Above them, islands of cloud gave flying chase through the sky. Here and there a dark smudge on the ice showed where a nokken or two had pulled themselves out of the water to sunbathe. But in the Great Bay in front of them, where the water was shallower and warmed more quickly by the sun, the children could race along as quickly as they pleased, with an eye out only for other boats and the occasional island.

Ferris, happy to be out on the lake instead of in the sweltering kitchen with her mother, no matter how delicious it smelled, decided it was time for a song. Avender and Reiffen soon joined in.

"Wind and lake!
Sky and peak!
The breezes blow! The mast goes creak!
And we go sailing fast and sleek
From Manor Neck to Bracken Creek!

"Trout and pike!
  Fin and tail!
  A dozen stickles in our pail!
  But fishing is of no avail
  Without a boat and sweeping sail!

"Crash and boom!
  Thump and roar!
  The falls ahead will crab your oar!
  But we can race away to shore
  With sails that bring us home once more!"

They flew on along the side of the wind. Behind them the Neck loomed like a wall at the foot of the lake, the gables on the Manor roof just now coming into view above the top of the stone. Past the Neck the spray from both gorge and falls rose in a thick white plume that curled up to join the clouds. Even well out on the lake they could hear the low rumble of the plunging water despite the crack of wind and sail.

Straight ahead, the usual traffic of farmers and fishermen crowded the town and bay, but the steady stream of people and wagons climbing the road to the Neck was due entirely to the feast. Beyond the road, green fingers of meadow stretched gently up into the more darkly wooded slopes of the Low Bavadars, the Hartrush tumbling out of the trees in a torrent of rock pools and short cascades. The pass into Firron had been free of snow for nearly two weeks, and First Feast was going to be celebrated right on time.

"Ready about," called Avender before they reached the town.

The boat swung round to the west, the bow turning past Thinwood and the Narrows. The children ducked their heads to avoid the swing of the boom and shifted their seats to the opposite side. Now they were facing the High Bavadars, where cliffs much higher than the Neck dropped sheer hundreds of feet to the ice. Smoke

---

from Spinner's farm rose above the spout of Teapot Hill on the other side of the gorge, but mostly the view was of jagged mountains white with ice and snow. Whitetooth stood taller than them all, its pointed peak showing clear in the distance against the sky.

The width of the lake stretched before them. Scattered rocks and islands dotted the dark blue surface: Big and Little Sheep; Goosefoot; Two Eggs; the Bottle. Some were covered in cormorants and gulls, others in sheep and the occasional nokken. Few had trees, as wind and sheep both did their best to keep all but the largest islands bare. And the nokken liked the islands better that way, too. Even the most agile finslapper was awkward on land, and preferred not to have anything close by that might conceal an enemy. Nokken Rock was one of the larger islands, with many stone ledges and flat rocks, perfect for sunning seals. On the west side a small cliff rose above deep water, where sometimes the pups liked to climb and dive.

As they had hoped, the children were able to make the island in a single long reach from the bay. They sailed on past a few lingering fishermen and grazing sheep, the blue lake foaming behind them. The fishermen waved as they hauled in their nets; the sheep paid the children no attention at all. But, when they neared the rocky island, half a dozen sleek brown bodies suddenly surged up from the surface around them. Sharp jets of water shot out across their bow from several whiskered muzzles. Avender brought the skiff into the wind at once, and Reiffen and Ferris quickly lowered the sail before they were blown back down the lake.

"It's the bachelors," said Reiffen as he unshipped the oars. Even with the sail down, the wind was strong enough to push them steadily northward, away from the island and back toward the Neck. This far west they wouldn't have to go far before being taken by the spring current. If that happened they would have their work cut out for them to avoid being swept back to the gorge and the falls beyond.

"I wonder why they're out today?"

As she spoke, Ferris leaned over the starboard gunwale and looked out at the closest nokken. The seals eyed the children in the boat carefully in turn.

"Steady, lads," barked the largest. "Hold water, there." Only their brown heads showed above the cold surface, like dark buoys bobbing in the small waves. The children all knew perfectly well that several more would be sweeping back and forth in the water beneath them.

"What's going on, Icer?" asked Ferris.

"No familiarity, there, human," barked the nokken gruffly. "State your business or move along. Skimmer! Hold your rank, there! You want 'em to think we're a bunch of eels?"

The other finslappers, having recognized the children in the boat, were having a little difficulty maintaining their formation. One of them, a bit younger than the others, had started to swim forward when he was checked by his sergeant's command.

"Hello, Skim." Avender gave the young nokken a short wave. Skimmer nodded back enthusiastically.

"Backwater, trooper," warned the sergeant. "I'll have your whiskers cut, I will, if you don't follow orders."

Skimmer returned quickly to his position, but his nose twitched playfully all the same. It was hard for any nokken to stay still for any length of time; and the other, older bachelors, who well knew that Icer's bark was worse than his bite, had also loosened up some at their posts.

Ferris looked back at the big nokken. "What's the problem, Sergeant?" she asked solemnly, following the seal's formality.

"No swimming today, humans," Icer replied. His long whiskers twitched as he spoke.

"We're not here to swim. It's way too cold for us. We're looking for Puphugger. Why are you out on patrol?"

"Trouble on the Rock, ma'am," said the sergeant. "Rock throwing."

"Rock throwing!" exclaimed Ferris. Avender and Reiffen were

equally shocked. Rock throwing was strictly forbidden anywhere near Nokken Rock, as was fishing, for that matter. Too many seals around to chance an accident.

"Who was it?" Avender wrapped his arms around the boom to keep the sail from flapping in the wind.

Icer's whiskers wiggled like a heavy mustache. "Strangers," he replied. "Five of 'em. Came out in a canoe first thing this morning and footed it around the Rock like they owned the place. When they started throwing rocks was when Puphugger brought us in from the fishing."

"Did you take care of them?" asked Reiffen.

"They were already gone by the time I had the troop mustered. Puphugger said they went off north, toward the Manor. We didn't follow, though. Not with the pups about."

"Good thing for them you didn't," said Reiffen. Nokken had been known to capsize boats for less. The bachelors especially tended to act first, and only afterward think about what they had done.

"Where is Puphugger, anyway?" asked Ferris.

"I can get her," barked Skimmer. "We've got your mussels for you. Three bags!"

"Watch your whiskers, there, trooper," warned the sergeant. "Did I say you could dive down? Left column, quick-swim forward. Hold on, you eels! Watch your ranks!"

"But they're here for the mussels, Icer!"

"That's 'Sergeant' to you, trooper." Icer glared fiercely at the smaller nokken.

"Aw, let him go," said one of the other seals. "There's no danger here."

"That's Giserre's pup," said another. "And Avender and Ferris. They're not going to be heaving rocks."

"Let's get back to the fishing," said a third.

The sergeant, losing authority by the second, gave a puffing splutter. "All right then. Skim, go fetch Puphugger. The rest of you lot go on back to your patrols. But I'll stay here to keep an eye on these three, just in case."

With a flip and a roll and no splash at all, the rest of the nokken disappeared. Some of them arrowed off in dark flashes just below the surface of the lake.

"Icer?" asked Reiffen. "Do you mind if I row us a little closer to the Rock? Those bags of mussels may be heavy, and I'd just as soon make sure we're nowhere near the current."

The sergeant gave his permission, so Reiffen pulled harder at the oars and started them closer to the island. The wind riffled the water around them. He rowed without splashing like the seals.

"I wonder who it was came out here and bothered the pups?" asked Ferris.

"Someone who didn't know any better," said Avender.

"Probably drovers from Firron up for the feast," suggested Reiffen.

"I wonder what they were doing way out here? Usually they're scared to death of the water. And the nokken. But who else would be so mean?"

"It's a long pull for drovers." Avender eyed the distance back across the lake to town.

They were much closer to the island when Skimmer and another nokken returned to the surface. Both carried sacks in their mouths. Puphugger was an older seal, almost as large as Icer, with a small scar across her left flipper. The fur around her ears and at the corners of her mouth was soft and gray, where Skimmer's was bright and brown. The two nokken swam up close beside the skiff. Reiffen held the oars clear of the water while the other two children pulled the sacks on board.

"Whew, these are heavy," said Ferris, trying not to soak herself with the dripping bag. "How do you swim carrying one of these?"

"It's easy," answered Skimmer, "if you know how to swim." Of course the children knew Skimmer meant that even the best humans were clumsy as bears when it came to water.

"I thought you said there were three bags," said Reiffen. He peered into the water to see if there was another nokken on the way up toward them from the depths.

For answer Puphugger turned to the sergeant. "Icer," she ordered, "fetch the third sack." As one of Longback's senior wives, she commanded much greater authority than a simple sergeant. Icer rolled forward at once and disappeared into the deep blue.

"So, Puphugger." Reiffen held the boat steady again with the oars. "What's this about strangers throwing rocks? Did you see them?"

Puphugger lifted her nose a little higher and peered at the three in the boat from slitted eyes. "I saw them," she replied. "They scared the pups right off the Rock. We haven't been able to get them back up since. And it's a fine day for sunning, too."

"You didn't recognize them?"

The nokken shook her head. Water rippled away from her neck as she moved in the lee of the skiff. Skimmer, freed from patrol duty, swam up behind the stern, where Avender was happy to scratch the slick fur at his throat and behind his ears.

"They must have been drovers," said Ferris, "if Puphugger didn't recognize them."

"Where's Longback?" asked Reiffen.

"Uplake." Puphugger pointed with her muzzle past the boat toward the south. "Those trespassers would need gills by now if he'd been here," she added grimly.

"You can be sure we'll tell my father what's happened," said Ferris. "He'll know what to do." All three of the children knew that relations between humans and nokken had not always been so cordial. The finslappers sometimes got touchy about their parts of the lake, especially when pups were around.

Reiffen pulled something small from inside his jacket, then reached over the windward side of the boat and offered it to Skimmer. Skimmer's whiskers quivered as he glided forward from the stern to see what the boy held in his hand.

Avender and Ferris were equally suspicious, though for a different reason. "What's that?" Ferris asked.

Reiffen only smiled.

Avender shook his head. "And you wanted me to give you some of mine," he said.

"Maple candy!" cried Skimmer delightedly as he recognized what it was Reiffen was offering. He lunged up out of the water at once for the treat. But Reiffen was too quick for him and pulled his hand back with a laugh before the nokken could snatch the prize with his small, sharp teeth. Skimmer slipped back into the water with hardly a splash; but when he resurfaced, he was eyeing Reiffen carefully, his head half-submerged like a floating log.

"Reiffen!" scolded Ferris. "You don't have to be so mean!"

"I'm not mean," said Reiffen with a laugh. "I'm the one giving him candy, after all. You ready, Skim?"

The nokken nodded. Reiffen looked away for a moment, trying to fool him, then tossed the candy quickly into the air. Skimmer never took his eyes off the boy. He was out of the water almost before the treat was out of Reiffen's hand. The nokken snatched the candy with his mouth close to the top of its arc, then dove gracefully back into the water. Puphugger eyed Reiffen with suspicion.

"Don't worry," he said. "I've got some for you, too." He pulled a second paper bag like the one he had given Avender out from inside his jacket.

"I can't believe you were actually complaining about the rhymer watching you," said Ferris. She shook her head as Puphugger swam under the boat and came back up for her treat. Puphugger was much too old and dignified to play catch for a piece of candy. But she was not so old that she would turn the offered dainty away. She took hers from Reiffen's open palm held close to the boat, her whiskers tickling his fingers.

"You stole it even with him watching you?" asked Avender.

"When I saw my chance, I took it," replied Reiffen over his

shoulder. Skimmer had resurfaced and was watching the boy carefully to see if another piece might possibly come his way. "You'd have done the same."

"Sure," said Avender. "But I wouldn't have pretended I didn't have any afterward. Especially if I'd already eaten someone else's without asking!"

"I'm telling you now, aren't I?" Reiffen reached into the bag and pulled out a handful of candy. "There are enough here for two apiece."

Each child took one. "Someday you're going to get caught," said Ferris, savoring the rich sweetness. "Then you'll really catch it."

"I don't see you turning me down."

At that moment Icer returned with the third bag, and Reiffen gave him a piece of candy as well. Then Puphugger and Skimmer lined up for more, and that was the end of Reiffen's bag, because the sergeant deserved a second piece as well. Avender offered to open his sack, but Reiffen stopped him before he could even get it out of his pocket.

"Don't give it all away," Reiffen said in a low voice as the nokken gulped down their sweets. Teeth made for feasting on fish were far less suited to chewing hunks of sugar. "We'll want yours for later."

Ferris handed Hern's bag over the side to Puphugger. She and Icer tickled their whiskers with their pink tongues at the sight of so much salt. The canvas bag had been oiled to make it watertight, so Puphugger could carry it off to wherever the nokken had their hidden rookery. There was even a loop on the end that allowed her to carry the bag over her neck, leaving her mouth free.

On another day the children would have lingered at Nokken Rock. They might have gone fishing with Skimmer, or taken him sailing. But Hern wanted them back as soon as possible and the stew would never be right if the mussels weren't a part of it, so they raised the sail again and were swept home on the front of the bracing breeze. Skimmer played leapfrog with the waves as the boat surged down the lake, but the catboat's fastest pace was nothing to

how fast a nokken could swim. He especially liked diving back and
forth over the bows just in front of the mast.

> *Crash and boom!*
> *Thump and roar!*
> *The falls ahead will grab your oar!*
> *But we can race away to shore*
> *With sails that bring us home once more!*

They were little more than halfway home when Skimmer dove
off into the dark blue lake and found something else to catch his interest. A school of brown darters, perhaps, or a smallish pike. The
children sailed on without him. Ferris had the tiller now, and the water bubbled swiftly as they raced along with the wind. Avender and
Reiffen were ready to catch the sail when she brought the boat
sharply about just outside the entrance to the little harbor. Reiffen
gathered the drooping canvas while Avender unhooked the boom
and unstepped the mast. Their momentum and the last of the wind
carried them into the cove; then Reiffen sculled the last few yards
back through the entrance to the cave. The bright blue daylight
faded behind them.

"Good wind out there, eh?" said Old Mortin, still in his chair.
Smoke curled up from his pipe to the ceiling.

"It was a good run all the way home," said Ferris, her cheeks still
bright from sun and wind.

"Got the mussels, do you?" Old Mortin peered hungrily into the
bottom of the boat as they brought it into the dock.

"Three bags!" Avender held up two in his hands, knowing old
Mortin would be able to see them better that way.

"Mmm-mmm. I can taste it already."

"You haven't seen any strangers pass through today, have you?"
Reiffen slipped the boat's painter over a cleat on the wooden dock
and cinched it tight.

"How's that?" Old Mortin's face wrinkled as he tried to follow what Avender was saying. "Strangers?"

"Someone was throwing rocks on Nokken Rock this morning," explained Ferris.

Old Mortin scowled and puffed hard on his pipe. "Throwing rocks!" he repeated. "We can't have any of that!"

"Exactly," Ferris went on. "Icer was out with a patrol. Puphugger saw them, but she didn't know who it was. That's why we're wondering if you saw any strangers."

Old Mortin rubbed his wrinkled chin. "No. No strangers. Mindrell's no stranger."

The children looked at one another suspiciously. For the second time that afternoon Avender remembered the attempt on Reiffen's life.

"Mindrell?" asked Ferris. "Was anyone with him?"

Old Mortin rubbed his chin a second time. "Come to think of it, he had two or three fellows along with him in the canoe. Rough-looking lot, they were. If there was any rock throwing, it would be them doing it, not him. A fine lad, Mindrell," the lakeman added. "Why, I've shared a glass with him, I have."

"They must be the ones," said Ferris to her friends.

"We should tell your father." Reiffen wasn't at all sad to have a convincing reason for his dislike of the bard.

Avender agreed. "He'll be the one who'll have to fix it if there's trouble."

The old lakeman went on, as the children finished stowing the catboat's gear, about how the men with Mindrell had been an untrustworthy-looking lot, and how he never would have allowed them past had they not been with the rhymer. "Sneaks," he said, his indignation rising the longer he talked. "The lot of 'em. I knew it soon as I saw 'em. Tell Berrel I say throw 'em in the lake. That's better than rock throwers deserve, if you ask me."

He shook his head firmly and knocked the bowl of his pipe clean on the side of his chair.

"We'll do that," said Ferris as she relit the lamp and led her friends to the stair. "See you at the feast."

It was always a long climb back to the Manor, much longer than the trip down. This time Ferris's shadow trudged rather than danced beside her in the flicker of the lamp. The mussels clinked loudly with every step, and the sacks grew heavier as they went up, despite the fact that they dripped water all the way from the bottom to the top of the stair. Ferris was dragging her bag behind her by the time they finally reached the kitchen.

"Thank you, dears." Hern gave her daughter a quick kiss as she took Ferris's bag and lifted it up onto the tabletop. Preparations for the evening must be going well, judging from her mood. "Now go on, the three of you. You'll just be in the way here and the sty's all fixed. Maybe Nolo or Berrel can make further use of you, because I can't."

They found Berrel in the Great Hall supervising the placement of candles on the chandeliers, both of which had been lowered to the floor for the task. They were massive old wheels of wood, black with age and the soot from long years of illumination. Each held a hundred tapers on its various spokes and rings, and three strong men were required on the ropes to raise and lower them. Just lighting the candles was a big job, but twice a year Hern insisted on fresh white tapers being set into all the holders. That was the real chore.

Berrel shook Ferris off the first time she tried to get his attention. But when he saw that neither she nor her friends were going to leave him alone until he noticed them, he finally turned around.

"Don't forget those last five in the middle there," he reminded the workmen. Then, to the children, "All right. Tell me what you have to say. But be quick. I'm busy here."

"Someone's been bothering the nokken at the Rock," said Ferris.

"Bothering the nokken? I know all about that." Berrel turned back to watch Toby Thwarting duck carefully under the second ring of lights and place a candle in the middle. "Mindrell told me this morning he thought he might have annoyed them. I hoped they would have settled down by now. I suppose I'll have to make a visit out there myself tomorrow. Did you get a good lot of mussels from Longback?"

"We got three bags," said Reiffen. "But we didn't see Longback. Just Puphugger and Icer."

"Icer had the patrol out guarding the Rock," explained Ferris. "That's how bothered they are."

"He did? The patrol? Well, maybe the pups were out. You know how nervous nokken get when the pups first come out in the spring. Just as long as they didn't try drowning anyone. Easy there, Toby. You're going to knock those ones on the right all off-kilter, and then we'll have to do them all over again."

"I told you we should have done this lot first," grumbled Toby.

"Sir." Reiffen politely caught Berrel's attention once more. "According to Icer, they were throwing rocks."

"What's that? Throwing rocks?" The steward turned back to the children.

"The rhymer didn't tell you that, did he, Father?" said Ferris.

"No, he didn't." Berrel frowned. "We can't have that, now. Still, I don't suppose he knew any better. He said he'd never seen a nokken and didn't want to miss the chance. But I'll speak to him all the same next time I see him. We can't have rock throwing. Longback and his folk are skittish enough by nature. It won't help to rouse them more. Mindrell's lucky he didn't get himself drowned."

The steward returned to the chandeliers, leaving the children free to look around. The hall was filled with people making ready for the evening. One group was setting up two rows of plank tables down the center of the room, with benches on either side. They had to work around the chandeliers until they were raised again, and were already quarreling with Toby in an effort to make him hurry up. A second crew, with Nolo in charge, was decorating the walls with garlands of freshly cut pine boughs, while under the balcony a number of the local farmwives were setting up tables. The cooking had been fierce for most of the week, and now the tables groaned beneath heavy platters of pies and tarts and, of course, Enna Spinner's famous maple candy. At the sight of Ferris with her hands empty, several of the women called her over to help. But Reiffen and Avender they wouldn't trust anywhere near the food.

Mother Spinner gave both boys a sharp look as soon as she saw them. Indeed, had they thought they could manage it, they would both have taken another try at the small brown parcels she was laying out on the table before her. But, now she had noticed them, she wasn't about to let either of them out of her sight. She pointed them out to everyone around her, and then there was no chance for either boy to stage any sort of raid, no matter how stealthy.

They were on their way out of the hall when Reiffen nudged Avender and nodded back in Mother Spinner's direction. "That's him," he said in a low voice. "That's Mindrell."

A tall, broad-shouldered man, who looked more like a famous captain than a bard, was chatting with the farmwife. He wore a lute strapped across his back instead of a sword, and struck up a conversation with the easy familiarity of someone used to making friends wherever he went.

"Look at that." Reiffen frowned in disapproval as the bard said something to the old farmwife that made her blush like a maid of sixteen. Gladly Mindrell ate the candy she offered him in return. "He thinks he's the cock of the walk."

"Nolo seems to like him, too," said Avender.

The Dwarf had left off hanging branches and hurried forward to greet the bard as soon as he saw him. They left Mother Spinner still giggling at some sally of Mindrell's; then the Dwarf guided the tall man off to where the evening's casks of beer and wine were set out beneath the gallery. Nolo tapped one barrel on the side with a thick finger and made a great show of pointing out to his new friend that this was the particular malt they should concentrate upon that evening.

"He doesn't seem to be watching you now," said Avender, who, after seeing the bard joke easily with everyone around him, had concluded Mindrell couldn't possibly be a murderer.

"Hmm?" Reiffen was too busy studying his new enemy to be paying attention to his friend.

"Mindrell. You said you thought he was watching you before."

"Well, he was. I guess he has better things to do now."

"Maybe it was your guilty conscience."

"That's what Ferris would say. But who was it gave all his candy away to the nokken?" Reiffen dismissed the idea that he might feel guilty about anything without another thought. "You're the one who's the greedy hoarder."

"You know I'm going to share them," said Avender. "Just as you finally got around to sharing yours. But that doesn't mean in the meantime I won't tease you the same way you teased Skim."

Reiffen grinned. They were very different, the two boys, but they had spent too much time growing up together not to be also very much the same. They watched as Mindrell charmed a second sweet out of Enna Spinner, who had never been known, by either boy at least, for her generosity. They left the hall feeling very virtuous about their own filching. "At least we're honest thieves," Reiffen said with a scowl. "We don't pretend friendship when all we're really interested in is sweets."

Avender agreed.

They wandered out of the Manor and into the orchard, hardly noticing the blossoms whose scent Redburr had found so pleasant earlier in the day. Eventually they found themselves on the path that led to Giserre's Tear. The constant thunder of the gorge and the falls beyond grew loud. Once they had both lived in the Tear with Reiffen's mother, after Avender's mother had died and before they had even become friends. But in the last few years they had shared a room of their own in the attic, one stairwell removed from the bear's. Nolo had built the Tear by himself, in Dwarven fashion, and the stone path that led down to it above the ravine, the first year he had come to Valing. The year both Reiffen and Avender had been born, and both their fathers died. Annelough, the Dwarf had called it: the Loud Place. But everyone in the Manor had taken to calling it the Tear because of the way the mist from the falls beaded on the windows, then ran down in long streaks against the glass.

They stopped at the entrance at the edge of the cliff. The Tear was hidden below, wrapped in twisting mist. Only the covered stone bridge that led from the stair to the hanging tower appeared now and again through the swirling clouds. Gulls coasted on the back of the wind above, soaring up and out of the narrow chasm. On the far side a thick fir wood rose up toward the low top of Teapot Hill.

"Redburr said you might leave soon," said Avender.

Reiffen watched the birds ride the wind. "Mother's been talking about it a lot. And she's had letters from Malmoret, too. More than usual."

"It won't be the same here, if you go."

"I have to. You know that. Mother and I are only guests in Valing. We belong in Malmoret."

Avender peered higher up into the sky and saw a fish hawk soar out toward the lake over the dark green trees.

"Has she said when you're going to leave?" he asked.

Reiffen shook his head. "Not yet. But I don't think we'll wait till summer."

Avender said nothing more. He wasn't one to ask for favors. What did he know of what mother and son had planned, or of what princes they would take counsel from along the way? Avender's parents had been heir to neither thrones nor titles. His home was here in Valing, with the lake and the mountains and the sky. Malmoret was for Reiffen.

Then Reiffen said, "I think if you ask her, my mother will let you come."

Avender's spirits rose. He turned to his friend. "Really? That's what Redburr said. But he thinks Hern might not like it."

"Hern knows little of the world beyond Valing," said Reiffen.

Then he added, "At least that's what Mother says. She says Hern's afraid of what might happen should I come under my uncle's hand."

"I'd be worried, too. I even thought for a minute he might have sent that Mindrell to get you."

"The bard?" Reiffen looked at his friend in surprise. "Did you see the way he was playing up to those old women? Old Mortin's scarier than he is."

Avender shrugged. "I only thought it for a minute. I guess it was in my mind because Redburr was talking about those murderers King Brannis sent, while I was grooming him."

"Redburr says the older I get, the less safe it is for me anywhere." As Reiffen spoke, the fish hawk dropped like a stone toward the lake and disappeared behind the Neck. "I can't stay in Valing forever."

Avender heard the reluctance in Reiffen's voice. He knew his friend loved Valing every bit as much as he did. Despite his lineage, Reiffen had known no other home. Together they had explored every nook and cranny of the great house, and most of the caves and tunnels beneath as well. They had climbed all the nearer hills, and sailed the entire length and breadth of the lake from Sothend to the Neck. But from his mother Reiffen knew of other things. His uncle sat king on the thrones of Rimwich and Malmoret, but only in Reiffen did the blood of both lines flow. Reiffen knew his duty lay in the lands of his parents' birth.

"Come on," he said, taking Avender by the arm. "We'll go ask my mother if you can come with us. That way we'll have all spring to persuade Hern to let you go. And maybe Ferris can come, too."

But they didn't find Giserre in the Tear. The princess was still making beds in the Manor. By the time they did find her the feast had already begun. And in all the excitement that followed they never did remember to ask her about Avender going with them to Malmoret.

3

The Feast

eyond the West, beyond the night;
Beyond the waning of the light;
Beyond Keeadin's fearsome waste,
Where eagles flee and wolves are chased;
Beyond the grip of Ossdonc's hold;
Beyond the grasp of greed and gold . . ."

By the time Mindrell stepped up to sing, the feast was nearly over. Plates and platters littered the floor; even the dogs were full. Dennol Long-bay was done juggling milk stools and Sally Veale had shyly sung "The Shepherd's Dawning." Even Letty Seedbuck had dared a jig with Tinnet Bullberry while the crowd clapped and cheered them on. Now no one had eyes for anything but Mindrell. They clutched their half-eaten slices of ham and empty bowls of mussel stew, and listened intently to his song.

Lute in hand, he jumped onto one of the long tables that filled the room. Smiling at the maidens and winking at the young men, he was a handsome sight in his bright green jacket and feathered cap. He started with a pair of well-known ballads to warm them up, "The King's Feasting" and "Widow's Lament," striding up and down the table as he sang. The Valings grabbed their plates and bowls as he stalked the board before them, his boots thumping on the wooden planks. Then he began a tune no one had heard before. A new song, he said, one he claimed they were singing more and more in the forest of the north. His audience listened rapt to his tale of the time, not so long ago, when Wayland and Banking had been at war and Mennon had found the Dwarves at the bottom of the world.

> ". . . And so the Wizard turned aside,
> Not knowing that the mountains hide
> The bones of earth, and all inside . . ."

At the mention of Wizards, every child sitting in the balcony felt a thrill of fear. Atty Peeks would have dropped his plate on the merchants below if Ferris hadn't caught it. Usseis, Ossdonc, and Fornoch: whenever a Valing farmwife wished to frighten her unruly children into silence, all she needed to do was mention one of the Three, or their fortress in the north. Even Reiffen and Avender, who had more reason than most to hate the Wizards, were enthralled.

> ". . . For down within the caverns blind
> The mansions of the Dwarves are mined;
> The lamps of Uhle glow undefined
> From deep within cut hearts of stone . . ."

Never in their lives had they heard such a rhymer. Mindrell seemed to live the different parts as he sang: pretending to draw Cuhurran's bow as mightily as Cuhurran himself; falling backward with a loud cry as Mennon was struck by the Wizard's shot. The bard waved his arms in the air before him and all who watched saw the broad river flowing southward far to the west, Mennon swirling in its grip. And when Mindrell turned from

Mennon to the Dwarves, he crouched and peered around the hall as if he were trapped in darkness beneath miles and miles of stone.

> ". . . And with him went a single friend
> With extra hands and eyes to bend
> The unknown darkness to their will;
> To find the path to what might fill
> The emptiness within Uhle's thought;
> The light imagined, but uncaught.
> For Nolo had learned much in craft
> Beside the forge of Uhle . . ."

"That's you, that is." Old Mortin slapped the Dwarf sociably on the shoulder. Wincing, the lakeman rubbed his stinging hand. Redburr, who was sprawled on the floor nearby, growled. The dogs around him pricked up their ears. Abashed, the lakeman wrung his sore fingers. Nolo's beard wagged as he tried to hold his laughter in check.

Mindrell paid them no attention. He placed his foot between an empty gravy dish and three apple cores, and stepped on along the table without missing a measure of his song.

> ". . . Then Bryddin nursed the wounded proof
> That rock and stone were more than roof.
> And more than stars and moon they learned
> From Mennon, when his strength returned.
> Cuhurran, known as Ossdonc's guise,
> And Fornoch, shown in Martis' lies,
> Were to their brother forced to run
> When first the Bryddin reached the sun.
> And even Usseis's spells,
> Full magicked from the coldest hells,

Will never quell the Dwarven might,
Now risen with the sun so bright
Above where even bats take flight;
Above the never-ending height;
Beyond the west, beyond the night;
Beyond the waking of the light."

There was a moment of quiet as Mindrell finished, followed quickly by a great roar of approval. The children whooped; the dogs barked and howled. Many guests thumped their mugs and bowls against the table. Even the fires in the twin hearths at either end of the long hall seemed to leap up in appreciation. Nolo banged his mug enthusiastically along with everyone else, only he forgot himself and smashed it into a hundred pieces on the second or third knock. He glanced around sheepishly, his deep-set eyes darting from side to side beneath his shaggy brows. But no one noticed his clumsiness, so he hid the handle inside his jacket pocket and turned to clapping instead.

Mindrell accepted his accolades, grinning enormously, then swept off his hat and bowed deeply to all four corners of the room. A cry went up for another song, but Mindrell knew how best to leave his audience. With a last bow he leapt nimbly to the floor, where he was swept up in a flood of congratulations. Old Mortin was the first to press a fresh glass into the bard's hand, almost teary in his apologies for his interruption.

"A grand tune, Mindrell. A grand one, mind you." He wiped a blurry eye as he pumped the bard's hand thoroughly in his own.

Up on the balcony with the other children, Reiffen, Ferris, and Avender agreed it had been a fine song, as good as any they'd ever heard. "I guess you don't think so badly of him now, do you?" said Ferris to Reiffen. Her eyes shone with delight, she had liked the song so much.

But Reiffen frowned the moment Ferris reminded him of his

suspicions. "He threw rocks at the nokken," he said with a scowl, "and that means there's something wrong with him. How well he sings doesn't matter."

"We don't know he's the one who threw the rocks," insisted Ferris. "It could have been one of the men he was with. For all we know Mindrell tried to stop them."

"You should have asked him that this afternoon when he was so busy helping you decorate the tables."

Ferris flushed. "Who told you that?"

"We heard Min Spinner telling Hern," said Avender.

"Well, it wasn't like I asked him to help me." Ferris flushed pink and looked down through her feet at the busy floor below. "He came over himself. And he helped everyone, which is more than either of you did."

With no hope of another song from the bard, the party began to thin. Berrel and Hern went off, leaving the cleanup for the next day. The few revelers who remained gathered in small knots among the empty tables. In the morning most of them would be found sprawled across the benches or slumbering on the floor. Redburr had already stretched his large, furry bulk out in front of the fire, a dozen dogs fast asleep around him, but Nolo was still drinking steadily with Old Mortin, Mindrell, and a few others.

"Look." Reiffen nodded toward the small company around the Dwarf. "That Mindrell's so full of himself he thinks he can match cups with Nolo."

Ferris frowned. "In case you didn't notice," she said, "he's not drinking as much as the rest of them."

Reiffen's scowl changed to a grin. "Really? I hadn't noticed. But then I guess I haven't been watching him closely enough."

Ferris's eyes narrowed dangerously, and Avender jumped in before she had the chance to rise to Reiffen's teasing. "Let's go see if any of Mother Spinner's candy's left," he suggested. Yawning mightily, he stretched his arms up toward the chandeliers.

Ferris pursed her lips tightly but said nothing. Reiffen, however, had already looked into the matter. "They were all gone a long time ago," he said. "Are any of yours left?"

Avender patted his pocket. Paper crinkled within. "The last three."

"Are you going to share them out?"

"Not now, please," Ferris broke in with a yawn of her own. "I'm too tired. And I'm filled to the gills. We should save them for tomorrow."

The boys agreed. With no room left for further eating, it was not long before they reluctantly decided the evening was finally over. They picked their way over the other children snoring contentedly on the floor and parted company in the hallway beyond. Ferris went straight back to the apartment she shared with her parents, but the boys were not quite ready to retire, and decided to take a last stroll outside. They went out onto the Neck through the passage at the end of the Great Hall and soon found themselves walking in the orchard. The afternoon's wind had died away and the air seemed warmer despite the nighttime chill. Around them the trees loomed like shadows in the darkness, the branches sleeved in sleeping blossoms. Soon they came out on the other side of the low wood and stood upon the same rock Redburr had sunned himself that morning. It was a good place, with a splendid view of the lake below in the daytime and the stars above at night. The Bear and the Hawk sparkled over the rounded tops of Baldun and the Shoulder. The moon had not yet risen, and the starlight was bright in the clear mountain air except for a thick line of cloud moving up from the south.

"Who do you think that is out there?" Reiffen pointed toward a small light that glimmered across the water.

"Some shepherd." Avender felt sorry for anyone who might have had to miss the evening's celebration to tend a sickly sheep.

"Looks like it's on Nokken Rock."

"It does."

"If I hadn't just seen Mindrell with my own eyes, I'd swear he was out there bothering Skim and Icer again."

"Well, he isn't."

For a while they talked again about leaving Valing and of what they hoped to see and do in the world beyond. They both liked the idea of traveling together to Malmoret far more than the thought of Reiffen going by himself. Someday they might have to part, but the longer they put that day off, the better they would like it. Without hats or jackets, they soon grew cold and decided it was time to go inside.

They were just starting up the stair to their room when Mindrell appeared on the landing above. Both boys stood aside to allow the bard to pass. Instead, he stopped and spoke to them.

"I seem to be lost," he said pleasantly. "Maybe one of you would like to guide me."

"Where are you going?" asked Avender.

"To the lower dock. Mortin and the Dwarf asked me to meet them there for a nightcap." Mindrell leaned lightly against the wall as he spoke, his lute slung over his shoulder.

"The entrance to the cellars is in the kitchen." Reiffen nodded back toward the front of the house.

"This way?" Mindrell pointed toward the wall behind the boys, seeming to miss Reiffen's gesture.

"No. That way." Reiffen pointed plainly in the other direction.

"I really think I need a guide." The bard hiccoughed and looked brightly at both boys. "Even if I make it to the kitchen, I have no idea where to go once I'm in the cellars."

"I'll take you," offered Avender.

"We'll both go," said Reiffen.

They led the bard back through the Manor. The hallways were silent now. Almost everyone not still in the Great Hall had gone to bed, though they did pass Wick Woolson holding hands with Min Spinner in a dark corner. The bard tipped his hat to them, which made Min turn her face toward Wick in embarrassment. Wick scowled at all three of them as they went by, his arm protectively around his sweetheart's shoulder.

"You lads'll be there in a few more years," laughed Mindrell after they had passed on. His dark eyes danced, a pair of darting coals. Reiffen frowned like Wick and quickened his pace, but Avender pretended he hadn't heard. Mindrell laughed again, a ready laugh full of much good humor. "Come now," he continued. "I know at least one of you likes the lass I saw you with all evening. Or is it both?"

His teasing felt ridiculous to the boys. He seemed like less the great bard because of it, and more like a leering mule driver encountered on the road. They hastened on to the kitchen. Stacks of dirty crockery towered around the room. A cat sniffing at the last of the mussel stew arched its back as they appeared and strutted away in disdain.

"After you," said the bard. He held the door to the cellars open as they passed, then followed behind. At the bottom of the steps a single pine torch lit the hall beyond, leaving the rest of the passage in gloom. Most of the doors on either side were closed and locked; Hern trusted no one in her cellars, whether there were strangers about or not. So both Avender and Reiffen were surprised when two men stepped out of an open doorway ahead of them and into their path. One had a bottle of Southy in his hand, looted no doubt from the room he had just left. The other was picking his nails with a long, sharp knife. There had been many guests at the feast that evening, and neither Reiffen nor Avender recognized either man.

The one with the knife frowned when he saw the boys and said, "I thought you said there was only one, harper?"

Alarmed by the fellow's knife and manner, Avender and Reiffen swung quickly around. Another man had come up out of the darkness behind them to stand beside the bard. Before either boy could do a thing, Mindrell grabbed Avender around the chest and held him tightly. The blade of a long, thin knife, nastier looking than the first man's, lay coldly along Avender's neck. All the boy's suspicions about Mindrell working for King Brannis came flooding back in a wave of certainty.

Reiffen started forward to help his friend, but the first two men grabbed him at once. Then Mindrell's words froze both boys.

"Come along quietly," he told them, his good humor vanished. "Otherwise I'll kill this one."

"But Mindrell," repeated the man with the knife. "You said there was only going to be one."

"Shut up, Boney," snapped the bard. He pushed Avender roughly forward. "It'll be easier this way. The other will be much more cooperative if he knows his friend's in danger."

Both boys trembled with fear. The knife felt thin and hard against Avender's throat. He wondered why Mindrell didn't simply kill them both at once and make his escape. Cautiously the bandits pushed their captives down the passage. Boney led the way. He was a thin, dirty man, with a nose almost as long as his fingers. The nose preceded his face as he checked around every corner and moved rodent-like from shadow to shadow. Once they heard a snatch of song from a storeroom close by. Apparently Boney and his friend weren't the only ones to successfully raid the cellars that night. Avender's hopes leapt at the thought that it might be Nolo or Red-burr rummaging through the bottles and casks, but neither he nor Reiffen dared cry out. The singers were left behind.

They came to the stair that led down to the dock. Mindrell took his knife from Avender's neck and pushed both his captives roughly down the dark steps. They stumbled forward and caught themselves on the hard stone walls. There was less hope for escape on that narrow way than there had been in the cellars above, knife or no. Boney again led the way with the other two villains behind. Mindrell kept to the middle with the lamp and his prisoners.

"You take care of the guard?" asked one of the other men.

"He's snoring in his cups in the hall," said the bard.

They moved quickly, now that Mindrell no longer feared any

sudden surprises, their feet slipping swiftly down the stairs. As they came out into the dim dampness of the wooden dock, small waves echoed across the stone. The only light was the one they had carried down the stairs themselves. The exit to the lake was as black as the water beneath the rocking boats.

Mindrell snapped out orders. "Boney, guard the stair. You two find some rope. We'll need to tie them up while we're in the canoes."

Boney's companion tossed his empty bottle into the dark water and followed his mate down among the boats. The hollow splash boomed off the glistening roof and walls.

"Where are you taking us?" demanded Reiffen, setting himself stubbornly in front of Mindrell.

"You'll find out soon enough," laughed the bard cruelly. "Your Majesty."

Somehow Mindrell had known which insult would anger Reiffen the most, the one the other children had learned to taunt him with when he was young. Reiffen's face turned black as the water.

Rope was quickly found, and Avender and Reiffen were taken down to the wooden dock, where their arms were bound tightly at their sides. Then Mindrell climbed back up onto the quay to raise the gate that covered the opening to the lake. While he did so, the two bandits still on the dock unfastened a pair of canoes from their moorings. The iron chain clanked loudly in the darkness as the gate lifted. Water dripped from the bars.

They loaded the boys roughly into the middle of the two canoes, making them lie on the bottom beneath the thwarts. Then the small craft rolled in the water as the bandits climbed in before and behind, Boney and Mindrell with Reiffen and the other two with Avender. Boney moved about carefully in the bow of his canoe, not sure of himself at all. But the other three bandits all seemed familiar with the awkward craft, and handled their paddles with a certain degree of skill. Both boats slipped silently out onto the wide waters of the lake, the paddle shafts knocking softly on the gunwales.

Outside, the night was as dark as the cave, but Avender could still feel the air open up around him. A little farther, and he saw the silhouette of the Neck rise up against the lighter darkness of the sky. To the south the stars lay concealed behind heavy thickets of growing cloud. There was still no wind and they made good time despite Boney, who paddled so poorly that Mindrell twice told him to stop before Reiffen was soaked with his splashing.

"And Mennon sank beneath the play
Of noise and night and cold and spray."

Mindrell laughed softly as he repeated the lines from his song. In the bottom of the other boat Avender lay listening to the cold gargle of the water, his fear growing with every stroke. The regular slide, slide of the canoes, usually so soothing, especially on a summer evening when the gilded water was as still as a sheet of glass, now became an ominous irritation. He wondered when Redburr and Berrel would realize he and Reiffen were gone. In the morning, perhaps, when they failed to show up to help with the cleanup. But not before.

Futilely Avender struggled to loosen his bonds; there was no give in the ropes at all. He was certain he knew what had happened. King Brannis had sent Mindrell to kidnap Reiffen and dispose of him in some way that would leave his disappearance a mystery forever. At any moment they would both be rolled out of the canoes into the water. First to drown, and then to have all trace of their drowning washed through the gorge and over the falls to the river below. Avender was just unlucky enough to have been with Reiffen at the time he was taken. Fearful and cold, Avender lay in the bottom of his canoe and watched the sky pass over his head, the clouds creeping northward behind him.

But the canoes kept on straight uplake without pause. Eventually Avender began to understand Mindrell was going well out of his way if all he wanted to do was drown them. The current was far off to their right and, if they were thrown into the water, their bodies would probably be found well before they were swept over the falls. Perhaps drowning wasn't going to be their fate. But what else could King Brannis want with them? Did he want to take Reiffen alive? And even if he did, what would the bandits do with Avender?

Then Boney spoke. Out on the lake his voice traveled easily; Avender heard him plainly at the bottom of the other canoe.

"There's the light," he said. "Looks like Ike ain't let us down."

"Keep your mouth shut," whispered Mindrell. "You have no idea how clearly sound travels over water."

"If sailors was what you wanted, you should've hired sailors," muttered Boney.

Evidently they were going to one of the islands. In the dark, Avender had no idea which one. At Boney's mention of a light, though, he remembered the unknown glimmer they had seen from the top of the Neck and wondered still if it had come from Nokken Rock, as they had supposed.

They paddled on for a few more minutes. Avender grew stiffer and more cold. Then he felt the bottom of the canoe grind roughly against a gravel beach as they were run ashore at their destination. Above him Mindrell's face came suddenly into view in a flickering light.

"All right." The bard's feet made a pair of soft splashes as he stepped into the water from the canoe. "Bring these two ashore."

Rough hands helped them out. A fifth bandit stood on the stony beach, a sputtering torch in his hand. There was splashing all around as the thieves stomped about in the shallow water with their captives, then dragged the boats farther up onto the rocky shore. The lake was icy cold where it poured in through the boys' boots. They looked around, trying to piece together where they were. But the island looked like any other in the dim torchlight. Beyond the meager glow all was blackness. Even the outline of the mountains was hidden in the cloudy night.

Mindrell took the torch from the newcomer and held it close

above the captives' faces. Avender wondered how many more bandits were hiding on the island.

"Ike, you and Boney take this one to the fire." Mindrell pointed to Reiffen. "Tipps, you and Hurl take the other to the cliff we saw this morning. We won't be needing him anymore to keep His Majesty quiet. You know what to do."

The one called Hurl broke into a rude grin. Tipps wiped his mouth with the back of his sleeve and looked as if he would have enjoyed another swig from his bottle.

Avender turned at once and kicked Tipps, who was closest to him, in the knee. A second well-aimed kick knocked the one called Hurl to the ground. But, just as Avender was about to try and run off into the darkness, Mindrell stepped forward and struck him hard across the head with his torch. The wood broke, sparks flying. Avender pitched forward on the ground, fresh lights starting before his eyes. He lay moaning on the stony beach, trying to remember how to see. Cold pebbles ground against his cheek. Dimly he was aware of hands gripping him by either arm and heaving him back to his feet. They led him, stumbling, through a field of rocks. More than once he banged his knees and shins, but there was no chance to rest and clear his head. In what seemed like a moment he found himself standing alone at the edge of another blackness. He sniffed once, and smelled the water below. Behind him someone gave a mocking laugh. Then a pair of hands gave him a hard shove and he toppled forward.

He hit the water with a loud splash. With his arms tied he rolled gently over and over as he continued to sink, bewildered by the blow to his head and the sudden shock of the cold water. He had no idea which way was up and which was down. He was still trying to figure that out when the cold finally got to him. The black water closed fast around him and his world became blacker still.

4

Inside the Rookery

t was the smell that made Avender realize he was alive. Water and wet fur and old, slimy fish: they were too real to be part of any dream. His nose twitched and he tried to rub it with his hand, only to find he couldn't move his arms. Fear gripped him; for a moment he thought he was still drowning. Then he realized he was breathing, or he would never have been able to smell a thing, and calmed down.

He opened his eyes, but it was just the same as if he had kept them closed. With a shock he remembered what had happened and the ropes tied tightly around his arms. Where was he? What had Mindrell done with Reiffen? His leaping thoughts were interrupted by a fit of bitter retching. When he was done he lay shivering weakly on the cold stone floor. But at least he was alive, which was not what he had expected after being dropped into the dark and icy lake. Were it not for the musky warmth of the dank air around him he would have been freezing.

Cautiously he tried to sit up, and cracked his skull on the ceiling. Groaning, he lay back down. He had no idea where he was. The smell of water was everywhere, along with the flavor of fish and fur, and the tang of wet stone. He wondered if he was back at the lower dock, but that wouldn't explain the fur. And, if someone had fished him out onto the wharf in Eastbay, then why the stony ceiling? He must be in some kind of cave.

Quietly he listened to the darkness around him and realized he was not alone. He heard people breathing—if they were people. The smell of fur remained very strong. And there was something about the snorts and coughs that went with the breathing that made him think of deeper chests and longer snouts than humans possessed. It almost sounded like he was in a barn.

Finally he guessed where he was.

"Skimmer?" he called out softly in the darkness.

"Here I am, Avender."

Something shuffled nearby, and he felt the tickling touch of the nokken's whiskers against his cheek.

"Skimmer," he whispered, "where am I?"

"In the rookery." Skimmer's voice echoed wetly in Avender's ear. "Those pirates tried to kill you."

For the first time Avender noticed his head ached in two separate places. One from Mindrell and the other, less painful, from trying to sit up a moment ago.

"What about Reiffen?" he asked.

"I didn't see Reiffen," answered Skimmer. "Was he there?"

"Yes," whispered the boy.

"I didn't hear any other splashes. Only you."

"Mindrell took him. We have to rescue him."

"Who's Mindrell?"

A fresh wave of dizziness washed over Avender as he tried to speak. He felt like he was going to be ill again and took a couple of deep breaths.

"A bard," he gasped weakly, as the feeling passed. A drop of water trickled from his wet hair into his eye, making him blink as he tried to clear it. He wished his hands were free to rub his face and sore head. "You don't have something I could cut these ropes with, do you?"

Much to his surprise, the boy heard Skimmer shuffle off. He hadn't really expected the nokken to have anything sharp in the cave. Around him other nokken grunted and snuffled in the darkness.

"How 'bout this?" asked Skimmer when he returned. He sounded as if he had something in his mouth.

"What is it?"

"A knife." Skimmer dropped it with a clatter on the stone close by. One of the nearer nokken shifted noisily at the sound.

"Where'd you get a knife?" whispered Avender.

"From the bottom of the lake." Skimmer's voice rippled like water when he whispered back.

"You'll have to pick it up again. I can't find it."

The boy and the nokken fumbled in the darkness as they tried to bring the knife up against the ropes. Avender's haste to get free so he could find Reiffen didn't help them at all. In the end they decided that Skimmer holding the knife tightly in his mouth was best, while Avender rubbed the rope against the blade. All they really needed was to cut one loop and he would be able to wriggle free.

"Why does a bard want Reiffen?" said Skimmer through his clenched teeth.

"It's not Mindrell who wants him. It's King Brannis."

"But why would King Brannis want him?"

"It's a human thing, Skim." Avender winced as he pricked himself with the knifepoint. But he could feel the strands of the rope beginning to part and kept on. "It's like what Longback would do if he thought one of the bachelors was going to challenge him."

"Longback fights his challengers," said Skimmer. "He doesn't send someone else to do it for him."

"It's more complicated than that for humans."

The ropes parted with a thin snap and Avender scrambled to pull them off. But the effort had taken something out of him, and his nausea returned worse than ever as soon as he was free. He bent double over the stone floor and gave up another large part of the lake. When he was done, he crouched gasping in the darkness. Some of the nearer nokken started to stir around him.

"Quiet over there!" came a voice. "I'm trying to sleep!"

"Not anymore," came an irritated reply.

A few angry barks and some finslapping followed from different corners of the cavern.

"Skimmer?" A softer voice spoke up from somewhere close beside them. Avender thought he recognized Puphugger. "Is that you? Who're you talking to? You should be asleep. It's a long day tomorrow, if we're going to get up to Stonehead for the eels."

"It's Avender, Auntie," said Skimmer softly. "I brought him to the rookery."

"What?" Puphugger sounded shocked, her hoarse voice rising shrilly. "Avender in the rookery? The Dwarf was bad enough, but a human!"

"Humans?"

"What's that?"

"Humans in the rookery?"

In a moment the entire cave was in an uproar. Barks and finslapping threatened on every side. Avender couldn't see a thing, but he could feel nokken lumbering blindly around him in the darkness. They shuffled awkwardly, their flippers slapping on the wet stone, and there were more than a few splashes as some of them darted in and out of what sounded like a pool in their confusion.

"Hunters ahead!"

" 'Ware harpoons!"

"It's coats for all of us, now!"

"Ork! Ork! Ork!"

"Belay that! Quiet in the hold! Bachelors to the pool! Aunties and pups to the upper decks! Finfist! Icer! Secure the rear hatch! Skimmer, report to the main deck!"

With his deep, bass bark, Longback made himself heard clearly over the bedlam in the cave. It still took some time for the bachelors and a few of the others to restore order; but, when the cave was quiet again, Avender sensed he was alone on his side of the secret chamber. Water slapped against unseen rocks in the darkness. Fish bones and discarded mussel shells dug uncomfortably into his side, but he kept silent and tried not to move. There was no telling what Longback and the rest of the nokken would do to him now they knew he was in the cave whose location they had kept secret from humans for so long.

"Skimmer!" barked Longback out of the darkness. "I hear you brought a human aboard."

"It's true," said another voice. "We can all smell him over there."

"I think I touched him," gasped someone else.

Avender spoke up. "I'm not trying to hide," he explained. "I just—"

"Pipe down over there!" roared the bull. "Skimmer's the one I'm talking to! Skimmer, did you bring this human aboard?"

"I-I did, Longback," stammered the younger nokken. "But the pirates were going to kill him if I didn't. They already clubbed him once—"

"You know the rules," cried someone from out of the darkness.

"That's right!" called another. "No humans in the rookery! It's the law!"

"But the humans have been our friends for years, now," cried Pu-phugger. "It's not like the old days."

"STOW IT!"

Longback's massive voice boomed out around the rookery as loudly as the great cataract itself. When the last echo had died away the cave was absolutely silent. Not even a pup barked. Avender sat holding his knees close to his chest and wished he could see what was going on. He was colder now that there were no nokken close by to keep him warm.

When Longback spoke again his voice, though not so loud, was still commanding. "In case you all forgot," he said, "we changed the law that time Nolo came to visit. We've had peace with the humans for longer than my grandfather's grandfather could remember. If the human's life was in danger, as Skimmer says, then we should at least take his bait before we decide what to do. But first, I think we need a little light. I want to take a look at this pup before I decide what's to be done with him."

A long moment passed, during which time there was more shuffling from Longback's side of the cave. Avender wondered why Skimmer had never told him about Nolo visiting the rookery. His question was answered when a warm glow suddenly filled the cavern. Firrit, one of Longback's younger wives, was balancing a Dwarven lamp on her nose. Close beside lay the bull, and in his mouth was the cloth in which the light had been wrapped before it was uncovered. Avender blinked and held his hand over his eyes until he grew accustomed to the brightness. It was a small lamp, but after the total darkness of the cave it seemed like a great deal of light indeed. Firrit moved slightly as she balanced the jewel on the tip of her nose, causing the shadows to swim gently back and forth across the walls of the cavern.

Longback dropped the cloth to the floor of the cave. "Step up, human," he called.

Avender crawled to the edge of the rock shelf. Before him a dark pool of water shimmered in the light. Several bachelors skimmed back and forth across its inky surface, eyeing the boy menacingly. Around the pool were other shelves and ledges of rock like the one Avender sat upon. But the others were crowded with nokken. Aunties and pups, bachelors and graybacks, their whiskers quivered as they stared at him. Avender had never seen so many nokken at one time before.

Longback and Firrit occupied a ledge close to the water on the other side of the pool. He was the largest nokken in the cave, with streaks of silver on his sides and thin, silver ears. Heaving himself up on his front flippers, he extended his neck and nose forward to give Avender a long, stern look. When he was done, he swung his nose down toward Skimmer, who lay all alone at the edge of the ledge in front of his captain.

"Now," said Longback. "Let's hear your tale."

Skimmer coughed into his flipper nervously. "Well," he began, "I was doing some night fishing off the Rock. The whitefins are spawning over there and it might be a good idea to check it out tomorrow—"

"Keep to the current, Skimmer," said Longback firmly.

Skimmer wriggled his whiskers and went on. "Um, like I said, I was fishing, when I saw a light moving on Nokken Rock. I went over to see what was going on and got there just in time to see two canoes come ashore. I couldn't tell who was in them, so I swam up a little closer to see what was happening. I thought it might be the rock throwers coming back to cause more trouble."

"Why'd you think that if you couldn't even see 'em?" called someone from the ledges above.

"Stow your gab!" roared Longback at the galleries. "I'll ask the questions here!" The muscles in his neck rippling as he moved, he looked back down at Skimmer. "So, why did you think that if you couldn't even see 'em?"

"I don't know." Skimmer shook his flippers meekly. "But why would humans come out to the Rock in the middle of the night? Especially during a feast? I didn't think they were up to any good."

"They were the same ones," called Avender from his side of the cave, thinking it would help Skimmer's story. "The same ones who threw the rocks this morning."

Longback glared across the pool at the boy for speaking out of turn but said nothing. On their ledges the nokken murmured among themselves. A few nodded their sleek necks, as if inclined to think better of Avender now they had heard he had also been a victim of the rock throwers.

"Anyway," continued Skimmer, "even when I came closer I couldn't see who they were. But I thought I'd watch 'em all the same, just in case they tried something. It wasn't long before one of 'em started fighting with the others. He knocked two down before the one with the torch broke it on his head. Then the leader ordered two of the others to take the one he'd knocked down up to the diving rock, while he took the others back to the fire. I couldn't see what was happening anymore, so I swam around to the other side to get a better view. But as soon as I got there, I heard a big splash. When I swam over to see what was up, there was Avender, down about a fathom and still sinking."

Skimmer twisted around to see how he was doing. Every eye in the cave was still upon him. He shook his long neck and went on.

"When I saw it was Avender," he said, "I grabbed him, and dragged him back to the surface. Then I swam out a little farther into the lake just in case the humans tried throwing rocks again. I tried talking to him, but Avender just hung in my mouth like a dead fish. I knew I couldn't take him back to the Rock, so I brought him here. I didn't know what else to do. I know I broke the law, but he's my friend."

"You were just hoping you might get another piece of candy," jeered one of the bachelors from the pool.

Skimmer ignored the envious swimmer and looked back across the cave to his friend sitting alone on the rock. "If I held you underwater too long, Avender," he said, "I'm sorry. I forgot you need to breathe more'n me."

"I'm okay," said Avender. He gave another small cough, though, and looked at Longback. "Do what you want to me, Admiral, but we still need to rescue Reiffen. Those bandits took him, too, and there's no telling what they've done to him. The sooner we tell Berrel and Redburr, the sooner they'll be caught."

"All in good time, human. All in good time." Longback preened a bit: he liked being called Admiral. "But you're not the one in the dock. First we have to deal with Skimmer's lawbreaking."

The bull returned his stern attention to the youngster. Skimmer crouched a little closer to the floor. "So then," said Longback. "I can see why you rescued the human. But why'd you bring him back to the rookery?"

"I-I didn't know what else to do," Skimmer replied. "He wasn't waking up. Usually when a human falls in the water they scream and shout a lot, but not this time. I didn't even know if he was still alive. So I decided to bring him here. I thought Auntie Puphugger might know what to do."

"You should've taken him back to the Manor." Longback leaned forward until his nose was just above Skimmer's head. He was at least twice Skimmer's size; and though the fur on his back was laced with patches of gray, there was little doubt Skimmer would be able to put up much more fight against him than a stickleback.

"Please, sir," said Avender. "That water was awful cold. I'd have died if Skimmer hadn't brought me ashore. I don't think he'd ever have gotten me back to the Manor quick enough."

Longback twisted his neck to look at Avender. His dark eyes were impenetrable across the cavern. For a moment he studied the bedraggled human, then looked up at all the nokken on the ledges around him, his neck swiveling from one side of the cave to the other. Most of the troop returned his gaze, though there were some who snuffled and turned their whiskers aside, unable, even in the midst of the group, to stand up to the bull. Not a nokken said a word.

"Here's my judgment," said Longback at last. "The human may live." There was a murmur from some, who swung their heavy necks in irritation. "But Skimmer is cast away for a full season. Till the ice returns he's forbidden to set whisker or fin inside the rookery."

One of the braver bachelors piped up from the water at the center of the cave, "But Longback! The law says—"

"The law changes!" roared the bull. He leaned forward and bared his teeth, old and yellow but still very sharp. "The humans are our friends! They've not killed one of us in the memory of our oldest grandfather's grandfather! Nor will we kill them in turn!"

"But if we let him go the humans will know about the rookery!" called out one of the older aunties from her ledge. "How safe will the pups be then? Even if the Valings are our friends, in time other humans will learn our secret. Not all humans are our friends."

The auntie looked knowingly around the cave and heard snuffles and snorts of agreement from all the other ledges.

"Who said anything about letting him go?"

All the nokken fell quiet. Firrit almost dropped the lamp from the tip of her nose. Longback craned his neck in triumph around the cave. In the silence the small waves of the pool lapped gently at the edges of the rock. Avender's voice sounded very small as he spoke.

"Please, Longback," he said. "I can't live here."

"Why not?" The bull rolled his neck proudly around his cavern. "There's everything you need here. Plenty of fish. Warmth. Nolo's lamp." Firrit almost dropped the lamp again when she realized everyone was looking at her. "You can sing us the human songs, and we'll sing you ours."

Avender bit his lip to keep from bursting into tears. It had been a long and terrible night. Reiffen was out there, in the hands of the bard and his bandits; and in the meantime he was the prisoner of the nokken.

"For goodness' sake, Longback," came Puphugger's voice from the auntie's ledge. "Let the pup go. We can't have a human living in the rookery."

More than a few of the other nokken nodded their whiskers in agreement. Puphugger bobbed her head wisely when she saw she had made her point. It was usually the bachelors who chafed the most at sharing the lake with humans.

"I'd gladly let him go," answered the bull. "But it's not a risk the rookery can take."

"I'll give you my word," said Avender. "You can have my solemn oath." He crawled forward until he was kneeling at the edge of the pool. One of the bachelors circling in the water rolled over onto his back and spat a long plume of water past Avender's shoulder before diving back into the depths.

"Your word's not enough," answered Longback sternly. "Not even from a friend. For years your kind hunted mine. We're at peace with you now, and I believe you'd try to keep your word. But weed grows even at the bottom of the lake, and secrets have a way of bubbling out of humans. Isn't it right your own father lost his life because humans couldn't keep secret where they'd hid their Sword? That's right, Avender. I know all about it. I know all about humans. So why should I trust you?"

The bull's dark eyes were easy to read this time as they bored into Avender. Longback might trust the Valings to live beside him along the lake the nokken had been born to. Especially if he had no other choice. But he would never give up his kind's closest secrets as long as there were alternatives.

"Please, Longback." All eyes turned to Skimmer as he looked up at the bull. "Couldn't we cover his eyes? If we covered his eyes he'd never be able to see where the rookery is if we let him go."

"Cover his eyes?" Longback looked down at the young nokken in puzzlement. "Cover his eyes? Cover his eyes with what?"

"With that." Skimmer pointed his nose toward the cloth that had covered the lamp and now lay on the floor at Longback's side. "I've seen humans do it with horses. They cover their eyes to keep 'em from seeing something that might scare 'em, like when they load 'em onto a boat or something. If we covered Avender's eyes, then he wouldn't be able to see where the rookery is. I could take him out my—"

Skimmer's explanation of his scheme was interrupted as two bachelors caught him in the chin with a pair of carefully aimed streams of water. Skimmer shook his neck and tried to get out of their way, but nokken spray water much better than they waddle and, try as he might, Skimmer couldn't avoid the bachelors' attack.

"Enough!" Longback glared at the squirters. "I'm the bull! Are you challenging me? Is that what this is about!"

The jets of water stopped immediately. The two offenders sank back down into the pool until only the tops of their heads were visible above the water. Longback continued to glare at them until they were properly cowed.

"Oh, let the human go," cried a voice from one of the ledges.

Longback glared at that nokken as well, then turned back to Skimmer.

"Explain this about covering the eyes to me again," he said.

It wasn't long before Longback was convinced he might let Avender go blindfolded at no risk to the secret of the rookery. And the sooner they let him go, before the lake was flooded with search parties trying to find out what had happened to Reiffen, the better. Some hours remained before dawn, and it was still dark enough for the nokken to safely bring Avender back out to the surface. Longback sent several bachelors out to make certain no early fishing boats were about, then ordered Avender to get ready to return to the lake.

"But what about Reiffen?" Avender reminded him. "Shouldn't we at least send word to the Manor that he's been taken?"

"I'll go," volunteered Skimmer.

"The troop'll do better than that," insisted Longback. "Icer, take a patrol out and see if you can find those pirates. Probably they're still on the Rock. Skimmer can go to the Manor."

Longback waved them away. Skimmer scooted across the slick surface of the ledge and disappeared into the pool without a splash. Icer and several other nokken dove down from the ledges above and also vanished into the dark water. Avender was left to tie the cloth tightly over his eyes himself. None of the nokken could possibly manage a knot with only teeth and flippers. The cloth was rough and stiff against his face, and smelled terribly of fish, which was made worse when Longback jetted a stream of water across Avender's eyes to make sure the blindfold was on tightly. Avender staggered backward as he was caught by surprise.

"Now, down the hatch with you," said Longback from the pool.

The boy knelt beside the ledge and slipped back into the water. It was terribly cold.

"Better take some deep breaths," warned the nokken captain. "Now grab onto my flippers. I'm right in front of you."

"Is it a long ride?" asked Avender as he reached for Longback. The bull's fur was much warmer and less slippery than the boy had expected and comforted him somewhat against the frigid pool. And though Longback smelled a little, the wet seal was certainly much more pleasant than the wet bear had been.

"Not too far," answered the bull. "But you'd better get a lungful. Ready?"

The water grew even colder as Avender's head submerged. The shock sent his memory back to the moment when the bandits had thrown him from the Rock; his bruises throbbed.

Then Avender was off on the strangest ride of his life. On the first attempt he fell off and had to be taken back to the rookery to start again. But the second was more successful. Before he knew it, the boy found himself racing through the dark, water streaming past his face. Bubbles boiled around them. He held on tightly, afraid he might accidentally be brushed off by the walls of the tunnel. But Longback swam as surely as he was swift, and Avender felt nothing at all but water against his back.

They descended at first, until the boy thought his ears were going to burst. Then they were scooting this way and that as Longback swam powerfully through the twists and turns of the entrance to the rookery. Avender hung on for dear life, his arms wrapped around the body of the nokken, just above the fins, and prayed he could hold his breath long enough for the journey to end.

The water around them became smoother as Longback shot out of the tunnel. The nokken captain burrowed on through the cold water, not wanting to come back to the surface too close to the rookery. Avender gritted his teeth and tried hard not to breathe. The pounding in his head grew worse, both from his bruises and from the strain on his lungs. He knew he was going to drown. And then, just as he felt his lungs were going to burst, Longback carried him leaping out over the water. Avender took a great, gulping gasp of air. He let go of the nokken and the two fell side by side back into the lake, Avender with a great splash and Longback with hardly a ripple.

The boy had only a moment's peace, gasping for breath, before Longback smacked him on the back of the head with a flipper.

"Did I say you could let go?" Longback demanded. "Do that again and I'll drown you. They probably heard your splash all the way to Bracken. Now hold tight and don't freeze to death. I have to take you to dry land."

Longback was much stronger than Skimmer and could carry Avender far more swiftly. So it wasn't long before the seal deposited the boy on the shore of some dark island. Avender was cold, but not completely numb, and was just barely able to remove his blindfold with his frozen fingers when told to do so by the bull. Hard stone lay beneath him as he pulled himself ashore. He lay still for a moment, staring at the night sky and the ghosts of color tinting the tops of the High Bavadars.

"My cloth," said Longback from the lake.

Avender tossed him his cloth. "I have something else for you, too." The boy reached into his pocket and pulled out his bag of candy. Wet sugar oozed all around his hand.

"Mother Spinner's?" Longback shook his head. "They would only melt by the time I got them back to the rookery. Keep them for yourself, boy."

Without another word, and with only a slight swirl of water behind his tail, the nokken disappeared, back to the rookery and his kind.

5

The High Bavadars

vender shivered on the rocky beach as the gray day crept across the sky. Clouds lay thick on the mountains, covering all but the lowest hills. He stared at what he could see of the western shore through the mist, his teeth chattering, then sat up quickly and looked around as he realized where he was. Longback had brought him back to Nokken Rock. For a moment he feared he might not be alone. Mindrell might still be lurking somewhere among the scattered rocks, or Boney with his wicked knife.

But there were few places to hide on the Rock. Avender soon saw, except for the sheep and a few curious gulls, he had the island to himself. The sheep trotted about quietly in the gray dawn; the birds picked at a dead grayling on the stones. Tiny wavelets rolled in silver curls across the stony beach. Cold though he was, he cast about the island for some sign of what had happened to the bandits and Reiffen during the night but found nothing. Even their fire was cold, doused completely. All that was left was a strange, foul reek that wafted faintly above the coals.

Crossing to the east side of the island, Avender sat back down on the beach and looked north to the Neck and the Manor. A whitefin nosed through the clear water at his feet, poking at the smooth pebbles. There wasn't a breath of wind, and the lake was still as glass. No breeze meant it would be canoes coming out from the lower dock to find him, not skiffs. So he hugged his knees close to his chest to keep warm and watched the lake for the first sign of approaching paddlers.

A small, dark head gently broke the surface of the bay. "Ork!" barked Skimmer. "Did you find Reiffen?"

Avender shook his head. "There's no sign of him, Skim. Did you get Berrel?"

The nokken nodded. The lake rippled around his neck, making the water shimmer in the thin light. "I had to go to Eastbay. No one was at the lower dock. They said they'd tell Berrel."

Avender rubbed the backs of his arms vigorously to try and warm them up. "How'd you know to come back here to find me?" he asked.

"Where else would you be?" The nokken glided back and forth across the little bay as he spoke. "Longback knew the humans would come here to look for Reiffen. So he brought you here, too."

"I'm glad you and Longback think alike," said the boy. "I don't want to stay out here wet and cold any longer than I have to."

"Of course we think alike." Skimmer wrinkled his nose in surprise at Avender's words. "He's my pap, remember?"

"Oh, that's right. I forgot." As far as Avender was concerned, Longback had acted like no father he had ever known. Banishing his own son from the rookery! But Avender also knew nokken family arrangements were different from humans', and that Longback had to be a bull first before he could be a father.

"It's too bad he sent you away for helping me," Avender said.

"I'm not a pup," said Skimmer proudly. "I catch fish on my own." He rolled over onto his back and glided close to the beach near his human friend. "I haven't slept in the rookery since that bad storm in Whitemonth anyway. Longback knew he wasn't really punishing me. Who wants to stay in a smelly old cave when it's spring!"

To show how little he cared about his exile, the nokken did several barrel rolls back out into the lake, dove deep, then zoomed abruptly up out of the water to land gracefully on one of the basking rocks along the shore that gave Nokken Rock its name. He gave himself a little shake. Drops of water flew through the air around him.

Avender scooted back across the beach to avoid getting even wetter. "I don't know how I can ever pay you back for rescuing me," he said.

Skimmer's velvet nose and dark eyes gleamed. "You're my friend. Give me a few pounds of Hern's salted pike and we'll call it even. Ferris and Reiffen wouldn't let me forget it if I let you drown."

Avender hugged his knees tightly, still feeling cold. He didn't want to think about Reiffen. Skimmer shook his long neck, ruffling the dark brown fur, and did a little grooming with his nose and teeth. The boy remembered the sticky packet in his pocket, and took it out.

"I don't have any salted pike," he said. "But I can give you this."

He tore the wadded bag open and spread the mostly melted mess out on the rock beside the seal. Skimmer's eyes brightened even more. With far less dignity than his father, the young nokken lapped up every bit.

The boy looked back at the lake. A pair of dark shapes had emerged from the mist in the direction of the Manor. Quickly they grew larger, the rhythmic sound of the paddles growing steadily across the water. Skimmer quickened his eating, then felt about the rock with his whiskers to be sure there was nothing he had missed.

By the time the two large war canoes came racing into the little bay, Skimmer was finished with his treat. He slipped easily off the rock and back into the lake. Humans and nokken might work together now in Valing, but water was always the best place for any finslapper to be when there were more than a few humans around.

The canoes surged to a halt, the lake foaming beneath their bows. Waves rolled across the beach. Before it was fully stopped,

Berrel leapt splashing out of the first canoe and hurried ashore. Nolo followed with a large pack and most of the other paddlers. They were all foresters, dressed in the dark green and brown that was as close as foresters came to having a uniform. All were hardy men, long used to days and weeks spent deep in the woods and mountains.

The Dwarf dropped his pack to the ground beside Avender and pulled out a thick blanket and dry clothes. "From Giserre," he said gruffly.

"Thanks," said the boy. "Where's Redburr?"

"He's already begun his search. He'll join us soon enough."

Behind them the foresters fanned out across the island. The sheep bleated anxiously and trotted about in alarm, and all the gulls took wing, complaining shrilly as they disappeared into the lowering sky. Berrel waited long enough for Avender to rub himself dry with the blanket before he asked to hear his tale. The boy told him everything as he dressed, from Mindrell's meeting them on the stairway to the moment when he was pushed from the cliff. From time to time the steward interrupted with particular questions, but mostly he said nothing. Occasionally he looked up at the gray sky to the east, as if he expected something or someone to appear from out of the clouds. When Avender came to the point where he awoke inside the rookery, the steward held up his hand for him to stop.

"Longback would just as soon you tell me as little about that as possible," he said.

There was a shout from the spot where Avender had found the fire. "There's been magic here," said the chief forester as they came up. He pointed out the stains among the rocks, and the withered look of the scrubby grass that had not been burned. "Some sort of potion, I'd guess. They poured it out on the fire when they were done."

"Aye, Ranner. I can smell it," said the steward. Beside him several of the other foresters sneezed.

"Spells, eh?" Nolo picked through the charred wood with his bare foot. "That means the bear was right. Mindrell works for the Three, not Rimwich."

"Either way," said Ranner, "his path is back through the pass and the Firron road. The Shaper will find them there. Here we won't learn much at all."

"Those are my thoughts exactly," said the steward. "And Redburr's. But if the bear has found anything he should be back by now."

Berrel looked uneasily up at the sky once more. A sudden gust of wind rolled over them from the south; Nolo tucked his beard into his belt to keep it from flying up into his face.

One of the foresters at the top of the cliff called down to those gathered at the bottom. "Redburr's coming!" he cried, and pointed towards the eastern sky.

The weak morning light was darkening quickly before the storm, but they could all see the large bird arrowing down toward them from the clouds. A very large bird. Nolo raised his arm stiffly from his shoulder and the bird, fully as tall as the Dwarf himself, descended to the offered perch in a great buffeting of wings and wind. Behind him the rain began to fall on the back of a second, heavier gust. None but Nolo was sturdy enough to hold the Shaper, but the Dwarf, with sinews strong as stone, provided a steady perch. Hard, cruel talons, each as long as a small knife, gripped his arm tightly.

"What news, Redburr?" asked Berrel after the great eagle had folded his wings.

The Shaper turned his head sideways to stare at the steward from one large, glassy eye. Avender had never seen Redburr take anything but bear or human shape before, and found this newest incarnation both interesting and strange. Except for the red tinge to the feathers about his head, there was nothing in the bird to remind anyone of either Redburr the bear or man, though he did seem a bit thicker through the middle than might have been normal for a bird.

Even his voice was different, sharp and shrill, as if it was harder for him to speak with his bird's beak and craw than it was with the muzzle of a bear.

"Cree!" he called. "There's no sign of them." It was impossible for him to talk without shrieking. "I flew all the way through the pass and up the road on the other side, both north and south. Even if someone met them with fresh horses they could never have gotten so far." He fluffed his wings and resettled on Nolo's arm. "I don't believe they've left Valing that way at all."

"There's no other way," said Berrel with a frown. "The mountains are impassable both south and west, and all the other ways are guarded."

"There was magic here, Redburr," said the Dwarf. He pointed to the remains of the fire at their feet. "Perhaps they used that in their escape."

The bird eyed the coals in his strange, sideways manner. "I'm no expert in spells," he shrilled. "But if they've escaped through some power of Usseis, we'll be hard-pressed to catch them."

Ranner wiped the rain from his face. "I don't think they used magic to get away," he said. "If they did, where are their canoes? They'd have had to leave the canoes behind if they left the Rock some other way."

"Then let's search for the canoes," suggested the Dwarf.

Redburr cocked his head and looked at the sky with his bright bird's eyes. "I can search from the air, again," he said. "But this rain will make it harder for me to see. And it'll take some time to circle the lake."

"You won't have to search the whole lake." Ranner scratched the back of his head and thought for a moment. "They can't have gotten much farther south than the Narrows even if they paddled all night."

"But why wouldn't they just head for the pass?" wondered the Dwarf as he wrung the rain out from the bottom of his beard.

"They might have gone up into the mountains to hide." Redburr cocked his head toward the Low Bavadars to the east. "Mindrell's smart enough to know he couldn't get far enough away before we'd be after him. Who knows what they might have done with their conjuring? They might have changed the boy into a mouse, or worse. For all we know they paddled back to Eastbay, changed themselves into a herd of cows with Mindrell as the cowherd, and are waiting for us to call off the search so they can sneak through the pass when we think they've already escaped."

"They could never hide as cows," said Berrel. "Strange cows would be noticed at once on any farm."

Nolo frowned impatiently. "Plainly they're hiding somewhere. All this talk won't help us find them."

"That's true," Berrel agreed. "Redburr, you'd better begin your search right away. The rest of us will paddle back across the bay. We'll raise the Home Guard and search every barn and goat shed in Valing until we find them."

"What about the western shore?" asked Avender. He had been thinking hard ever since Redburr suggested that Mindrell might be hiding in the mountains. "If you were going to hide, wouldn't you hide in the opposite direction you thought everyone was going to look?"

Berrel and the others looked at the boy in surprise. Having heard his tale, they had all but forgotten him. Ranner rubbed his chin and considered what the boy had suggested. "Well now, I might," he said, "if that didn't end up making my eventual escape that much harder. There's no way out of the High Bavadars except back across the lake. You know that as well as I do, lad. Mindrell won't want to cross the lake a second time to get away. No, if he's hiding, it'll be on the east side of the lake, in the Lows."

The steward laid a comforting hand on Avender's shoulder. "You've had a long night," he said, "and too many adventures already. When we rescue Reiffen it'll be because you persuaded Longback to send Skimmer out to find us. But—"

"Cree!" shrilled Redburr. "It may be unlikely, but the boy has a point. The very fact we're so ready to dismiss the idea shows the truth in what he says. We're dealing with the Three, after all. I for one am not ready to ignore any possibility. Ranner, how many trails are there on the western shore that Mindrell could have reached in the time he had?"

The forester scratched the back of his head again. "Only two or three. There's the High Trail back of Spinner's place, and Wallin's behind his. There are a couple others, but you have to know the lake and the mountains pretty good to be using those."

"We'll have to check them all," said Redburr. He turned to the steward. "I'll fly by Wallin's and the others on my way to Bracken, and maybe you can send one of the canoes over to Spinner's to look at the High Trail. Our quarry's probably on the east side of the lake, but I think we'll all be happier if we follow up every chance, no matter how remote."

So it was decided. Redburr nodded to Nolo, who tossed him into the air. The great bird flapped his wings and slowly began to rise south across the lake. Soon he was lost in the mist and rain. The rest of the company returned to the canoes, where Berrel told them off into two parties, one to go on with him to Eastbay, the other for Ranner to lead to Spinner's farm. The steward put as many men as he could into the first canoe, wanting to waste as few as possible on what he considered a wild-goose chase to the west. When it came time to choose a canoe for Avender, Berrel hesitated for a moment, then sent him off with Ranner.

"It was your idea in the first place," the steward said. "And I can't spare the seat in my own craft."

Deciding he needed to keep an eye on the boy, Nolo climbed into Ranner's canoe behind him. The four foresters with them hopped in at bow and stern, took up their paddles from where they had been left in the bottom of the boat, and pushed on rapidly across the lake. The rain hissed softly against the flat water around them; the only other sound was the muted knock of the paddles against the canoe's canvas sides. Avender remembered his last trip across the lake, bound in darkness beneath the thwarts, and wondered if Reiffen had been forced to endure a second silent passage of his own. Or had he really been turned into a mouse and kept quietly in Mindrell's pocket?

"Nolo?" The boy spoke quietly, his voice almost lost in the rain's wet whisper.

"What is it, lad?"

"How did Mindrell use magic? I thought only the Wizards could use magic."

"Others can cast spells and potions," Nolo replied. "But only if one of the Three prepares the way for them." He sat stiffly in the middle of the canoe, hardly moving. Rainwater sloshed around his legs. Should the Dwarf fall overboard Avender knew they would be a long time fishing him up from the lake bottom. "The Three guard their knowledge closely. But I'm told there have been times when they've trusted their slaves to do some small act of thaumaturgy for them."

"You mean anyone can do it?"

"If they have the knowledge."

"Even Dwarves?"

"No, lad. Dwarves can't. We're the children of Brydds, not Areft. Magic doesn't affect us, and we can't do magic. Not that any Bryddin has ever tried to brew a spell, far as I know. It's not a good thing, magic. Far too dangerous. Stone and water are what we trust."

"I hope Mindrell hasn't done anything too horrible to Reiffen," said the boy.

"Don't worry," Nolo assured him. "We'll find him."

At Spinner's dock Ranner left Avender behind to look after the canoe while he led the others ashore to inspect the farm. They were greeted by Spinner's dogs, who barked ferociously until Ranner approached them closely enough to be recognized. Avender sat on the dock with his feet in the canoe while the foresters hunted along the road toward the meadows above for any sign of Mindrell's passing. But the rain had already washed away whatever footprints might have been pressed into the soft dirt, and they found nothing. Nolo, who had no woodcraft at all, made his own search through the barns and farmhouse.

Most of the dogs followed the foresters, sniffing curiously, but one noticed Avender on the dock and trotted out to see what he was doing.

"Hello, Odo. Sorry, but I've nothing to give you today."

Avender scratched behind the dog's ears and under her chin. He and Reiffen had made friends with Spinner's dogs a long time since, just in case they ever had the opportunity to visit Enna Spinner's sugarhouse by night. The dog lay down contentedly on the dock beside the boy, not minding the wet at all if it meant a good scratching.

Avender was watching the raindrops on the water when Skimmer reappeared, his dark head emerging from the lake beside the canoe with hardly a ripple. Odo started to her feet and barked loudly at the newcomer, but Skimmer paid the dog no mind.

"Did you find Reiffen?" he asked again.

Avender shook his head. "He's probably on the other side of the lake, Skim, high in the pass."

"Then why're you looking here?"

Avender rocked the canoe slightly with his feet. "Because we have to look everywhere, just in case."

"I'll help."

"Sure, Skim. If you find their canoes let me know."

"Canoes?" Skimmer stopped swimming back and forth and rolled over onto his back. "What kind of canoes?"

"Regular canoes," replied the boy glumly. He was almost as wet again now as he had been after his ride with Longback. "From East-bay. If we find the canoes, then at least we'll know where they've gone."

Skimmer rolled back onto his belly and slipped underwater. His dark shape darted like a shadow beneath the large canoe. But he was back a moment later.

"There's two canoes under the dock," he said eagerly when he resurfaced. "Are they the ones you're looking for?"

"I don't think—" Avender stopped as he realized what the nokken had just said. "Two canoes? Under the dock?" He scrambled to his knees to peer through the dark water beneath the wooden boards. "Are they old?"

"I don't know how old they are," said Skimmer. "I just know there's two of them."

Try as he might, Avender couldn't see through the water beneath the dock. He looked back up at his friend. "You're sure there are two?"

"I can count, you know."

"What's keeping them down?"

"Maybe it's because they're filled with rocks."

Avender didn't wait to hear any more. He was sure the canoes were Mindrell's. He jumped up to his feet and began calling toward shore, waving for the foresters to return. Skimmer swam off a little farther into the lake as Nolo and the men came rattling back out onto the wooden pier. They got down on their knees beside the boy after he told them what the nokken had found.

"They have to be the ones we're looking for," said one. "No one sinks canoes for nothin'."

"We have to be certain." Ranner started to remove his jacket.

"I'll go," said the Dwarf, getting to his feet. "I can empty the rocks out of those canoes much faster than any of you can."

He stepped right off the side of the pier and plunged feetfirst into the water, sending up a tremendous splash. Avender and the foresters gathered around the edge and peered unsuccessfully into the depths to see how he was doing. Even Skimmer came dashing back to the dock to see if he could help, hurtling through the water like a bird.

A minute passed. The dull clank of stone rose dimly from below, but no one could see a thing. Skimmer tore back and forth around the dock. Then a waterlogged canoe rolled slowly up out of the water to wallow sluggishly beside the pier, and a second soon followed.

"Those are Eastbay canoes."

"And they ain't been down there long, either, or they wouldn't float so easy."

Nolo followed the canoes to the surface, climbing back up one of the pilings to the top of the dock. Water poured off him as he conferred with Ranner.

"We'll have to start after them at once," the Dwarf said.

"Aye." The chief forester peered through the rain back to the road behind the farmhouse that led up Breadloaf Hill. "They've got a fair start on us, too. Five, six hours easy."

"All the more reason for hurry," said Nolo.

"We'll have to send someone back to let Berrel know we're on the trail. That only leaves four of us to go after five, not counting the boy."

"One of ours is a Dwarf, though," said one of the foresters.

"We can send the boy back to the others with word of what we've found," said Ranner.

Nolo noticed the look on Avender's face. "No," he said. "Let him come with us. Searching the western shore was his idea, and he found the canoes, too."

"Actually, it was Skimmer who found the canoes," said Avender.

"Either way, you've earned the chance to come with us. We can send Skimmer back instead. He'll do it faster than any canoe."

Ranner eyed the boy grimly. "It'll be a hard climb," he said. "We've a lot of time to make up, too. We can't be waiting for laggards."

"He can do it. Can't you, lad?"

Avender nodded, though he was not at all sure he could keep up with foresters on the march. But he would much rather collapse on the trail than be left behind.

There was no more discussion. Skimmer received his instructions and darted back into the lake. Then the four men, the Bryddin, and the boy hurried from the dock back to the farm. They made a short stop in Mother Spinner's larder to scavenge a few provisions for the road, presuming Mother Spinner would approve, once she learned the reason. Avender hoped they might find a bag or two of candy as well, and assured himself that Reiffen would really appreciate such a homely treat when they found him. But Mother Spinner had taken all she had to the feast, and there were no more anywhere. Nolo did find a small cask, though, which he strapped to the top of his pack. That prize he had no intention of preserving until Reiffen was found.

It was a wet, cold climb, and Ranner drove them hard. The rain persisted as they slogged along the mountain road, which soon turned from path to stream beneath their boots. The muddy way led up through the lower pasture, where the Spinner cows were gathered placidly beneath a single oak in the middle of the field, and on to the upper meadows, where the huddled sheep had the fluffy look of fallen clouds. Beyond the sheep the wooded slopes began. Instead of the steady hiss of the rain on the grass, there was now the gloomy patter of thick drops striking the bare branches of the trees.

Quickly the path grew steeper and rougher. Beyond the farm the road was rarely used. Foresters on their patrols might travel through the mountains around the lake, but seldom would anyone else venture too deep among the lofty crags. Beyond a day or two's journey little was known of the mountains. There were strange tales about the High Bavadars, close though they might be to Valing. Strange storms that never troubled the lake could sometimes be seen scowling blackly above the farther peaks, and strange creatures were thought to hide in the most secret valleys behind the highest passes.

An hour's march brought them deep within the clouds. On a clear day they might have looked back and seen all the wide northern part of the lake spread below them, from Spinner's to Eastbay, sparkling and blue. But now, with the clouds settled thick upon the mountain, they could see little beyond the path beneath their feet and the jabbing fingers of the storm.

They were already far higher than Avender had ever been on the west side of the lake when they came to a scraggly fir by the side of the trail. A large, brown shape was perched upon one of the higher branches, which sagged almost to the ground beneath its weight. Only when they had come closer through the screening mist did they recognize Redburr's bird shape in the sodden lump.

"So you found us," said Ranner.

"There's only the one path past the Teapot," squawked Redburr. His feathers were heavy and wet; he looked as bedraggled as a bird could be.

"That's fair truth," the forester agreed. "Though we've seen little enough sign of our quarry along the trail. There's no other way they might have come."

The bird swept down on wide wings to alight on the small cask tied atop Nolo's pack.

"Watch your talons, there," warned the Dwarf. "We don't want to be drinking that just yet."

Not five minutes later they passed a low pine thicket by the side of the path. Redburr called for them to stop, his voice shrill even through the blanketing rain. Then he turned to the shrubbery and gave a piping call. For a moment nothing happened. He repeated the cry and a pair of finches poked their heads up from the short-needled boughs to trill a reply. Redburr answered, and the conversation sang back and forth, the finches obviously nervous to be speaking with an eagle. Several times they tried to duck their heads back down into the green cover, only to be called back to the task at hand by the sharp whistling of the larger bird. When they were done Redburr allowed them to return to their nest, then turned back to his companions.

"It's not easy speaking songbird when you're a raptor," he cawed. He shook his head as he spoke, as if to clear it. A fine spray spattered off his feathers.

"I did learn the birds saw the bandits," he went on. "They passed by here in the night, close before dawn."

"Did they see Reiffen?" asked Avender hopefully.

"Finches can't tell one human from the next. They can't even count. But there's no one else who might have been up here so early in the morning. You can be sure we're on the right trail."

"At least they haven't gotten themselves up as pike or something, and dived back into the lake," said Nolo. He wrung out his beard once again and, for a moment, the stream at their feet thickened across the stones.

On through the mud and rain they trudged. Redburr rode atop Nolo's cask rather than try to fly through the storm, bobbing like a cork with every one of the Dwarf's short strides. As they climbed higher into the mountains the rain lightened, but the clouds thickened. Often they were unable to see more than a few feet on either side of the trail. Sometimes the rain turned to snow and swirled fiercely around their heads; but the snow never lasted long, and the ground was too wet for any of the flakes to stick. They hurried onward, regardless of the weather, until Avender thought his legs would fail beneath him. But he was determined to prove Nolo's confidence in his ability to keep up, so he gritted his teeth and made no complaint.

Toward the end of the day they came out of the trees into the gray and stony wastes of the higher peaks. The wind strengthened; now the constant snow was driven into their faces or lashed against their backs as they plodded on. When darkness fell they hardly noticed, it had been twilight so long. But finally they were in danger of losing their way in the deepening gloom, or stumbling off the sides of unseen cliffs, so Ranner called a halt in a small hollow filled with stunted trees. All sank wearily to the ground.

They cleared a space beneath the rough needles and lay with their heads on their packs, the gnarled wood at the heart of the tiny copse too wet for even Nolo to start a fire. Avender had no pack, but he had the blanket Nolo had brought for him that morning. The Dwarf had kept it dry through all the day's long climb. The boy wrapped himself as snugly as he could and was almost warm by the time Ranner shared out a round of the dried meat and bread they had brought from the farm. Nolo passed the small barrel among them as well, which made them all feel warmer still, except Redburr, who couldn't manage a proper drink with his bird's beak. After knocking over the third cup set out for him, he cursed bitterly and flapped his wings.

"If I didn't think you'd need me as a bird tomorrow," he grumbled, "I'd go back to being a bear right now. A whole cask of lovely beer."

All but Avender and Redburr took their turn on guard, listening for real danger in the howls and shrieks of the windy night. The boy slept far more soundly than he could ever have imagined on the cold and muddy ground. Near dawn he dreamed of bandits and nokken and bards. They chased him through pool-filled caverns where the ceilings grew lower and lower until finally they were so low he was forced to crawl forward on hands and knees. When nothing was left for him but to fall forward into one of the pools and sink slowly downward into the darkness, he scrabbled for breath, then woke, panting in the night. For a moment he thought he was back in the rookery, with all the nokken snoring around him. Then he smelled the fresh scent of the scrubby pines rather than old fish and dank fur, and remembered that a long day had passed. It was mostly humans snoring around him now. He was still wet and shivering, but this time he was high in the mountains instead of deep inside a watery cave. He reached out cautiously and felt something soft nearby.

"Brawwk! Is that you, boy?"

Somehow Redburr's voice sounded more like it should in the dark, despite the squawk.

"It's me," Avender replied.

"Go back to sleep. It'll be another long day soon."

"Has the storm stopped?" Water no longer dripped from the trees, and the roaring of the wind had disappeared.

"The snow stopped some time ago, and the wind just died. I should have fine flying today. Now go back to sleep."

"Will we catch them soon?"

"We'll see."

Avender closed his eyes thinking he was wide awake. When he opened them again he could see every crooked branch clearly in the thicket above his face, and the rest of the company were scrambling awake around him. Ranner passed around another bite of food and then they pushed their way out through the stiff wood to stretch their legs on the clear ground outside. Only a little snow lay upon the gray stone. The rest had already melted or blown away. Sharp peaks rose toward the pale sky, the last storm clouds and lingering stars sharing the space between.

They marched off with the mountain morning throwing long shadows across the land. Avender's sore muscles soon loosened, but it took longer for the brisk wind to drive the last dampness from his clothes. At the first ridge with a strong breeze Redburr left them, leaping upward into the wind from the top of the Dwarf's head. For a while the Shaper soared above the long valley, searching for the rising air that would help him ascend. His companions watched him glide with widespread wings as they followed their own path across the arms and shoulders of the mountain, until he found the current he sought and wheeled away. Soon he was a black speck in the distance, disappearing between tall crests of rock and snow that gleamed in the golden light of the new day.

Nolo put a kind hand on Avender's shoulder as they watched the Shaper pass out of sight. "Ready for another day, lad?" he asked. "You're not tiring on us, are you?"

"I can do it," answered the boy stubbornly. "Reiffen's still somewhere up ahead of us, isn't he?"

Ranner led them on. They had long since lost any trace of the bandits. Their only hope now was that Redburr would be able to spot their quarry from the air with his sharp eagle's eyes. In the meantime they could do no more than follow the chief forester deeper into the western mountains.

The day grew warm. The last shreds of the clouds scattered among the jagged peaks. They climbed slopes of broken rock and picked their way carefully over valleys of pitted ice and snow. Pools of water filled the hollows and everywhere ticked the drip, drip, drip of ice loosened by spring. Twice they saw nimble mountain goats watching them from impossible ledges, but the morning was well advanced before Redburr reappeared. They were toiling along the side of a long ridge, steep cliffs on either hand, when he dropped like a stone from the cold blue heights. He swooped in a long, slow turn above the valley to their left before landing once again on the top of Nolo's pack.

"I've found them!" he cried in his bird's hoarse croak. A gleam of satisfaction shone brightly in his eye. "They're still heading west, but you're not too far from their trail. They took a different way around that mountain ahead of us."

Ranner nodded grimly. "They must have gone south on the ice field yesterday. Not a course I'd take in a thaw. How far behind are we?"

"About two hours. At the rate they're going, you should be able to catch them by the end of the day."

"Can you tell where they're headed?"

The feathers on Redburr's neck and shoulders ruffled in the wind. "Not yet. But they've come a long way if all they want to do is go to ground."

One of the foresters gave the bird an unhappy look. "You mean you think they're trying to cross right through the range?"

"It can't be done," said Ranner firmly.

"It has been done." Redburr gave the chief forester a sharp look. "I've done it myself, and not as a bird. But it was a long time ago, and I'm afraid I don't remember as much about the way as I should."

"If we're going to catch Mindrell by the end of the day," observed the Dwarf, "it hardly matters how far they're going. Gabbing about it just slows us down."

"Did you see Reiffen?" broke in Avender, unable to contain himself any longer from asking what he considered the most important question. "Is he all right?"

Redburr cocked a glassy eye. "I saw him, boy. He seemed to be dodging most of their kicks, as far as I could tell. But there are only four of the bandits now, counting the bard."

"Four?" Nolo tugged at his beard and turned to Avender. "Didn't you say there were five, lad?"

"There were," answered the boy. "Maybe Reiffen killed one."

"Cree! It'd be nice if he had, wouldn't it?" croaked the bird.

"More likely he fell through the cracks in the ice field," said Ranner. "It's a dangerous path when the bridges start to melt. That's why we're headed for the Girdle."

"The Girdle?" Nolo pulled at his beard.

Ranner nodded. "It looks bad, but Chimneyline and the Chutes are both worse. Long as the ledges hold, the Girdle's all right. And it's faster than the ice field on the other side. I'll rope us all together and we'll be safe as picnickers on Baldun. But the Girdle marks the end of my knowledge of the mountains. After that we'll be following your lead, Redburr."

There was nothing to do but press on as quickly as possible. Redburr took flight once more, leading them over the top of the ridge. Two hours' hike was no more than a few minutes' flying time for an eagle, and Redburr could flit back and forth between both parties with ease. They ascended on up the line of the ridge until they came to a place where their path seemed to fall off impassably into the valley below.

"There." Ranner pointed to the side of the mountain. "That's the Girdle."

At first Avender saw nothing. The trail appeared to end at the edge of the cliff before them. To their left the mountain towered huge and gray. Then he noticed a thin ridge of rock, wider in some places than others, winding across the middle of the mountainside. Redburr circled in the air above, but there were other birds wheeling through the sky below the slender path.

"That?" Nolo laughed at the sight of the narrow ledge. "That's nothing. You want a climb sometime, Ranner, come with me to Issinlough. When you've clung by your fingers and toes to the bottom of the world, then you've had a real taste of climbing."

"Wasn't me as said it was hard," replied the forester.

Several of his fellows pulled lengths of rope from their packs and soon everyone in the party, except the eagle, was tied together. Cautiously they started across the ledge. Avender found out soon enough that Ranner was right. The climb was not as hard as it looked. In some spots the ledge was two or three feet wide. Even at its thinnest there was still room for his entire foot to rest securely on the rock. In a howling wind and a storm like the one they had fought through the day before there would be real danger, but for the moment the only problem was that the ledge was broken in spots. And there were places where one ledge ended outright and they had to step over a fair-sized gap to reach the next. But Ranner and his fellows knew their business, and there was always Nolo bringing up the rear. With his strength and ability to grab onto the rock as if it were so much soft cheese, he was safer than the firmest anchor. "Dwarves don't fall," he always said. "How else could we live on top of the Abyss?"

The only bad moment came when Ranner stopped to test a bit of rock in front of him. Avender was halfway back along the line, safely anchored in the middle of the more experienced climbers, but the curve in the side of the mountain gave him a fine view as the chief forester took the long hammer from the loop on the back of his pack and tapped its thin head gently on the edge of the rock just beyond his toe. There was a crack, and a large piece of stone broke away to tumble down the slope. Other rock broke free below as the first bounded down the cliff, and all disappeared into the distant valley in a shower of gravel and dust. Redburr, who had been soaring nearby, swept in close to the mountain, as if he thought he might have to grab the forester in his talons. But Ranner was holding fast to the rope behind him with his free hand and stepped back quickly onto more solid footing without the slightest hesitation. A new gap was opened in the ledge, neither smaller nor larger than the rest. Carefully Ranner tested the new edge. When he was satisfied that it was firmer than the old, he stepped across it. The company moved on.

The rest of the day's march was much easier. Beyond the Girdle they untied themselves and followed the eagle up through another pass with the wind in their faces. They descended to another snowfield, and so on through several more passes, always climbing, as they advanced deeper into the High Bavadars. Now they found many traces of the bandits' passage: steps cut into the ice; footprints in the snow.

Even so, the afternoon had worn away by the time they climbed over the edge of one last ice field and followed its frothing runoff down to a steep, tree-filled valley. The sun was settling behind the western peaks as the Shaper urged them on, afraid they might not catch Mindrell before nightfall after all. By the time they reached the trees an ominous cloud had rolled in from the north above their heads like a spreading tide. Wearily they stumbled across the stones to a place where the stream met another, smaller brook flowing down from the direction of the looming storm.

"Cree! This way," called Redburr from a perch at the top of a tree above the second stream. "Hurry!" He watched for a moment as Ranner led the tired party up this new steep course. Then, with a flap of his wings, he launched himself back into the air and flew over the treetops beyond. A clap of thunder rang out through the valley. Close behind burst a sudden gust of wind. The thinner trees in the woods around them shuddered before the blast.

"That's no common storm," muttered the forester nearest Avender.

Nolo quickened his pace and began to leap quickly among the boulders after Redburr. The foresters, not to be outdone by a Dwarf in their own mountains, summoned the last of their strength to follow him. But they were no match for Nolo's endurance no matter how much longer their legs, and he soon outdistanced them. Avender, who had been in the middle of the company, found himself lagging to the rear no matter how hard he tried to keep up. He was young and sturdy but, unlike the men around him, had not spent the days of his life in constant climbing among the peaks and crags. The thunder rose and the stream began to chatter more and more loudly along its stony banks. The boy fell farther and farther behind.

Darkness dropped down across the mountainside as the storm swept over the trees. Branches rattled, first in the wind, then in the rain. Avender stumbled on into the teeth of the storm, his cloak lashing around him far more fiercely than it had the day before. Soon he found he could no longer safely follow the brook. The stream was rising quickly as every drop of rain from the valley above was channeled into the flow at his feet. He clambered up the nearest bank and continued on through the trees, but his progress slowed considerably as he had to make his way around every fallen branch and straining sapling.

The storm grew more and more ferocious. Finally there was a great clap of thunder, louder than any Avender had ever heard. The storm broke, its anger released in that single stroke. All was quiet again, except for the sodden pouring of the rain and the rush of the swollen stream. Avender almost fell on his face as the wind out of the north ceased abruptly. He hurried forward, though the urgency of the moment seemed to have collapsed as suddenly as the storm. The earth sucked wetly at his boots.

He came at last to a short cliff. Such was the torrent now, there was barely room to climb beside it. Somehow he managed to pull himself over the top, half-drowned and at the end of his strength. He stumbled on through the last of the woods to a meadow of thick grass. Scattered before him, he saw the foresters combing the field as if in search of something. The shorter figure of Nolo glowed in a thin light beyond a circle of tall stones that stood to the left of the stream. As Avender watched, the Dwarf bent down beside something hidden in the grass.

The boy hurried on. Heavy rain beat at him coldly. He noticed two figures that were not foresters, and when he realized they were being guarded by one of Ranner's men, his heart leapt at the sight of them. They had caught the bandits! Reiffen was rescued!

Avender hastened on through the gloom toward the lighted spot in the grass where he had last seen Nolo.

6

The Standing Stones

hat was that?"

Reiffen started as he heard the splash. It came from his left, beyond the looming darkness of the hill where the two bandits had taken Avender. Ahead he could see the dancing flicker of a fire. Mindrell and the other thieves were leading him toward the flame, carefully picking their way through the jumbled rocks. Quietly the bard sang, with some slight difference, the words Reiffen had first heard in the Great Hall what felt like days and days ago.

"And so he sank beneath the play
    Of wave and boat and cold and spray,
    Beyond the touch and feel of day."

Reiffen flushed but, instead of lashing out at Mindrell, listened hopefully for a moment as he stumbled forward. Maybe there would be a cry for help to follow the splash, or some further sound of struggle. But there was nothing. All he heard were scuffing feet as Mindrell led them through the rough stones to a low campfire at the center of the island. Small shadows swam across the rocks as Boney pushed his prisoner roughly to the ground. Reiffen sank down wretchedly, hardly feeling the warmth of the fire. A grim, empty feeling crept across him as he realized Avender was gone.

He gazed bitterly at the bard. "You said you wouldn't kill him."

Mindrell poked at the fire with his boot. "I said I wouldn't kill him in the Manor. I never said a thing about letting him live forever." Several sparks leapt up into the night, yellow stars beneath the clouded sky.

Boney bent to rub his thin hands in the heat of the fire.

"There's no time for that," said Mindrell harshly. He turned to the one called Ike and ordered, "Give over the pack."

From the darkness beyond the stones Ike brought out a large knapsack and handed it to the bard. Boney continued to crouch over the coals until Mindrell kicked him away. Then the rhymer told his two confederates to fetch fresh wood for the fire while he began to unpack the knapsack.

Reiffen had seen enough to be fairly certain they had taken him to Nokken Rock. He recognized the hill on the other side of the fire. But knowing where the bard had taken him was no help at all. There was nowhere to run, and no sign of any nokken to send for help. He leaned back miserably against the nearest rock, his arms still bound to his sides, and watched helplessly as Mindrell removed a small pot, several short sticks, and a carefully wrapped bundle from the knapsack. Opening the sticks into a small tripod, the bard set the pot beside them on the ground. Boney and Ike added the wood they had brought to the dying coals. When the flames were leaping once again, the bard set the tripod over the fire, poured water into the pot, and hung the pot over the burning wood. Then he carefully unrolled the bundle and added the contents one by one to his makeshift kettle, stirring the mixture with his knife all the while. First came some pale, powdery stuff, then what looked like a shriveled ear, and several whiskered roots. Lastly he held the knife to his left palm and, using the sharp point, cut a thin red line in his hand. One, two, three drops of dark blood dripped into the pot. Each drop hissed as it fell into the nasty broth. Ike and Boney backed away from the fire. Mindrell wiped his wound on his pants and wrapped a cloth tightly round it.

Reiffen shivered at the sight.

"You'll be warm again soon enough," said the bard with a shameless grin. He tapped the knife blade against the side of the kettle. The boy made no reply but swallowed hard in an effort to hold down the dread rising in his throat. What Mindrell was preparing looked like magic, or what Reiffen supposed magic might look like. Until that moment he had thought the only magic in the world was what was worked by the Wizards in faraway Ussene. But, if the bard was working for his uncle the king, what was he doing with magic?

Mindrell watched him carefully from beside the fire. He seemed to know exactly what the boy was thinking. "You're right," he said. "It is magic, Your Majesty."

Reiffen flushed again at the rhymer's mocking.

"It must be hard," the bard went on, "knowing what your life might have been. I know I wouldn't like it. But that's all going to change now. Maybe where you're going they'll let you brew a trick or two, yourself, like the one they've given me."

Reiffen's throat thickened fearfully. It was the Wizards Mindrell was working for, not his uncle. A terrible dread crept along his spine at the thought of why the Wizards might want him. No one ever escaped from Ussene. He was only going to live a little while longer than his friend.

Terrified, he watched as the bard let the potion cook a while longer, stirring it from time to time with the knife blade. When Mindrell was satisfied the mixture had cooked enough, he picked the tripod up with the flat of the knife and moved both pot and tripod away from the fire. Some of the potion tipped over the rim. The flames below spat and sparked, and sent up a burst of dark, stinking smoke. Reiffen sneezed violently: the smell was unbearable. His nose stung as if it had been rubbed in bitter charcoal. Ike and Boney also sneezed, but Mindrell had covered his nose with his bandaged hand and wasn't bothered.

"Ow, that's nasty stuff," said Boney.

"Glad it's not me has to drink it," said Ike.

"Spells is always nasty," Boney pointed out.

"Aye," his partner agreed. "I don't trust 'em."

Mindrell looked up from the pot. "But you trust the pay, don't you," he said with a smile.

"Sure I do," replied Ike. "Same as you. Gold don't take a tarnish, now, do it?" He grinned, his scruffy face leering evilly in the low light of the fire.

They waited a few minutes for the brew to cool. Avender might be at the bottom of the lake, thought Reiffen bitterly, but the bard still took care his prisoner didn't burn his throat on the vile potion.

"Well?" asked their leader when Hurl and Tipps returned.

Hurl squatted close to the fire and rubbed his hands. "That one's gone," he said. "Sunk like a stone."

"We pitched him in head-on," said Tipps. "Never did come back up."

"Pike be eatin' him now. Or one of them nasty waterpup."

Reiffen hung his head. The bandits' return left no doubt about Avender's fate. Not that it really mattered. Avender was probably better off drowned. At least that way he wouldn't be taken to Ussene.

Satisfied with Hurl and Tipps's report, Mindrell turned back to his potion. Gingerly he touched the side of the pot with his hand. First a quick touch, then a longer one, as he felt the concoction to be almost ready. Finally he dipped the tip of his finger carefully into the oily mixture and judged it sufficiently cool. Wiping his hand carefully on his pants when he was done, he brought the pot to Reiffen.

"Give me a hand here," he said curtly to his men.

Ike and Hurl stepped forward. Reiffen scooted backwards away from them and banged his head on the rock behind him. The two bandits took hold of him firmly by the neck and shoulders and forced him closer to the fire.

"Tilt his head back and open his mouth," said Mindrell.

They pulled Reiffen's head painfully backward by the hair. A filthy hand forced his mouth open. Above him stood Mindrell with the reeking kettle. The metal lip was still hot, but not scalding. The boy choked as the awful liquid was poured down his throat. The taste was even worse than he had imagined. Old mice came to mind, and the insides of insects, and dirt mixed with blood as he coughed and gagged. He swallowed despite himself, and enough of the mixture passed into his stomach that he soon felt horribly sick. Dizziness quickly followed. The glowing fire, the black sky, and the sneering faces of his captors all began to spin around him. They swirled faster and faster until finally they dissolved into a whirling mix that drained him off to some place far away. He thought for a moment of what Mennon must have felt as he was pulled down beneath the earth by the rush of the river, and then he no longer thought much of anything at all.

After that there was only a distant numbness. The bandits let him go and he fell heavily to his side. It seemed to take the better part of a midsummer's day before he finally hit the ground. The world was very far away. He could see it, but it had become so remote that seeing it really didn't matter. He was quite comfortable where he was. What happened in the world outside was completely unimportant. It had nothing to do with him at all. As far as he was concerned, he was asleep at home in his bed, the quilt pulled up snugly against his chin. The birds that nested in the eaves beyond his window were already busy with the morning. Any minute he would wake, and the sky would be blue, and boats would be flying freely across the lake below. And he and Avender would have many things to do.

Reiffen was almost surprised when he did wake and found no sign of his friend. Nor was there any soft mattress beneath him, and no cozy comforter pulled up to his chin. Instead he found himself lying cold and wet upon rough ground, all his muscles aching and sore. He felt as if he had been walking for days. But the worst ache of all was the one in his head. It throbbed painfully, far worse than the first time he and Avender had sampled Hern's best ale. With a groan he opened his eyes. Boney's grimy face stared down at him.

"He's wakin' up," said the thief. "Just like you said he would, harper. But I still don't know why you don't just put him out again."

"Because now we're too far away for him to try running off. Right, Your Majesty?" The bard's face loomed behind the big-nosed thief.

Reiffen remembered. He wasn't safe at home in the Manor, and Avender was dead. He had no idea where he was. Around him it was bright day, and the peaks of high mountains rose on every side. He sat up and found his hands were bound before him. Boney scowled and kicked him once, just to show he could.

"None of that." The bard pushed the bandit roughly aside. "You don't want to make our employer unhappy, do you?"

Boney ducked nervously at the mention of who had hired him and moved off to sit with the other bandits. They were camped in the lee of a high ridge, a jumble of fallen boulders around them. The sharp peaks above shone brightly with fresh snow. Reiffen recognized none of them, but he guessed they had to be somewhere in the High Bavadars, deep in the mountains where he had never been before.

Mindrell approached, blocking his view. Reiffen recognized the pack on the bard's back, and the handle of the lute protruding over his shoulder. "So, how's your head, King?" the rhymer asked. "Feeling much like a hike?" There was no real sympathy in his voice, so Reiffen didn't bother to answer. Instead he tried to stand up, only to sit right back down again as his head spun and the steep slope swirled around him.

"You'll be all right in a minute." As he spoke, the bard reached for the knife in his belt, and Reiffen started back in alarm. Mindrell laughed.

"I thought you were smarter than that, Your Majesty." With one stroke of the blade he sliced through the cords binding the boy's hands. "You already know I don't want to kill you. The one I'm working for requires you alive."

"You killed my friend," countered Reiffen sullenly. He would much rather have shown Mindrell he didn't care what was done to him, but the man's constant ridicule upset him, and he couldn't help but answer.

The bard shrugged and pulled the boy to his feet. This time Reiffen felt only a slight uneasiness. "We already went over that," said Mindrell. "What's done is done."

He turned back to his men. "Hurl," he ordered, "give His Majesty something to eat and we'll be off."

Reiffen rubbed his wrists where the rope had burned them. Still a little wobbly, he put a hand against the rock to steady himself. For the first time he noticed there were only two other bandits besides Boney.

None of the thieves made a move to do what Mindrell had ordered. He gave them a hard stare. "You heard me," he commanded. "Get on with it."

Reiffen, his head still throbbing, watched as the three bandits stood up. Hurl took a slight step forward. He was a stronger-looking fellow than Boney—almost as large as Mindrell. But there was something in the way the bard looked down at the thief that made the boy see Hurl as no more than half his leader's size. The bandit thrust out his chin and puffed up his chest, but he still stood with his comrades close behind him.

"The lads and me been havin' a little talk," he began, "and we made up our minds. We want what's comin' to us, we do. All of it. We don't want what Tipps got. We've had enough of mountains."

"That's right." Boney poked his big beak cautiously out from behind Hurl's back. "What's to say you ain't just leadin' us round in circles till we all fall an' break our necks, like Tippsy. Then you'll have all our pay to yourself."

Mindrell put his hands on his hips and faced his three mutinous associates. Reiffen watched closely. Perhaps he might find a chance to escape while they were fighting among themselves.

"So. You want it all," said Mindrell, still in command.

"That's right."

"We done what we hired on for. No one said nothin' about riskin' our necks in the mountains."

"You can keep the boy," said Hurl. "But like I said, we want what's ours. What you got on your belt, there, ought to do for a start." He nodded toward the meager-looking pouch that hung at Mindrell's waist.

"This?" Mindrell untied the pouch, keeping his eyes on the three men in front of him. Reiffen found himself wondering what Hurl and the others would do if he helped them. Somehow he doubted they would treat him any better once they got rid of the bard, whether he helped them or not.

Mindrell took a step closer to the bandits, and a step farther from the boy. "This?" he repeated, dangling the thin purse before their eyes. "You fools think I'm carrying something around in this? Here. It's yours."

He turned the pouch upside down; a few small coppers fell out onto the mountainside and rolled off down the slope, glinting in the sunlight. Hurl did his best to ignore them; but, when the other two went scrabbling greedily after each piece, he said over his shoulder, "We'll share that out later, lads. You know he's probably got more he ain't showin' us."

"I assure you, that's all I have." Mindrell dropped the pouch to the ground after the coins. "But if the three of you think you can overpower me, now's the time to have a try."

He held his arms carefully away from his sides. Something told Reiffen that Mindrell was quite ready for an attack from his direction as well. Glumly he realized he had never had a chance to escape at all. The bard was more than a match for the four of them.

"Maybe you can kill me," Mindrell went on. "Maybe not. But you'll have to kill me if you try, or I'll kill you. And, even if you do kill me, you'll still get no more than what I just gave you. If you want anything else, you'll have to come along the rest of the way. Where we're going is one more day's travel, and that's where you'll get what you have coming to you. Without me you'll never find the way yourselves, or the way home, either."

The three bandits muttered uneasily as they tried to decide whether Mindrell was telling them the truth. Reiffen could see it was a hard matter for them to balance their cupidity with their fear. On the one hand, they were tired of climbing through the mountains, afraid that what had happened to Tipps would happen to them as well. On the other, there was the promise of pay.

Slowly the bard lowered his hands. The moment of danger had passed. "Don't forget," he added with one of his easy smiles, "Tipps died when he tried to go his own way back there on the ice. Didn't I tell him that bridge would never hold his weight? Stick with me and you'll all be fine. You know you can't find your way out of these mountains without me. Or that the Boss would even let you, if you don't show up with the boy."

The last of the thieves' determination dribbled away. "Okay," said Hurl, still determined to save a little face. "We'll follow you for one more day, harper. But see here, if we don't get to where we're goin' by nighttime, well then that's the end of it. And we should be gettin' a little somethin' more for all our extra trouble, too."

"Deliver this one where I'm taking him," said Mindrell coldly, "and you'll get what I said you'd get. If you want to dicker with the Boss, that's your nightmare. In the meantime you'll do as you're told, or I'll kill you here and now. The boy will do what I tell him, with or without your help."

Hurl grumbled a moment longer, but his two companions were over their rebelliousness. With Ike and Boney still nosing around the rocks for any coppers they might have missed, Hurl grumbled and dug a chunk of stale bread out of one of the packs on the ground. He tossed it to Reiffen, whose hands were too stiff to catch it. But the coarse loaf tasted just as good once he picked it up. With the first bite he realized he was ravenous and wolfed the rest.

He was still working on the crust when Mindrell led them off westward along the ridge. It was early morning, and the sky was a clear, light blue, with a few thin wisps of cloud chasing one another through the peaks to the south. Had he not been a prisoner, Reiffen would have enjoyed himself immensely. He had never been this far into the mountains before. An eagle soared in lazy circles high in the air above their heads. At the top of the ridge the bard halted for a moment and shaded his eyes with his hand. He stared at the bird and the peaks around them for a long moment before leading them on.

They followed no trail. Deep in the mountains this far from Valing there were no trails. All the same, there were only so many routes one could follow through the lonely peaks. Everything else was impassable to all but mountain goats and birds. Steep cliffs and slopes made treacherous with broken rock forced the bard to follow the easiest way along the ridgelines and through the few passes that could be climbed. In the valleys far below Reiffen saw distant streams foaming through high falls and narrow chasms, with all the pent-up tumult of spring.

Mindrell led the way, with Hurl and Reiffen in the middle and Ike and Boney bringing up the rear. The ground beneath the boy's feet was an endless crumble of dirty ice and stone, except in the passes, where they found fresh snow. Strong winds buffeted them from the north whenever they came out of the lee of the cliffs, and in all the narrow clefts and chimneys the wind was funneled against them. The thieves' cloaks cracked about them like sails in a full breeze. Reiffen had no cloak, but his clothes dried quickly in the wind, which made him a little warmer. He realized it must have rained while he was under the bard's spell but had no memory of a storm at all, or even of how much time had passed since his friend had perished.

Pausing in the first of the passes, he looked back the way they

had come. A sea of peaks glistened behind him in the sunlight. The
lake was nowhere in sight. High as they were, the mountains
seemed small in comparison to the vast blue barrel of the sky. He
thought he recognized Whitetooth among the tallest of the mountains, but it was hard to tell, since he had never seen it from the west
before. Desperately he wondered what was happening in the
Manor. Had search parties already been sent out to look for him?
Had Avender's body been found?

His thoughts were cut short as Boney, who was next behind,
gave Reiffen the first of many shoves to get him going again. The
boy held his temper and moved on. Ahead the mountains loomed
taller than those behind, and even the sky seemed lost and small.
Somewhere in the midst of all those bright peaks was High Enossin,
tallest of all the mountains in the world. But Mindrell had said they
would reach the end of their journey before nightfall, and that was
surely far too soon for Reiffen to catch sight of the king of the
Bavadars.

They halted for a brief rest shortly after noon. Hurl handed out
another ration of stale bread and hard cheese. Reiffen did as the others and scooped up handfuls of the rapidly melting snow to quench
his thirst. It was their only stop of the morning, but Mindrell was
not pushing them hard. Reiffen was glad of that; he still had moments when his head spun slightly and his eyes glazed. He had been
glad of the chance to pick his way slowly across the pitted snow-
fields and up the steeper slopes. Even so, the boy was much more at
home in the mountains than the thieves, who slipped and fell con-
stantly, complaining all the while. Without Mindrell to cut steps for
them from the ice in the steepest passes, they would never have kept
up. And they frequently had to be reminded not to make too much
noise while they complained. Everywhere they went, higher snow-
fields loomed overhead, frozen crusts just waiting for the right
amount of thaw, or some sharp sound, to send them crashing onto
the slopes below. Reiffen wondered if perhaps he ought to try and

start an avalanche himself, counting on the snow to bury him in the mountains before he was buried in Ussene. But that would mean giving up, and he found he wasn't yet ready for that, no matter how frightened he was. He still had some hope of rescue. At that very moment, for all he knew, Redburr and Nolo might be in the pass behind him.

It was mid-afternoon when they began to descend. Reiffen followed Mindrell down a long arm of the mountain; below them a twisting net of steep valleys and deep gorges opened out between the peaks. To his right the slope fell sharply away into a wide chasm, a dark green wood lining the bottom. On the other side a much shorter drop led to a broad plain of cracked and dirty ice. Finding a spot to clamber down, the bard took them to the edge of the frozen field, where they picked their way carefully among great boulders and sudden fissures in the snow. Reiffen heard the sound of running water everywhere, though he saw no stream.

The ice ended suddenly in a steep drop to the valley. Mindrell was careful to keep away from the frozen edge, which looked to Reiffen as if it was about to crumble away from the top of the cliff at any moment. He followed the bard onto the bare rock at the side and looked out upon the prospect before him. Several streams gushed from the bottom of the glacier, bounding down the rocks to a small pool below. The path beyond appeared to be cut off, but the cliff was so filled with ledges and easy handholds that the climb down wasn't difficult, even for the thieves. Mindrell led them on a route that was fairly dry, the wind blowing the spray from the waterfall in the other direction. Not ten minutes later Reiffen stood at the base of the jagged cliff, the green line of the trees still in the distance below. Beside him the cascade crashed into a field of broken stone.

They drank quickly from the pool and went on. At first they

found the going easy beside the beck, despite the broken rock that covered the mountainside. But when they came to the wood, where the small firs shrouded them in a bright, piney scent, they found the only open path was right down the middle of the stream. Every stone was slippery and slick. Reiffen stumbled and fell into the water more than once, almost as often as the thieves. Only Mindrell never lost his balance, no matter how poor the footing. Boney and Ike complained loudly every time they dipped so much as a boot heel in the water, but Hurl said nothing. His mouth, however, grew tighter with each fresh wetting, and his scowl blacker.

They stopped again late in the afternoon at a place where a second, smaller brook from the north joined the stream they had been following. Thin birches grew along its banks. In among the rocks where the two watercourses met were a few small pools. Reiffen took another meager meal from Hurl, then went off to sit by himself as far from his captors as possible. He tried to look back the way they had come, but the trees had grown too tall for him to see more than a few yards up the course of the stream. His slight hope of rescue had faded completely as the long afternoon wore away. Numbly he gazed at the water. At the other side of the pool Mindrell lay easily on his back on a boulder, his hands behind his head as he watched an eagle in the sky.

Hurl, who was busy keeping an eye on the bard while he ate, squinted upwards a few times himself. He wiped the crumbs from his chin with the back of his sleeve and said, "That hawk's been up there a long time."

Reiffen, hoping for another quarrel he might be better able to take advantage of, watched the bandit carefully.

"It's an eagle," said Mindrell.

"Eagle, hawk, what's the difference. What matters is if it's a spy."

The bard shrugged. But it was the sort of shrug that suggested he did indeed think the bird might be a spy.

"It's too high to shoot at." Hurl shaded his eyes and looked upwards again. "But we don't have any bows, do we?"

The bard crossed one leg comfortably over the other. "The question is," he observed, "if the eagle is a spy, whose side is it on? Ours or theirs?" He turned to Reiffen. "What do you think, Your Majesty? Is that your Shifter friend up there trying to spy us out? Or is it someone my employer has sent along to make sure I do my job?"

Reiffen set his jaw firmly and made no reply. This time he was determined not to respond to the bard's mocking scorn. But Reiffen hadn't thought of Redburr looking for him as a bird, and for a moment his hope returned. He looked up at the sky. The eagle circled lazily, its feathers crimson and gold in the westering sun. Most likely it was just a hunting bird. Had it been Redburr, it would have swept down at once to save him. It was just like Mindrell to tempt him into getting his hopes up.

The bard laughed softly. "You're right," he said. "It's probably not your friend. Whatever it is, though, right now it can see the color of our eyes—"

At the other end of the pool there was a loud splash and much cursing from Boney.

"Now look what you've gone and made me do!" he exclaimed. He scrambled out of the pool, his clothes plastered against his skinny body. "Just when I was dry again, too!"

Mindrell sat up on his rock and looked at the aggrieved thief. "You've gotten your own self wet," he pointed out. "No one else had a hand in it."

"If you'd brought some decent grub I wouldn't have to try my hand at fishin' with my hat." Boney set himself down on the nearest boulder, water pouring off him. "Not my fault my foot slipped." He grumbled on as he removed his boots and poured two long draughts of water back into the stream.

Mindrell stood up and crossed over to the smaller beck. He didn't look back at the sky. "We've wasted enough time," he said. "This is the way we're going now. It's not much farther."

"So you've been here before?" said Hurl suspiciously.

"Of course I've been here before," snapped the bard. "How do you think I know the way?" He shook his head at the misfortune of having to work with fools and walked off up the stream, leaving the others to follow.

Reiffen eyed the other way, where the two streams flowed on down the mountainside through the trees. But Boney was a quiet one and before the boy could make up his mind about trying to make a run for it he felt the thief's wet hand poking him in the back.

"Get along, you," snarled the little man. "I've half a mind to push you in, too, just to keep me company."

It was nearly evening by the time they followed the second brook up a short cliff to the last of the woods. Through the trees Reiffen saw a high meadow that reminded him of the fields back home. He thought of the pasture that stretched up Baldun on the other side of the Neck from the Manor, and of the times his mother had held his hand and walked with him up that green slope when he was small, to the woods and his father's grave. For a moment he felt very sorry for himself. At least Avender had died quickly. No one had ever said the same about the Wizards' captives. Reiffen brushed his welling tears away, not wanting the thieves to see his weakness. But the sadness lingered all the same.

Not until he came out of the trees did he realize this wasn't a pasture like the ones back home. Halfway up the slope a circle of tall white stones rose ominously from the lush green of the grass, like the tips of some great and terrible claw buried deep beneath the meadow. Mindrell headed straight toward them. Already he had crossed half the distance and was walking steadily up the course of the stream.

Reiffen halted, wondering what was waiting for him at the center of the stones' frozen grip. Boney gave him another exasperated shove from behind. The boy, his patience finally exhausted, whirled around. Better to be killed here, he thought, than taken to Ussene. He caught the thief a quick blow on the side of the head. Boney staggered back and tripped across the rocks in the stream, cracking his shins on the stones.

The small thief had also had enough. Quick as a flash he pulled his knife from his belt and scrambled after Reiffen. "That's about it right there, that is," he said as he advanced. "You're gonna get yours now, boy."

Reiffen backed into the meadow, his heart beating wildly. He had never actually been in a real fight before, and saw at once that a training match didn't even begin to approach the desperation of the real thing. This wasn't the same as wrestling with Avender, or practicing swordsmanship with Ranner. Especially when he had no weapon of his own.

Ike rushed up from the woods below. "Hey, Bone!" he cried. "What's wrong with you? That's our meal ticket you're lookin' to slice."

Boney turned on Ike and menaced him with the knife in turn. "Watch yourself, friend. You just leave me be. I'm not gonna kill him. I'm just gonna leave him with a few marks to remind him of old Boney. Maybe I'll keep me an ear or two to remind myself."

He turned back to Reiffen and came forward slowly, his smile almost as sharp as his nose. Reiffen didn't doubt Boney knew his way around a knife. The boy backed deeper into the grass, trying his best not to trip over the thick clumps. And to keep from covering his ears with his hands.

Boney took another step forward. Reiffen readied himself to turn and run. There was a sharp, stinging sound as something whizzed quickly between the two of them from the direction of the tall stones.

"Okay, Boney. You've had your fun. Put away the blade."

Boney looked at Mindrell, who was standing close to the nearest stone, a second missile already in his sling. But Reiffen never took his eyes from the knife. He knew the brave thing to do would be to charge the thief while he was distracted, but at the same time he doubted he would be successful if he did. Letting Mindrell handle the situation seemed a much better idea.

"You keep off, harper," warned Boney, his gaze returning to the boy. "This ain't none o' yours. Ike saw him knock me down. It's about time His Majesty here got a taste of where he's goin'. I don't think the Boss is gonna care if he ain't got both ears."

"Now, that's just where you're mistaken." Mindrell walked forward, quickly cutting the distance between him and the thief. "Our employer was quite specific about the boy's condition. 'Untouched' was how he put it."

"I'm not gonna touch him," said Boney with an evil laugh. "It's my knife's gonna touch him."

He took another step forward. Almost immediately there came a loud crack as Mindrell banged a stone off the thief's skull. Reiffen saw the missile bounce high in the air after it struck. By the time it came back down Boney was stretched out flat on the ground.

Reiffen froze. The sound of rock on bone was worse than Avender's splash. He hadn't known then what the sound meant until after it had passed. This was different. This time a man had been struck down right in front of him. Ike started forward, to see if his fellow bandit was still alive, but Mindrell cut him short before he reached the spot where Boney had fallen.

"Leave him be. He's gotten his pay. Now there'll be more for the rest of us. Hurl, go on back and help Ike bring the boy up to the circle."

Mindrell went back up the valley toward the stones. Trembling fearfully, Reiffen tore himself free of his trance and turned to follow. Mindrell's skill with a sling had taken away any idea the boy might have had left about escaping to the trees now that there was only one bandit behind him. He got one look at Boney's body as he went by, and the sight of the dark blood oozing from the thief's head onto the thick green grass made him come close to fainting. He stumbled over the stones, not caring how wet he got as he lurched up the icy stream. His heart pounded as hard as before and his head spun, though neither knife nor potion threatened him any longer. Even the threat of Ussene paled beside the quick violence thrust so sharply into his life.

Somehow he managed to regain a measure of control by the time he reached the ring of stones. As he stepped between the slabs he forced himself to look at the circle, if only to get his mind on something other than Boney and Avender. The stones were tall and white, and unlike any rock he had ever seen before. Their smooth paleness was more like the bleaching of old wood at the edge of the lake than any rock he had ever seen. There were thirteen of them altogether, each half again as tall as Mindrell but not much wider, spaced irregularly around the circle. None had fallen, but only one or two stood straight. Mostly they leaned this way and that, left and right, forward and backward. They looked far older than anything Reiffen had ever seen. And then he realized that was what made them seem so odd. Exposed stone was always pitted and worn; the surface of the rock always showed the signs of age. But these stones, though they were smooth as his own face, were plainly very old. He couldn't tell how he knew, but still he knew it all the same.

Despite himself, he shuddered. The strain of his encounter with the thief would not go away. He sat down with his back to the nearest stone and tried to swallow, but his mouth was dry as bone.

Mindrell stood just inside the ring on the short, yellow grass, which was not at all like the lush growth of the meadow beyond. Much of it was blackened, and the earth blackened around it, as if recently burned. Here and there the ground itself had heaved and crumbled, as if whatever had seared the grass had not been content with the burning but had needed to rip up everything by the roots as well in some places, before trampling it all back underfoot. It was a dead, evil place. Even the smell was different, as if the very moisture of the air had been boiled away, leaving only dry dust in its place.

The wind freshened, ruffling Reiffen's shirt as it swept through the stone ring from the north. Hurl and Ike stepped warily into the circle behind the bard. Outside, the grass bent in waves of mottled green. An edge of dark cloud appeared behind the wind and began creeping toward them. Mindrell shaded his eyes with his hand and looked up at the thickening sky. There was no sign of the eagle at all.

Ike flopped down in fatigue with his back against one of the rocks, but Hurl looked about in evident anger.

"Is this where you been leadin' us?" he demanded. A clap of thunder rolled out of the north, though they had seen no lightning. "What're we supposed to do here? There's a storm comin'. Least we can do is get back under the trees."

"This is where we get paid," said Mindrell. He ignored the swiftly growing darkness to the north, and the wind whipping his dark hair around his face. "You have to expect a little weather when you work for the sort of people we do." He leaned back against the stone closest to Reiffen, careful not to knock his instrument against the rock. A heavier gust of wind swept over the ridge upon them.

Ike scuttled nervously back outside the edge of the circle. "I don't like this place," he said. "Maybe we should just take our pay and go."

Hurl said nothing but cast a careful eye around the stones. Whatever he was looking for, when he didn't find it his eyes narrowed and he looked at Mindrell suspiciously.

"Say, where is our coin, anyway?" he asked. "You said you had it here, harper. What'd you do, bury it?"

Mindrell remained at ease against the stone. The slabs seemed to grow whiter as the evening darkened.

"I didn't say I had the money here myself. What I said was you'd get what you're owed once we delivered what was wanted. Now we have to wait for our employer to show up. Judging from the wind, I don't think it'll be very long."

"Listen here." Hurl took an angry step forward, his temper breaking. "There's magic here, clear as can be. Now we don't care who we work for, long as the silver's right. And we're not afraid of anybody, neither. But we don't like all this moonshine and mystery—"

His voice was cut short by a tremendous bolt of lightning that struck the stone two over to his left, and a clap of thunder that made everyone's ears ring. Reiffen leapt up, his heart thumping in answer to the blast. Hurl also jumped about two feet, but when he came down he had his sword out and was facing the stone with the air of someone who expected something else to follow the thunder. Beyond the circle, Ike peered fearfully above the grass. Reiffen's eyes darted about in the growing darkness. He could see plainly enough something was coming. But how important that something was, or what it would be, he still wasn't sure. Then the thought occurred to him that another bolt might strike the stone behind him and he stepped deeper into the circle.

Mindrell remained unaffected. "You'd better put your sword away," he said to Hurl. "He won't like it if he thinks you're threatening him."

There was another bright flash of light and instant clap of thunder, this time at the center of the stone ring. Reiffen jumped backward and wondered if any place inside the circle was safe. He watched as Hurl turned round and round uncomfortably, trying to make sure nothing was sneaking up on him from behind. The air itself smelled burnt.

"He's here," said Mindrell.

Reiffen looked, but there was no one in the circle. He turned to the bard, who was no longer leaning easily against the stone but had regained his feet and was looking to the north. Reiffen followed his gaze and saw, out of the darkness, a tall man walking toward them. A very tall man, he realized as the figure entered the circle, his head higher than any of the slabs.

He knew at once it was a Wizard. Nothing else could be so large, or have such power. Awestruck, the boy crouched back against the smooth slab behind him, almost wanting to kneel more than flee. He wondered which of the Three had come to fetch him, and knew it hardly mattered.

Into the middle of the circle the Wizard strode easily, his hand resting on the pommel of his massive sword. Except for his great size, he looked no different from a human. He wore a doublet of dark velvet and loose trousers of the same material. A circlet of silver crowned his dark hair. With his beard trimmed short he looked every inch the powerful king, only twice the size. Even Redburr would look like a mouse beside him.

"Ah, Mindrell. You have completed your task." The air quivered as the Wizard spoke. His voice was as deep as the earth.

"Thank you, lord." Mindrell bowed low before his master, sweeping the ground with his cap. "It is my pleasure to do your bidding."

"Whom are these others you have brought with you?"

The Wizard's gaze flickered once outside the ring, where Reiffen knew Ike was cowering in the meadow, then turned back to Hurl, who still crouched at the ready in front of one of the stones. When the bandit realized the Wizard had turned his attention toward him, he dropped his short sword quickly. It looked like a stick-pin compared to the Wizard's blade.

"I had to hire others to help me, my lord," answered Mindrell easily. "The boy would not just come away. He had to be taken with force. They're waiting to be paid."

"Are they? With swords drawn?" The Wizard laughed and the sky rattled darkly along with his laughter. It was a vibrant laugh, filled with vigor and power, and rolled through the air like a swollen river despite the approaching storm. Reiffen was reminded of Cuhurran in Mindrell's song, and realized at once that this was Ossdonc who had come for him.

The Wizard stepped closer to Hurl. Drawing his great weapon from its sheath, Ossdonc sliced the bandit's head from his shoulders in one smooth motion before the bandit could move. So fast was his stroke that the blade remained unbloodied, flashing darkly as another burst of lightning crashed across the stones. Still chuckling, Ossdonc sheathed his weapon.

Stunned, Reiffen sat back upon the withered grass, his back scraping the stone. Behind him he heard Ike scrabble at the dirt, trying to bury himself; but the Wizard ignored them both. With great good nature he turned to his chief hireling.

"I suppose you want your payment also?" Ossdonc boomed, scattering the thunder with his voice like a hawk chasing sparrows.

Reiffen fully expected to see the bard's head fly across the ring after Hurl's, but Mindrell stood easily at one side of the circle, as if he were without fear as far as Ossdonc was concerned.

"I seek no payment, my liege," the bard replied. "Your goodwill is my satisfaction."

Ossdonc threw back his head and laughed again, his voice bounding back and forth between the stones. "You were always the cozener, Mindrell. Tell me what you will, I know you will never be pleased unless your pocket grows heavier from our acquaintance. Here."

Ossdonc held out his hand. A small pouch appeared between his fingers. Lightly he tossed the bag to the bard, who caught it heavily. In the Wizard's grip the prize had seemed a trifle, but Mindrell had to hold his sack of plunder with both hands.

"And what will you do now?" the Wizard asked.

Mindrell couldn't shrug under the weight of his reward, but he still managed to give the appearance of the gesture. "It will take some time to spend this, my lord. Your generosity is, as usual, greater even than that of the Bryddin."

"That is why you work for me and not them." Ossdonc put his hands on his hips and laughed again. The ground shook beneath his feet, and the thunder boomed against the ridges around him. "But perhaps you would rather return with me to Ussene?" The Wizard raised an eyebrow as he suggested this course to his hireling, as if he did not expect Mindrell to particularly like the invitation.

"I am yours to command, sire," replied the bard, playing to Ossdonc's vanity rather than his jests. Mindrell bowed his head in submission and spread his arms, his bag of gold falling to the ground with a thud that was lost beneath Ossdonc's fresh peals of laughter.

"Pick up your ransom," Ossdonc told him. "It offends me to see you neglect such treasure. I must begin my preparations and you, if you truly do not wish to return to Ussene, must leave the henge."

All this time, though the Wizard had paid no attention to Reiffen, it had not once occurred to the boy to try and sneak away. There was no spell over him, yet Ossdonc's presence was more powerful than any spell. Reiffen had seen what had happened to Hurl and had no doubt that escape was impossible. So he had sat with his back to the stone and watched in horror as the Wizard killed one bandit as casually as he might swat a fly, then toyed with Mindrell like a lion with an ant. He was still sitting with his back to the same stone when the Wizard turned and said to him, in a tone that was both enchanting and commanding:

"Come, boy. Stand beside me."

Ossdonc held out one hand, a king beckoning to his small subject. Reiffen rose at once. Were it not for the taunting in the Wizard's eyes and mouth, he might almost have appeared before Reiffen in benevolence. The boy barely noticed as Mindrell chose that moment to recover his bag and haul it heavily out of the ring.

With Reiffen beside him, Ossdonc drew his sword once more and pointed the blade toward the sky. Reiffen could feel the weight of it as the weapon passed before him. It was twice the size of any sword he had ever seen, black as cold iron. Nothing reflected in that blackness, not the flashes of lightning that increased and blazed around them as the Wizard raised the weapon, nor the face of Reiffen as he realized finally that no one was going to rescue him.

The great sword pointed toward the heavens. Lightning crashed and struck. Then Ossdonc began to speak. The constant thunder was so loud that even the Wizard's voice could scarcely be heard.

Reiffen felt it, though, in the rumbling that seemed to pass down Ossdonc's velveted legs and through the earth to freeze him to the ground. As the Wizard spoke, the sky began to whirl about his head and the flashes of lightning to swirl along with it. He gathered the tempest's power into himself, to use in the wizarding he would employ to take them away.

Their gaze was torn from the sky as a sudden rush of wind passed by them from the south, separate from the storm. Reiffen felt himself lifted and carried beyond the Wizard, who gave a roar of rage far more fearsome than any din of thunder. Great wings beat round the boy's face; a pair of heavy talons painfully pierced his shoulders. For a brief moment he looked up and saw the cruel beak and dark eyes of a huge eagle, and knew the bird was Redburr. But Reiffen had never seen those eyes look less human. They were jet-black, as black as Ossdonc's sword, and glared as fiercely. But their ferocity was for his sake, and his fear suddenly gave way to thrilling relief.

But he was too heavy for even Redburr to carry far. As the Shaper strained to lift them past the stone circle, a blast of light and thunder smashed against one of the bird's great wings. With a cry of pain the Shaper let go of the boy and fluttered clumsily on. Reiffen fell heavily to the ground, stunned by the twin shocks of his fall and the closeness of the Wizard's blast.

Ossdonc stepped forward to retrieve his captive. Redburr flapped weakly on the ground just beyond the stones, his left wing smoking. There was no sign of Mindrell or Ike, but all of a sudden a new figure came rushing out of the darkness toward the Wizard. He caught Ossdonc a great blow on the leg behind the knee. The tall Wizard howled with pain. Nolo, for it was the Dwarf who had come from beyond the circle, raised his axe for another blow. He was no more than a third of Ossdonc's height, yet such was the Dwarf's ferocity that the struggle seemed more than equal.

The rain began to fall in buckets. Ossdonc warded the Dwarf's second blow with his black sword, and the clash of the two weapons sent great sparks soaring upward against the storm. With a twist of his wrist the Wizard spun Nolo's weapon out of his grasp, but the Dwarf closed to grapple with the giant before he could be struck by the blade. The two of them locked tightly together as the rain poured down around them. Ossdonc twisted his sword arm free of the Dwarf's grasp and raised it for a mighty stroke. But even the Wizard's great strength was useless against the stony Dwarf. Nolo caught the blade in his hand—not even that weapon was sharp enough to cut through a Bryddin's skin—and twisted it away, almost knocking Ossdonc over in the process. The Wizard responded by catching the Dwarf a heavy kick in the side. Nolo swung off the ground like a rag doll under the blow but kept his grip on the Wizard's sword. Ossdonc swung the blade quickly from side to side in an attempt to dislodge him, but the Dwarf clung with all his strength even as he was waved back and forth above the burnt grass of the circle.

Reiffen rose groggily to his knees. His head hurt from the force of the bolt that had wounded Redburr, and his chest ached from his fall. For a moment he forgot where he was and what had happened to him as he tried to clear his head and catch his breath. He looked up just as Ossdonc kicked the Dwarf free from his blade with a blow that would have broken every bone in any human body. Nolo tumbled several feet through the air and landed on the broken earth at the far edge of the circle. With a cry of triumph the Wizard leapt at Reiffen and seized his arm. A look of anguish crossed Nolo's face as he called out, "Run, Reiffen! Run!" But he was too late.

A bolt of lightning knifed into the grass in front of the Dwarf; a clap of thunder boomed across the stones. Ossdonc jerked Reiffen to his feet and dragged him back to the center of the henge. He pointed his sword straight up at the sky and cried:

"RETURN!"

A single flash of lightning reached down out of the storm to lick the tip of the black sword. For a brief moment Ossdonc glowed brightly; Reiffen hung limply in his grasp. Thick gouts of flame boiled out from the standing stones towards the center of the circle, where they twisted together and spat upward in a writhing rope of fire. The heat blasted the Dwarf, drying him completely. Then fire and Wizard were gone, and Reiffen with them. Rain-soaked darkness followed.

ISSINLOUGH

And Areft, after he created the world,
created humans to fill the world.
And then he began to hunt them.

7

Ferris and Giserre

vender found Nolo cradling Redburr's limp head in the grass beyond the stone circle. There was no sign of Reiffen. Beside the Dwarf a pale gem shone thinly within the patch of trampled meadow. Its clear light revealed the feathers along one of Redburr's wings and up the side of his head were scorched all the way to the skin.

"Is he dead?" whispered the boy.

Nolo shook his head. He lifted the bird in his arms and carried him to the edge of the brook. With a cloth from his pack, he bathed the wound in the stream's cold water.

Avender followed with the lamp, the rain coursing down his head and shoulders. "Where's Reiffen?" he asked, hardly daring to breathe.

Nolo shook his head a second time. Avender's heart sank. Mutely he knelt in the soft earth, not knowing what to think or say. A cold, empty feeling swelled up inside of him as the Dwarf told him about the fight at the standing stones.

When he was finished, Nolo gestured toward the henge. The white rocks were streaked with dark patches from the rain. "Those stones are very powerful," he said. "They're Inach."

"Inach?"

"Heartstone in your tongue, lad. The True Rock, though it's far rarer to you on top of the world than to those of us below." Nolo smoothed a feather on the side of Redburr's neck; the quill fell away from the skin at his touch. The Shaper stirred and looked for a moment as if he might wake, then settled back into troubled slumber.

"What about Mindrell?" asked the boy, his eyes still lingering on his wounded friend.

"Ranner and the others are searching for him, but I don't think they'll find him."

They passed most of the night outside the circle of stone, camped with Redburr in the rain. The foresters, however, moved down to the shelter of the trees at the bottom of the dell. As Nolo had foreseen, they had lost Mindrell's trail in the stony ridge above the valley. But they still had two prisoners to watch, including one with a bloody bump on the side of his head where he claimed the bard had tried to murder him. Ranner, knowing exactly what Hern would say should he bring home an ailing Avender as well as no Reiffen, wanted the boy to come down with him out of the wet; but Nolo told him not to worry, that he would look after the boy. Then the Dwarf spent the rest of the night studying the stones.

The rain hissed on the sodden grass; Avender tried to keep awake at Redburr's side. Whenever the boy thought he was falling asleep in the dreary darkness he pinched his leg, but it didn't help. Only the faint odor of burnt feathers and skin assured him that Redburr was still close by in the matted grass.

He had been asleep for some time when he was woken by a loud thud. Jumping to his feet, he shouted out at once, thinking Ossdonc had returned. Nolo hurried over from the circle to see what was wrong. At his forehead his gleaming lamp bobbed; he had attached it to his iron circlet to leave his hands free while working. In the pale, shining light Avender was astonished to see that Redburr was no longer a bird. He had changed back to his natural shape, and now the smell of wet fur was added to that of rain, grass, and burnt feathers. The bear snored loudly.

"He'll heal quicker as a bear," Nolo explained at Avender's puzzled look.

"Was he awake?"

The Dwarf shook his head. Raindrops flicked from the tip of his soggy beard. "Sometimes when the stress gets to be too much for him, he just goes back to being a bear."

That the Shaper would heal more quickly as a bear reassured Avender greatly. He no longer needed to worry about losing a second friend. Shivering in relief, he realized he was soaked to the skin for the third time in the last two days. Nolo noticed his trembling and decided it was time to send the boy off to the foresters, regardless of how much he wanted to stay. Their warm fire glimmered through the trees at the bottom of the slope.

"He won't wake again till sometime tomorrow," said the Dwarf. "He'll be fine till then. You go get warm."

Redburr did look more comfortable stretched out on the dark grass as a bear than he had as a bird. The cold rain wouldn't bother him, now that he had his fur back. His wound looked much less serious as well. Though the Shaper had grown larger in the change, the burn on his shoulder looked smaller. He snuffled in his sleep, rubbed his nose with one of his large paws, and snored comfortably again. Completely forgetting the crash that had woken him, Avender went down to the fire and promptly fell fast asleep a second time. This time nothing interrupted him.

The rain stopped during the night; the morning opened wet and gray. Nolo came down from the meadow to join them for breakfast, leaving Redburr to sleep on alone. While they ate, the Dwarf and Ranner decided the foresters and their prisoners should start back for Valing as soon as they broke camp. Nolo and Avender would stay behind to take care of the bear, who might not wake for another day while he healed. But it was important that news of what had happened be brought back to the Manor as quickly as possible, especially the report that Reiffen had definitely been taken by the Three, and not by Brannis. As long as Giserre thought the king had stolen her son, she would never rest until an army was on the march to Rimwich to win him back. But Wizards were another matter.

After Ranner and the foresters left, Avender took his stale bread and went back up to the meadow to watch Redburr. Nolo followed, stamping loudly through the woods behind him. At the edge of the trees the boy noticed that two of the standing stones had been torn down. They lay like large coffin lids on the lush green grass not far from the matted patch where the bear was sleeping. Avender remembered the crash from the night before and wondered just what Nolo had been up to among the stones.

"I thought I'd start taking it apart," said the Dwarf as he came up beside the boy. "I think I've broken its power. Otherwise there was no telling when the Three might use it again."

"But what if we could have found a way to follow them?" asked Avender.

Nolo shook his head. "Magic won't work on me. And I don't like the idea of having so much power lying around while we're waiting for Redburr to wake up. It's better the way it is."

They built a stout shelter in the meadow while the bear slept, in case the rain started up again. Mostly that meant Avender fetched rocks and wood while the Dwarf knit both into a sturdy roof and walls against the sloping grass. The sky continued gray and gloomy all morning, and the bare branches of the trees showed like dark cracks in smoky glass while Avender gathered wood beneath them. There was no sign of life in the forest: no squirrels scampered; no robins or blue jays called. It was as if the magic of the day before had driven off everything that could flee.

Their shelter built, they spent the rest of the day in the meadow.

Nolo went back to work toppling the slabs while Avender watched. Unlike the Dwarf, he couldn't dig long trenches in the dirt with his bare hands. Instead he sat beside the stream close to the bear while Nolo, with brute strength and mining skill, sent the tall stones crashing to the earth one by one. Black dirt fountained high into the air as they fell, and the ground shook; but Redburr slept peacefully on.

He woke finally in the late afternoon, when Nolo was digging his sixth trench. Avender had returned empty-handed from a search for mushrooms in the woods and was lazily tossing bits of grass into the chattering stream when Redburr gave a sudden grunt and sat up. Avender turned to greet him, but, before the boy knew what was happening, the bear growled savagely and charged. Instantly Avender curled up in a ball on the ground. In the back of his mind he remembered Redburr telling him more than once never to run from an angry bear. Terrified, he waited for one of those huge paws to knock him into the rocky stream, or the powerful jaws to snap tight around his head.

But no attack came. His eyes shut tight, Avender tried not to tremble as he felt the bear lumber to a stop beside him. A low, rumbling growl seemed to rise out of the earth itself. Hot breath steamed against his cheek. Avender hugged his knees and wondered if the bear had gone mad because of the Wizard's magic. He held his breath as Redburr poked him with his muzzle and sniffed him from head to toe. Gradually the rumbling growl subsided. One huge paw rolled him over onto his back on the wet grass. A rough tongue licked his face.

"Open your eyes, boy. I won't hurt you now."

Avender opened his eyes. Redburr was sitting back on his haunches, licking his muzzle. He twisted carefully to look at his tender shoulder, and gave the wound a few swipes with his tongue. Then he turned to Avender and asked, "What day is it?" His voice was dry and rasping.

"Tomorrow," said the boy. He swallowed carefully and wondered if he really was safe again. "You didn't even sleep a whole day."

"Feels like I slept a month. I'm hungry enough. Did we save him?"

Avender shook his head. The bear scratched his belly and said nothing more. When he rolled forward onto his paws the boy scrambled to his own feet and took a couple of careful steps backward. Redburr ignored him and took a long drink from the brook. Thirst satisfied, he limped across the grass to what was left of the circle. Avender followed warily.

They found Nolo hard at work digging a pit in front of one of the stones. The five slabs he had already knocked down had been replaced by five deep gashes in the earth. In the middle of the henge the charred ground was a tumbled mass of turf and soil, as if some large child had been turning the dead earth with a shovel. Tall though the slabs were, half their length was buried in the ground. Nolo had been forced to dig deeply to upend them.

He looked up from his trench as they arrived and frowned as he caught sight of the boy. "What happened to you?" he asked, his hard hands black with moist earth. "You look like fresh-cut chalk."

Avender sat heavily on the grass without answering.

"I almost killed him," explained the bear. He sniffed at the closest slab, and the ripped earth. "I wasn't quite myself when I woke up. Luckily the boy remembered what I taught him."

Nolo looked up at the boy's face with concern.

"I'm okay," said Avender. "I'll be fine in a minute."

Nolo turned to the bear. "You could at least apologize," he said.

"Why would I do that?" The bear pawed at the grass. "Now he knows to be careful when I'm in a fighting mood. Remember that, boy. When the rage comes over me, it's best to keep out of the way. Especially if I'm hurt."

"I thought you were sleeping."

"I was. But if I go to sleep fighting, chances are I'll wake up fighting, too."

He licked his wound again and clawed up a large section of sod. Absently he began to eat whatever grubs he found clinging to the soil, his jaws chewing stolidly like a cow's. Then he walked over to the nearest slab and sniffed the stone once more.

"You know," he said, clods of dirt tumbling from his mouth, "I think I've smelled stones like these before."

Nolo looked sharply away from Avender, his concern forgotten. "You have?"

The bear nodded. His tongue swept around his heavy jaws, searching for any worms he might have missed. "I'm sure I have. In Cuspor. And maybe Simmas. Yes, definitely Simmas." He tore up another swath of grass. "And there's one in the hills north of the Ambore, too." He stuffed a second pawful of earth into his mouth.

"North of the Ambore!" Nolo climbed out of his hole and clapped the dirt from his hands, now keenly interested, as he joined the Shaper and the boy. "Really? How far north? Is it close to Grangore?"

"It's a few days east of Upper Crossing. There's a tribe of woodlings nearby who can take you to it. It's their holy place, though. I'm not sure how happy they'll be if you tear it up like this. Why are you so interested?"

"The stone is Inach."

Redburr shrugged his uninjured shoulder. "Stone's your work, Bryddin," he said, snapping at a fly that buzzed past his ear. "The forest's what I know."

"Inach is heartstone in the human tongue," Nolo answered. "It's what the Sword was made of."

Redburr forgot about insects and worms entirely. "Heartstone? If that's what it is, what's it doing up here on the surface? How did it get into the mountains?"

"Wizard's work, I guess. It seems the Three can shape Inach. We Bryddin can't."

"Stone the Bryddin can't shape? I don't believe it."

"It's true. We've never found anything strong enough to cut it. But that's all changed now."

"Changed?" The bear's black nose wrinkled in confusion. "How's it changed? All you've done is find more heartstone, not something to cut it with."

The Dwarf smiled and stroked his beard. He always enjoyed teaching something new to the bear. "How do you think we cut diamonds?" he asked.

"I have no idea. How do you cut diamonds?"

"With another diamond."

Avender saw what Nolo was suggesting at once. "So that means you can use this heartstone to cut other pieces, right?"

"Exactly." The Dwarf stroked his beard and beamed.

"But you must have found pieces of heartstone you could cut with before," said Redburr.

"That's just it," replied Nolo. "We haven't. Veins of heartstone are always huge. They're what holds us up over the Abyss, the bones of the earth. The only Inach any Bryddin has ever seen before is too big to be mined. But these slabs are perfect." He placed his hands on his hips and gazed eagerly at the stone laid out on the grass, as if he could hardly wait to get to work on it.

Redburr sniffed the nearest one once more. "It almost makes it all worthwhile," he said after a moment.

"It does," agreed the Dwarf.

This time it was Avender's turn to be confused. "All what worthwhile?" he asked.

"Losing Reiffen." Redburr nodded at the stones around them. "There's enough heartstone here to carve into a thousand swords."

Avender felt it would take a lot more than a thousand swords to make up for losing Reiffen.

"At least a thousand," said Nolo. "And there are those other circles you mentioned, too. Especially the one by the Ambore. That'll be easier to get at than this one here."

The bear growled softly. "And the Wizards led us right to it. Maybe Giserre will get her army, after all." His black eyes gleamed and his lips curled to bare his yellow teeth. Avender wondered if he was going to have to curl up in a ball on the grass again. "Only it'll probably come too late to save Reiffen."

"We're not going to give up trying to rescue him now, are we?" asked the boy, though he was afraid he already knew the answer.

"No one's ever escaped from Ussene, boy."

"But we can't just leave him there." Avender kicked a small stone at the edge of the pit. It struck the bare earth on the other side with a satisfying thunk. "We have to try."

The bear made no reply.

"What I don't see," said Nolo slowly, "is what the Three hope to do with Reiffen now they have him."

"That's plain enough," grunted the bear. "They'll use him to start a rebellion. That's always been their way. Sow discontent and reap the harvest after. There's no lack of ears in Malmoret willing to listen to any plan that rids them of Brannis. And Reiffen is the true heir, after all. Even in Wayland there are people who would join with him should he claim his birthright. The bloodshed that would follow would be terrible, far worse than the last war. No matter how it came out, the Three would have their way. The strength of Wayland and Banking wrecked, and the Wizards free to gobble up whatever's left. Even Valing would fall, in time. Mountains won't keep out Wizards, not if there's nothing else to stop them."

"But what about the heartstone?" asked Avender. "If we can make new swords, why would we fear the Wizards any longer?"

"It's not the Wizards we'll be fighting, boy, if they have their way. It's other humans, with Reiffen at their head, doing the Wizards' work for them. A sword's just a sword, as far as humans are concerned."

"Reiffen would never do the Wizards' bidding," said Avender stoutly. "They killed his father."

"And yours, too," added the bear. "But when you've watched the Three as long as I have, you won't underestimate their power. Mothers might murder their own children at Usseis's command. His skill lies in changing the nature of things, twisting them to his own purpose. Were it only Ossdonc we had to fight, we'd have won this battle long ago. But Usseis's skill is more subtle, and Fornoch's more cunning still. Who do you think it was slew my fellow Shapers? Reiffen will do whatever they ask of him, believe me. No one can withstand them, once they've fallen into their hands, except the Dwarves. And that's only because Dwarves are made of different stuff."

The bear turned back to the torn ground and clawed out another chunk of earth. He found no worms, and let the black sod crumble from his paw back into the pit. Avender lay in the meadow and looked up at the plain gray sky. A hawk spiraled through one corner of his view, circling in and out of sight behind the side of the western ridge. Each loop brought the soaring bird a bit less back into view, and each time it disappeared Avender found himself wondering whether it would return. And each time he had begun to give up hope that it would there it was, a dark silhouette, motionless except for the curving passage of its flight. It swung quietly across the sky, until finally it passed away beyond the hard gray stone.

He refused to believe Reiffen was gone, no matter what the Shaper said. There had to be a way to rescue his friend. On his own he wandered through the meadow and the trees for the rest of the day, dreaming wild plans. He would ride alone to the northern mountains and, wielding an Inach sword, rescue Reiffen and slay the Three! He would be a hero! Old Mortin would bang his cup on the table at the Bass and Bull and call for a song about him. His dreams comforted him for a while, but even while he was dreaming, he knew they were impossible. Boys didn't become heroes, especially not alone. Mostly they were captured, like Reiffen, and dragged away to die. Or worse.

He thought of one more question that night as he lay by the fire in front of Nolo's shelter.

"Redburr?" he asked. "How'd the Wizards get their power?"

"Hmm?" The bear rolled his head sleepily to the side and looked at Avender from the corner of one dark eye.

"How'd the Wizards get their power?"

Redburr looked at Nolo, who shrugged and poked the hot coals with his toes.

"You think I should tell him, don't you," said the bear.

"I don't know why you've kept the secret so long."

"It wasn't always a secret. Everybody knew once." Redburr rubbed at his wound with the flat of his paw. "Then too much time passed, and everybody forgot. I've had to remind stewards and kings exactly what happened more than once. It wasn't right for them to forget. But there was no reason to scare anyone else."

Avender waited patiently for the bear to go on. He was sure that, having started, the Shaper would finish. But it was a while before the bear finally spoke again. The fire crackled in the night and Avender had another a question ready when Redburr finally said:

"The power of the Three comes from Areft. Understand, boy, that Areft wasn't completely killed by the Sword."

Avender sat up in surprise. Thin fear trickled down his throat. "Wasn't completely killed? How can anybody be only partly killed?"

"There's always something left of Ina, boy. Like that right there." The bear nodded his heavy muzzle up toward the henge, dark shadows dancing in the firelight across the stone. "Inach is the bones of Bavadar. Just as the Bryddin are what's left of Brydds. And I'm what's left of Oeina. In the same way, when Areft died, he left behind the Wizards."

Despite himself, Avender peered fretfully at the shadows around them. He didn't like hearing Areft's name on a dark night in the wild mountains. Nolo reassured him with a grin.

"I don't see how anyone could forget that," said the boy.

Redburr's deep voice rumbled. "It was a long time before we knew for sure. We knew some of Areft's power escaped when he was killed, but it was hard to tell what shape that power would take when it re-formed. Years passed and there was never any sign of it, so most people forgot. All that was left were the tales old men and women tell around the fire at night, about how Areft would come back someday. Until Usseis finally showed himself in the north."

"When was that?" asked Avender in a whisper, still afraid to let even the dark night hear what he said.

"In King Essem's time, before the Separation."

"And before? When no one knew where they were?"

"More years than you can count, boy."

"But where were they all that time? Doesn't anybody know?"

Nolo chuckled. "You sound like Ferris, lad."

Avender frowned and dropped his eyes to the fire. "Ferris isn't here."

"So you have to ask the questions for her, eh? Nothing wrong with that." Nolo turned to the bear. "So where were they? The Wizards, that is."

Redburr shrugged, his forepaws sliding across his furry chest. "The world's a big place. We don't even know what's on the other side of the ocean. They could have been anywhere. Waiting, learning. Building henges."

"But how'd you know they were Wizards when they finally appeared?" asked Avender.

"They couldn't have been anything else. I did go north for a while to make sure my suspicions were correct about Usseis. He almost caught me, too, before I finished scouting out his fortress—even then he'd fashioned terrible new things. But I escaped, and came away having learned enough to know I was right. And when Ossdonc appeared soon after, there was no more guessing about it. Ossdonc has never been subtle."

"And Fornoch?"

Redburr shook his massive head. His dark eyes shone with yellow flame from the fire, matching the color of his teeth. "No one knows when Fornoch appeared. I knew there had to be three Wizards; but, until he revealed himself as Martis, I had no idea where Fornoch was. Don't believe for a minute, though, that Martis was his first disguise. There've been more than a few times in the past that might be explained if it turned out Fornoch had been here all along."

The Dwarf leaned forward and added a few more sticks to the fire. "The thing I don't understand," he said, "is why the Three bother with all this hocus-pocus instead of just killing everybody outright and getting it done with. That's all Areft did, according to the old tales, after he made the world."

"Because the Three aren't Areft," answered the bear. "They have other things on their minds. And perhaps they've learned that, if Areft can be destroyed by his own creations, so might they. After all, they're not Ina, no more than you or I, and they know it. Ossdonc might be happy with such a life, but not his brothers. Usseis, especially, seems to want to rule. Perhaps because he can't create the way Areft could, he wants to control everything instead. And ruling is much the harder of the two, when matched against outright killing. It's easier to kill a wild horse than tame it."

The bear stretched out along the fire and blinked sleepily. "Now, if you don't mind," he said, "I think I've answered enough questions. From both of you. The fire's nice and warm and I'm ready to go to sleep. We have to be on our way back to Valing early tomorrow."

Avender pulled his blanket close about him and crawled into Nolo's shelter. Stars stared brightly down on him from the top of the night sky. Though the Dwarf had toppled all thirteen of the henge's stones, the boy couldn't help but feel they were still too close to the Wizards' power. Areft's power. It was bad enough knowing the Wizards' strength was more than anyone else's; but now that Avender knew it was really Areft's, the thought of what might be happening to Reiffen seemed even worse.

They were three days on the return to Valing. They might have enjoyed the journey had so much sadness not been weighing on their minds. The season was turning, and the newly mild days coaxed up fresh flowers and filled the icy streams. Rock that had seemed barren a few days before now glittered with pockets of white cowbells and tiny yellow daisies. But the travelers' thoughts were elsewhere: Avender on the plight of his friend, Redburr on his next good meal and what he was going to say to Giserre, and Nolo on trying to work out some way to rescue Reiffen. He was a Dwarf. And being a Dwarf, Avender knew, meant preferring to pass the time in Bryddin fashion, digging about for ways to fix a problem.

Hern, Berrel, and Giserre met them at the lower dock on their return, with Ferris hopping impatiently back and forth behind them. Old Mortin was there, too, shaking his head mournfully. The lines in his face seemed deeper from an erosion of tears. "To think I shared a glass with that Mindrell!" he said with a doleful hiccough. "Charmed us all, he did. I should have known there was something wrong with that rascal."

Redburr bowed his head to Giserre as soon as he set his paws on the cold stone quay. Even on all fours he was almost as tall as she, and the Lady Giserre was not a short woman. "I've failed," he said.

"I have heard the tale," she replied. "You did what you could." She wore a simple dress, black as night; but it was a dress from Malmoret and outshone anything anyone in Valing might have worn, for all its plainness.

"Name your punishment, my lady," said Redburr humbly, "and I will accept it."

Giserre pursed her lips. "You lose my son," she asked, her anger cold, "and yet you propose I let you off with punishment? Perhaps you would like a dunking, or an afternoon in the stocks? No, Redburr, I will not allow you to escape so easily. What I wish is that you tell me the steps you intend to take to try again. What will you do to return my son to me?" She stared at the bear with terrible eyes. Her face might well have been cut from stone.

A sorrowful rumble escaped from Redburr's deep chest. "Your sentence is just, my lady," he answered. "But I doubt that raising an army to storm the north will achieve your aims."

Giserre's eyes flashed. "It is the only way," she said.

"Even were Brannis likely to raise a host to storm Ussene, Usseis need only slay your son in plain sight to defeat your purpose." The bear regarded her steadily, his small eyes intent and his large mouth closed.

"Here now," broke in Berrel, one eye on the children. "This isn't the place to discuss such things. Let's go upstairs."

He stood aside for Giserre, who lifted her long skirt as she swept past. Hern led them up the curving stair, lamp in hand. Through the cellars and up to the kitchen they went, where Hern told Ferris to help Avender find something to eat. "Anything he wants," she said, wagging a stern finger at her daughter. "Anything. After what he's been through I'm sure he's hungry as Redburr. There are pickled eels in the tub and some of last night's oatcake in the pantry. I'll be with Giserre and the others in the library, but if there's anything else you need, Avender," she added, "I'll try not to be too long."

In a swirl of white apron she bustled away. Avender sat down at the kitchen table and told the story of everything that had happened, from Mindrell meeting them on the stairs to Nolo digging up the stones, while Ferris and everyone else listened and helped him to whatever he wanted to eat. The only thing he didn't mention was that the henge was made of heartstone. Redburr had given him strict instructions not to speak of that to anyone, preferring that knowledge to be kept secret as long as possible. Most of the story had already been heard from the foresters, but no one minded listening to the tale again. Avender guessed it would be the end of summer before anyone in Valing began to tire of that.

"And you found no sign of that wicked harper?"

"I hope he fell off a cliff and broke his neck."

"He'll find it broke for him if he ever comes back here again!" Tinnet clenched his fist and scared even himself at the extent of his sudden courage.

Avender ate hungrily for a long time, but Hern had still not returned when he was finally done. So he went out with Ferris to Redburr's favorite sunning spot beyond the orchard, where they watched the fishermen on the lake casting their nets and lines. The ice beneath the western cliffs had melted almost completely in the week he had been gone, and large floes drifted on the current toward the gorge. A few dark shapes played in the water near Nokken

Rock. Ferris asked only a few questions, even when Avender mentioned what Redburr had told him about the Wizards.

"You have to take me with you next time," she said instead.

Avender tossed a pebble out from the cliff toward the lake below, its splash too small and far away to be noticed. "There won't be a next time," he said. "Redburr says it's impossible to rescue anyone from Ussene."

"That may be what Redburr says," said Ferris, "but he hasn't been stuck here with Giserre. You know she'll make him do something."

"Even if she does, they won't take me along. Berrel didn't want me to go this time. I wasn't much help, anyway. If anything I probably held them back."

"You found the canoes."

"Skimmer found the canoes."

"Skim wouldn't have been there to find them if it wasn't for you."

Avender shrugged. He couldn't completely deny his part, but he still didn't believe he had done that much.

"If there's going to be a war," he said finally, "they won't be bringing girls along. Or boys."

"That's what they think."

"It's not that simple, Ferris."

"I think it is." She set her hands firmly in her lap and looked out over the sparkling water. "There's no reason we can't go. Sword bearers and pages go to war, just the same as captains, you know."

"I'll let you try to convince them. Meantime I'll be out on the lake fishing with Skim."

She looked at her friend in sharp surprise. "You mean you don't want to go?"

"I didn't say that." He threw another stone out over the water, much harder than before. "I want to go as much as anyone. But at least I have the sense to know what's impossible and what isn't."

Ferris rolled her eyes. "Avender, you don't have any sense at all. If you did, you'd know we have just as good a chance of going along with whatever they're cooking up as anyone. You're part of this now, whether you think so or not. And I'm going to be part of it, too. With or without your help."

"You know I'd help if I thought it would do any good."

"If I think of a job you can handle," she replied curtly, "I'll let you know."

With a look that told him she no longer cared what he did, Ferris bristled back to the house. Avender wondered what she thought she could accomplish. He knew perfectly well, even if she did talk her way into coming along, she would be left safely behind somewhere on the way if anything important happened. Just as he would, if he were lucky enough to be asked himself.

He was still throwing rocks off the cliff when Anella came to fetch him to Giserre. He wasn't surprised, knowing that Giserre would want to hear his version as soon as possible. He followed Anella along the northern edge of the Neck toward the top of the gorge. From there a stone stair curved downward to a covered half bridge that poked out over the flume. At the bridge's end the Tear hung like a jewel in snow-white smoke above the chasm. Beyond and below, the water poured in a thick curve like the back of a leaping fish over the break in the northern cliffs, thundering down to the White Pool and the head of the river far below. Wreathed in swirling vapor that as often as not hid both stair and bridge, the Tear seemed no more than a bit of flying stone floating among the clouds.

They descended the stair. The roar of the gorge rose around them. Despite the warm sunlight, the covered bridge was chill and damp. Even with the heavy glass windows closed, the thick mist from the spring flood always found its way within. But the Tear itself was dry and warm. Two sets of heavy oak doors sealed the inner chamber from the ghostly plumes without. A fire burned brightly at the open hearth in the center of the room, the coals glowing. Beyond the stone-framed windows, the mists of the cataract swept and swirled. The small glass panes were streaked with tears as the mist melted back into the streaming cloud. The rush of the gorge thrummed below, but not nearly as loudly as it had outside.

Giserre was already packing. She sat by the hearth, the cushions around her strewn with neat piles of clothing. Several strands of dark hair had come free from the knot behind her head to hang down around her face. The loose hair made her look more like her son than Avender had ever realized.

She stood as the boy entered the chamber, and welcomed him. "Please," she said, holding out her long, pale arms. "Sit beside me, Avender. Tell me all that happened."

He continued to the middle of the room beside the fire. Except for the space taken by the double doors, the circling wall was filled with mullioned windows. From them five low tiers of stone stepped down to the hearth at the center of the chamber. Soft pillows and richly embroidered cushions covered most of the steps; when Avender and Reiffen had been small they had tried to sleep in a different spot among the pillows every night, while Anella and Giserre had kept to their places by the door.

Giserre moved an armful of dresses to a different couch to make room for Avender beside her. He didn't ask where she was going. Only Rimwich and Malmoret held any hope for her now that her son had been taken from Valing. He sat uncomfortably on the offered pillow, a large green one with the towers of Malmoret embroidered upon it in thread of red and silver, and told them the tale he had told Ferris and the others in the kitchen. Giserre made no interruptions. She and Anella worked quietly and without haste while they listened, as if there was nothing else on their minds at all. When Avender was done, the lady finished folding a dark blue scarf and added it to one of the piles before her. Anella also said nothing, waiting for her mistress to speak.

Giserre turned to Avender. "You have been a brave friend," she said. "I thank you, and all my line thank you also. Without you, I might not yet know Reiffen's fate."

She kissed his forehead. Avender didn't know what to say. Instead he remembered how she had always kissed both of them at night when he had first come to the Tear to be her son's companion.

Giserre looked down at the coals burning in the hearth and rested a hand on Avender's shoulder. "You are a second son to me," she said. "I am proud of you both. When Reiffen returns I shall tell him of all you have done."

"So it's decided?" Avender asked hopefully. "You persuaded them to keep trying to rescue him?"

Giserre took a slight breath. Had Avender not grown up with her, he might not have noticed the slight tightening of her jaw. "No," she said. "They have not. But there are others who might show more favor to the plight of the true king. My brother, for one, has always been his champion."

"If you're going to raise an army, Ferris and I both want to come, too."

The lady smiled. She was always at her most beautiful when she smiled. "You are a worthy friend," she said. "And Ferris also. But you have done your part. It is time for others to do theirs."

A heavy knock sounded on the wooden doors, as if someone had struck them with a club. Anella put down her work and hurried up the steps. It was no good calling out from within the Tear for anyone outside to enter. With the gorge thundering below, no one on the other side of the door could hear even the loudest shout. Redburr padded in, his long claws clacking on the stone. Nolo followed. Giserre rose from her seat, but this time her manner was not nearly so welcoming as it had been to Avender.

"You have had your say, bear," she said coldly, "both on the dock and in council. There is no need to force your views on me in private audience as well."

"There is, my lady." Ignoring her command, the bear descended the wide steps to the fire. "Especially when my private counsel is different from what I said in public."

"There is nothing you can say that will ever change my mind."

"Well then. Maybe I should let Nolo talk. It's his plan." Redburr started to settle himself comfortably on top of several dresses on the bench closest to the fire; Anella smacked him sharply and pushed him on. Grumbling, he moved back to the second tier, farther from the warmth of the coals.

Giserre turned her attention to the Dwarf. For the first time she allowed a small part of the pain she felt to show in her voice. "Please," she said wearily. "Just speak your piece and go."

Nolo set himself right on the edge of the fire, where anyone else would have burned, and rubbed his hands briskly in the flames. "I've been thinking, my lady," he began, "and I think I've found another way."

"Another way?"

"Another way to rescue Reiffen. An army won't work. That's clear as crystal. Redburr already pointed out the fault in that down at the dock. But there's more than one way to skin a bat. There are other ways to reach Ussene that might not occur to humans."

"Or Wizards, either," said Redburr.

"Come to the point, please, Nolo." Giserre returned to her packing, to show her visitors she only had time to grant them half her attention.

"It's quite simple, really." The Dwarf cracked a crooked grin. "We'll sneak in."

"The attempt has been made before."

"Not from underneath."

Giserre dropped the shawl in her hand; her fine, dark eyebrows creased in a frown. "Underneath?"

"From below," rumbled the bear from his bench. "From really, really far below. We'll underwhelm them."

Nolo grinned, but Giserre looked coldly at Redburr. "I thought you said this was Nolo's plan." She turned back to the Dwarf. "Please, continue."

"What I mean," said Nolo, "is that a small party might travel secretly through the Stoneways from Issinlough to Ussene. There might be some digging involved, but I don't think there's much chance the Wizards are prepared for an approach from that direction. There's even a possibility we might be able to tunnel our way right into the dungeons and whisk Reiffen away before anyone even knows we're there."

Giserre's composure nearly left her. Her mouth fell open. For the first time since their return real hope rose within her. She stared at Nolo for a moment, wondering at the simplicity of his plan. On the bench behind her Anella put a hand to her mouth, and Avender also started forward as he realized what the Dwarf had said. There might still be a chance to rescue Reiffen.

"Is that possible?" asked Giserre.

"Of course it's possible," replied the Dwarf. "It's just a matter of how much we have to dig. There are many paths through Bryddlough."

"But why not take an army?" asked Giserre as she thought the idea through more completely. "An attack in force might so surprise the Three as to destroy their fortress forever."

"You can't take an army through Bryddlough," said Nolo. "Not a human army. You'd never be able to feed them all. But a small group should be able to make their way up through the tunnels and come upon Ussene from below."

"Why not an army of Bryddin?"

Nolo shook his head. "There's no such thing. You might get a few score to answer a call to arms, but the rest wouldn't want to be bothered. Uhle and Dwvon can see the need, but until the Wizards actually make a move against Bryddlough, most Bryddin will never understand the need for fighting."

Redburr scratched his stomach with his great claws and rolled

152 | S. C. BUTLER

onto his side. A few feathers puffed up into the air, but otherwise the pillows beneath him held. "Nolo and I have talked about this for most of the last few days," he said. "A small party makes the most sense. That way we can move fast, which is as important as anything else now. The quicker we reach Ussene the better, as we all know."

"How many will you take with you?" Giserre changed the subject swiftly. No one wanted to think about what would happen to Reiffen as long as he was in Usseis's hands.

"Four or five would be best," said Nolo. "The bear and I, of course. And maybe another Bryddin or two to help with the digging."

"Who else? Ranner? A knight from Malmoret?"

"Our need will be for stealth in the Under Ground, Giserre, not fighting," said the bear. "And we'll need one other skill as well."

Giserre turned her head slightly to the side and waited for Redburr to go on.

"We'll need someone with us who can recognize Reiffen no matter what's been done to him."

There was a moment's silence after the bear finally voiced what everyone was thinking. Giserre clasped her hands firmly in her lap and straightened her back. "It is as I suspected," she said. "Well then. I have never done much campaigning. Indeed, I left Malmoret when I was barely more than a girl, and have not left this valley since. But I presume I shall be able to manage. It is for Reiffen, after all. No one else can recognize him so well as I."

Anyone else would have been abashed to contradict Giserre, and that would probably have been the end of the discussion right there. But Redburr was not in the least put off by her assurance. He sniffed once, his black nose twitching.

"Actually, Giserre, you're not the one I had in mind."

She did lose her composure then. Her eyes flashed and her chin rose. Though it seemed impossible, her back grew straighter. "Even you cannot have the audacity to suggest there might be someone who knows my son better than I!"

"Not better," the bear agreed. "But almost as well."

He turned and looked at Avender. The boy's face glowed with the red and gold of the fire.

"There he is right there."

Avender looked up in surprise. Giserre glared at him angrily, and Anella with disapproval. Nolo tried to give him a sly wink of encouragement. He had no idea what to think himself.

"Me?" he cried.

"You have surpassed even your usual foolishness, bear." Giserre's eyes flashed darkly.

"The thing is, Giserre," said Redburr, "we need you to keep the Wizards occupied while we travel to Ussene. They'll expect any fresh attempt to rescue the boy to come from you. If you come with us to Issinlough, I'm afraid it wouldn't be long before the Three guessed our purpose, and then we would no longer have the benefit of surprise. I think we can all agree it's better to have them looking elsewhere. Following you."

"This is no task for a child," she insisted.

"No, it isn't," agreed the bear. "But Avender has more than proven his worth over the last few days, and he's the only other person who knows Reiffen nearly as well as you."

The thought crossed Avender's mind that Ferris would strongly disagree with the bear's last observation. Especially after what she had just said on the cliff.

Nolo scratched his chin through his thick beard. "The only problem I see," he said, "is persuading Hern to let us bring the boy along."

"It's his decision, not hers," growled Redburr.

"He is not yet of age," pointed out Giserre. "Hern will claim the privilege of a parent."

"Well then, maybe we won't tell her." Redburr's small eyes narrowed craftily. For a moment he looked more like an enormous weasel than a bear. "We'll tell her Nolo's taking the boy to Issinlough for his education. She can't very well argue with that. And the fewer people who know what we're up to, the better. You can be sure there are spies in Valing, and they'll report back to their masters whatever we decide to do. But if all they see is Nolo taking the boy into the Stoneways for his education, what can they possibly suspect? Especially if you're somewhere else. That's why you need to keep packing. Let their masters' attention follow you to Rimwich and Malmoret. Call for Brannis and the barons to save your cub. Brannis will send you away empty-handed, but your brother and the barons might listen. And the Wizards will listen, too, thinking your pleading to be our real intent."

Giserre pursed her lips. "So I am to be offered as a stalking horse," she said. Avender could see she had hoped to take a more active part in the rescue, and do more than go begging at the court of a faithless king. But, if begging was what was required, she would swallow her pride and beg. The Lady Giserre had swallowed the better portion of her pride ever since she had first come to Valing.

"Yes, milady," said Redburr, "that would be best."

"It's what the Wizards will expect you to do," added the Dwarf. "And it'll give them one more reason to think that's what we're really up to."

"In the meantime we'll be hunting them from below," growled the bear. "But any success you might have with Brannis and the barons would help. A small force marching on Ussene while we're trying to sneak in through the basement would be the perfect distraction."

Giserre looked at the three of them, Dwarf and bear and boy, her dark eyes deeply serious. She made up her mind. "I believe you shall rescue my son," she said, accepting Nolo's plan. "I do not yet feel he is gone. He shall be king someday, that I have always felt, and I have felt it no less since he was taken away. But you must promise me"—she turned to Avender and held him close with her gaze—"that you will regard him carefully when you find him. You will study him, and assure yourself that he is the same Reiffen you and I both know and love. And after you have looked at him you will come to me, and you will tell me if you doubt he is whom he should be. For it would not be fitting, when he gains his throne, if he is not, in truth, Reiffen, but rather some poor Wizard's creature."

She spoke grimly, but the cruelty in her words was to herself for having to speak in such a way about her son. And when she saw she had made Avender afraid, even as he nodded and agreed to her bidding, her eyes softened. She laid her hand lovingly against his cheek.

"Do not be afraid, Avender. If my son is to be king, it will be by your grace and friendship. To you we will owe everything."

They ended their council with their plans decided. Giserre, with an escort of foresters, would travel to Rimwich and Malmoret to plead for an army to fight for her son. Hers would be the hardest task, for she would have to patiently pretend to play through all the intrigues of both courts, the Old Palace and Rimwich Keep, while all the time knowing the real tests were taking place deep below the ground. Nolo and Avender would travel by sea, as that was the quickest way, from Lugger to Mremmen, and then by land from Mremmen to Grangore and on to Issinlough. Redburr would travel with Giserre at first, accompanying her to Rimwich before going on by himself into the north to see if he might learn anything of what was happening in Ussene. They decided it would help their deception if he was known to be traveling with Giserre. That would give the Wizards' spies one more reason for believing that Giserre's mission was the important one.

They finished their preparations quickly; there were many reasons for haste and none for delay. The stewards understood Giserre's need to be doing something, but they were confused by Nolo's hurry. They pointed out that Avender had already had a grueling week, and that there was no reason for him to be off again so soon. Redburr finally told them that one of Nolo's purposes in going to Issinlough was to see what help the Dwarves might provide for any attempt to recover Giserre's son. After that Hern and Berrel gave up their objections at once, no matter how poor they thought the chances for success.

It turned out there was another reason the stewards might want Nolo and Avender to delay. In the late afternoon, the day before they were all to depart, the bear and the Dwarf brought Avender with them to the woods on the north side of the Manor to discuss their plans one last time. A thick pinewood grew between the house and the edge of the cliff, which was far higher here than on the side that faced the lake. To their left the gorge and waterfall thundered; to the right the steep green sides of the Shoulder rose up into the Low Bavadars. Redburr had picked a spot he knew near the edge of the cliff where the gray stone provided rough benches among the pines, and where they were unlikely to be bothered. So they were quite surprised when Ferris joined them not long after they arrived.

Redburr gave her a fierce look. "We're busy," he said. "Go on back to the house and help your mother."

"Oh, I'll go back," the girl replied with a large measure of satisfaction, "as soon as I've told you the news. I'm coming with you."

Nolo's thick eyebrows rose in surprise; Avender brightened. Much as he enjoyed Redburr's and Nolo's company, having Ferris along would make the trip even better.

Redburr growled. "No, you're not," he said.

Ferris ignored his tone. "Yes, I am. Mother said I could."

"Your mother has nothing to do with it."

"You know better than that. She thought it was a wonderful idea for me to come along, after I told her it was fine with you. She said I could use a trip to Issinlough, just as much as Avender. She said it would help take my mind off all the terrible things that have happened."

The bear climbed down from his rock to stand beside the girl. His dark nose came uncomfortably close to hers. She smiled primly.

"It's not fine with me," he said. "You're not coming."

She was so close to the bear Avender was surprised she didn't keel over from the smell of fish and beer. But Ferris was undeterred.

"If I can't go with you," she said sturdily, "I'll tell Hern what your real plans are. And then Avender won't be allowed to go, either. I know you wouldn't be bringing him along if you didn't need him."

The bear glanced angrily at the boy. "What have you told her?"

"I haven't told her anything!"

"He hasn't," said the girl. "He didn't have to. But I know the three of you are up to something. And Giserre, too. She was in a much better mood after you talked to her yesterday. She even smiled at dinner." She gave Avender a narrow look. "I told you I was coming with you this time, no matter how hard you tried to keep me away."

"I didn't have anything to do with it! I would've told you everything if they'd let me!"

"Quiet, boy. I'll deal with the girl." Redburr shouldered Avender aside, then turned and studied Ferris carefully. "You don't really know anything, do you. You're just guessing."

"I know enough to tell Hern there's more to your plan than you've told her. What will you do if she starts asking questions? You know she'll see right through you if you start to lie."

"The lass is right, Redburr." Nolo didn't even try to conceal his grin. "We all know you can't lie to Hern. Remember that time you got into the October ale and broke two casks? You didn't fool her for a second. And there were those beehives of Darny Uphill's, too. Let the lass come. She already has permission."

"You know I'm right," said Ferris confidently.

The bear growled once more, and even bared his teeth. "I should call your bluff, girl. I can always take the boy with me, with or without your mother's permission. But it wouldn't be so easy for you."

"It wouldn't be so easy for you, either," said Ferris boldly. She was trying to keep up a brave front, but Avender could see she was starting to fear she might be left behind after all, for all her careful planning. It hadn't occurred to her that the bear might not be as afraid of her mother as she thought.

Redburr stared hard at Ferris a long moment, his teeth still showing. Then suddenly, much to the surprise of the other three, his mouth relaxed and his anger disappeared.

"On the other hand," he said, "we do want to keep our real purpose as quiet as possible. And it might even be better this way. You can come. But this isn't a picnic to Nokken Rock. You'd better hear what you're getting yourself into before you decide to join us." He turned his heavy head to Nolo. "If I'd known convincing Hern would be so easy, I might have asked the girl along from the first. Better to have two of them with us when we get to Ussene, in case something happens to one."

"Ussene?" A horrified look burst across Ferris's face. "You're going straight to Ussene?"

The Shaper grinned wickedly. "Proud of yourself, aren't you, now you've found out what it is you've gotten into? Where'd you think we'd go to rescue the boy, the Pearl Isles? You can always stay home if you like." His small eyes flickered cruelly.

Ferris caught herself with a deep breath, but was still white as a sheet. She swallowed before she spoke. "I said I'd come, and I will. But I thought you were going to Issinlough first to get help from the Bryddin. I didn't think we'd be going straight to Ussene."

"We are going to Issinlough, lass." Nolo gave the girl a kind look. "And we'll use what help we find there. But we won't be taking any armies to Ussene, Bryddin or otherwise. The task's for us alone."

A gust of wind swayed the tops of the dark green trees. Last year's needles were swept off the side of the cliff in a brown swirl. Ferris sat down on the gray stone between the Dwarf and the bear and listened to their plan.

8

The Three

Everything was quiet. The thunder of the storm had disappeared. The slashing rain and spears of lightning were gone. Only Ossdonc's iron grip on Reiffen's arm remained to remind him of everything that had happened. His last chance of rescue was gone, snatched away in the single moment Ossdonc had cried out:

"RETURN!"

Once again he found himself standing within a circle of tall stones. Only this time there was no blackened earth or grass beneath his feet. This time he stood firmly on a smooth rock floor. Ossdonc loomed beside him, a dark shadow against the night. Reiffen hardly had time to look around before he was pulled along by the Wizard to a set of steps that led down beneath the floor. He caught a glimpse of a star or two in the night above, and the shadows of what might have been mountains beyond the circle of stones. Then he was dragged down into the deeper darkness. The upper world was left behind.

The walls closed in around them. No light sparked their long descent. If there were any windows along that spiral stair, no stars or moon shone bright enough to reveal them. Terrified, Reiffen struggled not to fall as the Wizard pulled him along, the only sounds the thud of Ossdonc's great stride and the slap of Reiffen's smaller steps behind.

Abruptly the stair came to an end; Reiffen tripped on the unseen floor. His arm was nearly wrenched off as Ossdonc jerked him forward in a new direction. This time there were no stairs and no turns, just a hurried run forward behind the Wizard's own fast walk. Although Ossdonc's great bulk blocked most of the high-ceilinged passage ahead, gradually Reiffen began to notice the gray stone of the walls on either side, and found he was trotting along in the wake of the Wizard's long shadow.

The light increased. Reiffen found himself pulled into the sudden brightness of a large room, where smoking torches burned in brackets on the filthy walls and soldiers stood idly about. The Wizard threw Reiffen across the room toward them, and the soldiers snapped to attention as the boy fell at their feet in a jumble of arms and legs. He quailed at their cruel, hard faces, small reflections of their master's. Even indoors they wore heavy helms and armor of leather and black iron, and carried short, heavy swords.

Ossdonc's voice boomed. "Take this one to the dungeons!" Without waiting for any sort of reply he turned and left as suddenly as he had arrived.

Two soldiers seized Reiffen's arms and dragged him roughly off down a different passage. There was no chance to fight them. And even if he should escape, where would he go? They pulled him along to another room filled with guards, and from there descended many levels into the dungeons. The boy lost all track of the twists and turns and branching corridors they followed. By the time they tossed him into a dark cell and slammed the heavy door behind him, all he knew of where he had been taken was that it was somewhere deep beneath the world.

The key rattled in the lock. Footsteps receded down the hall. Reiffen lay still in the darkness, terrified of what might be done to him next. He knew that no one who had ever been taken to Ussene had ever come out again. Or, if they had, that they came out completely different from whom they had been when they went in. Where else could he possibly be, but Ussene?

He cried. His tears wet his cheeks and the grime on the ground beneath him. When he stopped it was only because he lacked the strength to keep on. Exhausted, he lay on the floor, his wet face sticking to the cold and dirty stone. Knowing his crying would do him no good, he did his best to swallow his fear. But it remained, nonetheless, a tight little knot that gripped his stomach.

He wiped his nose with his sleeve and, to keep from crying again, explored the cell around him.

It wasn't large. He felt no furniture, just a pair of iron manacles hanging from the back wall, and a wooden door in the front. His fingers traced a thin crack at the bottom of the door, but not a glimmer of light shone in from that direction. His lip began to tremble and he bit the inside to keep from crying again. No other sound disturbed the darkness. After a while he surprised himself and fell asleep, fatigue finally overwhelming his terror. He slept for a long time on his side on the cold stone floor, his knees pulled up to his chest and his arms wrapped round his knees.

He was dreaming of his mother and the blue lake shimmering beneath the Manor when he was startled awake by the sound of the key turning once more in the lock. Quickly he sat up and rubbed his eyes with the backs of his filthy fingers. The door opened and an arm with a torch was thrust inside.

"Come on out, you," said a harsh voice. "No hangin' back, there. You're wanted Upstairs quick."

Cautiously Reiffen went to the door. It was small and he had to bend to pass through it. Ossdonc could never have fit. A rough hand grabbed his shoulder while he was still in the doorway and dragged him out into the torchlight. He shielded his eyes against the glare.

Up they took him, back through the long maze of corridors and passages, past other guards, not all of them human, in rooms where coal and twisted bits of wood burned in metal braziers. At last they came to a part of the fortress that seemed less forbidding, where the halls and corridors were much larger than they were in the dungeons below. Large enough, Reiffen supposed, for the Three to pass comfortably through them. He felt small as his guards prodded him along beneath the high ceilings, thick candles sputtering in brackets along the walls. Here he also saw people other than soldiers for the first time. Most of them kept their eyes to the floor and never even tried to look at him. Guessing they were slaves, he wondered how long they had been in that place, and whether his fate would be the same as theirs.

They arrived at a long hall where the light came not from candles but from lamps that seemed crude imitations of Dwarven skill. The lights were set atop heavy iron sconces and bore no resemblance to Nolo's delicate, gleaming jewels; these gems were too large for the dim light that flickered from them. Weak shadows followed the soldiers as they pushed the boy forward to a pair of huge iron doors standing closed at the far end. Even Ossdonc would look small before them.

The doors opened. The guards stepped back. Reiffen moved forward without being told. Behind him the portal closed silently. Trembling, he fought back the urge to turn and throw himself against the exit. He had no wish to appear as frightened as he felt. All the same, when he advanced past the circle of tall columns into the chamber beyond, his heart nearly leapt from his chest and his legs all but betrayed him.

He found himself in a great, circular hall, larger than any he had ever imagined. The dome of it arched high above, lost in the gloom, and the far side was also indistinct. In the middle, on a dais raised three tall steps from the floor, were the Three.

Although he had seen only Ossdonc before, and that in the midst of tempest and tunneled darkness, still he was able to recognize each of the Wizards. Usseis, the chief among them, was plainly the one seated on the throne. He was tall, the same as his brother, but much less massive. Where Ossdonc gave an impression of enormous vitality and strength of body, the sight of Usseis was more subtle. From the simple silver crown atop his head to the long white robes that covered him, he appeared the very picture of the wise old king. His throne was a stone bench, tall and heavy to suit his size, but completely unadorned. He sat with one hand folded in his lap, leaning on the other. But, when Reiffen came closer, he saw that Usseis's eyes were black as the heart of the darkest storm, without any white. Currents coiled, unseen but felt, within them, just as a thunderstorm can be felt in the stillness before it arrives.

Behind him stood Ossdonc, his hands folded atop his great sword. He remained all in black, but his clothes were changed from what he had worn before, a short tunic over leggings this time, with ruffles at his throat. And at the foot of the dais, in gray robes that were otherwise the same as Usseis's, sat Fornoch with his staff laid on the step beside him.

They were the Three: the White; the Black; and the Gray. Reiffen stopped and faced them at the foot of the dais. His heart shivered as he did so, but the powers laid down deep within the very rock of that chamber left him no other path.

He did not set foot on even the lowest step. Fornoch sat on that step. Above him Usseis bent forward, a thin smile on his lips. Now that he was close enough to see their faces Reiffen could see that they were, indeed, brothers. They all shared the same black eyes, eyes that projected great power and strength, while at the same time masking the thoughts that lay within. They were not human eyes. They could not be read in the way that a man's or woman's might be read. Not that it mattered. Reiffen saw at once that the desires of the Three were always plain upon their faces, and varied little. Power and greed and cruel amusement flickered between them, with small room for any other feeling.

Reiffen trembled before them. At first his mouth was dry, his imagination shuffling back and forth between the thought that he was about to be blasted to a cinder, or his heart torn horribly from his chest. For a long while he stood like that, beneath their piercing gaze.

Then Usseis settled back upon his bench and spoke. "Welcome, Reiffen," he said. His voice was less horrible than Ossdonc's, which crashed and boomed with the power of wind and mountains. Usseis's voice was calmer, the oil poured over rougher waters. And it was smooth, like oil, as well, and penetrating. It washed over Reiffen, spreading slowly across him, leaving no part of him untouched.

"Welcome," Usseis repeated. He raised his hand as if offering the room around him to his guest. "Welcome to Ussene. Is it not formidable? Are we not the Three?"

Behind him Ossdonc rolled his head back and laughed so loudly that the echoes he sent racing round the room seemed almost to come alive. But Fornoch said nothing.

The laughter faded. Usseis placed his hands beside him on the bench and leaned forward. "You should be honored," he said, and again Reiffen felt the words roll down him, coating him thickly. "It is not often that all of the Three come together to greet a guest. Our affairs are pressing, and can only be neglected for the most compelling of reasons. Your presence, therefore, is very compelling." He smiled again, a smile Reiffen could not help but feel would be most at home at beheadings, or vivisection.

"Come," Usseis said. "There is no need for you to be afraid. Had we wanted you for other purposes, you would not be with us now. My brother was perhaps a little brusque in his treatment of you upon your arrival, but that is his way. Let me ease your mind."

The Wizard raised his hand and held it palm forward toward the boy. At once Reiffen's heart ceased its trembling. His tongue no longer stuck dryly to the roof of his mouth.

"You see," said Usseis, "we are your friends. Great injustice has been done to you by other, lesser folk. We have brought you here to help you."

Ossdonc chuckled, almost to himself this time, the noise was so much less than it had been before. "Just think," he said, his voice breaking loudly across the room. "I might have been your great-uncle. The queen Loellin was your mother's aunt, you know."

"Queen Loellin would have thrown herself into the sea had she known she was married to you," answered Reiffen hotly. Then he tensed and almost took a step backward as he realized he had insulted a Wizard.

But Ossdonc boomed his laugh again, and Usseis also smiled. Reiffen found himself wondering if the words he had spoken had been his own. Only Fornoch continued silent at his seat at the foot of the dais.

"Do not worry, young friend," said Usseis, his eyes glinting. "You speak your own mind. My arts may have loosened your tongue somewhat in easing your heart. But I have done nothing to your mind . . . yet."

Usseis glanced at Fornoch as he spoke. Fornoch met his gaze but still remained only an observer.

"Why did you bring me here?" Reiffen blurted out. He was still astonished that he could ask such a question, despite Usseis's explanation. And, though he did not quite know why, he knew there was something wrong in bandying words with a Wizard.

Usseis extended his arms wide in virtuousness. "Have I not already told you? It is as I said. My brothers and I wish to help you. We are here in answer to your desire."

"My desire?" Reiffen's brow knit in confusion.

"Yes. Your desire."

The White Wizard folded his hands and held them beneath his chin, his eyes still intent on the boy. "I know that you have always pretended, while in Valing, that you have no wish to be king. But you may shed that pretense here. We are your friends. Here you may speak freely about what lies truly in your heart. Here you may allow yourself the comfort of your dreams. And we, as true friends should, will help you."

"You're not my friends," said Reiffen stubbornly. "My friends are back in Valing, mourning my death."

"Ah. There you are wrong." The Wizard smiled from one corner of his mouth, as he might had he just removed the color from a butterfly's wings. "Your friends are actively planning to rescue you. They meet in council even as we speak, and show only their foolishness as they try to plot some way in which I might be forced to return you. But they have never been your friends. Have they ever helped you in your heart's desire? I think not. They spend their time trying to persuade you to do what they want, not what you want. What sort of friends are those?"

Usseis smiled sadly. "The bear especially," he continued, "will never help you. Always has he been against those who wish to better themselves. His counsel will ever be for his own benefit. For all his friendliness he would just as soon you humans sank back into your hovels in the woods and left his animal friends alone."

"Redburr isn't like that at all." Reiffen raised his face and looked the Wizard in the eye but found that a dangerous thing to do. Blinking, he drew himself back from the sudden plunge into darkness he had been about to take, and remembered, on the back of his tongue, the foul burning of the potion Mindrell had fed him on Nokken Rock.

"Redburr isn't like that," he repeated. But now he was almost mumbling, and his eyes fell to the gray stone at his feet. "He would have rescued me if he could."

"Would he?" The Wizard's heavy gray brows arched above his fearsome eyes. "Then why did he try to rescue you in the guise of a bird? Surely, had his real intent been to save you, he would have attacked my brother in his strongest aspect. He knows that he is not nearly strong enough to fight Ossdonc, so he arrived in the shape of a bird, not a bear, that he might make his escape more easily."

"You're just saying that to frighten me." Reiffen was not about to allow the Wizard to trick him into thinking badly of his friends. But, all the same, the question of why things were done one way and not another was now planted in his mind, no matter how much he ignored it.

Usseis shrugged, and the dangerous glittering in his eye subsided. "As you wish," he said. "But you will only have yourself to blame when you learn the truth. You could be king of all the lands from Firron to the Blue Mountains with my assistance. King in your own right. Or," and Usseis smiled cruelly at the thought, "you could simply be the instrument through which my brothers and I exact our revenge."

"I'd still be your instrument either way," said Reiffen. "You're not really giving me a choice at all."

"I assure you, boy. I am." The black eyes bored more deeply into him than before, and Reiffen found himself forced to look down at the floor like a disobedient child.

"Return him to the dungeons," suggested Ossdonc loudly from his place behind his brother. "On one of the lower levels this time. That will make him know his own mind."

"That is one possibility," agreed Usseis. "The lamentations of his fellows might affect him greatly. I had so wanted to show him every courtesy, though."

"Then do so."

For the first time Fornoch spoke. His voice was different from both his brothers', a whisper from behind. But it was a strong whisper, without timidity, and could be heard at any distance. Almost it sounded to Reiffen like a voice within his head, a calm and reasonable voice suggesting always what was the calm and reasonable thing to do. But it was not a kind voice and was, in its way, every bit as cruel as the voices of its brothers.

"Show him every courtesy," said Fornoch. "Allow him the freedom of Ussene." He looked upon Reiffen as if the boy were a book or a map or a goose quill pen. "He cannot escape. There is no worry there. After a month he will see the practicality of what we offer. And the impracticality of any other course of action he might devise. Now, however, he is too full of the deep waters and fierce independence of Valing to appreciate the nature of our gifts. A little time will purge him of his past."

Ossdonc scowled as Fornoch spoke and, once his brother was

finished, spat out his disagreement. "Bah!" he exclaimed. "As usual, Fornoch, your words are those of an old woman. Your intrigues have failed before and will fail again. I say throw the boy into one of our deepest holes and allow some of our pets to play with him for a while. Either way, we'll have what we want when we bring him out again." He slapped his hand against his belt to reinforce the rightness of his approach.

Usseis kept his gaze fixed upon Reiffen, who felt his fear begin to rise again beneath the Wizard's eye.

"And what do you think?" asked the White Wizard of the boy when the Black had finished speaking. "Whose suggestion shall I follow? Which of the two alternatives would you prefer?"

Even though Reiffen was still looking carefully down at the cold stone floor, he felt the black eyes of the Wizard boring two small holes into the top of his head.

"N-Neither," he said, swallowing hard before his mouth dried up completely again. His earlier bravado had passed. He was just a boy once more. "I-I just want to go home."

Ossdonc roared. "See, Usseis! He begins to break already! Throw him in with the other prey! By tomorrow he will do whatever we say!"

Usseis leaned back upon his stone bench. "No. I will give him another chance. We will try Fornoch's plan. Let the boy see for himself what our friendship means. If he should still persist in his foolishness we can always pursue the other course. But, boy"—Usseis narrowed his eyes and Reiffen found himself forced to look upon the Wizard's face against his will—"think well of what we may choose to do should you make us force you. If you are king in your own right, then you will have some say in who will die and who will not in the world to follow. But if you are no more than a puppet, we shall have no reason to do other than as we see fit."

With a wave of his hand the Wizard dismissed him. And Reiffen, without even noticing what he was doing until after he had already done it, turned and left the room.

He found himself standing in the outer hall, beyond the monstrous doors. A single soldier led him away through the upper levels of the fortress to a small room at the end of a long, empty passage. A low bed was the only furnishing. Smudges of dark soot smeared the bare rock walls. A rough wool blanket lay wadded at one end of the filthy mattress. It seemed he was still a prisoner, for all Fornoch's offer of courtesy.

Reiffen was glad he was still a prisoner. Had the Three spoiled him with comfort and gifts from the start he would have been far more nervous. Even so, he sat on the hard bed for a long time, his chin cradled sorrowfully in his hands, and almost wished that Usseis had buried him in the deepest of his dungeons. At least then he would have been spared the torment of brooding in an empty cell about the horrors yet to come.

To keep from doing just that, he decided to test what the Wizard had said about allowing him the freedom of the fortress. Cautiously he reached for the door latch, half-suspecting some sort of trap. But the handle didn't turn into a biting serpent, or burn the flesh from his hand. The door opened easily. Across the passage stood a second door similar to his own. It took a while for Reiffen to summon the courage to open it; he realized it might be hard to wander freely about a place where all sorts of terrors might lurk behind every closed door. But, when he finally did open it, he found only another small cell like his own on the other side. Nervously he glanced up at the ceiling, half-expecting some bony imp or grinning gremlin to drop upon him from above. But there was only the same dirty rock as the walls.

He went back out into the corridor. A single candle sputtered between the doors. It occurred to him he might prefer being eaten by some horrible creature in the darkness, rather than cowering in his cell. At least then the waiting would be over. So he set off down the corridor to explore, his heart in his mouth as he wandered through the Wizards' fortress alone.

He soon discovered that Ussene was a very empty place. The

stone hallways echoed with his footsteps, and the candles on the walls were few and far between. He groped his way between the islands of dirty light, wishing he had brought along the candle from his room. Few turns interrupted the long passages that led back and forth and up and down without ever seeming to go anywhere. Each corridor looked the same: long stone lanes with thick candles sometimes flickering at the intersections and the corners. He was soon lost, but he hardly thought the Wizards had brought him all this way just so he could die of thirst in some forgotten corner of their fortress.

Eventually he came to a broad set of stairs guarded by several soldiers. They challenged him sharply the moment they saw him and, when he didn't know the password, roughly carted him off down a different corridor to what appeared to be a barracks. There he was brought up before the very same officer who had escorted him to his new cell. He was a short man, fat and strong. At his feet a small slave was busy polishing his boots with a blackened rag.

"Couldn't stay in your cell, could you?" the officer sneered. He stood up and kicked the slave into a corner. "No, you have to take Him at His word and go exploring." With a curt wave, the officer dismissed the soldiers who had brought Reiffen to him.

The boy said nothing. A nasty light appeared in the officer's eye.

"Too good to talk to me, are you?" he said.

Without warning he cuffed Reiffen across the face, knocking him backwards to the floor. Then he put his hands on his hips and stood over the fallen boy. "They may have decided to let you run loose around the place, but no one said anything about giving yourself airs. When They're not around, I'm the boss here, and you'd better not forget it. Now get out of here. The password of the day is 'Darkness' the next time someone asks you. And if you forget it I'll be happy to give you a real thrashing the next time they bring you back."

Reiffen rubbed his cheek. He was angry and embarrassed that

the man had knocked him down so easily. As he backed out of the room he told himself next time he wouldn't be caught off guard.

Still fuming, he walked off without a thought for where he was going and promptly got lost again. At the next intersection, he came to a passage that went both left and right, but neither way looked any different from any of the others he had explored that day. The only thing he knew for sure was that he didn't want to go back to the guardroom, so he went left, for no other reason at all.

He came to a set of stairs. A thin flicker of light in the distance showed the steps ascending into the gloom. Perhaps this was the stair that led back to the place where Ossdonc had first brought him, where he had last seen a glimpse of the sky. Candles high on the wall lit the way as he climbed, still few and far between. But there was always some small flicker ahead, no matter how dark his current footing, so he kept on. The thought occurred to him that had the stair been leading him down instead of up, he might not have been so eager to continue. But, in going upward, there was at least the chance he might come out into a place where he could see the sun.

The stair ended and he found himself in another square room with smoky walls and an exit on the far side. An empty brazier stood in the middle of the room, but it had been so long unused there were no ashes in it at all. Reiffen crossed the room and kept on, determined to make some sense of the long, empty passages around him.

The new corridor lined straight on through long troughs of gloom. He quickened his pace, all the while careful to make sure that nothing would catch him unaware. Then he came to a spot where there was no further light ahead to guide him. He crept forward slowly, hoping the glare of the lamp behind was hindering his view ahead. His shadow stretched out across the dusty floor, merging finally into the darkness. He wanted very much to go on, though he was also well aware that the darker crooks and crannies of Ussene were probably just the places best left unexplored.

He peered forward into the gloom one last time. Just as he was about to turn back, he thought he felt something different in the air. Was there some sound at the edge of his hearing? Was something moving in the darkness? A light touch brushed his cheek and he started quickly in alarm, until he realized he had felt the air moving past him in the passage. What was more, there was a different odor on the breeze. Slightly wet and cool, and almost clean, and thoroughly lacking the smoky thickness of the air he had been breathing since he first arrived. It was almost the smell of outside.

He moved cautiously forward, one hand touching the wall so as not to lose his bearings. He looked behind him every few steps as well, to make sure he could still see the last candle. But all the same, he moved steadily forward toward the source of the sweet breeze.

Sooner than he had expected, the wall beneath his hand fell away. The hall had opened into a larger room. The draft felt fresher now: it ebbed and flowed across his face. For a moment he stood in the dark entrance and tilted his head this way and that to see if he could learn anything more from the air.

It was while he was standing motionless in the doorway that the darkness began to take some pattern before him. There seemed to be a square ahead that was different in its darkness from the rest. There was no hint of light, but there was a difference of texture. Black velvet is different from black canvas, and that was the difference here. And, more than that, the breeze seemed to be coming straight from the different spot as well.

He took a few more steps forward. Soon he realized he was looking at a tall window open to the night. A few more strides and he was standing at the sill. The window began at his shoulders and extended well above his head, a window for tall Wizards. He gripped the edge in both hands and leaned forward on tiptoe to take his first breath of fresh air since coming to Ussene.

It was raining outside. That was why the slight breeze in the passage had smelled damp. Raindrops fell refreshingly against the top of his head. He leaned as far out the window as he could, to feel as much of the delicious night as he might.

He found himself looking down from a high cliff into a narrow valley. The stone dropped almost sheer below. At the bottom, very far away, he saw the flickering of tiny lights. Some lay at the bottom of his own cliff, while others seemed to lie on the other side of the chasm. At last he had found a gate back to the outside world. Not one he might use to escape perhaps, but one he might use all the same to gain a glimpse of the world from which he had been taken. Somewhere out there under the same night sky were his mother and his friends.

He pulled his head and shoulders back within the frame and ran his fingers through his damp hair. Afterward he stood for a long time watching the darkness and the shadow of the rain. He wondered how long he would have to wait to see the dawn, and supposed it would be too much to ask for the window to be facing east. But little matter. For the moment he was happy just to lean against the massive stone sill and breathe in the cool wet of the night. Even in the heart of his fortress Usseis could not spoil the sweetness of a spring rain.

"Please, sir," said a voice from the dark behind him, "it is wonderful to look out on the world, isn't it?"

Reiffen whirled around, but it was still far too dark to see a thing. The hairs on the back of his neck prickled in fright as he pressed closely to the wall beneath the window.

"Don't be scared, kind sir," said the voice, which sounded much more fearful than Reiffen. And sad as well, as if its fear was not that Reiffen would hurt it, but rather that its approach might be spurned. "Molio won't hurt you."

"Who—who are you?" stammered Reiffen, his back still braced against the wall.

"Only Molio."

"Who?"

"Molio. I saw the captain knock you down. He is very strong, like all the soldiers." There was a shudder in Molio's voice, as if he was remembering the strength of the soldiers firsthand.

Reiffen recalled the little slave who had been blacking the captain's boots when he was brought back to the guardroom. "Is the captain the one who gave me the password?" he asked.

"Oh, yes. He's the one," said Molio eagerly. "He's the one who gave you the slaves' password."

"Slaves' password?" Reiffen relaxed a little now that he knew who was behind the voice. Surely the little bootblack couldn't hurt him.

"Oh, yes. He would never give you the Masters' password. That's why Molio knew you were one of us. That, and when he hit you."

"Why did you follow me here?" The thought came to Reiffen that perhaps the little man was a spy.

A moment passed before Molio answered him, which only increased the boy's suspicions. Then the little man said, in a low, lonely voice, "Molio thought maybe . . . maybe you would be his friend."

"You weren't sent to spy on me? To tell them everything I do?"

"Oh, no, sir! Molio is too unimportant for spying!" The little man's voice quivered with fear. "Only the quickest and strongest can be spies! Molio is only a slave, fit for cleaning and candles only." The voice in the darkness dropped to a whimper. "Molio wanted only to help."

"Help me?" asked Reiffen in a bitter voice. "How can you help me?"

"Oh, Molio can show you many things, sir. Molio knows all the ways of the fortress, sir."

"Can you show me how to escape?"

"Escape?" squeaked the little man. "Please, sir, don't even say such a thing. There is no escape from the fortress. Many things are not allowed here. We shouldn't even be here!"

"No?"

"No! They come here sometimes. And They get very angry when someone is where they're not supposed to be."

Reiffen didn't need to ask who "They" were. And, since he had no wish to see Them again any time soon, he was more than happy to allow the little man to lead him away. They hurried back down the hallway that had led up to the room with the window, Molio in front. As they approached the last light the little man came slowly into view. Reiffen found himself wondering at the fellow's strange appearance: his pointed little head; his tiny ears; and his arms and legs seeming too small for his round little body. His face was mousy and thin, with a sad little mustache and dark eyes that seemed to have little white. Reiffen had heard rumors about the sorts of things that Usseis did in his laboratories, and wondered if Molio and the rest of the people he had seen so far in Ussene were the end result.

Their return along the passage and the stair was much shorter than the boy remembered. Apparently he hadn't ascended as far as he had thought. At one point Molio stopped beneath one of the flickering candles and, producing a long taper from somewhere among the folds of his ragged clothing, lit the end at the candle's small flame. Then he marched on down the stair with the flame shielded behind his hand. At the darkest spot between that light and the next he stopped again. Reaching once more into some hidden pocket of his cloak, he produced a short, thick candle similar to the others Reiffen had seen throughout the fortress.

"What are you doing?" asked the boy. "I thought we were in a hurry to get away."

"Molio still must do his job," said the little man.

With a practiced eye and a little jump he tossed the candle up into the darkness. The taper gave off just enough light for Reiffen to see the candle had landed atop a small ledge high on the wall. Molio raised his long lighter and, applying it to the wick, soon had a fresh light going. The little man was more than just a bootblack.

Had it not been for Molio, Reiffen might never have learned to find his way around Ussene. He would have been left to sort things out by repeatedly running into the guard, who eventually would have knocked most of his teeth out of his mouth for the trouble he gave them. But Molio taught him the ways around the guard posts, and showed him the few spots in the fortress that were of any interest. All the boy had to do was follow his guide around on his regular routes with his bag of stubby candles and his long taper. For that, as it turned out, was Molio's main job in Ussene. Blacking boots was only a sideline, initially thought up by the soldiers to add to his torment, but now one of the little man's few pleasures, since he was actually good at it.

Reiffen never went with Molio, however, when it was his time to go to the guardroom. Instead Reiffen would generally go to the places that most interested him, which also happened to be the same ones that most scared Molio. Like the Front Window, which, once he discovered it was rarely used by the Three, Reiffen visited at least once every day. There might not be any lake in view, or so much as a single blade of grass growing on the barren cliffs. But at least there were mountains, harsher than even the High Bavadars but mountains all the same, and blue sky, with stars at night when it wasn't raining.

But even more than the room with the window, Reiffen liked to go to the Library. The first time he found the place, Molio had tried desperately to stop him. "Fornoch's place! It is forbidden!" he had cried, while struggling to hold back the larger Reiffen by the arm. But Molio was as weak as he looked and sounded, and had finally let go when he realized he was in danger of being dragged down the hall to Fornoch's place himself. Reiffen, who had gone a long time since seeing the Wizards, was not quite as frightened of running into them as he had been that first night by the Window. In fact, he feared Fornoch the least of the Three. Fornoch was the one who had suggested Reiffen be given the freedom of the fortress, and a chance to change his mind. Had Molio warned him away from Oss-

donc's place he would have instantly obeyed. But for a glimpse of
Fornoch's he was willing to take a chance.

So he left Molio moaning behind him and continued on down
the corridor. The passage ended in a door, another door that was
twice as large as normal in order to accommodate Wizards. Reiffen
hesitated before trying the knob: though he had grown bolder in his
days of roaming the fortress, still this was the apartment of a Wizard. Even if no doorknobs had yet bitten him, and he had yet to fall
into any pits teeming with snakes or poisoned stakes, he had no desire at all to burst in on even the weakest Wizard.

The knob turned easily in his hand. He cracked the door slightly
and put his eye to the opening. Books were what he saw. Shelves and
shelves of books. Huge, enormous books like layered chests, and
tiny books that could not possibly hold more than a letter a page.
Books lying open on tables and books stacked on the floor in uneven piles. Dusty books and books so new they had never been
opened. And, here and there among the books, an amulet, or a
wand, or the skeleton of a toad.

Reiffen wanted very much to enter that room. He didn't care
how many Wizards might be waiting inside for him. Just a minute in
that library would be worth anything Usseis might think to do to
him. So much to see and learn! His forehead bumped against the
jamb as he tried to get his eye as close to the crack as possible. Holding his breath, he listened for anyone who might be within. It was
like waiting for the start of a feast, or for morning to come after the
first snowy night on the Neck. Time slowed while he struggled to
keep himself from entering. More than once he told himself the
room wasn't safe, that it was exactly the sort of place that Wizards
would visit often. If he went in he would be caught. And, if he were
caught, then terrible things would happen.

But he also reminded himself that Usseis had said he was to have
the freedom of Ussene. If they really wanted him not to go somewhere, they should have told him.

The door opened easily once he made up his mind. There was

no squeaking, not even a creaking from the hinges. The whole beautiful room opened up to view. He stood silently for a moment in the doorway, taking it all in. Then he crossed the threshold into a world completely different from the rest of the barren fortress.

Cautiously he peered at the first book he saw, a medium-sized volume with dark leather binding and silver scrollwork along the spine. The title was inscribed in silver letters: *The Dictionary of Names.* Reiffen stopped himself just in time from dragging his finger along the open edge of the cover. Reluctantly he left the book untouched, feeling he had already risked enough in coming through the door.

He went around the room, reading the titles of the books on the tables. Most of them he didn't understand. Not all were about magic. Of the few he could understand there were some simple atlases and histories. One he even recognized as a history of Banking he had often read with his mother.

When he finished examining the books on the tables, he started to look at those on the library shelves but was soon distracted by all the other things gathered there besides books. A delicate spiderweb stretched across an ornate wooden frame, as if it were a work of art on exhibition, a fat black spider as big as the end of his thumb sitting in the middle of the web. A spyglass that seemed to have been carved from a long piece of hollow bone lay on its side on a pair of ivory holders. A strange round contraption with numbers inscribed around the edge and a pair of levers pointing at the numbers ticked like half a cricket.

The shelves covered all four walls of the room. There were no windows: the only opening was the door through which Reiffen had entered. Soft light glowed from an unseen ceiling. Except for the tables, the tops of which were level with Reiffen's chest, there was no other furniture in the room. All of the strange objects were set on the shelves, and none of them were very large. As he came to each, he had to fight the urge to pick it up.

With one he could barely restrain himself. It was the last thing he encountered on his tour around the room. A small green stone, no larger than a pigeon's egg, lay on a shelf close to the door under a small bowl of glass.

At first he almost missed it. The stone was dark green, almost black, and seemed no more interesting than a pretty pebble you might find in a shallow stream. He was going to ignore it, but, as he passed it by, the color of the stone seemed to lighten. Intrigued, he returned for a second look. The stone grew lighter once more as he came close to it. Other than the spider, which had seemed to lift its head and study him even as he studied it, the green stone was the only thing in the room that seemed to do anything. Everything else just lay about, mysterious and silent.

Reiffen tried different things with the stone. He waved his hand in front of it, but the stone remained the same. Only when he moved his whole body close did the color change, and then it was not so much the color changing as it was that the heart of the stone grew brighter. It was not like a Dwarven lamp, where a clear gem would cast its radiance all around a room. The green stone was dark, and its light just enough to gleam within its depths and lighten the blackness of its outer shell. It lent no color to the clear glass bowl around it. And, when Reiffen remained close to the stone, he found that the light began to pulse, faster than his breathing.

With a shock he realized the stone had joined the rhythm of his heartbeat. He jerked back from it as if stung; at once the stone darkened back to greenish black. Cautiously he reached out with his hand once more; but, again, there was no reaction from the stone.

He was both fascinated and repelled. He had never heard of such a thing. All the other objects in the room were things he recognized, things that, if not common in the human world, were at least familiar to it. Except that round, ticking contraption. But never had he heard of a piece of stone that seemed to be alive. He wished he could show it to Nolo. Nolo knew everything there was to know about stone.

Reiffen pushed at the upside-down bowl with his finger. It

moved easily across the shelf, but he pulled back before he had moved the bowl more than a finger's breadth. Did he really want to touch the stone, whatever it was? He was close enough to it again that it began to beat regularly once more in time with his heart. Its pulsing made him more aware of his own heart thumping against his chest with excitement. There was so much to learn! If only Usseis didn't want to use him to further the Wizards' plans. What he wouldn't give to learn the green stone's purpose! And to read every book in the room as well.

There was a small noise at the door. Reiffen glanced up in alarm. The green stone pulsed very quickly and much brighter than before as it sensed his sudden fear. But it was only Molio, peering around the bottom of the door. His mustache drooped even more than usual.

"Please, sir," he whispered. "Can we go home?"

The moment was broken for Reiffen. He stepped away from the stone and it stopped its beating at once. Secretly he was glad it had become a plain old rock again. He didn't know why, but he didn't want Molio to notice it. Reiffen just knew that the thought of the little man touching the stone made him angry. Just as he had been angry when Avender had first come to live with him in the Tear.

He stepped forward to cut off any view Molio might have of the stone. "Okay," he said quickly. "We can go."

The little man put his finger to his lips, parting his mustache in the middle. "Don't let Him hear you," he whispered. "He knows everything that happens in His room." He hurried off down the passage still talking, once he made certain that Reiffen had closed the door tightly behind them. "Not even soldiers go there," he said. "Molio isn't the only one scared of His place. Oh, no. No one likes to go there. No one at all."

"You weren't so scared that you couldn't come get me," said Reiffen. He gave the little man a curious look.

"You are Molio's friend. Molio should never have shown you His place. He'll know who showed you, then Molio gets in trouble, too. It is bad to be a slave, but there is worse."

The little man shook his head but would say nothing more about what might be worse than being a slave. Reiffen thought he knew, though. There was a certain level in the fortress below which Molio refused to take him. There he might find all the things that were worse than being a slave. But nothing Reiffen could think of could persuade the little man to take him there. If he wanted to learn what was in that part of the fortress he would have to go alone.

9

The Road to Grangore

erris took a deep breath, savoring the strange smells of the sea. For a brief, happy moment, rescuing Reiffen was the furthest thing from her mind. It was their first day out of Lugger and she was still getting used to how different the tumbling ocean was from the lake. There was a wildness to the sea the lake could never have, not even when the fiercest winter storms howled down from the Bavadars to crash in thin white waves along the base of the Neck. The world was much larger than she had imagined, and she had imagined it big to begin with. Avender had been on a chase through the mountains, but this was the first time Ferris had ever been more than a day's hike or sail from home. Sothend and Bracken were the only places she had slept besides the Manor, until now. And the fact that she was missing her regular chores was thrilling, too.

They had spent three days on the Lugger road, pushing the horses hard the whole time. Giserre and Redburr had traveled with them at the start, past Baldun and Firtop and through the pass between. But, at the first junction in the road, the lady and the bear had turned south through the mountains for Wayland, while Nolo and the children had followed the eastern way to the pine forests and farms of Firron. Ferris guessed Giserre was halfway to Rimwich by now, while *The Other Side* carried Nolo, Avender, and her across the ragged blue water to Mremmen.

Around them the wind kicked a steady spray off the tops of the rolling waves. Gulls swooped and soared. *The Other Side* was a trim craft with a single mast, blue and yellow striped sails, and a small raised deck astern. Atop the deck the captain stood with his arms on the heavy tiller as he steered his small vessel southwest, through the mild waves of the Inner Sea toward the Toes. If all went well, he had told them, they would reach Mremmen in less than a week. And, with a strong wind out of the north to fill their sail, everything was already going well.

Ferris and Avender spent the day on deck, mesmerized by the break and roll of the ocean around them, but Nolo mostly remained below. When he did come up he made sure he was holding fast to the mast. Only once did the Dwarf approach the railing, and that was to see a dolphin that had popped up out of the sliding seas to race for a while beside the foaming bow.

"What's that for?" asked Ferris as the Dwarf tied one end of a strong rope around his waist and the other to the mast, before approaching the side of the ship.

Nolo pointed to the dark blue water. "I don't know how deep it is," he said. "If I fall in I'll never get back to the surface."

The ship's crew chuckled at the Dwarf's misgivings. Ferris was certain none of them had ever seen a Dwarf before because of the way they had stared when Nolo came aboard. She guessed they didn't believe his excuses at all. Whether you had actually seen one or not, everyone had heard how tough Dwarves were, and Nolo probably wasn't the first landlubber to be petrified by the thought of crossing the open ocean. All the same, he kept close to the middle of the ship throughout the voyage. Whenever he went near the side, he made sure he was securely tied down.

"It's not that I'll drown," he explained at supper that night to both children and crew. "But I can't breathe underwater like a fish.

184 S. C. BUTLER

Sooner or later I'll run out of air. Then I'd never get up off the bottom." He shook his head and drained a cup of grog, to which he had taken quite a fancy. "Down there I'd be just another statue with fish swimming in and out of my mouth. And not a drop to drink but water. A Bryddin shuts down if he's smothered, and doesn't wake up till he can breathe again. Morm fell overboard once on Lake Cammas, while he was fishing, and it was a week before anyone found him. He was right as rocks, though, soon as they dragged him up off the bottom and woke him up. But I'll stay right here in the middle of the boat, if it's all the same to you. Water's a lot deeper here."

The next day the weather turned, and strong squalls drove them back and forth across the gray-green waves. Ferris and Avender thought *The Other Side* would founder at any moment, but the captain seemed hardly to notice the change at all. They spent a rough night and most of the next day rolling back and forth in the hold beneath a swinging oil lamp. Ferris tried to make herself feel better by remembering that Reiffen was going through much worse but only managed to make herself more miserable instead.

She and Avender were both glad when the storm began to clear the third evening out from Lugger. They had reached the Toes, the halfway point of their voyage. Both children knew enough about sailing to understand that no captain worth his salt would ever take a ship through such an archipelago at night, but Nolo chafed at the delay.

They anchored beside a low, green isle, its shoreline thick with trees. Tangled vines trailed across the sandy beach to the water. To the west, the sun emerged for the first time all day as an orange ball below the thinning clouds. Other islands loomed low against the evening. When the captain ordered the mate and two sailors ashore for fresh water, Ferris wanted to go with them, but Nolo insisted she and Avender remain on board.

Ferris's eyes narrowed. "Are there rebels on this island?" she asked.

"Rebels? Who said anything about rebels?" Nolo snorted to show what he thought of rebels.

"I heard all about the rebels in Lugger while you were hiring the ship. Lots of people said we had to watch out for rebels if we sailed south."

The captain shaded his eyes against the setting sun and watched his crewmen row ashore. "There are renegades in the Toes," he admitted, not noticing Nolo's sour look. "Not everyone in Banking accepts Brannis as their king. More than a few have come here to hide out among the fishermen. They claim they're waiting for Prince Reiffen to come of age and lead them. But I guess that's not likely to happen now, is it."

"You heard what happened?" asked Nolo.

"Aye. The news reached Lugger two days before you."

"Don't you think someone will try to rescue him?" asked Ferris without thinking. Avender scowled, and she realized at once she had said the wrong thing. Drawing attention to what they were trying to keep secret wasn't a good idea. Nolo frowned at her severely from behind the captain's back.

But the captain didn't seem to notice her friends' annoyance. "From Ussene?" He shook his head. "Not likely. I've heard no one who goes in there ever comes out again. But what am I saying?" He looked more closely at the girl. "You look about the prince's age. Was he a friend of yours back in Valing?"

"Oh, we knew him," said Ferris with a matter-of-fact frown. "But I don't think anyone would ever call us friends. He was a prince, after all."

Avender's scowl deepened, but Ferris knew she had to make up for her mistake. The only way she knew to do that was to act as if she didn't know much about Reiffen at all, even if it was unfair to make strangers think he had been putting on airs in Valing. Nolo sighed softly, his beard fluttering.

"Kings and queens are different," agreed the captain, with an understanding nod.

Avender rose to the defense of his friend. "It's still terrible, what happened to him."

"Aye, that's plain truth." The captain watched his mate lead the sailors ashore and pull the boat up the beach behind them. "I suppose the rebels'll have nothing to fight for, now. They've taken a ship or two, and held a few travelers for ransom. But without Prince Reiffen to make their cause, they'll be no more than pirates."

Nolo eyed the distance from ship to shore. "Are you sure we're safe here?"

"Safe enough, with a Bryddin aboard, I'd say. Even renegades know better than to try and fight Bryddin."

"That only works if they know I'm here."

"I guess that means you'll have to sleep on deck tonight so they can see you." Ferris looked up at the clearing sky and hid a smug smile. The captain wasn't giving Reiffen's rescue a second thought. "At least it'll be a good night for it."

Anxiously the Dwarf peered over the side. "I guess it's not too deep. I won't need to worry about finding the bottom here. If I have to, I can always walk ashore."

They talked for a while about other things as the stars crept out from behind the thinning clouds. After supper the crew, their pipes gleaming red in the darkness like drowsing sparks, told tales of the sea. Islands that floated and water that burned, the mariners did their best to astonish the children with the strangeness of their windblown world. Both Avender and Ferris peered cautiously overboard as the sailors described the stranger creatures of the deep, birds that swam and fish that flew. And both hoped they might see at least one or the other before they went ashore.

That night, as Ferris had suggested, everyone slept on deck. She scanned the shore for rebel campfires, anyway, before she settled down.

"Avender?" The Dwarf had already begun to snore on her left. "Do you think Reiffen knows about the rebels?"

"I suppose." The boy lay wrapped in his blanket, his hands behind his head as he watched the sky. "But I don't think so. He probably would have said something if he did."

"I'll bet Giserre knows."

"I'll bet she does, too. She gets letters from Malmoret all the time."

Ferris listened to the waves rolling along the shore. Sleeping on an anchored boat, she decided, was much different from when it was under sail. The the ship had seemed to strain against the sea, and the waves had tried to hold them back as the wind had flung them forward. But tonight the swell rocked them as gently as the lake back home.

"Do you think Reiffen should be king?" Ferris asked.

Avender paused for a moment before he answered. "Redburr's always said Reiffen shouldn't try to be king," he said finally. "He says it would start a war."

"Well, I don't think there should be a war." Ferris remembered how much the two boys had fought when they were small. Redburr had been forever growling at them and forcing them apart. "But I do think Reiffen should be king. He is the rightful heir. And everybody says Brannis is doing a terrible job anyway. Maybe when we, you know . . ." She looked around to see if anyone was listening and lowered her voice to a whisper. "When we bring him back from Ussene we can help him be king, too. Maybe we'll defeat the Wizards and everyone will be so happy that even Brannis will see Reiffen should be king."

"Maybe," Avender said. But Ferris knew he didn't really think anything could ever be so easy. Especially not becoming a king. They were still a long way from Ussene.

She rolled over onto her side between the Dwarf and the boy and tried her best not to think of all the questions crowding her mind. Had the ship not rocked so gently, she would certainly have failed. But it did, and it wasn't long before her snores were mixing with her friends' across the crisp spring night.

As the captain had predicted, they sailed into Mremmen on the morning of the seventh day after leaving Lugger. To the north, the

Blue Mountains raised distant peaks across the top of the sea. To the south, the water swept unchecked to the sky. Before them the Ambore flowed through a gentle valley, the new town building against the hills behind the southern shore. Ferris leaned on the ship's rail and tried hard not to miss a thing.

"Someday," said Nolo, as he watched their arrival from the safety of the mast, "Mremmen'll be a port to rival Far Mouthing. There's a lot to trade among humans and Bryddin."

For now, Ferris saw only a jumble of docks and ships and houses, with great throngs of people elbowing one another out of the way as they hurried about the crowded streets. There were Dwarves in Mremmen, and both children looked about eagerly in hope of seeing one. But Nolo was anxious to be off upriver on the same tide that had brought them in and, before they knew it, had booked passage to Bridging on a small sloop. Avender and Ferris understood the need for haste, but they wouldn't have minded a look around the town all the same. It wasn't every day they got to visit a brand-new city.

Ferris could barely contain her disappointment as they said good-bye to their shipmates and stopped in the bustling town just long enough to buy fresh provisions. Wistfully, as their new ship started upstream, she watched the noisy streets fade down the river behind them. The blue and yellow sails of *The Other Side* disappeared beyond the first broad turn.

To Ferris's way of thinking, the river passage was more like a sail through the Narrows and down to the southern end of the lake than it was like their crossing of the Inner Sea. Mremmen's open bay closed swiftly into the Ambore's sluggish current, the water slow and brown. Long woods brushed by on either bank. Willows swept their early leaves in screens of pale green along the shore. On the ship there was hardly any room for passengers: every square foot was buried beneath sacks of grain, or barrels of salted fish, or coils of rope. The craft going upstream beside them all appeared as deeply laden as their own, but those sailing down floated high above the water.

"Why are those boats riding so much higher than ours?" asked Ferris as another lightly loaded wherry raced by.

"A bag of gemstones doesn't weigh as much as twenty barrels of flour," answered Nolo.

"Since when is a bag of gemstones worth only twenty bags of flour?"

"Since humans started working some of the upper mines. I've heard children in Malmoret play with rubies now instead of cat's-eyes."

The sloop's captain spoke up from his place at the stern. "It's not gemstones folks are looking to bring back with them anymore from Grangore. It's lamps and Dwarven arms."

"Arms?" Nolo's heavy brows rose questioningly. "Bryddin are crafting arms for humans?"

"Not Bryddin," admitted the captain. "But human smiths who've learned the Bryddin skills. There's more than a few forges in Grangore, from what I hear. And, like as not, there'll soon be more. Not that I've actually been there myself."

They reached Bridging near noon the next day. The children marveled at the town, which was built upon a low stone bridge where it crossed a shallow stretch of the river on a series of five heavy piers. Tall, narrow houses covered both sides completely, all crammed so closely together their wooden sides leaned crazily out over the curling water in search of extra room. Not one looked anything like any of the others. Some had balconies with clothes hung out to dry; others bristled with smoke and chimneys. Rickety stairs led from floor to floor and house to house, and the bottom of every pier was thick with boats, barges, and bales. Both children were eager to explore this odd town, with its single busy street that crossed the bridge between the buildings, even more than Mremmen; but once again Nolo hurried them on. The closer they came to

Grangore, the more impatient he grew. He knew how far they still had left to travel.

"But how could it hurt to stop for just a minute?" Ferris's eyes lingered on a pair of Dwarven lamps offered for sale in one of the shops. The gems glowed dully from inside small wooden boxes, their soft light swallowed up by the daytime.

"How would you feel, lass," called the Dwarf over his shoulder as he pushed forward through the crowd, "if we got to Reiffen just that one minute too late? We've got the hard part of our journey ahead of us now. No more easy sailing. Just weary footwork for miles and miles."

Ferris couldn't help but grumble, though she knew the Dwarf was right. Avender, who had been eyeing a fine sword in another stall, said nothing. He flashed Ferris a guilty look, and she knew he was telling her they had been enjoying their trip too much. Who knew what dark cavern Reiffen was cowering in, and here she was pouting because she couldn't take a stroll through the Bridging market. She hiked her pack higher on her back and hurried after the Dwarf. This time she didn't look back at the curiosities she had to leave behind. By the time they reached the woods, the straps of her pack were already chafing her shoulders.

Their road soon became little more than a narrow track as it climbed swiftly into the northern hills. At first they passed through forest filled with elm and ash and hickory; but, as the path took them higher and deeper into the woods, the ground grew hard and rocky. The trees turned to balsam and spruce. Ferris trudged along after Nolo in the wooded gloom, Avender close behind. Rarely did the path follow a straight line for more than a pace or two, so broken was the land by rock and root. Only the occasional flitting of birds, or the swish of a branch behind a leaping squirrel, disturbed the stillness of the trees.

Nolo pushed them hard. Though his short legs would never keep up if Avender and Ferris set off at a run, the Dwarf could stick to a fast walk far longer than they. Each morning he roused them cold and stiff before the sun was up and kept them marching all the long day until there wasn't enough light left in the forest to see by. And each evening they fell back exhausted to the ground with hardly the strength to remove their packs. Often they were asleep before Nolo had even started their campfire or served out their ration of bread and cheese. Ferris had worked hard all her life in her mother's house, but, by the middle of her second day on the road, she was ready to go back to baking bread and sweeping floors. At least at the Manor there was some break to the routine. You could take the sun on the porch for a minute or two, or take a taste from the stew pot. Here, at the edge of the Blue Mountains, there was nothing but trudging and trees.

They passed no one on the way.

"Where is everyone?" Ferris shifted her heavy pack for the twenty-seventh time and reached for a sapling to help her over a rough spot in the path.

"Most travelers keep to the water," said Nolo without turning round. "But it's slower. The river takes a wide bend westward just past Bridging. The road's the straighter path. But you can't get a wagon over the road, so hardly anyone comes this way anymore. And then there's the woodlings."

"Woodlings?"

"Aye, woodlings." Nolo poked his hairy chin at the trees. "They're kin to the Keeadini, even though they live in the forest. They know we're here, you can be sure of that. But I doubt we'll see any more of them than we did the rebels in the Toes. They won't bother us while I'm along."

"Why not?" Ferris shifted her pack again.

"Because woodlings and Bryddin are great friends. They were the first humans we met after Mennon helped us find our way up out of the ground. If it was humans you were traveling with, well, that would be another vein completely."

"What would happen then?"

"At the very least you'd have to pay a toll."

Ferris tugged at her pack for the twenty-ninth time and peered suspiciously at the dark woods around her.

She slept little that night, though Nolo and Avender snored away easily on either side of her by the fire. Every slight sound signaled a stranger's approach, as far as she was concerned. But they never did see any woodlings. Nolo told her they were definitely out there, watching from behind mossy boulders and rough-barked trees; but Avender insisted it was just her imagination every time she thought she saw something moving in the woods.

Uphill and down they went, never seeming to make much headway in either direction. All the brooks and streams they crossed ran west toward the long curve of the Ambore, now many leagues away. But nowhere was there a height of land or a ridge to climb to get a sense of what lay beyond the forest. All was thick pinewoods and lichen and stone, with the sky barely seen through the heavy branches above. And it was always cool and damp, the sun as effectively shut away as if they were inside a mossy cave.

On their third afternoon in the forest they came out of the trees close beside a deep gorge. Far below ran a wild and foaming river. A thin bridge of blumet and stone spanned the chasm in a clutch of metal as fine as woven cloth. Twin pairs of carved giants stood at either end, their stone backs bent beneath their heavy burden. Each held a blumet cable in its thick stone hands. The two cables looped across the gorge, the slender span suspended below them on silver strands that gleamed in the late-afternoon sunlight. Ferris thought the thin mesh of the roadway was far too frail to hold her or Avender, let alone a Dwarf, but Nolo set his heavy foot upon the delicate path without the slightest hesitation. The children followed carefully. The way was wide enough for a large cart, but they kept their course to the middle all the same. Far below, the river stormed through the chasm, a splashing ribbon of wild white and blue. Small shrubs and stunted trees clung to the steep cliffs at either side, and everywhere the stones were thick and green with moss and fern.

Beyond the bridge their track joined a second, wider road that led them shortly to the village of Upper Crossing. Geese and chickens wandered the muddy streets; curious dogs barked at their arrival. Ferris felt immediately at home. All the houses were framed in dark wood, their upper floors projecting out slightly into the street, like the houses in Bracken or Eastbay. They passed the night comfortably in the local inn, though it was so crowded they had to sleep in the barn; but Nolo had them up again before dawn the next morning, with no more than a cup of hot soup and slice of fresh bread to greet the day. Then they were off once more, rubbing their eyes sleepily as they started on the final leg of the road to Grangore.

The highway was busy: the traffic from the river had returned. Wagons rolled past in both directions along the smooth Bryddin road. The three travelers made good progress even though everyone they passed insisted on stopping to bow respectfully to Nolo. Despite his anxious hurry, he had to bow solemnly to them all in return.

"What a nuisance!" he grumbled, his beard wagging in exasperation. "All this formality."

A sense of growing urgency had begun to nag at all of them as they came closer and closer to Grangore and the entrance to the Stoneways. Nolo had told them that, even when they reached Issinlough, they would still be less than halfway to Ussene. They had been two weeks on their journey, and every new day was a chance for the Three to do something terrible to Reiffen, if they hadn't already. The leaves budded and spread their green canvas above the road, and Ferris and Avender worried more and more about what might happen to their friend.

That night it rained, and though Nolo dug a quick burrow for them in the side of a hill, they still spent a wet and muddy night. Water seeped down through the roof of their makeshift cave, dripping from the matted roots above their heads. In the morning

Ferris woke with a stuffy nose that was only made worse by her filthy clothes. When Nolo refused to light a fire so she could spend the morning drying out, she threw a small tantrum.

"We'll be in Grangore tomorrow," said the Dwarf mildly, despite the rain pelting his head and shoulders. "You can get a hot bath there."

Ferris sneezed and kicked her pack. Endless dull traveling was hardly what she had expected when she had insisted on coming along. "Great," she complained. "I can hardly wait. By that time I'll have a fever and we'll lose a whole week while you have to nurse me back to health."

"No, we won't." With a good-natured grin, the Dwarf picked the girl's pack up off the muddy ground. "We'll just leave you behind."

Ferris's jaw dropped. "What? You'd leave me all alone in the middle of nowhere?"

"Not the middle of nowhere, lass." Nolo held the pack as Ferris tied her long braids around her head and slipped her arms through the grubby straps. She felt as filthy as the road. "There're folks in Grangore I'd trust you with. But if you can't keep up now, it'll only get worse in Bryddlough."

Ferris wrinkled her upper lip to hold back another sneeze. Grit and grime trickled down her neck. She was cold and she was miserable, but she wasn't going to be left behind no matter what. She noticed Avender watching her with some concern as she scratched her nose with a dirty hand, his hair hanging in dark strings across his face. She supposed she looked just as awful.

"If you want," he whispered as they set off after the Dwarf, "we can put some of your things in my pack."

She shook her head and flipped up the hood of her cloak. The rain wasn't coming down that hard, just a cold and steady drizzle. Although she couldn't control her sniffles, she didn't utter another word of complaint the rest of the day. The rain stopped in the early afternoon and Nolo built a warm fire first thing when they camped that evening. Determined not to get sick, Ferris wrapped herself in

her cleanest, driest clothes and fell asleep close to the flames without even bothering to eat. She woke once, in the middle of the
night, to find the fire still burning strong and the Dwarf beside her
feeding fresh wood to the flames.

I n the morning her sneezing had turned to a harmless cough. Ferris
wrapped a dry scarf around her neck and followed Nolo and Avender up the steepening trail. Now every hill climbed brought another
and taller one beyond. Leafy maples and hemwood spread their new
leaves above the road, but the travelers were still able to catch their
first glimpse of the mountains before lunch, the sun gleaming on the
upper peaks. But it was late afternoon before they finally rounded the
spur of the Egg and entered Grangore from the south.

All three crags loomed high above the valley. To the west rose
Ivismundra, sharp as a wolf's tooth against the weathering sky.
Aloslomin's rounded crest faced it from the east. Between them, at
the head of the vale, Aloslocin climbed more gently than its two
companions, but to a taller height. Snow glinted on the upper
slopes, and the lower meadows were speckled with blooming snow-
bells and yellow henbud. Dark forests ribbed the lower ridges with
rows of tamaracks and firs.

They climbed up into the valley. Beside the road the Ambore,
now no more than a swift mountain stream, clattered away. Road
and river ran side by side through the center of the vale, past scattered farmhouses and newly cleared pastures stubbled with the
stumps of trees.

Grangore itself was even newer than Mremmen or Bridging,
and as filled with people and wagons as Eastbay on market day. The
sharp scent of fresh wood being planed and split, and the ring of
hammers and humming saws, filled the air. Wagons laden with food
and forage filled the street. Had Nolo not been with them, the children would have had to put their chins down and fight for position,
or been jostled from the road. But unlike an Eastbay market, the

people wandering about were from everywhere in the world. Savage nomads from Keeadin with their painted faces and feathered hair; rough seamen from Cuspor with tattoos of fish and leviathan on their foreheads and hands; silent Dremen from the far west, sailed all the way south around Fetland on the rumor of rubies and gold; and others whom neither Avender nor Ferris had ever heard of, let alone seen in person. News of Bryddin wealth had traveled far and wide in the years since Uhle had first dug his way up from stone to sun. Several humans passed by carrying light wicker baskets, with Hissers hidden inside for sure. Ferris thought she saw the long forked tongue of one slithering out from between straw slats to taste the world. The whole town bustled and busied itself as if everything had to be done today, to make way for all the new things that had still to be done tomorrow.

But nowhere did they see any Dwarves.

"Where are they?" asked Ferris with a slight, impatient cough.

"Where are what?" Nolo arched his heavy brows.

"The Bryddin, of course," she answered crossly. She knew that he knew perfectly well what she meant. "We haven't seen one yet this entire trip. I thought Grangore and Mremmen were supposed to be full of Bryddin."

"They're here." Nolo kept them going steadily towards the center of town. "How full of Bryddin do you expect the place to be, anyway?"

"Enough so we might see a few," put in Avender, who was just as curious as his friend. "You're still the only Bryddin we've ever met."

"How many are there, anyway?" asked Ferris. "In Grangore, that is."

"Nine, the last I heard."

"Nine!" Ferris glared at the crowd around her. "Why, that's hardly any!"

"Nine Bryddin outside Bryddlough is a lot," said Nolo. "How many Bryddin do you think there are in all the world?"

Ferris shrugged, not thinking that was a question she should rightly be expected to answer.

"Eighty-seven hundred and thirty-nine," said the Dwarf.

"That's not so many," said Ferris. "I think almost that many people live in Valing."

"How do you know the number so exactly?" asked Avender.

"Because Brydds told us how many we were when he made us." Nolo stepped aside to avoid the back of an overloaded mule. "From first to last we've always kept count. That's why Yddin is called as he is. Yddin means last in our tongue. And I know I was the three hundred and seventy-eighth to come up out of the dark into Bryddlough."

At that moment, as if the meeting had been planned, there was a buried shout from the crowd in front of them. The throng parted to reveal another Dwarf hurrying forward.

"Nolo!" shouted the newcomer. He was shorter and thicker than their companion, but his hair was curlier and less gray. Like Nolo, he wore a thin circle of iron around his forehead. His face broke into a beaming smile.

"Huri!" called Nolo.

Everyone in the crowded street stepped back respectfully as the Dwarves bowed once, then clasped one another in a grip that Avender and Ferris knew would crush any human to jelly.

"You've returned!"

"I couldn't stay away forever."

"So right, my friend. No matter how much Abben calls, there are always the Veils."

They held each other at arm's length for a moment before embracing once more. Then Nolo disentangled himself to introduce his companions. Avender and Ferris stepped forward and bowed as the Dwarves had done. Huri accepted their gesture with one of his own before cheerfully offering his hand human style. The children took his grip gingerly, but Huri knew better than to squeeze too hard. Ferris thought shaking his hand was like holding a stone that moved.

"Well," he said, peering at her and Avender, "I take it you're on your way to Issinlough."

"We can't wait to get there," said Ferris truthfully.

Huri shaded his eyes and looked up at the afternoon sun. "It's too late in the day to be starting out for the Sun Road. You'll have to spend the night with us in the lough. I'll show you the way."

"Actually, Huri, we have to step into the Lamp and Candle, first."

"None of that now, Nolo," said the other Dwarf with a twinkle in his eye. "The ale in the lough's every bit as good as that at the Lamp. No need to make extra stops along the way."

"It's not what you think, Mr. Huri," interrupted Ferris. "We're supposed to meet a friend there."

"Just plain Huri, if you please." Huri looked up at her thoughtfully and stroked his glossy beard. "A friend, you say?"

"I think you know him," said Nolo. "Big fellow, name of Redburr."

"I know him," began Huri. "But there was this problem—"

"What's the fool done now?" Nolo threw up his hands. "That bear has as much sense as a lump of mud."

"Hold on." Huri caught his old friend by the shoulder as Nolo was about to rush off to the inn. "He's already waiting for you at the lough. It was just a little matter of an unpaid bill. I already took care of it. The price of a pint's a bit higher at the Lamp now than it was the last time Redburr was in town."

"Redburr's been here before?" asked Ferris.

"He has, lass. And very helpful he's been both times. Now, if you'll all just follow me." Huri turned and started up the street. The crowd parted magically before him, as much, perhaps, for fear of the pain of bumping into him as out of ordinary respect.

Nolo and the children followed.

10

An Underground Evening

The Dwarves' lough was set in the side of a small hill at the north end of town. A pair of humans in Bryddin armor guarded the open doorway. Carved birds flocked tightly along the dark stone arch, with a great eagle in the middle and gulls and owls and pigeons wheeling and banking on either side. Such was the skill of the Dwarves that Ferris kept expecting one or another of the birds to turn out to be real and fly away, especially the pigeons. Below them, running down the single columns of stone on either side, were tangled together all the other animals of the forest, from squirrels and bats and raccoons scrambling close beneath the birds, to bobcat, and fox and skunk. And clustered happily at the bottom, three or four tiny moles snuffled at the feet of a pair of great bears. On the left the bear stood on its hind legs, its forepaws reaching up for a beehive, bees darting about its face; but on the right it was on all fours, curled around the column, its eyes intent on a fish leaping clear of a tangle of frogs and salamanders in the pool just beyond its reach. A wolf rested nearby, its bushy tail tucked beneath its belly. Ferris had to stop herself from trying to stroke its stony fur.

"Those bears look just like Redburr," she said, peering back and forth between the carvings.

"Of course they do." Huri wiggled his bushy brows. "He was the model."

The guards saluted the Dwarves as they passed. "Wish we could get them to stop that," whispered Huri when they were inside. "It's bad enough needing them at all. Just the sort of thing that makes Angun think he's right."

"Not all humans are thieves," said Nolo.

Huri shrugged. "Until we hired the guards, the lamps were stolen regularly."

Inside the hill everything was bright as the passage descended into the earth, despite the lack of windows. Dwarven lamps set atop delicately carved sconces lined both walls, each lamp a single bright jewel the size and shape of a small bird's egg. At the end of the hallway they came to a long room with many doorways opening out on either side. Some echoed with the clang of hammered metal and the chink of chiseled stone; others gave off heat and hinted at great furnaces. Two Dwarves emerged from a passage on their left, their conversation interrupted by the appearance of Huri and his guests.

"Nolo!" cried one.

"You're here?" said the other sourly. "We weren't expecting you yet."

"You weren't?"

"I told them you'd be another day at least," said a third voice.

As he spoke, the Shaper climbed up to join them from a set of stairs at the other end of the hall. In one hand he held what was left of a whole chicken; his other thick fist gripped a large mug. He made a very large human, both tall and wide, with thick tufts of red hair bulging out around his jacket at the neck and wrists, and a long red beard that fell most of the way down his round belly.

Ferris rushed down the hall to give him a hug, and coughed

slightly when he hugged her back. He looked at her carefully but said nothing as she and Avender were introduced to the two new Dwarves, Nurr and Angun. Ferris thought Angun didn't look half so pleased to meet them as Nurr, or as Huri had outside in the street. Angun bowed stiffly to the children but didn't shake their hands. He was taller than the other three Bryddin and wore his beard trimmed close against his chin.

"Don't mind him," whispered Redburr to Ferris through a mouthful of chicken. "He thinks the Bryddin should close the Sun Road and go back to living alone on the bottom of the world."

When the introductions were finished, Nurr turned to Redburr and asked, "Is there anything left to eat down below, or have you consumed it all?"

The Shaper waved his chicken back toward the stairs. "There's a little left," he said. He drained his mug and wiped his mouth on his sleeve. "But more's always a good idea. And bring a little soup, too," he added, eyeing Ferris once again. "For the girl."

"That's what I thought. I'll go help Beadly bring out another round. Meantime, Huri, why don't you and Angun take our guests downstairs."

Huri led them off toward the staircase at the other end of the hall. Angun followed just behind, his mouth pursed in a manner that suggested he didn't approve of bringing humans any farther into the lough, no matter how friendly they were.

The broad steps disappeared into darkness. Ferris hesitated, afraid of stumbling where she couldn't see. Nolo offered her a stony hand.

"You'll get used to it," he said gruffly. "There's a lot of darkness underground. And this isn't really the Abyss. Only an imitation."

Feeling momentarily like a small child, though she was taller than the Dwarf, Ferris took Nolo's hand. Avender did the same on the Dwarf's other side. The next moment the roof cut off the light behind them. They went on blindly, but Nolo didn't slacken his pace. The stairs ended after a few more steps; Ferris felt as if she had entered another large room. Her footsteps echoed faintly from unseen walls. From somewhere in the darkness came the clear tone of water trickling drop by drop into a deep pool.

"Look up," said Nolo.

Ferris raised her eyes. For a moment she thought she saw the stars twinkling in the sky. Then she remembered it was still late afternoon outside and realized the glimmering light was the result of some Bryddin craft.

"Here we are." Huri's voice came strangely out of the darkness in front of them. "You'll find benches and a table if you come forward a little more."

They groped their way on, and were soon sitting on hard stone benches, their elbows resting on a stone table, both as smooth as bone.

"Look," said Ferris, pointing upwards at the glittering ceiling. "There's the Bear. And the Throne."

"And the Falls," said Avender.

"And the Serpent, and the Hawk."

The children ticked off each constellation as they found them in their proper places across the rocky heaven. The lights shimmered the same as real stars and, had they not known it was still afternoon outside, both Ferris and Avender would have been certain they were standing under a true night sky.

"It's beautiful," Ferris whispered.

A light came on in the darkness beside them; the shining ceiling vanished. Huri set the lamp he had taken from his pocket atop a thin stone candlestick on the table. Nolo did the same with his. Several empty platters and bowls lay scattered about in the thin, cold light.

"You might have done that earlier," grumbled Redburr. "Humans need their light. Not to mention bears."

Huri chuckled. "I know. But then they would never have seen our stars. Welcome to Minabbenett. Our night sky underground."

"A dreamer's fancy." Angun frowned, stepping forward out of the darkness to join them in the light. His silver circlet sparkled.

The lamps lit the table and the faces around it, but not much more. The rest of the cave remained dark and unseen. Water continued to fall softly somewhere out of sight. Ferris could only guess at the cave's size, and realized the Stoneways might not be as pleasant a place as she had imagined. The dark beyond the light might hide many things. And there was the Abyss to think about, as well.

Nurr returned with a small, stout man, the two of them loaded down with platters of mutton and cabbage and mushrooms, and not a few pots of beer. They set out the food and everyone promptly helped themselves, Redburr leading the way. His chicken was long gone. The meal was hot and wholesome, and Ferris and Avender both fell in with a will. She especially enjoyed her soup, which cleared her thickened throat and nose, and warmed away the last chill from the road. Now if she could only get a hot bath.

When the edge was off everyone's appetite, except, perhaps, for Redburr's, the Dwarves began to talk about the road ahead, and the changes Nolo was sure to find upon his return to Bryddlough.

"The Sun Road's a regular highway, now," said Huri, helping himself to another mushroom. "There's even an inn along the way."

"An inn?" Nolo looked up from his mug. "That I hadn't heard."

"Unfortunately," said Angun stiffly, "you're not the only one among us to find he can no longer do without the comforts he's picked up on the roof of the world."

"There's a lot Bryddin and humans can learn from one another," answered Nurr.

"I'll drink to that." Nolo raised his cup. Huri and the Shaper joined him.

"Yes," said Angun with a frown. He had only eaten mushrooms for his meal, and was only drinking water. "Like fighting, for instance."

"It's not all fighting, Angun," said Nolo easily. He clapped his fellow Bryddin on the back. "Spend a little more time up here and you might find a lot you like."

"You're hardly the one to talk, Abbening."

Nurr and Huri both chuckled, and even Nolo smiled.

"Abbening?" asked Ferris.

"I've been away from Bryddlough so long, lass, my old friends have started calling me Abbening—the Sunburnt One."

"But you're not sunburnt."

"It's a joke," said Huri, winking broadly at Ferris across the table.

" 'Funny as a Dwarf' is never going to be a popular saying," said Redburr as he gnawed on the last of the mutton. "But not all humans like to fight, Angun. Most of them hate it. It only takes one side to start a war."

"Yes," said Angun. "But humans always do seem to find that one side, don't they?"

"Being a human is much more complicated than being a Bryddin." Redburr put down his mutton bone and wiped his fingers on his already filthy jersey. "They started life under Areft's hand, not Brydds'. And there are the Wizards. It's one thing to wrestle manders. Wizards are something else entirely."

"We have been lucky," agreed Huri. "We are the gift of Brydds."

The Dwarf raised his cup to the hidden darkness, then drained it in a single pull. The other three Dwarves joined him in his toast. When they were done, all four began to sing, their voices deep and resonant. Redburr took the lamps from their candlesticks and covered them on the table beneath a dirty bowl. The cave returned to dimness; the stone stars glimmered above their heads once more.

The Bryddin sang in their own tongue, their voices low and sonorous, the sorts of voices Ferris thought caves might have if caves had voices. The words they sang were thick and rough and hard as stone. The harsh consonants ground together, clashing and smashing against one another. Ferris didn't understand a word, but in her mind rose a picture of great beauty and sadness, a world without sun or sky. A lonely world, without a blade of grass or single flower, but filled nonetheless with a darkness strong as light that all but illuminated the buried rocks with shadow. The voices rumbled back and forth across the chamber, and rose up until all the hall was filled with a wealth of music.

When they were done Redburr took up a part of the song in his own deep voice, singing in the human tongue.

"*Dim.*
Dim.
Dim.
Brydds draws breath.
Another he sends
Upward
Through the darkness.
Father-born in utter blackness,
He gives us life.
In that moment of each shaping,
He gives his heart,
And breath,
And craft.
Torn from him,
We cling to him,
And to no other.
Too short the span when child exults
With father.
Then,
Wisdom given,
Fearful parting.
Blown upward on the breath
Of his expiring,
We fly in fear through the Abyss;
Eyes still sightless,
Fingers empty.
Stone unfelt
And yet imagined,
Hearts of earth still far above.

And yet,
As for something lost and missing,
Bryddin cry out for the father
Left in darkness
Deep below.
He who taught us;
He who wrought us;
He who with his breath
Hath brought us.

"Pale.
Pale.
Pale.
To each
His heart in portions
Cast;
His strength in pieces
Parceled outward;
His spirit hewn apart among us.
Deep he sleeps
With breath unbidden.
Shadowed Ina,
Emptied by his own hand's giving.
Still he lies
So deep below us.
How we call him!
How we miss him!
How we wish that
We might show him
What we fashion from his knowledge.
What we mold
From his forbearance.
How we light his prison's window.

Lamps to lift his heavy darkness.
Fire to warm his empty body.
He who lies in sleep
Believing
That he lives
In our conceiving,
Knows that we can resurrect him
Through the strength of all our building.
Through our hands
His own are making.
Would that we might make him happy.
He who taught us;
He who wrought us;
He who with his breath
Hath brought us."

Redburr's singing ended. There was no sound in the cave except water dripping. For a time the darkness was, once again, overwhelming. Ferris began to understand why everything the Bryddin did was done with such care.

"We miss Brydds," said Huri finally.

"And Hodi," said Angun.

"And Finlis," said Nurr.

As the Bryddin began to speak the human tongue again, the darkness seemed to lessen. It was a warmer darkness once more, with shining stars above. Ferris and Avender felt their hosts beside them at the table.

"Tell us about Finlis, Nolo," said Huri at length. "He and I worked long together upon the Halvanankh. Perhaps you might tell the tale of his breaking."

"We've waited a long while to hear you tell it," added Nurr.

"It is a sad tale," acknowledged Nolo. "And sadder, too, perhaps, for some among us."

Ferris turned to Avender, but she couldn't see him in the darkness. Lately she had noticed, whenever someone started up "The Lay of Ablen," that Avender usually slipped quietly from the room before the singer was past the first verse.

"Avender and I have heard the story an awful lot," she said. "Maybe someone could show us around the lough in—"

"It's okay," Avender interrupted. "Nolo was there. I've never heard him tell the story. Giserre always told Reiffen and me not to ask."

With a clatter of glass, the Dwarf poured himself a fresh cup of ale. "Well then," he began. "If the boy really doesn't mind, I won't, either. His father was with us that day. And Reiffen's. And Seedin, who was steward then with his wife in Valing. It was Seedin who led us through the caves in the Neck to Pittin's Pool."

He stopped for a moment, gathering the threads of his story. His feet scuffed across the floor as he settled himself on the bench; drinking from his mug, he swallowed loudly.

"I suppose I should start from the beginning. It was after we defeated the Bankings at Rimwich and buried Mennon and the other dead that King Brioss declared he would go to Valing to retrieve the Sword. You know about the Sword?"

"We've heard the tale," said Angun.

"The sword Pittin used to kill Areft?" said Huri.

"That's the one. Brioss wanted it to sanctify the joining of Banking and Wayland into one kingdom. Valing's where it's always been hidden."

"Brioss was a wise man," said the Shaper. "Unlike his brother."

Nolo paid no attention to the interruption. "Brioss's son, Prince Ablen, went with us," he continued, "and Queen Loellin of Banking with her consort, Cuhurran. And Princess Giserre, first cousin to the queen. Brioss wanted the prince and princess to marry, to seal the union of the two lands. Martis, whom we all thought then was only the king's counselor, came, too, and many others from both Rimwich and Malmoret. Finlis and I rode along with them, to see more of the northern lands. But the rest of the Bryddin stayed behind in Rimwich to help rebuild. If we'd only known then that Martis and Cuhurran were really both Wizards, Finlis would probably still be with us.

"It took us a week to travel from Rimwich to Valing. We went overland along the north road, through the forest and the Low Bavadars. At night we camped beneath the stars. Ablen and Giserre were often together, as the king hoped. They started off cool to one another, but Giserre was very beautiful. Still is, I'm told. Even Finlis and I could see that Brioss's hopes were coming true. And Loellin was also content. Any marriage between her cousin and the king's son would keep her line on the throne the same as his.

"They were a finely forged couple, the prince and princess. We were happy for them, especially since their marriage would help settle down the two kingdoms. It was Ablen's courtesy to her, and Loellin, too, that made Giserre fall in love with him. He was wise, like his father, and wooed her as a friend, not a conqueror.

"It was all settled by the time we reached Valing. Ablen and Giserre wanted to marry at once. Martis, however, advised the king that such an important wedding had to be done in Rimwich. But Giserre and Ablen couldn't wait. They persuaded Seedin to marry them secretly, with only Finlis and myself to witness the ceremony. I'm sure Seedin got permission privately from the king for the union, or he would never have performed it. But the result of Martis's counsel was that the marriage was secret, and never recognized in Rimwich. That's why Brannis became king after his brother's death."

"I'm sure that was Fornoch's plan all along," said Redburr. In the dark, Ferris thought his rough voice sounded no different from when he was a bear. "Of all the Wizards, Fornoch has always been the subtlest."

"Fornoch's plans are deeply delved," Nurr agreed.

"We suspected nothing at the time," said Nolo. "It was one long celebration. The long war between Banking and Wayland was over.

Soon there was going to be a wedding in Rimwich. Perhaps if you'd been with us, Redburr, we might have been more on our guard."

"I doubt it. Martis fooled me as much as anyone."

"Either way, Brioss wanted to fetch the Sword at once, despite all the feasting. But Seedin explained it was hidden in such a way that some of the tunnels beneath the Manor had to be drained before we could retrieve it. There are some sound tunnels in the Neck, my friends. Not so well planned as our own, but as well carved as anything I've ever seen by humans. It took three days to drain them, then Seedin led us down. The king and everyone else followed behind. Giserre wasn't with us—the queen wouldn't permit it. But Loellin was there, and Martis and Cuhurran, too. Finlis and I brought up the rear, along with a forester named Vender."

Ferris grew more conscious than ever of Avender sitting beside her. In the dark she couldn't see him react to hearing his father's name; but she thought she could imagine him sitting, as he always did when anyone spoke of Vender, with his head bowed and his eyes cast down at the floor. A name was all Avender had ever known of his father.

"Vender was the rear guard," Nolo went on. "He had to stay with us while Finlis and I lagged behind. As you can imagine, we were a lot more interested in the stone than in our destination. There's some honest rock in the Neck." Here Nolo went into a discussion of geology that only the other Dwarves could understand. But he soon resurfaced, before Redburr and the children were completely lost.

"Finally we came to a cave that was right beside the gorge. Around us the rock shook with the weight of all that water rushing by on the other side. We entered at the lower end of the hall and followed the slope upwards. At the other end, stone steps led into a narrow crevice.

"We stopped at the steps. In the crack beyond, a wooden door was roughly fitted between the rock walls. Seedin took a silver key from his pocket and slipped it into the lock. He pushed the door open and a fine spray blew in from the flume. The roar of the water was deafening. Seedin had to point to Loellin and King Brioss to get them to follow him outside. The rest of us remained behind.

"They were gone a few minutes. The mist blowing in through the doorway soaked us while we waited. When Martis stepped back further into the cave, I thought he was just trying to get away from the damp.

"Loellin returned first. Seedin and the king followed, both struggling with either end of a heavy chest. Vender and Ablen came forward to take it from them, but Seedin waved them off. Together he and the king carried it down the stair and set it on the floor. While they were opening it, I decided to climb the steps and take a look outside. It was an impressive sight, even more beautiful than the falls at Cammas. The water boils through the chasm in a sheet of foam, and thick clouds and rainbows fill the air. There's nothing like it in all Bryddlough—it's much wilder than the Veils.

"When I turned back to the chamber, I found Brioss bending over the open chest. He took out something heavy draped in thick blue cloth. Carefully he unwrapped it to reveal a large sword, at least twice as thick as any sword I'd ever seen. I could see at once it was made of Inach.

"That was when things went wrong. I saw Cuhurran laugh, though I couldn't hear him in the thunder from the open door. He grabbed the Sword from the king's hands and waved it over his head as if it was his own. The prince and Vender started against him, but that only made him laugh again. He kept on laughing as Ablen and Vender, poor humans, drew their weapons. Vender gave Cuhurran a blow on the shoulder, but his blade shattered as it struck. Then Martis, who was behind them all, raised his hands and gave a great cry that even I could hear. A sheet of flame swept the cavern and out the door behind me. It was hot as mander's fire, and only lasted a moment. But when it was gone only Finlis, myself, and the two Wizards were left. The others lay like lumps of, um . . . Well, let's just say they got burnt pretty badly. The future of Wayland and Banking was gone.

"As surprised as Finlis and I were at what had happened, I think the Wizards were even more amazed. They couldn't believe the two of us were still standing. I think that was when they first realized Bryddin can't be touched by magic. The four of us stood that way for a moment, two Dwarves and two Wizards, and stared at one another while we tried to figure out what to do.

"Martis, or should I say Fornoch, was the first to decide. He took the Sword from Ossdonc and swung it at Finlis. Finlis snatched a blade from one of the bodies on the ground. But Fornoch had the more powerful weapon. It cut right through Finlis's blade and caught him a blow on the head. Such was Fornoch's stroke that, even though the Sword was made of Inach, it broke in two. But Finlis was also shattered, and crumbled to pieces on the floor.

"I cried out, not thinking to defend myself at all, as the Wizards turned to me. In a way, I was as broken as Finlis. I couldn't believe he had shattered. Before I could pull myself back together, the Wizards were upon me. It was Ossdonc who moved first. I think he was jealous of Fornoch and wanted to be sure he killed me himself. He pulled his sword from his belt and flung it at me with all his strength. I was still too stunned to move. Fornoch, I think, guessed what would happen and leaped forward to stop him. But he was too late. Ossdonc was too quick for him. The sword struck me in the chest. Of course it didn't hurt me, or I wouldn't be drinking with you today. It was regular steel, not Inach, after all. But Ossdonc is very strong, as I was reminded just the other day. The blow knocked me off my feet and out the door. I landed on the slippery ledge and, before I knew it, slid off the rock and into the flume."

"You fell?" exclaimed Nurr in astonishment.

Nolo sounded somewhat shamefaced as he answered. "I was still so staggered by what had happened to Finlis. That and the fact you can get a little sloppy up here on the surface, where there's always something under your feet. But falling's what saved me. I was carried over the waterfall down to the river below. Even the Wizards couldn't follow. By the time I dragged myself out from beneath the water and climbed back up to the Neck everyone left at the Manor thought I was dead. And the Wizards, of course, were gone. A woman on one of the upper floors said she saw a pair of huge ravens fly up out of the mist and into the western mountains. Each was carrying something long and thin."

"The pieces of the Sword," guessed Huri.

"That's what we've always thought," said Redburr. The plates clattered in the dark as he swept them aside and leaned forward on the table. "Now we know where they went. Flying to the henge would be easier than flying all the way back to Ussene."

"The henge?" asked Nurr.

Then Redburr took over the tale of what had brought them all the way to Grangore, and Giserre to Malmoret. He said nothing, though, about what their plans would be once they arrived in Issin-lough. Instead he told them how Giserre would try to raise an army in Banking to rescue her son, while he and Nolo would see what help they might receive from the Bryddin.

"It would seem," said Angun when the Shaper was finished, "that those among us who counsel sealing the Sun Road will feel the truth of our argument more strongly than ever once this tale is generally heard."

"You can't den yourselves up forever," growled Redburr. "No matter how much you might want to. Now the Three know you exist, they'll never let you be."

"Let them come. The Abyss is deeper than they know."

"You can be sure that, if they come, they'll not be frightened of a hole in the ground."

"The Abyss is no hole," said Angun.

"And the Wizards are more than manders," answered Nolo.

"Enough," said Nurr. "Each Bryddin will do as he wishes, as we always have. I, for one, would prefer not to meet the Three either under Abben or above the Abyss. In the meantime, I'd like to hear the end of Nolo's tale. He still hasn't told us what he did with Finlis."

"Finlis has a tomb," said Nolo. "The same as Hodi."

"Where he fell?" asked Huri.

"No. It's better hidden than that. There are passages beneath the Manor humans will never find. That's where Finlis lies."

The cave grew silent, as silent as Ferris imagined Finlis's tomb to be. Then everyone noticed the faint echo of the water again. The dark ceiling once more became a reminder of the velvet sky.

Beside her, Avender was glad to have heard Nolo finally tell the tale. Both had lost someone close to them that day, even if Nolo had known Huri for entire lifetimes, while Avender had never even met his father. But he was sad, too, not simply for his father, but for his mother as well. Remembering his mother brought Avender sharper anguish than any memory of his father ever would. His father was only another story about the past, like Mennon; but his mother had kissed and hugged him six whole years before she died.

That night, he and Ferris stumbled wearily off to the guest rooms of Granglough. It was nice to sleep in a bed again, even if it was a stone ledge carved out of the wall. At least there were no roots poking them in the back, nor beetles to wake them up at dawn by crawling across their noses. The mattress and blankets were human enough. Ferris, however, had not gotten the bath she had been hoping for, and only complained.

Avender fell asleep dreaming about swords and Wizards, and the earth opening up beneath his feet. But it wasn't a nightmare. The Bear and the Throne sparkled in the sky above, and his father and Brydds waited for him in the darkness below. Along with the stars

and the darkness, he heard over and over the low hum of deep
voices singing:

> "He who taught us;
> He who wrought us;
> He who with his breath
> Hath brought us."

11

The Sun Road

n the morning Ferris's cough was much better, despite not getting her bath.

"I should've asked Nurr," she said. "I'll bet he'd have found me a tub somewhere."

"It's too late now," Avender replied. "You know Nolo's always in a hurry in the morning."

They went up to breakfast in the Minabbenett, where they found Redburr, Nolo, and Huri deep in conversation. The Shaper was shaking his large head vigorously, his red beard wagging across his chest. "No, no, you're out of your minds," he was saying between generous spoonfuls of fried mushrooms and bacon. "It's too dangerous."

"With the work Nolo and I've done on the brakes, it'll be fine," replied Huri.

"That's easy for you to say." Redburr's cheeks bulged as he made room in his mouth to speak. "You're not the one who's going to be banging along in the back. And with your hard head, a bad spill wouldn't matter anyway. It's the rest of us who'll get hurt."

Ferris heard Huri mutter something under his breath about Bryddin not being the only ones with hard heads as she slid onto the bench beside him. She reached across the stone table for the milk. "What are you arguing about?"

"Huri and Nolo think they've come up with a way for us to save some time on the Sun Road." The Shaper took a slice of toast in his large hand and covered it with butter. "Only it won't be much of a time-saver if we never get there."

"It's thirty leagues from Uhle's Gate to Vonn Kurr," argued Huri, "downhill all the way. A rolling wagon'll get you there a lot faster than your own feet. You could save more than two days."

"It's safe." Nolo pulled easily at his beard as he tried to reassure Redburr. "Huri and I figured we could strengthen the brakes by lining them in leather. Do you really think I'd go along with this if I thought it'd put the lad and lass in any danger?"

"If it gets us there faster," said Ferris, "I think we should try it." She poured herself a cup of milk and reached across Redburr's plate for the toast. "It'll be just like sledding on the Shoulder."

"Just like sledding," said the Shaper. "Except that it's sledding on hard rock instead of soft snow."

"Or ice," pointed out Avender, who also liked the idea of racing along for miles and miles in a runaway wagon. "Ice is just as hard as rock, and sometimes we sled on that."

"Hard or soft, it hardly matters," said Nolo. "We're not going to crash. It'll be easy as sailing to Eastbay for a pint at the Bass and Bull."

Redburr grumbled and groaned for the rest of the meal, but by the time they were finished he had given up arguing. All the same, when they inspected the wagon Huri and Nolo had worked on during the night, a heavy cart with high sides and solid wheels, the Shaper took one look and went back into the lough without a word. When he returned, his arms were filled with blankets and pillows scrounged from the guest rooms.

"At least we'll be comfortable when we break our necks," he said as he tossed the bedding into the back of the wagon.

They hitched an old, tired horse to the cart and started on the road out of Grangore. It was a gray day, with rain in the offing and all three peaks hidden by cloud. Yellow cut-nots and bluebells bloomed bravely beside the road, but even their brightness faded once the travelers climbed up into the shade of the old forest. The stone path curled up Aloslocin's gentle flank between great beeches and gnarled oaks, small stone bridges fording every stream.

While they walked, the Shaper told them about his own journey, for he had been busy while the children had been sailing south across the Inner Sea. He had traveled with Giserre part of the way to Rimwich, then, after changing once more into an eagle, had flown off into the north to spy out what was happening in Ussene.

"Did you see any sign of Reiffen?"

Avender looked up hopefully at Ferris's question.

Redburr shook his head. "I saw a band of Keeadini crossing the plain with prisoners from the river, but nothing of Reiffen. Ussene's dungeons are buried deep beneath the mountains, girl. There was no time to linger. A pack of Usseis's creatures came at me as soon as I reached the fortress and I had to fly south as hard as I could to get rid of them."

Ferris shuddered at the thought of what sort of flying creatures Usseis might employ. Batwings came to mind, and the snarling jaws of wolves. Sighing, Avender looked back down at the ground.

"But I did learn we've chosen the only possible approach," the Shaper went on. "We'd never get near the place aboveground. All paths to the fortress are watched. No one can get anywhere close without being seen—not even in the air, as I found out. And there are more watchers than ever before. More of everything. More towers, more guards, more iron. The Three have been busy in the years since they stole the Sword, and we've been unwary too long. It's plain enough now the Bryddin can give us only so much protection. Angun's not entirely wrong. The Three are our fight more than theirs."

"Angun speaks for himself," said Huri, "like all Bryddin. But there are many who don't agree with him."

A squirrel pattered overhead, its bushy tail swaying. Branches swished as it leapt from tree to tree. Avender kicked a stick off the side of the path.

Ferris crossed the road to walk beside him. "Are you thinking about Reiffen?" she asked.

"I think about him all the time."

"I do, too. But we're going as fast as we can. That's why we're taking the wagon."

Avender shrugged. "He should have been here. It's not the same, going to Issinlough without him. Do you know how many times we talked about doing this?"

"You can go later," she said, trying to be cheerful. "After we rescue him."

"I suppose. But it'll never be the same."

Ferris looked off through the trees. The leaves on the mountainside were barely budding, and the woods seemed stuck in their winter sleep. Back home in Valing she used to listen to Reiffen and Avender talk about the things they would do when they grew up, the places they would visit, and the battles they would fight. She could only imagine how much more they might have said to one another when she wasn't around.

"I miss him, too, you know," she said.

Avender looked up at Ferris instead of the road. "You're right," he said. "I should be looking on the brighter side. But when you asked Redburr if he'd seen Reiffen, it just reminded me how horrible everything's been. I wish we were back home, fishing with Skim."

"So do I. This adventure isn't what I thought it would be at all. And we haven't even come to the hard parts yet. At least I'm not coughing anymore."

He smiled, but the sadness lingered in his eyes. Ferris missed

Reiffen terribly, but she knew it was worse for Avender. He and Reiffen had been closer than brothers. They had all three been close, but it had never been the same for her. At the end of the day she had gone back to her mother and father, while Reiffen and Avender had gone back to Giserre. Even as a little girl Ferris had known there was a difference, however much she had wanted there to be no difference at all.

A steady drizzle had begun to fall by the time they arrived at Uhle's Gate, halfway up the mountain. They were all looking forward to finally getting underground and out of the wet. At the sight of the travelers, the two guards standing at their ease just inside the entrance hurried back to their positions in front of the door. The road ran straight past them into the mountain, where the warm glow of Dwarven lamps illuminated the passage beyond.

"Morning, Mr. Huri," they said as the party stopped in the shelter of the trees just outside the gate. "Morning, sir," they said to Nolo. They looked curiously at the children, for few human children ever passed that way, and the Bryddin had none of their own.

Avender and Ferris unhitched the tired horse from the cart and tethered it to a nearby branch. The animal began to nibble at the few shoots of new grass poking up between the roots of the trees. While the children were busy with the horse, Huri helped Nolo and Redburr push the wagon into the mountain. Unlike the entrance to the lough, the door to the Sun Road was bare of carving. A long, black block of stone was etched in the rock above the entrance, its point hanging downward. Otherwise there was no ornament at all. And the ceiling beyond was so low that Avender could almost touch it with his upraised hand.

"Ah," said Nolo, happy to be in Bryddlough once more, if only at the very edge. "The Abbenaia."

"The what?" asked Ferris.

Nolo pointed at the road around them. "The Sun Road," he explained. "Thirty leagues it runs, in great spirals to Bryddlough." He laid a hand against the smooth stone walls, far smoother than the rough carving of the tunnels that ran through the Neck. "It's changed a bit, though, since the last time I was here."

Huri winked and turned to Ferris. "We were both here that day, Nolo and I. The day Uhle first broke through."

"It must have been amazing." Her eyes shone as she looked at the wide passage around her.

"It wasn't so big, then, miss. More what you'd call a muddy hole. But the sun was bright enough. That's why we call it the Abbenaia. Abben's Bryddin for sun, you know."

"Is it? I didn't know that. Thank you, Huri."

Huri beamed. Ferris saw Avender was about to ask how she could possibly have forgotten one of the first Bryddin words Nolo ever taught them when the Shaper grabbed him firmly by the neck and pushed him on toward the wagon.

"Help me line up the cart, boy," Redburr growled. "Even if we are going to regret it later."

With Nolo directing them, Redburr and Avender rolled the wagon into position beside the left-hand wall. The slope of the road began just past the entrance, but the tunnel wasn't so bright as it had looked from the dim day without. A single lamp hung on the outer wall just past the doorway; beyond that the passage curved down and to the right in a growing gloom.

It was a wide road, despite the low ceiling. There was no room for a horse and rider, even if someone had been cruel enough to want to bring a horse so deep beneath the earth. But three wagons would fit easily across the passage, and donkeys, more used to mines, might easily pull them down and up the slope.

Huri held the wagon to keep it from rolling down the road while Redburr and the children clambered into the back. The cart creaked reluctantly on its wooden springs. Redburr, with his pillows and blankets, took up most of the space. Ferris and Avender had to squeeze in between a large sack of leather scraps and a heavy bucket of grease for the axles. The ceiling was too low to stand, so everyone had to sit on the bottom of the cart, which crowded them even more.

Redburr shared two of his pillows with the children, then wrapped the rest around himself. "If I had any sense at all," he grunted as he settled in, "I'd turn myself into a bat and avoid all this nonsense."

"Whoever said you had any sense?" said Nolo as he scrambled up into the driver's seat. "That's all we need, a talking bat to tell everyone the Shaper's on his way to Issinlough. Probably scare everyone we meet on the way half to death in the process. Not to mention bringing us more attention than we need."

Redburr gave the Dwarf a warning look. Nolo paid him no mind and set himself for his driving instead.

"All set?" called Huri from the back of the cart.

"All set!" answered Nolo.

"Good-bye, Huri!"

"Good-bye, Ferris! Luck to all of you!"

Ferris grabbed the wagon's wooden side and held on tightly. Huri gave them a firm shove and let go. The cart picked up speed at once, and Ferris felt a rising thrill as they began to rattle and bang along. Nolo steered with a tiller he had rigged to the front wheels, but there wasn't much call for steering other than to keep along the bend of the tunnel. There was little traffic and no obstacles at all; everyone on the road heard the clatter of their approach well before they came into sight. The few travelers they passed were well clear of the way as soon as the wagon rolled into view. All of them pressed their backs safely up against the inner wall, their picks and shovels at their feet, and stared at the strange sight of a cart careening down the road.

The wind rushed past Ferris's face. Redburr's and Nolo's beards streamed back over their shoulders and everyone's cloaks whipped in the breeze. It was far more exciting than the iciest slide on the Shoulder; because the cart was so much higher off the ground than a sled, Ferris felt she was speeding along much more quickly than she ever had sped before. The wall barreled by beside her. The wagon shuddered and shook. But no cart had ever been built to go that fast, and it was soon rattling everyone's teeth and bones. Ferris closed her eyes and buried her chin in the single pillow the Shaper had given her, trying in vain to cushion herself against the banging. She thought about insisting he share the rest of his bedding, but, before she had a chance to say a word, he began to unwrap himself from his coverings and pushed forward to say something to the driver. Not caring whether Redburr noticed or not, Ferris snatched up a second pillow as soon as his back was turned.

Redburr tapped Nolo on the shoulder. "You think you should try the brakes?"

"What?" The Dwarf strained to hear what Redburr was saying, but the cart was moving so fast the Shaper's words were whipped away as soon as he spoke.

"The brakes!" Redburr shouted. "Don't you think it's time to try the brakes!"

"I was just thinking that myself!"

His left hand holding on to the tiller, Nolo leaned over to grab the brake with his right. He missed his first attempt, which made the wagon wobble slightly. Ferris dropped her pillows and made a sudden grab for the side of the cart. She swallowed hard and tried not to seem concerned as Nolo brought the wagon back under control. Short as the Bryddin was, he had to stretch all the way across the seat to reach the brake handle. But he succeeded the second time and the leather brakes rasped at the wheels with a slithery hiss. Gradually the cart began to slow. The pounding of Ferris's heart slowed as well. Nolo pulled hard on the lever until finally they were rolling along at no more than a fast gallop. The brakes hummed against the wheels.

"What's that smell?" asked Ferris, wrinkling her nose and trying not to sound as if she had ever been scared.

"I think it's the leather burning," answered the Shaper.

"Is that bad?"

Redburr stood up gingerly and leaned out over the inner side of the rumbling wagon, careful not to bang his head on the ceiling. The cart tilted dangerously, much worse than before, and this time

Ferris was sure they were going to crash. But Nolo quickly released the brake and put both hands back on the tiller to steady their course. The wagon leapt forward, almost throwing the passengers out the back and into the road. Ferris thought her arms were going to be pulled from their sockets as she strained to hold on.

"Watch out there!" called the Dwarf angrily to the Shaper over his shoulder. "You're too fat to go hanging over the side! Do you want to wreck us?"

"I'll show you fat," grumbled Redburr. But he moved back to the middle of the cart just the same, almost tripping over the blankets he had left wadded in the bottom. Nolo brought the wagon back under control, then reached for the brake once more. This time he kept the pressure up until they stopped completely. Ferris grew uneasy as the smell of burning increased, and waited for the wheels to burst into flame. The wagon came to a shuddering halt, the stone of the Sun Road strangely quiet once the loud clattering of the wheels had ceased.

"Finally smartened up, eh?" said Redburr. His deep voice echoed along the curving walls and ceiling.

"Just a few quick adjustments. Hold on to the cart there, will you." Nolo waited for Redburr to climb out of the wagon before releasing the brake and hopping off the seat. The cart rolled forward a foot before the Shaper set himself firmly in the road and held it fast. "Hand me down that sack of extra leather, will you, Ferris? And maybe the grease bucket, too."

Working quickly, the Bryddin lashed the tiller in place so the cart wheels were set for a slight curve. "Now the wagon'll follow the turn in the road without my help," he told them when he was done. Next he looked at the brakes, and pulled at his beard with some concern when he saw how much the leather pads had already worn away. He cut fresh ones from the spare strips he had brought and spread new grease around the shafts. Then he and the Shaper climbed back into the cart and the wagon rolled off once more.

"That should do it," Nolo said confidently as he took his place at the brake. "Just stay away from the right side, Redburr, and we'll be fine."

This time the cart steered itself in a wide circle along the spiraling way, while Nolo attended to his braking. He let the wagon get up to a comfortable rate of speed, then held it there with a constant pressure on the wheels. The air filled again with the smell of burnt leather as they coasted on, deep below the stony feet of the mountain, but this time Ferris didn't worry about what might be happening at all. She trusted that Nolo had fixed everything, and rode with the wind in her face and the rush of their descent gleaming with the Dwarf light in her eyes. And the shaking wasn't so bad, now that she had two of Redburr's pillows and they weren't going quite so fast.

In time even Redburr, who had never liked sledding, enjoyed the ride. It was loud and jarring, but the wind felt lovely in their faces as the lamps flashed by along the walls. Occasionally they passed dark doorways and spots where small fountains bubbled into cisterns along the inner curve of the road. Less often they passed another party toiling up or down the stone way. The lamplight rose and fell as they rushed along, as if they were rolling through many short days and nights rather than just one long morning. There were only two or three lamps for every full turn in the road, and the gloom was deep between them.

"This is the way to travel!" cried Ferris as they raced past yet another group of astonished miners. She leaned forward close to Nolo, the wind buffeting her face delightfully. "Why doesn't everybody do it?"

"How would they get the wagons back to the top if they did?" replied Nolo in amusement.

"You could have donkeys haul them up. Miners use donkeys in caves all the time!"

"And how would we feed the donkeys, lass? You can't grow hay underground!"

Ferris frowned, wishing she had thought about that before asking the question. But a moment later any disappointment she felt was whisked away in the sheer joy of racing through the Stoneways like a log through a flume.

They had been running hard for the better part of an hour, their bodies limp with bouncing, when Nolo announced they had to stop again so he could replace the linings on the brakes.

"We must be close to the Axe and Ruby by now," offered Redburr, wiping his dry mouth with his hand. "Huri told me it was about a third of the way down the road. I've been looking for it the last ten minutes. I say we stop there."

So Nolo kept the wagon clattering on a little longer, until they saw a change in the road ahead. A walled pool of water extended halfway across the stone floor, a large doorway on the inside wall and a smaller tunnel on the outer. Several men sat by the pool or loitered by the door. Nolo pulled hard on the brake and the wagon skidded slowly to a stop, well past the pool.

Redburr threw off his pillows and scrambled out. While Nolo set to relining the brakes a second time, the Shaper led the children back up the Sun Road to the inn. A crowd had gathered outside as the cart had clattered by and it seemed every miner in the tavern had an opinion to share about how the travelers were all going to break their necks. But the innkeeper and his wife welcomed Redburr as an old friend from the days when their place of business had been aboveground, and plied him with questions after sending their equally curious customers back to their stout and stew. He answered very little while saying quite a lot, and told them he was taking the children on a grand tour of Bryddlough as part of their education. A few minutes later the three friends were back on the road again with a bag of fried mushrooms and a small cask under the Shaper's arm.

"That's an odd place for an inn," said Ferris as she opened the bag and sniffed at the mushrooms. "Mmmm. . . . These smell delicious."

"The Upper Mines are only a few miles down that passage." Redburr nodded toward the smaller tunnel across from the pool. "Humans can't mine as well as Bryddin, of course, but they still free up the Dwarves to do other things. And the gems down here are a lot better quality than they are nearer the surface. That's why Thickner persuaded the Bryddin to let him set up his inn here. From here on the loway's mostly empty."

"Loway?" asked Ferris.

The Shaper grinned, and held out his hand for a mushroom. "That's what the miners call it," he said as he popped the tasty morsel into his mouth, barely chewing before he swallowed. "If it's a highway up on the surface, they figure they ought to call it a loway down here."

Ferris rolled her eyes, but Avender smiled for the second time that day. "What?" he said when he saw the look she gave him. "I think it's funny."

"I'll drink to that," said Redburr, patting his cask.

"The next time I go adventuring," said Ferris with a small shake of her head, "I'm making sure there's at least one other girl along. Maybe that way I won't be the only one who understands when it's time to wash."

Nolo had finished his work and was ready to go when they returned. They ate their mushrooms and a few slices of ham they found at the bottom of the sack once they were under way. The eating wasn't a problem, but after spilling the contents of their canteens all over themselves while trying to drink, they gave up that part of the meal. They settled back to enjoy the ride, well used now to the experience. Redburr, with the children's help, even made up a little song, which they sang loudly as they raced down the tunnel.

"The wheels are rolling
The wagon is bowling
And we are not strolling
Along the Sun Road!

"We're bouncing and jouncing
And quaking and shaking
And swerving and curving
On down the Sun Road!

"No one comes near us
With Nolo to steer us
Because they can hear us
Far down the Sun Road!

"But how will we stop
At the edge of the drop
As we roll from the top
Along the Sun Road?

"We don't know, we don't care
We'll fly through the air
With the Dwarf and the bear
On down the Sun Road!"

The stone walls flew by. Other tunnels appeared now and again on either side, leading to who knew what mysterious places. Twice more Nolo stopped to replace the leather in the brakes and grease the cart's wheels. On and on they went, twirling downward like a paper boat swirling through a very long drain.

But the ride was enjoyable for only so long. Eventually it was all they could do to keep from being jarred to jelly by the wagon's endless shaking. Sitting was no good, even with Redburr's blankets and pillows to cushion them, because then every bone in their bodies was rattled by the rushing cart. But standing was impossible, with the ceiling as low as ever, so there was nothing to do but bear the jouncing as much as possible and hope the ride would soon be over.

Even Nolo was relieved when he finally peered into the gloom

ahead and announced they were close to the end. With both hands
he pulled hard on the brake, and the cart began to slow. Gradually
they came to a stop beside the next lamp on the curving wall, its soft
radiance sending thin shadows across the smooth stone floor ahead.

"All out!" called the Dwarf.

He slid briskly down from the high front seat and held the wheel
to keep the cart from rolling farther down the road. Groaning, Redburr and the children followed. After the long ride, the loway felt as
unsteady beneath their feet as the deck of *The Other Side,* so used
had their legs become to the shaking wagon. They hobbled about,
trying to recover their balance, while Nolo undid the lashings holding the front wheels in place and dragged the cart over to the inside
of the road.

"I don't know if I'll ever be able to ride in a wagon again." Ferris
groaned as she tried to twist the kinks out of her neck and shoulders.

Avender arched his back and touched his toes. "What are you
going to do with it now, Nolo?" he asked. "I hope we don't have to
haul it all the way back up the Sun Road on our way home."

"I don't think it could stand the trip, lad." Nolo showed them
where the edges of the wheels were splintered and cracked, the
wood warping. With one sharp tap he knocked the nearest wheel
off its axle and that whole side of the wagon sagged toward the
floor. "We'll leave it here. Someone can always use the wood. But
we're in too much of a hurry to bother ourselves."

"I think we've hurried enough," said the Shaper. "I need a little
something to settle my stomach first before we go on."

He sat on the floor with his legs stretched wide. In between was
the small cask he had brought from the Axe and Ruby. For a moment he wrestled with the stopper at the side of the barrel; then
there was a great explosion and a geyser burst suddenly up between
his hands. He was drenched in an instant, the foam coating him
from head to foot before the barrel spun out of his grasp and onto
the loway. Avender and Ferris jumped to avoid the wild spray as the

cask whirled about; then the barrel caught the angle of the road and, with beer shooting out behind, scooted out of sight around the turn.

Redburr was stunned. For a moment he sat befuddled in a puddle of suds. "My beer!" he gasped.

Nolo shook his head. "If you'd think for just a little bit before trying to fill your belly, you'd remember that beer doesn't take well to shaking."

But the Shaper wasn't listening. He stared at the wet trail that traced the barrel's passing, then jumped to his feet and sloshed nimbly after it.

"Come on," said Nolo when Redburr was almost around the turn. "We'd better follow him. Let's hope he doesn't run right off the edge of the road."

They had barely gone a hundred paces and were only just starting to feel their legs properly again when they came to the last lamp and an abrupt end to the passage. Redburr was on his hands and knees at the edge of a yawning gulf, his beard dripping beer as he peered sadly down into the darkness. Nolo and the children came up behind him, but only the Bryddin went all the way to the edge. Avender and Ferris remained a step or two behind, neither of them quite ready to stand on the brink of that immense pit. Craning her neck, Ferris saw stretched out below the vast deep of Vonn Kurr, lights sprinkled across its depths like stars reflected in a quiet sea. Some flickered like open fires; others shone pale and steady as befitted the lamps of Uhle. Close by, a small stream rang clear as a set of tiny bells, reminding her of the hidden pool in Granglough. But here the sound was different, for the Granglough pool was a shallow basin compared to the depths of Vonn Kurr. Farther off she heard the deeper tones of heavier falls cascading into deeper bowls, and, farthest away, at the bottom of the pit, more felt than heard in a low bass rumble, the thunder of a mighty cataract.

"This has changed," said Nolo. He stood on the edge of the

precipice with his hands on his hips and looked critically out into the blackness.

"It's very beautiful." Ferris took another brave step forward to stand close behind him.

"It's starting to come together." Nolo pointed toward the wonders of the gulf. "You can't see as well in the dark as I can, but the waters have all been gathered into one stream at the bottom, and there's a deep pool in the floor. When Vonn Kurr is finished it will rival even Issinlough."

Redburr sighed at their feet, but clearly not for the beauties of Vonn Kurr. With a last longing look at the gulf, he stood back up beside them. Beer dripped from his clothes and a few flecks of foam clung to his hair.

Ferris wrinkled her nose. "You smell terrible," she said.

"Don't tease me," whimpered the Shaper. "I've suffered a terrible loss. Thickner's a master of the art."

"No use crying over cracked stone." Nolo turned away from the deep and walked toward the right-hand wall. "Huri told me there've been some improvements since you were last here, Redburr." He looked closely at the stone a few paces back from the edge of the road. "Ah! Here it is."

Hidden in the gloom along the inner wall Ferris spied a metal door. It slid back into a pocket in the wall without a sound as Nolo applied his strength to it. But opening the door only revealed another, smaller pit she thought looked every bit as bottomless as Vonn Kurr.

"A lift?" asked Redburr, raising one of his sodden eyebrows.

"Aye, a lift."

"What's a lift?" asked Ferris. She held on to the side of the doorway and peered into the dark hole. It smelled damp, like the top of a deep well.

Neither Redburr nor Nolo answered. Instead Nolo raised his arm and, with a whirring sound, something small and dark flitted down to him. He stepped back from the opening, a small bat suspended from his sleeve. Its black eyes gleamed. Nolo tapped the small creature once upon its ugly nose with his thick finger. Immediately it let loose its perch beneath his arm and flew off into the dark gulf. Nolo followed it to the end of the road, took off his pack, and settled himself on the edge of the cliff. His legs dangled over the side as comfortably as if he were seated on a bench in Valing.

"Its a long way to the bottom of Vonn Kurr," he said. "Even for a mistrin. Let's hope the lift's a little closer."

"What *is* a lift?" repeated Ferris impatiently.

"Haven't I ever told you about lifts?"

"No."

"Well, then." Nolo placed his hands on the stone beside him and took a deep breath of the darkness. "A lift is just what it's called, a flat platform used to raise heavy objects up and down. It's the same principle as a canal lock. You've never seen a canal lock? Well, then, let's forget about canal locks and just say a lift's a platform that rises and falls with the water below it. Let more water in, and the lift goes up. Let the water out, and the lift falls. It's simple, really."

"Simple if you're a Bryddin," grunted Redburr, who was licking his fingers after running them through his beard. "But still only something a Bryddin would ever think of." Once or twice, when he thought no one was looking, Ferris saw him suck on his sleeve.

"And that little bat?" asked Avender.

"The bat? That was a mistrin."

"An underground carrier pigeon," explained Redburr.

"When it shows up down below," Nolo went on, "the liftkeeper will know someone wants to use the lift. He'll give it some food, and then it'll probably come back long before the lift does. But at least we'll know then the lift's on its way. Either way, the lift's a lot faster than taking the stairs."

The bat did return long before the lift. It fluttered back and forth above them, a dodging shadow in the dim lamplight. Ferris tried to coax it down with a last bit of mushroom she had saved for later snacking. It came quickly to the offered food but flew off again at once, refusing the mushroom and not even bothering to hang from Ferris's arm the way it had with Nolo.

"Wrong kind of food," said Redburr. "She only eats crickets. But I'll take it off your hands."

"Bats are pickier than bears," laughed Nolo.

"Where do you get crickets underground?" asked Ferris.

"Cave crickets," replied the Dwarf. "There are lots of those in Bryddlough. There's more life down here than you know."

A hollow bubbling behind them signaled the arrival of the lift. Now there was a floor instead of a hole in the small room beyond the metal door. The floor was also made of metal, and their footsteps rang hollowly as they stepped inside. Avender and Ferris had expected something that would wobble and shake like a raft; but the floor only sank a little under Redburr's and Nolo's weight, and didn't wobble at all. Once inside, Nolo raised his hand again for the mistrin, then tapped her nose to make her fly away. When she was gone he closed the heavy door behind them. Pulling out his lamp, he set it on the middle of the floor.

It was a few more minutes before the lift began to descend. With the door closed, the smell of damp was even stronger than before. They sat on the cold metal floor away from the walls, their packs on the ground beside them. Ferris only noticed the lift begin to move by the way the walls began creeping upward, the newly exposed sections glittering wetly in the lamplight.

The air grew wetter the deeper they went. Soon rain began to fall on them from above. It wasn't a pleasant feeling, for the drops were large and had a rusty odor. Ferris shivered as the first few struck her head, thick and wet, as if there were birds perched on the walls above. She pulled the hood of her cloak up to protect her hair, though it was already filthy from weeks of travel. By the time they reached the bottom they were all as wet as Redburr, who now smelled like a pile of rusty fishhooks instead of a wet dishrag from the Bass and Bull.

A second door appeared in the wall beside them. Slowly the lift came to a stop. A large metal wheel was set in the middle of the door, and Nolo had to spin it several times before the passage would open.

Out they stepped into a world shimmering with pale light and booming like thunder. A fine mist filtered past them from the right, where a huge waterfall churned a glowing pool. Droplets glistened like tiny pearls where they caught unbroken in the wild mats of Nolo's and Redburr's beards. Through the clear water, Ferris saw that the bottom of the pool was filled with lamps tumbling about in the current as they lent their cold illumination to the rushing stream. A small river poured rapidly away through the deep, while all around rose the tiers of Vonn Kurr itself, sparkling in the light of many lamps and fires. Other falls leapt back and forth across the cliffs, until they joined at last in the final cascade some forty or fifty fathoms from the bottom.

"It's like the White Pool," Ferris breathed. The seething water splashed lines of rolling shadow across her face. "Only it's night-time, and someone's thrown magic fire in the stream."

"There's still a lot more work that needs to be done," said the Dwarf. "But it'll do, lass. Eventually."

He led them away from the pool before Ferris was done gazing upon it; they followed the road alongside the swirling river. The Kurren, Nolo called it: one of the Seven Veils. His eyes shone as he spoke; his pace quickened as they crossed the soaring cave.

Ahead of them both road and river entered a tunnel in the far wall. Other people were working at the bottom of Vonn Kurr, both human and Bryddin; but all were too far away from the travelers to do more than wave. They entered the passage along a wide way, as wide as the Sun Road; but the ceiling here arched much higher above their heads than it had along the upper path, and the echoing rush of the Kurren was much more pleasant than the rattling of the wagon had been. Rather than the usual brackets bearing lights along the walls, this road was lit by a series of round glass globes that hung from the ceiling, as if the passage were illuminated by a series of small, soft moons.

They came to a place where the river disappeared into a dark culvert, the road crossing the stream on a wide bridge. A plain column of marbled stone stood in the midst of the span, dark gray rock ribbed with narrow streaks of white and crimson. Nolo stopped and bowed solemnly. His companions gathered quietly beside him.

"Now we're come to the land as I left it," he said, raising his face to gaze upon the polished shaft. "This is the Tomb of Hodi, the first among the Bryddin to be broken and lose the breath of Brydds. His stone marks the beginning of Issinlough. Beyond is the Uhliakh, Uhle's Stair in your tongue, which leads to the city. Until the coming of Mennon and the carving of the Sun Road, few but Uhle and I ever came this way through the Under Ground."

He led them across the bridge to the far side of the Kurren. In a moment the bright chatter of the river dimmed to a murmur behind them.

Soon the road changed once more and they found themselves at the top of a long staircase. The passage remained as grand as ever, but now it descended so steeply that the ceiling was more a wall in front than a roof above. The first stair was fifty steps, but the second, which came soon after, was a hundred and fifty. Beyond that the way was mostly stair. It wasn't long before Ferris was as weary as she had ever been, her legs cramping at the long descent and her toes chafing painfully in her boots. She was relieved to see that Avender was also struggling down the steps beside her: it would never do if there was any part of this journey in which she couldn't keep up. After a while even Redburr was panting, his skin flushed almost as red as his hair. But always the way was broad, and lit by the softly glowing moons.

When she felt she could go no farther, she saw below a spot of blackness at the end of the steps. Tiny stars sparkled along the far edge and, as they descended, both stars and darkness grew. At first

Ferris thought she was looking at another deep, like Von Kurr. Then the lights began to draw together and she realized she was seeing the reflection of a splendid city in a midnight pool. Tall towers soared above shimmering spires and gossamer pathways, each tower twinkling with many windows and winding galleries. Silver bridges looped back and forth between the towers, arcing in long curves across the darkness. Issinlough! she thought. It had to be.

Eager to get a closer look, she forgot her fatigue and hurried down the stair. More and more details of the city came quickly into view. She saw lamps that shone from the very tops of the towers, terraces glowing with lights from below, and windows gleaming with colored glass. She had never seen anything so beautiful. Down she rushed, Avender beside her, both of them eager to reach the pool and see Issinlough itself, not just its reflection. Already they could see people moving back and forth across the bridges and paths.

Suddenly Ferris didn't feel so well. The people she was looking at were right side up when, if she was looking at a reflection, they were really supposed to be upside down. She sat down heavily on the stair, unsure for a moment which was the right way up herself. Avender thumped onto the step beside her. Together they rubbed their eyes as they tried to straighten out what it was they were seeing.

"It does take some getting used to, at first."

Redburr had stopped on a lower stair, his head level with the children's. The rusty water from the lift had dried enough that he was back to smelling like sour beer. "But don't worry," he went on. "It's Issinlough that's upside down, not the Dwarves. Those aren't towers you're looking at, they're unnerets. And that's the Abyss below them, not the sky. You're looking through a hole in the bottom of the world, not a reflection in a pool of water."

As the Shaper spoke, the image behind him seemed to right itself, and Ferris found she could look at the sparkling city again without feeling like she was going to fall on her head. Those weren't terraces lit from the bottom she had seen, but regular terraces with lights above. It was only the towers that were pointing the wrong way: straight down. She realized that looking at Issinlough was like looking at a wasps' nest. Except Issinlough hung from the bottom of the world and not the branch of a tree, and light and life shone from every wall and window.

Nolo stood lightly at the edge of the hole and gazed happily at his city. He seemed to have no thought at all for how far he would fall if he slipped. Softly he sang:

> *"Falling waters break the night;*
> *Silver's shine slips into sight.*
> *In the darkness, deep below,*
> *Lies the light of Issinlough."*

Still a bit unsteady, Avender and Ferris followed Redburr down the last few steps to the bottom of the world.

12

The Upside-Down City

They found themselves at a wide opening in the rock, perhaps thirty or forty feet across, and not much deeper than Redburr was tall. Through this shallow well the upside-down city glowed, brilliant with lights against the blackness beyond. Darker than anything Ferris had ever imagined, the Abyss loomed like a thick, black curtain drawn closed beneath the world. Typically for the Bryddin, there was no railing. Ferris and Avender remained on the last step of the stair, reluctant to come any closer to that terrible fall.

Nolo, however, was planted firmly on the very edge. Eagerly he pointed out the sights of his home. "That's Dwvon's unneret, the Rupiniah, there. And beyond that are Ullough and Innising, the unnerets of Uhle and the brothers Filt and Falt. And over to the right, just under the lip of the well, is the Wavening. We could see the Kurren if we crossed over to the other side. But here—we'll get a much better view of everything if we just start down the stair."

Without another word he slipped over the lip of the well. Ferris caught her breath as Nolo disappeared, but Avender's caution faded in the face of the Dwarf's excitement.

"Come on," Avender said, turning back to Ferris after he had taken a few steps toward the hole. "There's a stair, here. It looks scary, but if it can hold Nolo, you know it'll hold us."

Ferris took a deep breath and started forward. The full glory of Issinlough emerged from under the stone ledge like a starry sky from behind a clouded night. Unnerets hung from the rock before her, laced all about with swirling ribbons of footpath and stair. Carefully she set her foot on the first rung of the slender spiral that led down from the side of the well. To her relief, it didn't tremble beneath her weight, or sag when Redburr followed heavily behind her. Reassured, she grasped the slim railing and passed below the bottom of the world.

She found herself on one side of the shining city, the Seven Veils draping the dark around her. Nolo named each of the glistening cascades: the Kurren and the Glinnet; Ovallen and Dinnet; Beesen, Wavening, and Issin. All shimmered in the lamplight, as if their waters were filled with falling jewels. And at the center of the city and the Veils around it hung the thick finger of the Halvanankh, ribbed with rock and the delving of the Dwarves.

The stair turned to a grated footpath suspended from the stone roof on thin shafts of blumet. The clamor of forge and furnace echoed from the workshops in the thick rock above their heads; but the unnerets, so slender and delicate they looked as if they might break free from the roof at any moment and dive deep into the darkness below, were quiet as a village at night. Here and there a figure moved along a bridge or path, but, except for the noise, mostly the city seemed empty.

From the footpath Nolo led them into the top of the nearest upside-down tower. They passed into a rich hall, the marble floor gleaming in the lamplight. Stairs led both up and down. On the other side of the hall the path widened into a broad avenue that led to the next unneret. This time Nolo brought them to a halt in the middle of another marbled passage. The floor was so finely polished Ferris could see her reflection in the stone.

"Now," said Nolo, pulling thoughtfully at his beard, "the question is where's Dwvon? Up or down?"

Redburr slid his pack to the floor with a tired shrug. "You look for Dwvon," he said. "I'd rather find a warm fire and something to eat."

"We need baths, too." The dirty shower Ferris had gotten in the lift had only reminded her how much she needed to wash away the grime of two weeks' traveling. She didn't even want to think what her hair would be like when she undid her braids.

"Bear with me a moment." Nolo held up a hand for quiet. At first Ferris thought he was listening, until she noticed the Dwarf's large, bare toes wiggling slightly on the floor. She realized Nolo was feeling with his feet for what was happening in the stone. The Dwarf pointed toward the ceiling. "I think Dwvon might be right upstairs."

Redburr sighed but came with them as the children followed Nolo up a set of wide steps back into the bedrock above. Ferris didn't completely forget about the bath she needed, but she was willing to put it off for the chance to meet the first Dwarf. Almost at once they came to a large chamber that appeared to have been carved from the rock. The walls were straight and smooth, and the roof vaulted above their heads.

"Dwvon's workshop," explained Nolo. "He's very good with stone."

Lamps hung high upon the walls, casting dim shadows about the hall. Pale or dark, swirling with color or plain as slate, cut stone of every sort and kind lay about the cavern: marbles and granites, sandstone and schist. The slabs were of all shapes and sizes, some as large as small houses, while others were small enough for Ferris to pick up by herself. All were in different states of fashioning, from freshly mined rock to finished carvings. Splinters and dust littered the floor, and along the walls and ceiling ran various winches and pulleys and heavy chains. Through this Bryddin moraine Nolo led

them on a winding course, until they came upon a Dwarf and two
humans standing beside one of the larger blocks of granite suspended from the roof by a loop of chain.

The Dwarf looked up. "Ah, Nolo!" he called. "You've arrived!
Hello there, Redburr. Hold fast a moment, and I'll join you."

"Dwvon!" said Nolo in surprise. "You knew we were coming?"

"Huri sent a mistrin ahead with the news. Uhle's going to meet
us later in the Rupiniah. We can talk there. Just let me finish this lesson and we'll be on our way."

The travelers sat down to wait on a cast-off block of stone.
Dwvon turned back to his human apprentices, who didn't seem
much interested in the new arrivals. They were more concerned
with what the Bryddin could teach them about cutting stone. Students and master wore heavy leather aprons that hung below their
knees, and held iron spikes and short-handled hammers in their
hands. A thin coating of powdered stone had settled evenly across
their heads and shoulders. Despite her awe at meeting the oldest of
the Bryddin, Ferris thought Dwvon looked a lot like Nolo at the
start of a snowstorm back home in Valing. Snow never melted on
a Dwarf, not unless he was standing in the middle of a very hot
fire.

"Now then, Femmet," said Dwvon to one of his students.
"Where would you strike? Remember what I've told you. Choose
your spot carefully."

Femmet stepped up to the stone and studied its smooth surface.
After a moment's consideration he found a spot he liked and swung
his spike up sharply against the rock.

"Here," he said, looking back to the Dwarf for confirmation.

Dwvon looked to the other man, who, after examining his fellow's choice, gave an affirming nod. Nolo frowned and shook his
head slightly, but neither of the pupils noticed.

"What about there?" suggested Dwvon. He pointed to a spot
above the one Femmet had selected, higher than Dwvon himself

could reach and more than halfway up the side of the slab. Femmet moved his spike as instructed. This time Nolo nodded.

"Good," said Dwvon. "Now strike as you've been shown. One good hard blow."

Femmet aimed his hammer carefully. With a full swing he rang it down upon the blunt end of his spike. Even in that large cavern the sound of the blow was sharp and clear. Close behind came a longer, but not louder, crack. A single straight line opened up across the middle of the stone.

"You didn't hit it hard enough," said Dwvon, but there was a note of approval in his voice all the same. "The time will come, though, when you will. Strike again."

Femmet knocked home a second blow, as hard as the first. There was another crack, but no second line appeared in the stone. Indeed, there didn't seem to be any further change at all.

"Excellent." Dwvon stepped up to the rock and, with Dwarven strength, pushed the two newly formed pieces a few inches apart. Light from the back of the cavern showed through the fresh split. "The line is straight," he announced as he eyed the space between. "No secondary fractures, either. That first point you chose would have caused some flaking in the lower left front quadrant. I don't think you noticed the softness in that part of the stone. But otherwise an excellent strike. Now then, why don't the two of you each have a try on these new pieces and I'll take a look at what you've done when I return."

Then, without removing his apron or dusting himself off, Dwvon came over to Nolo and the children. There were introductions all around. Dwvon bowed to Redburr in the proper Bryddin fashion, but he shook hands with Ferris and Avender. He gave them both a broad smile as some of the dust shook off his beard and onto their arms.

"Redburr," he said, turning to the Shaper. "It's good to see you again."

"I told you I'd be back. You can't get good redbrick stew up above."

"Redbrick stew? That's easily taken care of. But if that's the only reason you're here, I'll be surprised."

With a shrewd glance at the children, the first of the Bryddin led them back down to the unneret below. Past the marble hall, the stair curved in and out of the upside-down tower. Sometimes they descended the unneret in an open gallery, all of Issinlough revolving into view as they circled the tower. Other times the passage curled inside along the outer edge of some large hall, or wound in tight spirals like the stair to the lower dock in the Manor. Ferris would have been completely lost had they not kept coming back outside. Once Dwvon stopped and showed them the Bryddsmet, a great silver dish suspended beneath the Halvanankh from the longest of the unnerets on three gleaming cables. But inside the tower there was little to see. Bryddin liked to build and delve, but they were never much for filling what they built. Having shaped the stone around them according to their will, they almost always moved on.

They came at last to a passage that led back into the center of the tower. An irresistible smell drifted out toward the children; something delicious was simmering within. Redburr's eyes brightened as he sniffed the air.

"Ahh," he sighed. "This is what I've been waiting for. Even the wagon ride was worth it."

Dwvon chuckled. "Mother Norra went right to work as soon as she heard you were on your way."

Ferris and Avender could not have been more surprised when a few more steps down the hall brought them to a cozy country kitchen, where a stout gray-haired woman stood stirring a large pot in front of a cheery hearth. A long stone table occupied the middle of the room, separating them from the fire, and a pair of curtained windows looked out onto the city and the night around them from the walls on either side. Redburr had to duck his head to keep from knocking it on the pots and pans, and bags of mushrooms and hams, that hung from hooks in the low ceiling.

Nolo was as astonished as the children. No one like Mother

Norra had ever lived in Issinlough in all the long years before he left. He had told Ferris and Avender more than once that there were no lady Bryddin.

"What's this?" he exclaimed. "A cook in the Rupiniah?"

Redburr rubbed his hands, his eyes bright and hungry. "Mother Norra's better with mushrooms than you Bryddin are with stone."

Nolo looked around the kitchen with fresh appreciation. "I wish you'd told me. I'd have come back a lot quicker, if I'd known."

"Get on with you." Mother Norra waved off Redburr's compliment with a flick of her apron. Old she was, but also hale and hearty, and a good deal larger than either of the children. She dropped a heavy curtsy to Nolo, and burst out as she stood back up, "Mr. Redburr! Welcome back to Issinlough! And two young 'uns with you besides! Garlic and beer! No one told me there were young 'uns coming!"

She dropped her iron spoon into the simmering pot and bustled forward, wisps of hair falling away from the thick bun at the back of her head. "Come along, dears," she said to the children. "You've been on that damp lift, I'm sure. Just because those Bryddin never catch cold they think the rest of us are just the same. I've told them a hundred times that contraption's too wet. Now, come along, both of you. I'll have you right as rocks in no time. Nothing a little hot stew won't cure. Suppose you tell me your names. Ferris? Avender? Both from Valing, are you? Well, I'm Mother Norra, and though I've never been to Valing I happen to know they'd like redbrick and flinny stew there as much as they would anywhere. . . ."

Still talking, she ushered them through a second door beside the one they had come in by, and up a second set of stairs. Ferris allowed herself to be pushed along in a mild daze; she couldn't quite shake the feeling that somehow she was no longer in Issinlough but on a visit to a long-lost aunt's house in Bracken instead. Upstairs she found a pair of large bedrooms with deep feather beds and framed samplers on the walls. A deep stone tub and shallow basin occupied the back of each room. Mother Norra left Avender in one room, then began to fill the tub in the other with hot water from the tap in the wall. "Now don't hurry yourself," she told Ferris as she trotted back to the hall. "The stew'll be ready by the time you come down. I'm sure a nice hot bath is just what you've been dreaming about for days and days. Beets and taters, but I wonder what men think about sometimes."

By the time Ferris had peeled off her dirty clothes, her tub was filled. She turned off the taps and climbed inside. Her sore feet and aching muscles began to relax as soon as they felt the steaming bath. Despite herself, she drifted off into a short doze, the water lapping comfortably at her chin. But she woke with a start not five minutes later, remembering that Dwvon was waiting for her downstairs. And that stew had smelled delicious. By the time she had finished washing and drying her hair, she was ravenous.

She met Avender in the hall when she was done.

"That took long enough," he said. "What did you do to your hair?"

"I washed it, of course. Who knows when I'll get the chance again?" She flicked a few loose tresses back behind her shoulder. "I can braid it in the morning."

Avender gave her a curious look, and followed her down the stair. Together they hurried back to the kitchen eager to sample the steaming stew. The Shaper rubbed his large hands hungrily as they arrived, and would have taken an early taste had Mother Norra not eyed him carefully. Beyond the wide windows the unnerets of Issin-lough hovered above the Abyss. There was no glass in the window-panes as there was no weather to keep out, so the room wasn't nearly as hot as it might have been despite the glowing coals. And it was a Dwarven hearth, after all, with firestone instead of wood glowing red in the grate, and most of the extra heat carried away up the flue.

"Take a seat, dears, take a seat." Mother Norra strained to lift the heavy pot from its place before the fire, but scowled Nolo back to his seat the moment he rose to help her. From the shelves above she selected several large stone bowls. "This will warm you well enough," she said as she ladled out the first portion from the steaming pot. "Always a little chill down here in the Stoneways, wet or no."

"Thank you, ma'am." Redburr reached for the bowl with both hands. Mother Norra rapped him sharply across the knuckles with her spoon.

"Children first," she scolded. "Then maybe we'll talk about trying to fill your bottomless pit."

The Shaper nursed his sore hand, but his eyes never left the stew pot until he had his own bowl before him on the table. Their hostess served each of her guests in turn, supplying them all with spoons pulled from the deep pockets of her apron.

"Here, dears," she said to the children as they tried to cool their first mouthfuls. "Have some juice. It's only mushroom, but it almost tastes like milk. Well, milk mixed with acorns, maybe, and dusty acorns at that. But it's the closest a body can come to milk down here. No grass for cows, you see. Pigs don't mind not having sunlight, but I wouldn't mind a cow or two, or even a goat. And don't worry, Mr. Redburr. You can be sure I've a drop of something for you and the Bryddin as well. . . ."

She drew off three pints for Redburr and the Dwarves from a small barrel at the front of the room. Avender eyed the beer longingly, but Ferris thought the thin, white juice tasted better than it looked. Everyone ate hungrily, while their hostess settled down at the end of the table and watched them happily. Nor did she wait for them to ask for more before she was up and filling their bowls brimful a second time. The stew was delicious, thick and hot, with chunks of mushroom and fish swimming in the gravy. Ferris kept up with Redburr bowl for bowl, at least for a while. And as they ate, Mother Norra talked at them. Somehow, though her guests hardly spoke a word, she had heard all about their journey before they had finished their first three bowls.

"Mother Norra," said Nolo with a grateful nod, "I had no idea redbrick could taste so good."

"It's the seasonings," beamed the cook delightedly. "You never ate 'em with a little pepper and sage before, I reckon. It's a pity I can't get 'em fresh, but . . ."

And, before anyone could stop her, the kind old woman was off on a lecture about Wayland herbology.

They were all starting on their fourth helpings, except Ferris, when Uhle arrived. Mother Norra noticed him first; the others turned round to greet him after she had jumped up and crossed to her cupboards to find another bowl.

In some ways it was harder for Ferris and Avender to meet Uhle than it had been for them to meet Dwvon. Dwvon may have been the first of the Bryddin, but Uhle was far more famous. Without Uhle there would be no Sun Road and the Bryddin would most likely have remained among their unnerets and tunnels forever, lost to the sun and stars. Nor was he covered in a thick mantling of dust to mask his grandeur. His tunic was of soft leather, belted around the waist and with only a few pockets for tools. Around his forehead he wore a golden diadem that gleamed in the firelight, and not the iron circlet of Nolo or Dwvon. He was tall for a Dwarf, almost as tall as Avender, and his hands were large, with long, fine fingers. Like Angun, he wore his hair and beard neatly trimmed. Were it not for the roughness of his face and the usual bare feet of all Bryddin, Ferris thought he might almost have passed for a fine lord of Malmoret, though on the short side. His dark eyes were stern, rather than open and merry like Nolo's, or Dwvon's for that matter, hidden deep beneath a thickness of brow like twin caves in a mountainside.

Ferris remembered what Redburr had told them once, that Uhle was ever the fire of the Bryddin, always striving upward. "Dwvon's more the deep pool inside his folk that never seems to change," the Shaper had said. Now that she had met them, Ferris saw clearly what the Shaper had meant. Mother Norra's kitchen seemed to have grown more serious the moment Uhle arrived.

"Nolo," said Uhle, bowing to his friend in greeting. Nolo rose from the table and bowed formally in return.

For a moment they stood without saying a word. Dwvon and Nolo may have looked alike as two brothers, but Ferris knew it was Uhle and Nolo who had searched together for the surface of the world.

Uhle spoke again. "I'm glad you've returned."

"I'm glad I'm back, too," said Nolo.

"I gather you won't be staying long. It's a sad tale you bring from the surface, friend. But Huri's mistrin revealed only the barest trace of what has happened. You must explain it all."

Mother Norra hastened forward with another brimming bowl. "None of that now, Mr. Uhle. No talking on an empty stomach. Have a bite and a sip first, and then everything'll be a deal clearer after."

So Uhle sat down beside Ferris and had a bite and a sip. She was glad to see his soup got caught in his mustache the same as Nolo's, though not so much as Redburr's. Somehow that made Uhle seem less of a legend, and more a real person, no matter how formal he was.

As they ate, Nolo and Redburr told the full tale of what had brought them to Issinlough, despite Mother Norra's disapproving frowns. Good as her cooking was, it wasn't enough to distract Bryddin from their regular habits. They had to come straight to business. Dwvon and Uhle listened attentively, without interrupting, as Nolo and Redburr spoke. The tale of Reiffen's abduction didn't seem to affect them much, but they both took notice when Nolo described the henge.

"Inach, you say." Dwvon ran his thick thumb absently along the smooth surface of his spoon.

Uhle nodded thoughtfully. "So," he said. "Some good will come of this, after all."

"That's what Nolo and I believe," said Redburr. "But we have more than stone to deal with first. First we have to rescue the boy."

"You're certain that's necessary?" Dwvon looked at Nolo as he asked the question.

Nolo nodded. "There's no other possibility. Reiffen is too dangerous a tool to leave in the hands of the Three."

"Then why journey all the way to Issinlough?" asked Uhle. "I doubt that even the strength of all Bryddlough is sufficient to attack Ussene. Two of them alone were enough to break Finlis, and they almost did the same to you."

"They were wrong about that," Nolo answered.

"There's no question," said Redburr in answer to Uhle, "that a frontal assault would fail. And even if we were strong enough to win the fortress, the lives lost would achieve Usseis's purpose almost as much as any civil war."

Uhle frowned. "Humans take the rule of blood too seriously," he said. "Why should anyone follow a boy because of his parents? Especially one in the hands of the Wizards?"

"Not all will want to believe he's in their hands," said Redburr. "And there are those who would follow even the Three against the current king."

"Humans do have a unique ability to do the very thing that hurts them most."

Dwvon nodded. "I've seen something already of what you say, Nolo, in the brief time humans have been here with us in Issinlough. Their lives are too short. They strike in haste, with no thought for the shape of the stone after."

"We're not all like that," said Ferris stoutly.

Dwvon turned to look at her, a smile cracking at the corners of his mouth. His dark eyes sparkled like his city against the night. "No," he said, still smiling, "I don't suppose you are."

"Always remember," said Redburr, "that all Bryddin are brothers. But humans don't share such kinship, and there are many more of them, as well. You're few, and have all of underearth in which to carve your will. The humans are many, and their lands run up one

against the other. Their ways of living together are more complicated, and more formal, than yours. And it's not as if all Bryddin are
of one mind, either. I met Angun in Grangore, you know."

Uhle frowned, and the creases in his forehead deepened. Frowning made him look more Bryddin to Ferris, and less like a stocky
man. "As you say," he said. "But Bryddlough is vast. There are many
places for the Abbenander to go if they wish to remain in the darkness. I shape their purposes no more than they shape mine."

"Let's hope the disagreements of the Bryddin always have such
easy solutions," said Redburr.

Dwvon tugged at his beard, causing the dust clinging there to
scatter farther down his front in a miniature snowfall. "Your philo-
sophical ruminations are all very well, Redburr," he said, "but I'm
sure you're eager to be on your way."

"We are in a hurry," Nolo admitted.

"The Wizards' arts are different from ours," said Redburr. "Experience suggests that we try to rescue the boy as soon as possible."

Avender and Ferris both shuddered, as they always did, at the
thought of Reiffen cold and miserable in some deep dungeon of
Ussene. Or worse.

"What will you do if you find you've arrived too late?" asked
Uhle. Ferris could see it was always Uhle's way to look at things dif-
ferently from anyone else, Bryddin or human. He was the one who
had sought the sun in utter darkness, after all.

For a moment no one answered his question. Ferris knew she
and Avender had never thought of such a possibility, but plainly this
was not a new idea to Redburr or Nolo. The Shaper looked silently
down at the stone table; the Dwarf rubbed a finger on the fringe of
beard beneath his lip.

"We've chosen not to think about that," said Nolo finally.

"Perhaps you should."

"We'll do what we have to, if the need arises," growled Redburr.
Ferris glanced quickly at Avender, horrified by what the Shaper was
suggesting. The boy's expression showed he was thinking the same.

It had occurred to neither of them that the success of their quest might lead to further complications.

"In the meantime," Redburr continued, "we should not discuss it. Tomorrow we start for Cammas."

"And then?"

"And then we'll march from Cammas to Ussene." Redburr's voice strengthened as he strove to dispel the disquiet that had come over them. "Nolo tells me Delven has been exploring in that direction and we'll find most of the way clear. The journey will take a few weeks. Which is why we have to start as soon as possible."

"That's your plan?" Dwvon's eyes wrinkled with concern. "The four of you will journey all the way to Ussene, and attack the fortress alone?"

"That's just it," answered Nolo. "We're not going to attack Ussene. As everyone has already pointed out, we'd never succeed. We're going to sneak in."

"Sneak in?"

"Yes. Like moles. We'll do it from below, where the Three will least expect us. What better way could there be for a Bryddin to sneak into a fortress?"

A broad smile spread slowly over Uhle's face.

"Abbening," he said, "this is most interesting. Apparently the time you've spent among humans has led to much subtle thinking."

Dwvon sighed. "Angun won't think so," he said.

"I care as much for Angun's thoughts as he for mine," said Uhle.

"He'll say we should leave the affairs of humans alone. That there's no need for us to take sides. That the Three mean nothing to us and we should leave them alone."

"Angun's a fool," said Redburr.

"We know that," said Uhle. "But there are some who don't. I think it would be best if as few as possible know why you're here."

"That's fine with us. We'll leave tomorrow. Nolo might want to spend more time in Issinlough after being away so long, but we all know the need for haste."

"It's a long way to Cammas." Uhle stroked his chin thoughtfully with one of his long fingers. "And almost as long from Cammas to the roots of the northern mountains. You have a long journey ahead before you reach Ussene."

"It is a long way," acknowledged Nolo. "And we are in a hurry. But there's no other way. If we traveled aboveground we'd be spotted long before we arrived."

"There might have been no other way when you left." Uhle folded his hands upon the table, pushing his empty bowl aside. "But now there is. Many new things have been learned beneath the world, as well as above, since the Sun Road opened. Grimble has been working with balloons."

Dwvon's eyes brightened. "That's right," he chuckled. "Grimble."

"Grimble?" Nolo's thick eyebrows bunched in alarm.

"Yes, Grimble."

"Don't worry, Nolo," said Dwvon. "I don't think it'll blow up again. Gammit's fixed everything. This isn't another Iron Frog."

"Blow up?" asked Redburr with some concern.

Dwvon began to explain about Grimble and his balloon. Unfortunately for Ferris and Avender, that was the moment when Mother Norra, who had been fidgeting for some time, decided the children had had enough.

"Oh, no," she said as she stood up. She wagged her spoon threateningly at Dwvon, towering over the Bryddin. "That's about enough. After all I've heard about kidnappings and blowing up, you're not going to scare these poor things any more today. Look at the dears! Ferris can't hardly keep her head off the table, and I've seen Avender rub his eyes twice already. There—he did it again! It must be long past midnight upstairs. If you want to get started early tomorrow it's time I took these two off to bed."

"But we really want to hear about the balloon," pleaded Ferris. Then she yawned again despite herself.

"You'll see it soon enough tomorrow, whatever it is. You need your rest. Stonechip and buttons, but I'd like to know what your mums were thinking, letting you two go off with Mr. Redburr like this. You listen to your Mother Norra. I reached Issinlough fast enough, for all I came here on my own two legs, thank you very much. It's bed for the two of you, and there's an end to it."

Had either of their friends backed them up, Ferris and Avender might have made more of an argument. But neither Redburr nor Nolo had any intention of getting in Mother Norra's way. Redburr hid his face by picking up his bowl and pretending to lick out the last of the gravy, which everyone knew he had already done long before. Nolo looked up at the ceiling and stroked his beard. Plainly, as far as they were concerned the less the children heard about Grimble or his inventions, the better. Ferris showed her temper by stomping all the way up the spiral stair. But the well-laid stone of the Rupiniah didn't echo half so obligingly as the wooden stairs back home in the Manor, and she was still in a terrible mood even after she had lain down between the soft sheets and pulled Mother Norra's quilt up beneath her chin.

She turned to Avender the minute the old woman had left the room. "Who does she think she is, ordering us off to bed like that! She's not my mother! And just when things were starting to get interesting, too! I had a lot of questions I wanted to ask. What do you think those balloons are anyway, that Uhle was talking about?"

"Balloons?"

Ferris snorted. "You were falling asleep, weren't you? You're the reason we got sent to bed, you know. I could've stayed up all night."

Avender's mouth opened in a long yawn. "Maybe now that we're here we should just go to sleep. This bed's about the most comfortable I've ever slept in."

"Is that all you can think about? How comfortable your bed is? I'm sure Reiffen's bed isn't comfortable at all." Even as she was complaining, Ferris had to admit the sheets felt smooth and cool against her wiggling toes. For a moment she rubbed them cozily against the bedding. Then she remembered another of the questions she had meant to ask.

"What are we going to do if Redburr and Nolo decide Reiffen can't be rescued?"

"Hmm?" Avender blinked sleepily. "I don't know," he mumbled. "But I guess he won't be Reiffen anymore if they decide not to save him." He gave another mighty yawn. "Just some creature of the Three who happens to look like Reiffen. If he's still himself we'll be able to tell."

"Of course we'll be able to tell. That's why Redburr brought us along. But I don't see how he could ever not be Reiffen. The whole reason the Wizards took him in the first place is because of who he is."

A low snore from Avender's bed stopped her before she said anything more. She had half a mind to wake him up again and make him listen, what they were talking about was that important. As far as she was concerned, some part of Reiffen would always be there, whatever the Wizards might do to him. Even if it was the tiniest part of all, that would be the part she would see. She doubted she would ever be able to see it any other way.

Avender snored again. Ferris decided to let him sleep. Truth be told, she wished she could sleep herself. It was a perfect night for sleeping, just cold enough for snuggling deeply into a soft bed beneath a pile of quilts and blankets. With a start she realized it would always be that way in Issinlough. The endless night was always the same at the bottom of the world, for all the lamps the Bryddin made. But Ferris was too anxious; every time she closed her eyes she found herself confronted with a vision of Reiffen lying on the ground before a vengeful bear. So she lay in her bed and listened to the empty dark, her thoughts with her wretched friend. Beyond the window the lights of the gleaming city seemed less brilliant now. The curtains lay flat, motionless as the stone walls around them. There were no breezes in Issinlough. Everything was still as stone.

She was still awake when Redburr came up to the room and

tumbled heavily into the last empty bed. Though the Shaper insisted he knew as little about the matter as she, Ferris pestered him all the same with questions about Grimble and balloons and what they were going to do when they woke, until finally she had bothered him so long she woke Avender as well. They both threw pillows at her, but that only made her more annoying.

"I guess the only way to get you to be quiet," said Redburr, "is to tell you a story. Then maybe I'll get some rest."

"Something about the Bryddin?" she asked hopefully, burrowing comfortably beneath her covers. A story would at least take her mind off Reiffen, even if it answered none of her questions. "About Dwvon? Or Uhle?"

"Whatever it takes." Redburr settled himself wearily in the soft darkness. His great bulk loomed as a darker shadow in the gray room. "Maybe I'll tell you about Dwvon and the mander. It's a fine tale. And it'll give you a fine sense of the Stoneways, too."

He paused for a moment, and when he began to speak again his voice seemed to rise more from the room itself than from his own throat, as if the unneret were the one actually telling the tale of its fashioner.

D wvon felt Brydds' breath upon his face," Redburr said, "and that was when he woke. Such it is for all Bryddin. Their father's breath pushes them up through the darkness, but they have no idea where they're going, or where they came from.

"How long the journey lasts none of them know. It only ends when each Bryddin feels the rough stone against his face and hands. Then the warm breath ceases and the knowledge of up and down is revealed as they start to fall for the first time. In fear their hands grab at the hardness above. Their fingers squeeze the rock. Their feet kick up until their bare toes can gain a hold as well. And then they hang for a while, in the darkness at the bottom of the world.

"So it was for Dwvon, first among them. He rested, and felt the solid rock around his fingers. He smelled the stone as he pressed his face against its hardness. He liked its roughness and its cold. Slowly, as his fear of falling subsided, he realized that Brydds had sent him to this place for his delight, and not for his destruction.

"He grew curious. Reaching out, he discovered the stone continued around him in all directions. On clinging hands and feet he crawled carefully across the bottom of the world. He knew the surface that held him was stone, because Brydds had put the knowledge of stone in his mind before he had sent him up into the world. But he knew nothing at all about the shape of the stone, or where it would take him as he clambered across it.

"He came to a place where the rock turned beneath his hands, and began to climb upward. Now he could cling to ledges that held his weight on their own, and did not have to feel the pain of the stone as he gouged it with his fingers and toes. Up he climbed, fearful that the rock would soon close in over his head again, until he came to yet another strange place where the rock curved away beneath him. He found himself lying on the stone, which lay now between him and the Abyss, rather than above his head.

"For a time he rested again, glad that he had not come into a place where he had always to hurt the stone to keep from plunging back down into the void. And afterward he rose up and explored the cave he had found. Great was his wonder when he came upon a narrow trickle of water. Try as he might, he could not catch its softness with his fingers, and so he learned that water was not something he could shape to his own design but only channel.

"He brought his hands to his face and sniffed at this strange new thing, so different from the rock and air he had previously known. He found it cool and refreshing. He bent low over the trickle and drank deeply, and came alive as he drank, the water seeming to replace something inside himself. He followed the stream back up the cave, hoping it would lead to other good things. Soon he came to a pool, where the water was deeper than he could reach with his arm. And there were things moving about in the water, both at the bottom of the pool and within the water itself. He could feel their motion with his hands. And on the far side of the pool, when he had examined its roundness, he found soft things that squashed beneath his fingers unless he touched them with great delicacy. And because they seemed more like the water than the rock in their softness, he tasted them and found they were also refreshing. He felt renewed, with an even greater sense of fullness than the water had given him.

"He decided this was a good place, and that he would make it his home.

"So it was that Dwvon dwelt in the beginning in what he called the Lough a Issen, the place of water. And he explored all about his lough, both within and without the cave. And in his exploring he discovered all the different sorts of stone that filled the darkness: the olath, which is the strongest of stones; and the c'charr, which can be polished into many different grains and colors; and the nirrin, which is the frozen ropes of molten stone that flow in pockets through the world. And he found Inach also, the True Stone, which was once the bones of Ina, and is far too strong for Bryddin hands to shape.

"Then Dwvon learned to work the stone with his hands. With his strong fingers he shaped it into vessels for holding water, and smooth places for him to lie when he took his rest, and cunning traps to catch the fish and crabs within the water. Much he found in that dark world that was good and made him strong. But always were his creations made only with his hands. For though he had found the veins of gold and blumet in the stone, he had not yet found the fire that would let him bend the metals to his will.

"Many other caves he found in the bottom of the world around him, and other streams as well. Some were torrents that spouted out from holes in the stone, and some were damp seepings from the rock like tears. And once, as he ventured farther and farther from the lough, he found a stream where the water was warm. And he marveled, for the Bryddin are all cold as the rock around them. And the fish and crabs he caught were also cold, and the water that held them. Indeed the only warmth he had felt so far was in one of the flying creatures he sometimes heard darting through the air. For once he had chanced upon one that had wounded its wing and lay shivering on the floor. And it had been warm to his touch, much warmer than the water or the stone. Carefully he had mended the creature's delicate bones, and nursed it back to health with portions of his food. And afterward the creature had brought its fellows to share his bounty, and always there were five or ten or a score of them hanging from the ceiling of the lough. But this was the first time he had felt the warmth of the world in something else, and he was eager to learn more about this fall of water. Could it be the source of the heat in his warm-blooded friends? For even as he played with his hand in the stream, he could feel the warmth flowing up from his fingers to his arm and into his chest. And the warmth was a feeling that was good, but different from the water and the food.

"So he tunneled through the rock above the warm flow until he came out into a wider passage. Beside him he heard the water racing through the narrow cavern, and even the air here was warm, like the water. And the stone was warm, and slick with dampness. Long he continued beside the stream. Sometimes he walked upright through wide caverns. Other times he pulled himself through narrow tunnels where there was no room to breathe. But always he came out in wider chambers. And always the water grew hotter as he went forward. And as the water grew hotter he became aware that the air had changed as well. In it now was the smell of fish or crabs left too long uneaten. But also with the taste of nirrin to it, and warm like the water.

"At the end of the cavern he came to a place where the stream burst upward through the floor. And here the water was hotter than anything Dwvon had yet felt. All the rock in the floor of that part of the cavern was Inach, and Dwvon despaired at ever finding the source of the heated flow. He could neither descend through the fountain nor tunnel through the heartstone around it. And in his hopelessness he lay prone upon the rock and felt the throbbing of the stone beneath him. For the very rock pulsed like a beating heart, and in his sense of the stone around him he knew that he was very close to one of the secrets of his world.

"So it was that Dwvon determined not to give up his search. He decided there must be another way through the rock. He began to tunnel his way through the wall of the cavern, away from the heartstone. And all the time he could feel the stone beating furiously around him. Slowly he worked his way deeper into the rock until at last he came to a place where the heartstone itself was riven. And between these ribs of stone was a narrow plug of nirrin, as smooth to his touch as if he had fashioned it with his own hands. His heart beat furiously in his chest in time with the pulsing of the stone, and he dug quickly and carelessly. So it was that, in his haste, he was unprepared when the nirrin gave way beneath him and he fell down into a fiery cave. He caught at the heartstone to catch himself; but the heartstone was stronger than Dwvon, and his fingers could not pierce it. And so he tumbled through the rent and into the fire below.

"Now did Dwvon feel true heat. He burned with pain as he fell into the heart of the molten nirrin. And great as the pain of his burning, greater even was the pain in his eyes. For the pool of flaming nirrin into which he had fallen gave forth a brightness such as he had never imagined. Always had he lived in darkness, with only sound and touch and taste and smell to recognize the world. But now his eyes, whose need he had not understood before, cried out at the sudden use.

"He flailed about in the liquid stone. But the stone was far thicker than any water, and he was able to swim upon its surface. And as he swam the pain in his eyes lessened, and he realized that he might look about him.

"So he climbed out upon an island of heartstone to gaze upon the seething nirrin. All was a boiling sea of red and golden stone. Bubbles burst forth in molten crowns. Steam rose in thick white columns. Blots of darker heartstone marked other islands amid the tongues of yellow flame. Dwvon began to cough and gasp: the smell of spoiled fish was far stronger than it had been in the chamber above. His body burned as the heat ate at him both inside and out. Eventually he understood that, though he might endure the pain, in the end he would be consumed by the fury of the earth about him. And yet he was reluctant to leave this land of light. Now that he could see, he finally felt complete and whole.

"He searched the heartstone above for the crack through which he had dropped into the fiery cave, but it was beyond his reach. Peering through the pale smokes and choking mist around him, he sought another exit. Then he saw the mander for the first time.

"It lay crouched on another island in the burning pool, its tail pulled up along its inky body, its four legs tucked beneath it. Its long tongue curled out from between its jaws and licked along the line of its small, sharp teeth. And eyes like his own, though small and black, glimmered back at him through the smoke. Gold and red reflected in the scales on the back and sides of the beast. Then the mander uncurled its tail and disappeared into the boiling liquid.

"Dwvon watched the stretch of pool between the two islands, but there was no sign of the creature. He did not know what to expect. Nothing before had he known in the world that came close to him in size. Fish as long as his arm; crabs broader than his hand. But nothing larger. He knew nothing of manders.

"It came at him from behind. Beneath the surface of the burning pool it swam to scrabble up onto the back of the island. But Dwvon heard it and turned to face its charge. Together the two crashed back into the fires. Dwvon found himself wrestling with the monster beneath the melted stone.

"Terrible was that fight between mander and Bryddin. Through the sulfured pool they gripped and grappled. Great was the surprise of the mander at the strength of Dwvon. Always before had it preyed on weaker creatures. The monster sought Dwvon's head with its powerful jaws, but biting Dwvon's head was no more useful than biting stone. With its sharp claws it raked the Bryddin's belly, then cried out in pain as its talons snapped against its stony prey.

"But Dwvon could no more hurt the mander than it could hurt him. He tried to break its spine beneath his grip, but it twisted back and forth within his arms. He smote the creature with his fists, but his blows fell to nothing against its scales. He gouged at it with his hands, but it was too slippery for his grasp.

"They struggled futilely through the burning stone. Then the mander realized that the lava weakened Dwvon, and so the beast forced him deep within the molten pool. Down it pushed him, using its bulk to force them both to the bottom of the viscous stone. Twice Dwvon broke free from the monster's grip and fought back toward the surface. But each time the beast wrapped its thick tail around him and dragged him back to the bottom. Around them the nirrin was whipped into a fiery froth with the fury of their battling. Dwvon's struggles began to weaken as he realized the monster's strength was greater than his own, here in its lough.

"The Bryddin are not creatures of fire. They have need of air and water. For a moment Dwvon ceased his struggling and readied himself for a final test of strength. The mander crushed him all the more fiercely as it felt his vigor flagging. Then Dwvon realized he lay atop another plug of nirrin in the heartstone. A gleam of hope brightened within him. Twisting suddenly in its grip, he caught the creature completely by surprise and began to tear at the softer stone beneath him. Two or three great handfuls he pulled up out of the naked rock before the mander realized what he was doing. By then it was too late. For then the pressure of the molten stone blew both Dwvon and the plug out into a surging stream beneath. Behind him the beast had to use all its strength to keep from being sucked out of its lair into the frigid water as well.

"Swiftly the current pulled Dwvon away as fire and water met in a fierce storm. His strength was almost finished. He had not breathed since the creature had first pulled him below the surface of the fire. Then the stream burst out in a fountain of steam and water into an open cave.

"Long lay Dwvon stunned upon the floor. Cool drops falling

upon him from the ceiling above washed away his pain. Long it took before he was willing to rouse himself and look about him. He did not think the mander had followed.

"When he finally rose, one thought still burned within him. Though the fire was yet guarded by the beast within, still he knew he must learn its secret. How the world had opened before him with the golden flow of light! What he might do if he could see! But he was not going to risk himself to another battle with the mander. There were other ways to learn what he desired.

"He returned along the course of the stream until he had found a bed of olath. Then he fashioned for himself a long-handled scoop and chain of stone links, and returned to the cavern of the fountain. There he gathered some of the nirrin that had been expelled from the geyser, and fashioned it into two small bowls that fit neatly together. With these tools he crawled back up the passage he had dug to the crack in the roof of the molten cavern.

"The slit in the heartstone remained open. Dwvon's heart quickened at the sight of its reddish glow. Fresh lumps of nirrin had gathered around the side, spat up from the frothing heat below. Yet there was still a space through which he could lower his long-handled spoon. Carefully he placed his eye to the vent, and felt the heat from the fires below against his face. There was no sign of the mander. He attached the ladle's handle to the last link of the stone chain and lowered it into the burning pit. Link by link his scoop descended. The spoon dipped into the seething red and gold. Quickly he pulled the chain back upward, before any sudden onset of the beast might deprive him of his treasure.

"But the mander did not appear. Dwvon poured the flaming nirrin into the bottom of one of his bowls and closed the other above it. With a fine pressure from his fingers he sealed the two together. The heat and light were trapped within. If he hurried, he might be able to return to his lough before they cooled back to darkness.

"The nirrin, though much reduced, still glowed when he poured it out within his cavern. The mistrin hanging from the ceiling whistled and fled before the light. But all the lough was filled with a flickering bath of red and gold, a pale reflection of what Dwvon had seen in the cave of fire. His stonework gleamed and sparkled in the light, which ran before the first shadows ever to dance across those walls. The calm pool gleamed in red and gold.

"Dwvon reached for a morsel of fish from a dish close beside the bowl of fire. He was hungry after his long battle and had not eaten since first finding the warm spring. As he took the fish, a small piece of fatty skin fell atop the glowing coal. Briefly it spurted into light. And Dwvon stopped with the fish uneaten before his mouth at the thought that the fire might seek nourishment the same as he.

"So intent was Dwvon upon this new thought that he neither saw nor heard the mander as it crept forward into the lough. For the creature had more than one passage from its lair. It had come by different ways, following the scent and taste of the Bryddin upon the rocks. Until it found him at last, deep in thought above his stolen treasure.

"With a roar the beast leapt out upon the thief. Once more the two grappled, this time in the dimmer light of a single fire. Their shadows twisted against the cavern walls, as if they were but one pair in a multitude of battling hosts.

"Into the depths of Dwvon's pool they fell, where the fight was much more equal. For just as Dwvon had felt weakened by the clawing fire in the cavern of the mander, so too was the creature weakened by the clinging cold of the pool. It thrashed its tail wildly, trying to clear the water away. Steam rose from its sides as its fires were stilled. Round and round they fought, each trying to bring its own strength to bear on the other. Thrashing and splashing, they rolled closer to the edge. Beyond them lay the dark Abyss.

"Dwvon, who knew there was nothing beyond the lip of his pool, began to force his foe in that direction. He had no hope to destroy the beast in any other fashion. So it was, with each twist of their bodies and each thrash of the creature's tail, he brought them closer to the edge. And then they were fighting beside the low wall he had raised to dam the stream. For a moment Dwvon allowed the beast to gain the upper hand. Its great jaws snapped and slavered. Its heated breath assailed him. Then Dwvon brought his legs up beneath the creature's belly. With a great double kick he sent the beast flying up and through the air. And the mander, so bent upon its prey, paid no attention to the blackness beneath. For though the creature had seen many deeps and darknesses in the underearth, it had never yet found the Abyss. It knew not that nothing lay below. And so it grabbed instead at Dwvon, fearing its prey would escape it as it fell. Dwvon warded off the clutches of its short claws, but he was too slow to escape the last curl of the great tail. The creature caught him about the wrist, and both were dragged forward and over the edge of the pool. Dwvon's toes found no purchase on the stone. Together they were swallowed by the darkness.

"Except that something caught Dwvon by the ankle as he fell. And so he hung that way, with the mander's tail gripped tightly around his wrist, and something unknown clinging to his leg above. He was whipped back and forth as the mander thrashed about, trying to raise itself back to the stone. He could not see it in the darkness, but he could hear the snap of its jaws and the hiss of its panting breath. Long he hung that way, taut between two vises. And then at last the mander's strength began to fail. The grip of its tail began to slip. Dwvon could feel the coil slide free from his wrist. Until at last, in silence, the creature fell. A long, long plunge, with only a distant howl of despair as the beast finally realized there was no bottom here.

"When it was gone, Dwvon felt the grip around his ankle quicken. He was pulled back within the Lough a Issin. His fire had spilled out from its bowl and been extinguished by the stream, and he had no way of knowing what had rescued him until a voice spoke from the darkness.

" 'I came to your light,' said the voice. 'I am Uhle.'

" 'I am Dwvon. The son of Brydds.'

" 'I also am the son of Brydds,' said the voice. 'I have known for some time I was not alone. But in the darkness I could not find you.'

" 'Come with me,' said Dwvon. 'I'll take you to the place of light. Now that the beast that guarded the cave is gone, we can learn all the ways of the fire.'

"Together Dwvon and Uhle returned to the Abbenough, which is what they called the cave of fire. And soon after, they brought new flame to the Lough a Issin. Then the first of the lights began to gleam above the darkness of the Abyss. And Angun soon joined them, following the light as Uhle had done, and many other Bryddin after. And in time they built this city, Issinlough, in the place where Dwvon and the mander fought, and filled it with the light they had found. And in time Uhle came to believe that there were other lights to find, and began to search for them. But that is another tale."

Redburr finished and looked across the quiet room at the children. Avender, he knew, had fallen asleep long before the mander had ever appeared in the story. But he was glad to see that Ferris was finally slumbering as well. She lay on her back with her dark hair spread out across the pillow, one hand outside the coverlet across her chest. Care and worry had passed from her face, and she slept like the child she had been at the start of spring, before Reiffen had been taken away. Redburr rolled quietly into his own bed, careful not to wake her, or Avender. There might never be another time when they slept so easily again.

13

Molio

I n Ussene, the days passed in a deep gloom broken only by the flickering of the candles along the rough stone walls. Reiffen followed Molio on his rounds through the grubby passages, but when he wasn't with Molio he found himself drawn more and more to the Library, no matter how hard he tried to resist.

Usually the little man came to wake him when it was time to set off on the day's routine, tapping lightly at his door. "Sir," Molio would whisper in a voice almost too timid to hear. "Would you like to go with Molio today?" His small eyes glittered happily as Reiffen sprang up and rubbed the sleep from his own, both of them glad Reiffen could avoid the temptation of the books for another day.

But often Molio was called away for extra duties and Reiffen was left to himself in his dark room. Even then he generally went first to the Front Window, where the sight of the mountain shadows gliding gradually in brown shrouds across one another, or a chill rain driving through the steep valley beyond, might be enough to keep him from going to the other place. But more and more often it was not.

There was something comforting to Reiffen about the Library. It wasn't like the rest of Ussene. The light was brighter there than it was anywhere else; sometimes the room even seemed cheery despite the spider and the pulsing stone. In the Manor he had spent many happy hours alone in the bookshelved dens; this library was very much the same. The smell of the leather bindings. The volumes beckoning in long and secret rows. The rest of the fortress was all boredom or torment, but in the Library at least he might remember what his life had been.

He tried to stay away. He knew the place was evil. These were not the books he read in Valing. These were the work of Wizards. So he followed Molio as often as he could and sometimes even searched for the little man, roaming the halls cautiously alone.

For his part, Molio was happy to have a friend. In his worshipful way he never failed to tell Reiffen that he was the first and best friend Molio had ever had. "Kicks and beatings," he said as he rubbed the memories that lay beneath his wax-covered coat. "All Molio has ever had is kicks and beatings. Friends are better."

One day they found themselves near the long tunnel that ran from the Front Gate back into the depths of the mountain. Molio's usual route was through the back stairs and side passages of the fortress, where they rarely saw anyone else; but once in a while they came out into the busier tunnels. This time they found themselves nearly running into a company of sissit leading a line of prisoners into the heart of the hill. It was the first time Reiffen had ever gotten a good look at sissit other than as pictures in a book, and they were far more horrible in person than on the page. Nothing was right about them, though they might have passed for human at a distance. They were short and thick, with arms and legs not long enough for their bodies. Their skin was terribly pale, as pale as the white of an eye. A few thin wisps of hair wagged at the tops of their heads, as colorless as their skin. Their clothing was ragged, mostly filthy pelts and hides. But they were strong, and pushed even the largest of their prisoners easily along, their flat feet slapping loudly against the stone floor with every step.

Molio tugged at Reiffen's sleeve. "Please, sir," he whispered. "Not good for sissiti to see us. They are always hungry."

But, as Reiffen allowed the little man to draw him backwards, one of the captives started toward him. The prisoners were all joined together by a long rope that bound their hands, and this particular prisoner could not go far before he was pulled to a stop by his restraints. All the same, he stretched forward as far as possible and peered at Reiffen through the wild tangle of his hair.

"Reiffen?" he croaked. His lips were cracked and dry. "Is that you?"

For a moment Reiffen thought it was Avender who was standing before him. Then, through the layers of dirt that covered the other, he realized the boy was too old. It wasn't Avender. Avender was dead.

Molio tugged again at his sleeve and whimpered, "Please, sir. It's not good to be watching new ones arrive. Sissiti get angry."

Even as Molio spoke, the nearest sissit gave a sharp pull on the rope that sent the prisoner stumbling on after the others. "Don't you recognize me?" he called unhappily as he was pulled away. "It's Rib. Rib Clammer. Don't you remember?" A puzzled look came into his face as he saw that Reiffen's hands weren't bound. "Aren't you a prisoner?" he asked. "Aren't they taking you down into the pits with the rest—"

Before Reiffen could answer, the sissit guard hit Rib heavily across the back with his spear. The boy fell forward against the prisoner in front of him and gasped for breath as the guards dragged them away. But Reiffen remembered him now. He was a farmer's son from Eastbay, and had left Valing the summer before, apprenticed to a Wayland merchant.

The slap of the sissit's feet echoed down the tunnel; the prisoners disappeared into the gloom. A large rat took advantage of the stillness to scurry across the path in hope of finding something left behind. Reiffen stared after them long after Rib and the others had disappeared.

"Friend?" asked Molio in his small, soft voice. He peeked out from behind Reiffen and peered down the tunnel as well.

Reiffen nodded. "From home," he said, feeling strangely tired. "I thought he was somebody else for a moment."

"Molio is friend," whispered the little man kindly.

"Yes, you are," said Reiffen. He might have patted him on the shoulder, only Molio was not much cleaner than the sissit. "My last friend in the whole world."

"You miss friend? You miss home?"

"I do. I miss them both." But Reiffen was thinking of Avender, not Rib Clammer, and of the way the surface of the lake sometimes reflected the white peaks of Valing in the evening, when the winds died down and everything was still.

Shouldering the little man's bag, which he sometimes carried for him, Reiffen followed him back up to the empty tunnels above. But he was troubled by the look he had seen on Rib's face as the older boy was dragged away. Plainly Rib had thought Reiffen might not be a captive at all. It was natural enough. There was Reiffen, unbound and apparently wandering freely through the fortress. What other conclusion might have come to a prisoner? Reiffen didn't at all like the idea that anyone might think he was in Ussene of his own accord. He had been captured and brought here just like anyone else. It wasn't his fault they wanted him to be something more than an ordinary slave. He would escape if he could. But there was no way past the guards at the Front Gate, and no way to climb down from the Front Window.

He tried not to think about the Library.

Two days passed before Reiffen made up his mind to go look for Rib in the dungeons. He spent all his time with Molio, who would have been delighted with his company had Reiffen not been brooding about what Rib thought all the while. They spent most of the second evening at the Front Window watching the colors of the sunset bathe the valley beyond. Molio had never known to watch a sunset before and was enchanted by the sight. Even after the last shadows of red and orange had faded from the cliffs he stood leaning with his hands and chin against the sill, watching the sky be slowly salted by the stars.

Reiffen sat by himself against the far wall in the growing darkness. He had kept away from the Library since seeing Rib, but that hadn't made him feel any better. He knew he had to do something more, to prove to himself that he really was doing everything he could to upset the Wizards' plans. And it was important the other boy understand that Reiffen, too, was the Wizards' prisoner. Maybe he might find a way to bring Rib back Upstairs with him. Molio was nice enough, but he wasn't someone who would ever help Reiffen come up with a way to escape.

His thoughts were interrupted by the little man, who had finally left the sill and come back through the darkness to sit beside his friend. "Sunset is beautiful," he said. "Stars, too. Thank you, friend."

"Hmm?" Reiffen wasn't thinking about the stars. "You know, Molio," he said after a moment, "I think I'll go Downstairs tomorrow and look for Rib."

He felt Molio stiffen beside him.

"D-Downstairs?" the little man whispered. He tucked what little chin he had between his knobby knees. "N-no one goes there. Y-you can't help friend there."

"Maybe I can. I can't know till I try."

"Molio doesn't want to lose kind friend," he whimpered. "Not now." He brushed a tear from his eye and left a waxy streak across his face. "Molio has never had friends before."

"No one's going to hurt me, Molio. Usseis made that quite clear. Besides, you told me yourself you used to live Downstairs. But here you are, alive and breathing all the same."

The little man shivered and went quiet at the mention of his own time Downstairs. Reiffen could see Molio was thinking hard of what he might say to convince his friend not to go. "Bad things happen," the little man said finally. His voice remained fearful in the thick night that had fallen through the window. "Many bad things Downstairs. Only lucky ones ever come up. Even soldiers."

"I've made up my mind. Fine friend I am if I don't even try to do something for Rib." Though Reiffen knew as he spoke he wasn't going for Rib's sake, but for his own.

Not wanting to give Molio any further chance of talking him out of his purpose, he stood up and turned down the tunnel away from the Window. The lights in the passage glowed dimly before him, disappearing into the depths of the Wizards' fortress. Molio followed miserably behind.

The next day Reiffen waited long enough to get the new password, then set off for the lower levels. His friend made no attempt to stop him, or go with him.

Soon Reiffen came to the main tunnel. The road was empty now, and there was no one to challenge the boy as he turned to the left and marched deeper into the heart of the dark stone. It was a large passage, large enough for ten men to walk abreast, and tall enough to allow the Wizards easy passage. Here and there other tunnels branched off on either side. None of the side ways were lit and from them all Reiffen sensed a guarded deadness, as if each path led straight to the bottom of a graveyard. Garbage lay piled along the walls, broken weapons and other things Reiffen didn't want to think about. Large insects skittered through the shadows. Everywhere the rough stone was dark and dirty. The weight of the fortress above seemed to press down upon him, choking the air. Heavy torches burned along the walls, and the whole passage reeked of smoke. Reiffen walked quietly and listened carefully for any sign he wasn't alone. But even the rats were careful to keep out of his way. For all they knew he was just another hungry sissit.

He walked for quite some time before he noticed a light in the passage ahead that seemed stronger than one of the usual torches. Soon he was close enough to see it came from a fire burning in a

raised brazier. A group of sissit were standing around the fire roasting potatoes and other, less wholesome things on the ends of their
daggers. The sissit's pallid skins glowed red in the light of the fire.
The main passage ended here, but on the other side Reiffen saw a
second, smaller tunnel that angled downwards into the stone beyond like a black chute.

Reiffen steeled himself and stepped out of the shadows into the
room. The sissit turned his way at once, their shabby arms clanking
as they moved.

"Yah, that won't help you here," said the sergeant after the boy
had spoken the password. He jerked his knife back the way Reiffen
had come. The legs on whatever it was the sergeant was eating wiggled as he waved the skewer about.

Reiffen swallowed uncomfortably. Usseis's assurances seemed
less absolute here in the deeper parts of his demesne. "Usseis said I
could go where I—" the boy began, but he was cut off by a sharp
blow from the back of the sissit's hand. His teeth caught the inside
of his cheek and his mouth turned salty with blood.

"Don't go usin' the Boss's name down here," hissed the sergeant. "You ain't got no password! You ain't goin' nowhere!"

"Maybe we give 'im a little tour, anyway, eh, Blinks?" suggested
one of his mates with a snicker. "We're gonna get 'im down here,
soon or late. Might be fun to tinder 'im up."

"Yah?" The sergeant scowled darkly at his fellow. His pale skin
looked soft beneath the dark leather of his jacket and breeches. Had
he owned a tuft of hair anywhere upon his head or face he might
have almost looked human. "And who's gonna tell th' Boss we didn'
foller orders? You, maybe?" He bit off one of the legs wriggling on
his knife; dark juice dripped down his chin.

Reiffen backed up a step. Explaining his situation to Rib seemed
much less important now than it had been the night before. The
Front Window, or even the seclusion of his own small cell, was suddenly much more attractive. What was done was done. Rib and he
would both have to follow the paths set out for them. Antagonizing

the sissit was not going to help either of them. He took a second step backward.

"Look at 'im," said a toothless one, coming forward. His voice sounded like boots being pulled from thick mud. "Scared a'ready, he is. Hope I'm the one 'ut gets to hold 'im down when he do finally come down the Holes."

He waggled his dirty knife in Reiffen's face and grinned. The rest of the troop laughed horribly, their dark humor echoing across the walls. They kept laughing as Reiffen turned and hurried back the way he had come. It was a long time before he no longer thought he heard the echo of their guffaws. Evil flourished in all the parts and passages of Ussene, but there was no question it grew stronger the deeper one went into the darkness.

His heart pounded in his chest. He thought the sissit were following him, until he realized the footsteps he heard were only his blood thumping in his ears. His chest heaved; he put out a hand to steady himself against the wall. He felt better after a moment and was ashamed to have been so thoroughly scared by a few sissit soldiers. The heir to the thrones of both Banking and Wayland might have shown a bit more courage in the face of a few fat sissit. But he was only a boy, and Giserre's pride commanded little respect in the dark pits of Ussene. He was glad that Molio had not been with him; he would not have liked Molio to see him so frightened. The little man's high regard allowed the only shred of self-respect Reiffen still possessed.

He turned off the main way into the passage that would take him Upstairs, but after that he paid no more attention to where he was going. He walked on listlessly past the guttering candles and moldy walls. The dark tunnels around him all looked the same. He was not at all surprised when he found his unguided footsteps had taken him to the Library. On his last visit he had come across a book, *Magic's Aspects,* and his curiosity had finally overcome him. He had read the first few pages but had slammed the cover swiftly shut once he realized what it was he had found, a book that explained the nature of magic and how to do the most basic spells. To be so close to the power of the Wizards had frightened him. But now, with other, simpler terrors behind him, the Library welled up before him as a refuge.

It was always peaceful among the books. Reiffen had never seen anyone else in the Library, and this time was no different. Even though he was afraid of it, he had come to think of the room as his special sanctuary.

He found the book where he had left it. Its cover fit perfectly in his hands as he picked it up from the table closest to the door. It was a medium-sized volume, with a soft leather binding. Just the right weight. Just the right shape. There were no chairs anywhere, but the table was at the perfect height for him to stand while reading. His elbows rested on the dark wood on either side of the opened pages.

"Magic," he read, *"is the art of using the world. All the world's creatures contain this art within them, in one fashion or another, either through talents of their own or through long study of the nature of the world itself. Examples of the first sort of magic can be seen in the ability of the Oeinnen, or Shapers, to transform themselves into almost any sort of creature; or in the power the Bryddin wield over all things of stone and earth. But all creatures have the ability to work magic, to some degree, because all share the same common connection to the world around them. Only the Bryddin, born of Brydds in the void beneath, are not affected by the magic of Areft's world. They are, by their nature, of different stuff."*

As he read, Reiffen forgot everything that had happened to him in the tunnels below. He forgot the time. He forgot where he was. The world he was exploring was far more interesting than the one in which he lived. There was much in the book that he had already learned from school, or from Redburr and Nolo. But never before had it all been connected. Never before had all the various bits of knowledge in the world fit together so exactly. Everything was part of the whole and, as such, everything was related. It was just a matter of assembling the power and knowledge necessary to follow the paths between the things of the world to perform magic. The book made it all seem so simple.

He had read past the first chapter and was well into the second when the feeling came over him that he was no longer alone. Drat that Molio. Here he was looking for Reiffen once again at exactly the time when Reiffen wanted to be left alone. He had just come to a passage describing the basic differences between fire and water and bird and bee and was beginning to wonder if there were any spells or potions that might be simple enough for him to learn right away when he had to turn and see what Molio wanted.

He stopped short. Fornoch, in his gray robes, stood beside the spiderweb, one finger thrumming lightly on a corner string. His eyes were on the spider, not Reiffen; but that didn't make Reiffen feel better at all. How long had the Wizard been there? Why had he not spoken? Reiffen swallowed hard, trying to hold back the fear welling up within him, and closed his book. He was really in for it now. The spider clung tightly to its line as the net trembled beneath the Wizard's touch. Then Fornoch looked up and, noting that the boy had noticed him, left off bothering the spider. He smiled.

This time his smile was not like his brothers'. It was almost human. It didn't send shivers up Reiffen's spine, or make him want to look and see what was about to strike him from behind. It was a warm smile, almost like Giserre's when he returned to the Tear after a long day of sledding or hiking through the mountain meadows. Despite himself, he almost calmed. Maybe he hadn't reached the end.

"I was waiting for you to notice I had joined you." Fornoch came forward, his finger stroking the head of the spider gently as he passed. Reiffen realized the Wizard hadn't been toying with the spider. He had been playing with it, the way one might play with a favorite kitten.

The Wizard looked over the boy's shoulder at the book lying upon the table. Reiffen stepped out of his way. But the Wizard took no offense.

"I thought you might appreciate that," he said. "I put it in a place where I thought you might find it. I had to be careful about making it too obvious, though. I knew you would not want to pick up the books that were lying about. At least not at first."

Reiffen was confused. "Y-you mean it's okay for me to be here?"

"Of course." The Wizard crossed his arms within the drooping sleeves of his cloak and smiled once again. "Why do you think the Library is here? Do you think I need it?"

Reiffen looked around the room with a fresh understanding. It seemed impossible that all this might have been created for his benefit.

"Usseis and I hardly require something like this," Fornoch continued. "Magic is as natural to us as opening a door is to you. Ossdonc might occasionally need some sort of reminder, but only when he is in a hurry. No, Reiffen. This is your room."

"But Molio said . . ."

"Molio knows only what he has been told. Or thinks he has been told."

"But why would you make this room for me?" Reiffen looked for a moment at the wonders assembled on the shelves around him. He hated the Wizards and everything they stood for, but all the same he couldn't help but think how wonderful it would be to read every book in that room, and learn the purpose of every object.

"You know the answer to that question." There was almost a tone of disappointment in the Wizard's voice, as if he was proud of what Reiffen could learn when he used his brain hard enough.

"You're still just trying to make me join you," Reiffen decided at once. "You're showing me what might be mine if I decide to do what you want."

He wasn't sure, but Reiffen thought Fornoch's eyes twinkled, as if he had given the Wizard the answer he wanted. Fornoch pursed his lips and spoke again. "I would not quite describe my purpose in just that way," he said. "I would prefer to say that I merely offer you an example of what you stand to gain, should you decide to see things our way. It is not as if your other choices are as generous."

"Then is what this book says true?" Reiffen looked down at the book upon the table. "Can anyone do magic?"

"Yes."

A thrill of excitement raced through him. Someday he might hold in his hands the same power that had murdered his father.

"But that power can only be yours if I choose to teach it to you," continued Fornoch, as if reading Reiffen's mind. "There is no other way to learn."

"And if you do teach me," asked Reiffen with sudden daring, "what's to stop me from using that power upon you?"

Fornoch smiled again, finding the boy's ambition amusing. "Nothing. Nothing at all. Once the power is gained, there is no other control upon it. You will always be your own master, if you come to us freely. But if you force us to bring you to our will, then your life will cease to be yours. Once extracted, a will can never be returned."

"I'll never follow you freely!" said Reiffen with sudden passion. "Not if you offer me everything in the world!"

"But that's precisely what I am offering."

The Wizard crossed the room to the place where the green stone lay beneath its bowl of glass. The Library, which had seemed very large without him looked much smaller now that Fornoch was in it. He lifted the bowl with one hand and picked up the stone with the other. It remained lifeless and dark, a small pebble cradled in fingers. But when he returned to stand before the boy the rock began once more to pulse and glow.

"Do you know what this is, Reiffen?" asked Fornoch softly. He held the stone up before the boy, who felt the heart of the rock beating in time with his own. He was unable to speak, his eyes fixed on the pulsing stone, so he shook his head instead.

"It's a simple thing, really." The Wizard turned the rock between his fingers, displaying all its sides. "The bearer of this stone will live forever. I fashioned it for you."

Reiffen wondered if Fornoch could read minds. First the Library, where even a human boy could learn magic. And now this, a talisman that would allow the bearer to live as long as Nolo or Redburr. Think of what he could do then!

"Of course, if I were to take it away from you, then it would stop working." Fornoch withdrew his hand and the stone with it. Immediately the stone went dark again, its heart shrouded in hardness. "That's why you can't just carry it around with you. You have to keep it inside you, where it will always be with you. Guarding you from within."

Reiffen followed the green rock with his eyes. Slowly the Wizard brought it closer. The boy reached out and, as his fingers drew near the stone, he felt it even before he touched it. It was not that the stone was hot. It was more like the way that a thick wool jersey, when rubbed quickly, would sometimes spark his finger when he brought it close. The stone, however, didn't shock him. It was cold to the touch, colder than the air in the room around him.

He pulled his hand away. "No," he said firmly. "You're not going to get me that way, either. Kill me if you want, but I won't help you at all."

"As you wish."

Fornoch wrapped his hand around the stone and withdrew his offering. He didn't appear upset, or disappointed. "You will not be killed, of course," he said. "But we will use you. There is a certain amount of pain involved in Usseis's procedures. The end result, however, will be the same. Not from your point of view, perhaps. But that is your choice."

Reiffen stood stiffly by the table. Now that he had rejected Fornoch's offer he expected his freedom to be at an end. But Fornoch had other thoughts. He ignored the boy and returned to the bookshelf to replace the stone beneath its case. The bowl slipped back over the dark green gem and the tension in the room lessened at once.

"I'll leave you to think about what you can and cannot do," said Fornoch. "The choices are yours."

He drew his cloak about him and disappeared. Reiffen blinked, but his eyes were not deceiving him. Fornoch had vanished. And there had been none of the thunder and noise of the journey from the henge with Ossdonc. Fornoch's cloak had twirled around him and twisted into a thin line that had suddenly no longer been there. Reiffen was left alone in the room, the books still available to him, the spider and the stone still at hand.

After that Reiffen wasn't the same. His talk with Fornoch left him uneasy and unsatisfied. He knew he had done the right thing and that no good could come from accepting anything offered by any of the Wizards. All the same, he couldn't help but feel he had missed something. That an opportunity had slipped through his fingers. Now his thoughts were always on the Library. Everything he did reminded him of what the Wizard had offered. When he was at the Front Window, craning his neck for a glimpse of the sun between the narrow gaps in the cliffs and ridges overhead, he thought about the books. When he was in bed, waiting for the hour or two of sleep that was all he had anymore, he thought about the Wizard disappearing from the room with a single sweep of his cloak across his body. And when he went out with Molio on his rounds, he saw the green stone in every lamp and candle touched by the little man, their dim yellow flames twisting up into the dark green glow of the stone.

Even Molio was aware that something had changed. He had always been very respectful of Reiffen, but now he seldom spoke unless Reiffen addressed him first. As a result, much of their time together was passed in silence, Reiffen alone with his thoughts and

Molio not wanting to disturb his only friend. The little man began to look troubled when he was with the boy; the eager smiles that had always filled his face became fewer and fewer.

Reiffen barely noticed. He was too busy trying to keep himself from returning to the Library. He was afraid that, if he did, he might finally succumb to Fornoch's gifts. And who knew what would happen then? What if the green stone was a trick, an easy way for Usseis to take control of him? All he knew about the world, young as he was, told him the Wizards were not to be trusted. And yet he was sure that Fornoch had not been lying. It was as if he had understood that Fornoch did not need to lie.

He tried to remember all he had been taught about the time when Fornoch and Ossdonc had assumed human form and lived among men and women. His father had met them both then, many times. Ossdonc had even married his mother's aunt, the Queen Loellin, and had ruled for years over Banking as her consort. Fornoch had cast himself in the part of Martis, the king of Wayland's most trusted counselor. Together they had kept the two kingdoms at war with each other for years. By the time the Dwarves had arrived on the scene, Banking and Wayland had been on the verge of collapse, and all because of the policies the two Wizards had whispered into the ears of queen and king. Ossdonc had been simple in his counsel. Banking was the greater land, and deserved to rule all the world. Wayland was in the way. And Queen Loellin, ever vain and subject to the flattery of those around her, had followed easily along the path her magicked husband had laid out for her. But Fornoch had ever been more subtle, persuading King Brioss that he was in the right to defend his homeland against the wicked predations of his neighbors. Always had he led Wayland down a path of apparent righteousness to a place of death.

And whenever Reiffen worked it all through in his head he knew he was right. The thought of his mother and father, and what the Three had done to them, comforted him. Thinking about them helped him shrug off Fornoch's tempting, and kept him from the Library. Because he was sure that the more he visited that place, the more easily he would be turned to Fornoch's purpose. He told himself that Fornoch had been mistaken to tempt him, because now he had found the strength to resist.

Then one day, as he had dreaded, the officer he had met with Molio came to summon him to another audience with Usseis. Reiffen was watching the sky from the Front Window, reminding himself there was more to the world than dusty passages and sneering sissit. But all hope of ever seeing any of that again died when the officer called sharply to him from the edge of the room, where as little of the sunlight as possible would bother his weak eyes. Reiffen took one last look at the sky, wishing he could say good-bye to the stars as well, then joined the officer at the door. Guards fell in behind and before Reiffen, and led him away.

The Wizards' vast chamber was the same as he remembered it. The doors opened noiselessly once again; he walked through the circle of pillars alone to stand before the dais in the middle of the room. Fornoch was once more seated on the lowest step, while Ossdonc stood guard behind Usseis with his heavy sword girded to his belt, his long black cloak pulled aside to show the glint of his weapon.

Ossdonc grinned as the boy stood before the dais, more an ogre than a Wizard, but both Usseis and Fornoch appeared sad. They stared at Reiffen for some time as if expecting him to be the first to speak, giving him one last chance to change his mind. But Reiffen refused to give them that satisfaction. He waited impatiently for them to begin whatever it was they were going to do.

In the end Usseis spoke first. "It seems, Fornoch," he said, "that your plans have failed. Always you are too subtle."

"You are too impatient, Usseis. If you will only continue to wait you will have what you want in the end."

"Bah," growled Ossdonc, his hand on the pommel of his sword. "All we did was wait the last time, and see what happened then. Had you permitted me to loose my war bands upon the land there would have been nothing left for the cursed stone men to rescue."

"Peace, Ossdonc," said Usseis. "Though what you say is true. Even now, Fornoch, we might be treating with the Bryddin instead of needing to devise new ways to ruin them. And the Three Kingdoms would pay us proper homage."

"All that will come, Usseis," said Fornoch. "All that will come. If you hurry the process with this boy, however, it will take much longer."

Ossdonc crossed his arms impatiently across his broad chest and rolled his eyes.

"We both agree that, willing subject or not, the boy will be what we need."

"Yes," said Fornoch. "But we also agree that, if he joins us freely, there will be far fewer difficulties later on."

"Areft would never have been so patient," growled Ossdonc. "He would have crushed them all." And Ossdonc, as if imagining himself in the role of his forebear, reached out his massive hand to crush imaginary victims in the air before him.

"Areft was destroyed by humans," Fornoch reminded his more savage brother. "They are capable of much more than you are ever willing to understand. That is why we must be certain we have our nets wrapped about them completely before we take the next step."

"Enough." Usseis's voice brought the attention of the other two Wizards back to himself. "I have made my decision. As the two of you are always quarreling, it is up to me to choose our proper course." He leaned forward. A brutal smile blazed across his face. "Think you, boy, that we cannot bend you to our will? If such a one as Mindrell can enthrall you, what then can I not do? Great gifts we have offered you, yet you see fit to reject them. Perhaps you need a taste of the other side of our nature."

The Wizard lifted his hand until it was pointed, palm forward, at Reiffen. The fingers were spread wide apart, and through them Usseis's eyes shone. Reiffen felt something jerk within him, as if his heart had been fetched forth and was now caught writhing within the Wizard's hand. Slowly Usseis closed his fingers one by one around that unseen part of Reiffen now clutched in his magic grip. As each finger closed the boy felt bars of iron being laid across his chest. The last finger folded in. Usseis's hand was now a fist pointing past Reiffen towards the doors behind him.

"Go," ordered the Wizard. His voice had become deep and commanding, and rang out among the pillars as loudly as Ossdonc's ever had. "Do as I would wish. When that is finished you are released."

Then the Wizard waved his hand as if he were dismissing a dog. Or a bootblack.

Reiffen turned sharply and marched back across the towering room and on to the hall outside. Only this time his enchantment was much worse than it had been under Mindrell's hand. This time he was aware of all he saw and did, as clearly as if he were still completely in control of himself. He felt his boots scuff across the dusty floor, and smelled the thick candles burning on the walls. He felt his heart pounding in furious fear inside his chest, and tasted the dryness of his mouth. And, worst of all, he knew exactly what his Master had ordered him to do, and followed the workings of his own mind as he, not his Master, decided upon the best way to accomplish the task that had been set before him.

He tried desperately to make himself stop. With every step he ordered his arms and legs to cease working. He tried frantically to close his eyes, so he wouldn't be able to see where he was going, or find his prey. But his eyes, no more than his legs and arms, refused to obey him. In his anger and frustration he tried to scream, but he could neither say nor do anything that was not permitted. Anything that was of his own will was prevented. Only Usseis's desire was allowed.

And so, outwardly purposeful but inwardly desperate, Reiffen watched himself hunt for Molio through the caves and tunnels of Ussene. It wasn't hard to find him. All the time he had spent with the little man gave him a good idea just where Molio might be, and he soon found him setting new candles out on their holders in one of the corridors near the officers' mess.

"Molio," said Reiffen's voice cunningly, even as the rest of him tried to cry out in warning. "Come with me. I have something to show you."

"Something to show Molio, sir?" The little man's eyes brightened eagerly. Maybe his friend had recovered from his sadness, and would be the way he had been before. "Something for Molio, sir?"

"Yes," said Reiffen. "Something for Molio."

But inside his head Reiffen was screaming, No! No! No! and trying as hard as he could to get his body to do what he wanted. But Molio could see nothing wrong, and trotted along happily behind his friend. No one had ever wanted Molio to see anything before. This was going to be a special day.

Reiffen led the way through the halls to the long passage that led to the Front Window.

"Are we going to the Front Window, sir?" asked Molio with some fearfulness. "No soldiers there?"

"No, Molio. There won't be any soldiers there."

"Is that where the thing is, sir? The thing you want to show Molio?" The little man's eyes glowed. His look reminded Reiffen of the time he had teased Skimmer with the lumps of maple sugar back in the canoe near Nokken Rock. But this time what he would do was far worse.

"Yes, Molio," he said. He tried, once more without success, to bite his tongue. "That's where it is."

Molio bounded up the stair. Reiffen had never seen him so happy and excited. The little man raced ahead, then thought better of it as they approached the windowed room. It was broad daylight outside, and the soft gray light spilled forward down the corridor through the Window. But Molio's instinctive caution had returned, and he let Reiffen pass on ahead of him before he followed.

Reiffen went straight to the Window.

"Is this what Molio is supposed to see, sir?" asked the little man, as if the Window itself was the most extraordinary thing he had ever beheld, now that Reiffen had taken such pains to show it to him. "It is beautiful, sir." The little man caught his breath with joy.

"No, Molio," said the false Reiffen. Inside he wanted to curl up into a ball and die. "It's outside. Come and see."

Molio, trusting his friend completely, scurried across the room. He put his small hands on the sill and stood on tiptoe to look out like a little child. "Where, sir? What is Molio looking for, sir?" he asked expectantly.

"Here," said Reiffen. "Just below the Window on the other side."

"Is it birdies, sir?" asked the little man. He scrabbled at the wall in his haste to climb onto the sill. "Molio's never seen birdies, sir. I hope it's birdies!"

"Let me help you."

He seized the little man by the back of his tattered coat and, instead of helping him safely up into the Window, pushed him over the edge. Only as he began to fall did Molio even begin to sense his danger. He trusted his friend completely. "Sir!" he cried out. "Sir! I'm falling!" And then his shriek trailed off as he sailed out into the narrow slice of sky between the jagged cliffs. He weighed no more than a bird himself and Reiffen was able to fling him far beyond the Window. Even so the little man struck the face of the cliff several times before he hit the bottom, his short arms and legs waving frantically as he rolled and spun through the air. The false Reiffen made himself lean far out over the edge of the Window to watch the entire fall, and to hear Molio's piteous cries. One glance had Reiffen of the little man's face before Molio was gone, and in that moment the boy saw all the hurt and sorrow that had ever befallen his friend. Molio's small eyes glistened mournfully. His wretched life was complete. Then he was gone, like a stone dropped into the lake from the top of the Neck.

Reiffen tried to tear himself away from the Window; he tried to close his eyes. But he still had no control over himself. Only at the very end, when Molio had landed soundlessly on the ground so far below, and the guards at the Front Gate had emerged to see what had happened and were pointing upward as they clustered in the courtyard, was the boy finally able to throw himself back into the room.

He shuddered. He moaned. He rolled in his misery along the dusty floor until he was filthy with tears and dirt. For a long time he was not himself, so complete was the shame of what he had done. It was his own mind that had tricked and cheated Molio. Usseis had given him no instruction. His only command had been to kill the little man. Reiffen had conceived the rest. From his own heart had come the means of the little man's dying. Reiffen had known Molio would follow him blindly to the Window and never even try to save himself. Reiffen was his friend. And the knowledge that he could do such a thing left the boy trembling on the floor. A cold wind from the Window scoured the room around him.

It was a long time before he came to his senses. And when he did his first thought was to throw himself after Molio. But, as he raced to the Window, he felt Usseis's hand upon him once more and his body stopped short of his purpose. And then he knew there was no escape for him, and wept bitterly again. Only this time his weeping led to exhaustion as well as despair.

He awoke in darkness. For a long time he lay on the floor, forgetting where he was and everything that had happened. Then he felt the chill breeze from the Window and remembered it all. He tried to cry again, but there was nothing left.

Something whispered softly. Reiffen started, thinking Molio's ghost had risen from the stony depths to creep back into the fortress and haunt him. Then he felt the wetness in the breeze and realized he was hearing rain beyond the window. The pattering drops were soothing; it wasn't long before he had fallen asleep again. He was young, and nightmares were still only dreams to him, dreams that could be forgotten, if only for a little while. For a long time he slept, troubled only by the nagging at the back of his imagination that, when he woke, there would be an uncertain price left for him to pay.

When he did wake the rain had stopped. A clear dawn filtered through the Front Window, leaving a soft square of light upon the hard stone floor. Wearily he rose. His entire body ached, as if he had spent the previous day slaving away in the stables or being taught how to wrestle by Redburr. And he was still very tired despite having slept the better part of the previous day and night.

He was completely beaten. There was nothing left within him with which to fight the Three any longer. He felt withered and unclean. Without even thinking about where he was going, he wandered off from the Front Room and back into the main parts of the fortress. For hours he wandered aimlessly, barely even noticing the guards.

In the end he found himself at the Library door. He had known he would come here eventually. For a moment he stood reluctantly outside. He really didn't want to go into the Library now. That was a change from the way he had been before, because before he had always fought with himself to stay away. Now that he had no other choice, the itch no longer plagued him. Maybe some other day he would be able to take up the struggle again. Now he lacked the strength. There was no fear. His hand didn't even tremble as he twisted the iron knob and passed inside, to the books and the spider and the stone.

USSENE

Ossdonc, Ossdonc
Cut off his arm
If his sword can't touch you
He'll do you no harm.

Usseis, Usseis
Cut off his head
If his spells aren't spoken
Then he'll soon be dead.

Fornoch, Fornoch
Cut out his heart
Hold on to your own or
He'll get a new start.

—WAYLAND NURSERY RHYME

14

Balloons Below Bryddlough

Ferris never did figure out how long she and Avender slept. Without any morning to wake them, they might have snoozed away the week. But Redburr, once the smells drifting up through the window from Mother Norra's kitchen grew too powerful to ignore, roused everyone in plenty of time for breakfast.

Uhle and Nolo were waiting at the table when the Shaper and the children came downstairs. "Back to his stonework," Nolo replied when Ferris asked where Dwvon had gone. The table before them was spread with large platters of scrambled eggs, mushrooms, bacon, and small fish called swippers that Redburr said were delicious. Both Bryddin were already hard at work at the meal, and the Shaper, in his haste to join them, nearly knocked over Mother Norra as she bustled to the table with a pitcher of clear, cold water from the Issin.

"Pickles and pike," she scolded. "You're worse than a small child."

"Sorry," mumbled Redburr, looking scared to death she might decide to punish him by keeping him away from the food. He sidled carefully out of her way towards the table.

"Those eggs look delicious," said Ferris, half out of politeness and half to help Redburr escape his predicament. And they really were, she discovered, as soon as she joined the Bryddin at the table, with a rich flavor she had never tasted before.

"Aren't they, lamb," fussed the cook, one eye fastened on Redburr. "Our flickers are as good as any in Issinlough."

"Flickers?"

"A large lizard," said Nolo. Bits of egg covered the front of his beard. "They like to nest in small caves at the top of unnerets."

"Very tasty roasted," added Redburr through his own mouthful. "Taste like chicken."

Ferris stared horrified at her plate. "You mean I'm eating lizard eggs?"

"I'll have yours." With great relish Avender shoveled the last of his portion into his mouth. "Why're they called flickers?"

"Because they have long tongues," said Uhle, "that flick out all the time to taste the cave around them. They don't have eyes at all."

Ferris shuddered and pushed her plate away completely. She decided not to eat the bacon, either. Who knew what pigs dined on in Issinlough? But it was hard not to eat in front of Mother Norra, who saw what was wrong at once. Before Ferris knew what was happening, the kind woman had placed a fresh plate in front of her, piled high with a stack of griddle cakes topped with rich black jam. Redburr looked on enviously.

"No butter or syrup, though, dear," said Mother Norra as Ferris tucked into her new meal. "I've been after Mr. Dwvon you don't know how long to trade a few of those lamps of his for a cask of fine Valing syrup. Maybe you can bring some along with you, next time you come to Issinlough. I do miss a good maple syrup. And the candy! Biscuits and butter! I remember there was one goodwife on the lake who made the best—"

"Speaking of lamps." Uhle set a pair of small pouches on the table before the children. "I have something for you. Ferris. Avender. You're children of the sun and moon, used to the light. You're not

used to the darkness of the Under Ground. So, to help light your
way through Bryddlough, I've brought a lamp for each of you."

He emptied the pouches on the table. Out clattered a pair of
bright, glowing jewels. Shadow and light danced around the walls as
the gems rolled to a stop. Precious they were, and more specially
precious as gifts than for their worth. Ferris curtsied properly, and
made a pretty speech of thanks before she reached out to take one
of the shining stones. In her hand it felt exactly like any other rock:
hard and cold. No heat accompanied the glowing brightness; the
sharp points of the gem pricked her fingertip as she rolled it back
and forth upon her palm.

Avender, who had never owned anything more valuable than a
pair of boots before, could only stammer and stare at the brilliance
in his hand.

"Even Bryddin need light in Bryddlough," said Uhle. "Set your
lamps on the rock beside you and you'll see most caverns well
enough. But I could make you some small headbands, if you want."

"I'd put them on walking sticks," suggested Redburr as he
picked through the bones for any final scraps of fish.

"Whatever you do, don't lose them." Nolo took Avender's and
studied it at arm's length. The gem wasn't terribly bright, but it still
wasn't something Ferris wanted to bring up close to her eye. "You
could buy two or three farms in Bracken Creek with one of these,"
he added as he returned it to the boy. "Not to mention every barrel
of maple syrup in Valing."

They thanked Uhle again; then breakfast was over and it was
time to go. Mother Norra gave both children huge, smothering
hugs when they said good-bye, as if she were trying to squeeze the
food back out of them, and wiped her eyes with the corner of her
apron. "We could use a few more young 'uns down here," she
sniffed. "Brighten the place up considerable, it would."

Ferris was sad to leave; in Mother Norra's kitchen she had felt
she was home again. Now the strangeness of the Stoneways would
be all the keener for their having rested in a place that reminded her

so much of Valing, flickers or no. And it might be a long time before she got another bath. Shouldering her pack, she followed Avender and the others outside to the winding stair.

They followed Nolo up the Rupiniah and across another footpath to the Halvanankh, the lone relic of the old, wild cave that had been all the beauty in Issinlough before the Bryddin began to build. Up a circling stair cut from the rough rock itself they climbed, back into the bedrock above. Now and again a window opened along their path to give a moment's view of the city below, allowing the bottom of the world to loom once again in a patchwork of shadow and stone. But most of the time they traveled through smoothly carved tunnels that ran straight as a diamond's edge through the rock, or turned in the sort of perfect curves that only Bryddin could fashion.

Grimble's workshop was some distance from the main city, beyond the rim of the Veils. Nolo explained that the experiments performed there were of such a kind that both Grimble and all the other Bryddin preferred it that way. Unexpected explosions and sudden stinks were best tolerated as far as possible from the city proper. As it was, the travelers heard the workshop long before they reached it, and smelled it only a little later. Even by Bryddin standards the thumps and booms that echoed along the passage were exceptional, and the sulfurous smell was something entirely new. It reminded Ferris of freshly manured fields—or the same fields shortly after being burned. Neither were odors she had ever expected to find underground.

Odor and noise both worsened the moment the company entered the workshop. Here they found another large chamber, so filled with machinery and jumbled equipment that the far end was completely lost to view. Coils of wire wound among piles of tanned animal hides, bolts of canvas and large barrels rose in tall towers to the ceiling, and thick metal pipes strangled everything in their looping grip like untended vines. Here lay a stack of wooden planks discarded on the floor, there a forgotten pile of pig bladders. Through it all boomed the sound of metal being hammered and bent, the roar of the furnaces along the right-hand wall, and the hiss of air rushing through the throbbing pipes.

They threaded their way through this jungle of junk, stepping over the odd hammer or broken barrel stave, until they finally arrived at the end of the cavern. Where the back wall was supposed to be, they instead found themselves facing out into the Abyss. A large ship floated in the darkness just beyond the edge of the floor, like a great, fat fish in an inky pool.

"Is that the balloon?" asked Ferris. Nolo nodded. "What holds it up?"

"Nothing holds it up," answered the Dwarf. "It's an airship."

"An airship? What's an airship?" Ferris gasped as she figured out the answer to her own question. "You mean we're going to fly?"

Nolo nodded. Ferris gaped at the floating vessel. Dozens of questions rushed to her head, but she couldn't find her tongue to ask a single one. The idea of flying was too enormous, and too exciting, to allow anything so commonplace as talking to get in the way.

"Lucky us," grumbled the Shaper as he stood beside her.

Avender whispered to Ferris as they followed Nolo forward, "Aren't you even a little scared? What if we fall?"

Ferris shook her head. Falling was the furthest thing from her mind. Rather, she was entranced by the thought of flying through the air like a bird. Or a cloud.

Heavy cables, moored to large stone cleats set into the workshop floor, held the craft down. Men and Dwarves scurried about, busy with last-minute tasks. The vessel was much larger than *The Other Side;* instead of wood it was built of canvas stretched around some sort of frame. A pair of short, stubby fins ran along either side. Several of the metal pipes the company had clambered past in the workshop snaked into the vessel just below the fin facing them, their far ends connected to the blazing furnaces along the wall.

Waves of heat rolled across the room from the forges, over the edge of the workshop, and into the darkness beyond.

On the narrow part of the vessel's tail a Dwarf was making some last-minute adjustments to a large metal pinwheel mounted close to the main body of the ship. He finished his work as the company arrived and set the wheel slowly spinning with a push of his hand. Then he noticed the new arrivals.

"There you are." Nimbly, the Dwarf stepped between two of the spinning blades and inspected them from another angle. "You'd better get on board," he called over his shoulder. "We've been waiting for you so we can leave."

He waved them toward the ropes that looped around the canvas hull and indicated they should use these to climb aboard. Ferris drew close to Nolo.

"Is that Grimble?" she whispered, finding her tongue once more.

"No," said Nolo. "That's Gammit."

"Isn't Grimble the one in charge?"

"Grimble?" Nolo cocked an eyebrow at her in surprise. "No one would go anywhere with Grimble in charge."

"You should have explained to them about Grimble," said Redburr as he came up beside them.

"They'll find out soon enough." Nolo grasped one of the ropes firmly and led the way up the side.

Wondering what it was that was so mysterious about Grimble, Ferris followed. The ship dipped slightly under their weight as they left the ground, especially when the Shaper pulled himself aboard; but it settled gently back toward the roof once it had adjusted to its new load. Its moorings stretched tautly. The rough canvas throbbed and thrummed beneath their hands with the force of whatever was being pumped inside.

At the top of the curving hull they found a small deck set below the level of the canvas. Standing there was a Bryddin with snow-white hair. Ferris had seen Bryddin with black and brown and gray hair, but this was the first time she had seen one whose hair was white. He wore a long-sleeved smock covered with pockets: the smock would have been almost as white as his hair had it not needed a good laundering.

He paid no attention to Ferris or anyone else as they came up to the top of the ship, and made no room for them in the crowded cockpit beside him. Instead he stared closely at a piece of paper he held in his hands. After considering it for a moment, he held it out at arm's length in front of his face and dropped it. It twirled lightly through the air, a spinning child's toy revolving beneath a pair of paper wings, and landed on the metal deck like a wilted flower.

Nolo pushed into the cockpit beside him. "Hello, Grimble," he said. "Still working at flying, I see. Guess we'll see how your airship works soon enough."

"Hmm?" Grimble looked up distractedly from his toy. "What's that? Airship? Oh, yes. We're on it now."

He stooped and picked up his paper plaything. For a moment it looked as if he had already forgotten that Nolo had spoken to him. Then he looked back up. "Hello, Nolo," he said. "Who are your friends?"

The rest of the company crowded down onto the deck beside the Bryddin and were introduced to the inventor. For a moment he seemed almost ordinary, bowing to each of them in the proper fashion, and shaking their hands as well. But it soon became clear he had absolutely no idea why they were there. "Come for a voyage, have you?" he asked. His white eyebrows, as bushy as Nolo's, narrowed in confusion. "I didn't know there was going to be a voyage."

"Yes, you did." Gammit clambered up along the ropes from the stern to join them. "We're on our way to Cammas."

"Ahh. Cammas." A look of understanding crossed Grimble's face. "Are we going to study the fungi?"

"Not this time," said Gammit.

Grimble nodded, though Ferris saw quite plainly that the white-haired Bryddin still had no idea what was going on as he sat down on the edge of the cockpit. Although the vessel was large, there was little room on the narrow deck for them all, especially when one of them was Redburr. Much of the space was taken up by large sacks filled with stones and jammed in along the sides of the platform. Below them the inside of the ship was crammed with many large, bulging bags, the nearest visible through the grated decking at their feet.

"What are those for?" asked Ferris, getting down on her knees to poke at one with her finger. The rough canvas felt as hard as a Dwarf's skin.

Gammit glanced cautiously at Nolo.

"It's okay," said Nolo. "They're not going to give away any secrets."

Gammit appeared unconvinced, and gave Ferris a narrow look. "They're what keep us from falling," he said.

"How do they do that?"

"That gas pumping into them is lighter than air," Nolo explained despite Gammit's continued frown. "Gammit makes it in the furnaces."

"Lighter than air? How can anything be lighter than air?"

"Why shouldn't something be lighter than air?" asked Grimble, suddenly joining the conversation. His eyes brightened as they focused for the first time on the children. "Air's lighter than water, isn't it? And water's lighter than rock. It only stands to reason that something should be lighter than air."

"Nothing has to be lighter than air—" began Ferris, but Grimble interrupted her immediately.

"Exactly." His paper toy fluttered unnoticed to the ground as he turned completely to this new interest. "Nothing is lighter than air. Nothing is lighter than anything."

"But air *is* nothing," insisted Ferris.

"That's where you're wrong." Grimble wagged a finger at her. "If you blow into an empty wineskin it fills up, doesn't it? Well, if air was nothing, then the wineskin wouldn't get bigger, would it? But it does. The fact is, there are all sorts of things in air, even if you can't see them. Once you separate out the different parts you can discover a lot."

"All right, all right." Gammit raised his hands to interrupt them. "That's enough for now, Grimble. You'll have plenty of time to give away your secrets on the voyage. Right now we have to leave. We're supposed to be in a hurry, remember?" He looked to Nolo as he added this last remark, and Nolo nodded in agreement.

Cupping his hands to his mouth, Gammit bent over the side toward the workshop and shouted loudly, "All right! Shut off number two! Shut off number two, I say!"

The bags in the hold ceased their trembling. The pipes were pulled free of the ship with a slight popping sound and the open section of canvas closed. Grimble and Gammit climbed out on either side of the hull, while Nolo and the others settled themselves as comfortably as they could on the cramped deck. No matter how Redburr arranged himself, it seemed something was always poking him somewhere, or he was poking someone else.

"That's my shin you've put your pack on."

"Sorry."

"Watch your elbows!"

"I'm trying. There's no room!"

Gammit looked across the cockpit at Grimble. The white-haired Bryddin lay on his back on the hull, his feet in the air. "You remember what to do?" Gammit asked.

"Yes."

Gammit turned and gave a last shout back down to the workshop. "Okay, that's it! Cast off there! We're set to go!"

Ferris held her breath. Bryddin and humans bent to the cleats on the floor below and soon the ship was untied. Almost at once she felt a slight heaviness, and her knees flexed. She looked down and saw the ropes that held the vessel slither serpent-like away from the sides. Slowly the workshop seemed to fall away. Or rather the ship began to rise. Above her, the stone roof descended steadily.

"Watch your heads," warned Nolo.

On the other side of the cockpit, Gammit lay down on his back in the same manner as Grimble. Together they caught the stone roof with their feet as the ship drifted upward. Their legs flexed against the stone, and the ship stopped rising.

"Too much gas," said Nolo.

Gammit gave him a dirty look. "I told Grimble the humans wouldn't be so heavy."

He turned back to Grimble. "Steady there. Let's walk it out till we balance."

They started to push the airship forward across the ceiling. Left foot, right foot: they marched the ship ahead. It was the strangest sight, two Bryddin strolling along with the bulk of their ship beneath their backs and the weight of the world above their feet. Ferris smiled. Only in Bryddlough, she thought, would anyone ever have to work hard to keep from falling up.

"That's better," said Gammit when they had gone so far that he and Grimble were tiptoeing along the ceiling. They rested in shadow, now that the bulk of the airship was between them and the light from the workshop window. The weight of the ship was perfectly balanced now, and the craft had ceased to rise.

"Nolo, I need you to come below and give me a hand with the engine." As Gammit spoke he rolled into the cockpit and disappeared through a small opening beneath the canvas toward the stern. Nolo followed him after a moment, wiggling past the bulging bags.

They left the airship hovering silently just below the world. Grimble remained lying on his back as if he were sleeping. On closer inspection, Ferris found he was actually studying the rocks in the roof above. Redburr pulled himself up off the floor and sat on the edge of the hull, where he had more room. They rested in cool twilight, for the ship was blocking the furnace heat as well as the light.

"A little light would be nice," said the Shaper from the gloom.

It took a moment for Avender and Ferris to catch his meaning. Then they fished through their packs for the lamps that Uhle had given them. The light from the two small gems was just strong enough to lend a glow to their faces and deepen the shadows on the ceiling above. Grimble gave his head a shake as the light washed across him, as if he had needed a reminder of where he was. A moment later he had rejoined them in the cockpit. From one of the many pockets in his smock he pulled a thin spyglass, and snapped it open. Putting it to his eye, he surveyed the darkness around the ship.

A series of loud clanks rang out from below, followed by a low hum. Beneath them the airship started to shake gently.

"I think we've begun to move," said Redburr.

The children looked up. The ceiling slid slowly past their heads, though they felt no motion at all. It rose away from them as well, soon to vanish beyond the meager glow of the lamplight. Ferris thrilled at the notion they were flying through the air like a butterfly or a bird. A soft breeze sprang up against her face as they glided forward, growing in strength as their pace quickened.

Avender held on carefully to the side of the cockpit and looked over the curving side. "What's making us move?" he asked.

Redburr looked to see if Grimble was going to answer the question, but the white-haired Bryddin was still patrolling the empty sky with his telescope.

"It's the propeller," said the Shaper, when he saw that any explanation would be left up to him.

"What's a propeller?"

Redburr poked a thumb back toward the stern. "That large wheel Gammit was working on when we arrived. It's like a giant screw. When it turns it pushes the ship through the air."

The workshop reappeared behind them as the Shaper spoke, its large window a bright, golden brick in the darkness. Already they were farther away than Ferris would have thought. The short figures of Bryddin and the taller ones of humans stood waving at them from the edge. The window dwindled from a golden stone to a glimmering eye, and the waving people to small specks within. Before it winked out altogether, a new and much brighter set of lights emerged behind it. The airship had descended far enough to clear the ledge of rock that hung between Issinlough and Grimble's workshop, and now the suspended city appeared sparkling in the darkness beyond. It looked like nothing so much as one of the massive chandeliers from the Great Hall at the Manor in Valing, though of far finer fashioning. Its slender towers and silvery pathways glistened against the empty night.

"Why's it shimmering?" asked Ferris.

"I think that's one of the Veils between us and Issinlough," said Redburr. "The Kurren, maybe. Let's hope Gammit can fly this thing well enough that we don't go ramming into it. Or any of the other Veils."

Around them the darkness thickened. Ferris's eyes glittered as the ship circled the shining city and its curtain of flickering falls. Like a great fish in the depths of an empty ocean, the airship burrowed onward through the Abyss, north toward Cammas.

When the city had shrunk to the size of a single bright star hanging low in the sky astern, Nolo poked his head up from below and called for Avender and Ferris to come down for a tour of the ship. Redburr was too large to squeeze along with them through the narrow passageways in the hold, so he took the opportunity to stretch out on the deck in solitary comfort instead. Grimble, with his spyglass still glued to his eye, hardly counted as company.

Though they were thinner than the Dwarf, the two children had a hard time following him through the narrow tunnel to the airship's stern. He wormed his way down, slithering between gasbags and metal girders, while the children behind him felt so tightly packed they could barely breathe. The humming grew louder as they descended, and the gasbags throbbed more and more, until at last they tumbled out of the snug passage into a small cabin at the very stern. There they found Gammit hard at work pumping a large two-handled crank. Behind him the gears and flywheels of a complicated engine rattled and whirred.

"Beautiful, isn't it," said Nolo admiringly. He stood on the metal deck with his legs spread sturdily and his hands on his hips as he studied the mechanism before him. Gammit huffed and puffed as he worked the heavy crank, his mustache fluttering with every breath. But he was a Bryddin, and would be able to turn that crank a long time before he grew tired.

"It'll be your turn again soon," said Gammit to Nolo. Gammit's beard flew up and down as it caught the handle in front of him with every stroke. "I'll have to look to the ship soon. But only one of us needs to work the engine now we've got our speed up."

"Maybe we can help," offered Avender.

Gammit looked to Nolo, who shrugged and grinned. "All right, then," said Gammit. "Have a try."

He stepped back from the crank, which pumped on without him, the flywheels still turning. Avender, sure of his own strength, stepped forward. Ferris didn't like Nolo's grin. Obviously he expected Avender not to be able to master the mechanism at all.

The boy spat on his hands and rubbed them together before reaching for the nearest end of the crank. Catching his fingers on the upswing, the bar pulled him swiftly forward. Up and down it swung, his arms jerking uselessly behind. Avender could barely keep up, let alone add any push of his own. He might as well have had the largest pike in Valing running out his line in the deepest part of the lake, for all he was able to control the crank in any way. He let go of the bar and pulled back his arms, an embarrassed look reddening his face.

"Don't worry, lad." Still grinning, Nolo gave him a friendly pat on the shoulder. "There's not a man in Valing could work that lever for more than a minute or so. It's built for Bryddin strength."

"You might have warned him," said Ferris crossly. She checked to see if Avender had hurt his hands or arms, but the only thing injured was Avender's pride.

Gammit resumed his post at the engine, a large grin cracking his granite beard. "That's all right," he said. "At least you took a try. But if you want to lend a hand, go on forward and turn on the bow lamp. I'm sure Grimble's forgotten to do it."

Nolo led Ferris and Avender off along another tight passage through the middle of the vessel. In a second small chamber in the bow they discovered a large cabinet with a handle on the side. The handle clicked once when Nolo pulled it, but nothing else happened. The Dwarf, however, seemed confident he had accomplished something, and led them back to the top of the ship. There they found a broad beam of light shining from the bow, its hollow glow swallowed by the darkness. Grimble was staring transfixed into its pale gleam, but the fan of cold light revealed nothing. Not even a mistrin flew out of that long night under stone.

"You two keep a lookout up here," said Nolo. "We don't want to go crashing into some ankh in the darkness. Call us down below if you see anything. When you get tired, wake up Redburr and make him relieve you."

"What about Grimble?" asked Ferris. The white-haired Bryddin hadn't moved since they had come back on deck, and was still staring into the empty beam of light.

Nolo shrugged. "Even if he saw we were about to crash, he'd probably be more interested in watching than stopping it."

Slowly the hours passed. Issinlough's single star faded behind them. The initial excitement of flying dampened as the children realized the trip would be made in darkness. In every direction the void was the same: thick as a blanket and twice as stifling. There was no way to tell how fast they were going or where they were. Somewhere overhead the world hung in heavy ridges of stone, but whether it was six fathoms above or six hundred was impossible to know.

Below lay nothing at all.

Deep he sleeps
With breath unbidden.

Late in her watch, Ferris remembered the words of Dwvon's song. She leaned out over the side, but the curve of the airship prevented her from being able to see straight down. Not that she supposed straight down would look any different from forward or backward, or left or right. How deep did the Abyss go? Was there really no bottom?

"Do you think he's still down there?" she asked, nudging Avender with her elbow.

"Who?" A look of understanding crossed Avender's face as he followed her glance. "The Bryddin think so."

"Do you think he knows we're here?"

"He's supposed to be sleeping."

"I wonder." Ferris leaned out again, but the view below hadn't changed. "Do you think we could fly deep enough to find him?"

Avender shrugged. "Even if we could, we don't have time to find out now."

With a twinge of guilt, Ferris turned away from the dark deep. It had been too long since she had thought about Reiffen. Locked away in the dungeons of Ussene, any darkness he faced was sure to be much more horrible than this. The Abyss was mysterious but empty; the fortress of the Three was most likely filled with horrors. She shivered and pulled her cloak closer about her shoulders, but she was feeling more than cold.

The sound of scraping made Ferris turn back to the side of the ship. Gammit scrambled up into view, clambering around the vessel's skin like a squirrel on the trunk of a tree as he inspected the ropes and canvas. Redburr stirred in his sleep and rubbed his nose. To take her mind off Reiffen, Ferris asked Gammit what the ship was called.

"Called?" he repeated testily. "It's an airship. You'd think you'd be able to see that yourself, even if you are a human."

"I can see it's an airship," said Ferris reasonably. She had grown used to Gammit's irritability. "But it ought to have a name. You and Grimble have names. Why shouldn't your ship?"

The Bryddin glared at her, his beard blowing back over his shoulder in the wind. Having no answer for her question, and to show he had no more time for such human nonsense anyway, he dropped back down out of sight over the side.

"I still think it should have a name," grumbled Ferris.

"Then give it one." Redburr, who wasn't sleeping as soundly as she thought, opened one of his small eyes.

"All right." Ferris thought for a moment. "How about *Nightship*?" she suggested.

The Shaper shook his head. "Too gloomy."

"What about *Floater*?" said Avender, who was still keeping a lookout ahead.

"That's just boring," scoffed Ferris.

"If it was up to me," offered Redburr, "I'd call it the *Airfish*. It looks like a fish, after all, but there's not much eating in it."

They were still trying to come up with a name when Nolo rejoined them. Except for an occasional deep breath, he showed little sign of having worked the engine with Gammit for hours and hours. Under his arm he carried a large bundle. Redburr's nose twitched and his other eye opened as soon as he caught sight of what the Dwarf was holding. A moment later the Shaper was up off the deck and lumbering forward.

"Hold fast there, friend," said the Dwarf. "You'll get your share, same as the rest."

He unfolded the bundle and spread the contents out on the deck. Mother Norra had sent them boiled eggs (clearly marked "chicken"), cold ham, and large slices of broiled mushroom that tasted almost like roast beef. To drink she had packed both ale and a sweet mushroom cider. They leaned against the side of the canvas hull as they ate, munching hungrily as they watched for any sign of danger in the darkness around them.

"Now if we just had some wood for a fire," said Redburr contentedly, his mouth full of ham. "Then this voyage might almost become enjoyable."

"No fires," said Nolo emphatically.

"A fire would be nice," said Ferris, rubbing her shoulders. "It's cold down here."

"No fires," repeated Nolo. "Not on this ship. We'd go up in smoke at the first spark. The gas in the bags doesn't mix with fire at all."

"Then you should've had Mother Norra pack more beer." Redburr drained the last drop from his bottle, and brought it up to his eye to make sure he had missed nothing. "Then at least our bellies might stay warm."

"There isn't enough beer in all Issinlough to keep your belly warm."

"True."

They argued some more about what to name the airship and, after a great deal of discussion, finally decided on *Nightfish*. Ferris thought the name fit perfectly: she imagined the ship as a great pike sliding slowly through the darkness, its bright nose cleaving the way. But then she was the one who came up with the name.

Redburr took over the watch after the meal. The children tried to rest, but, unlike the Shaper, they found it difficult to sleep with the deck thrumming steadily against their cheeks and bags of rocks poking them in the back. They dozed fitfully, their shallow dreams filled with long falls and hissing manders. Finally they gave up the attempt completely and went back to watching the emptiness surrounding them. At least if they were awake they would be able to tell if any of their bad dreams actually came true.

Ferris knew they were getting close to their destination when the breeze began to soften against her cheeks; the airship was slowing down. A few more minutes passed; then Nolo came up from below with a lamp glowing at the end of a long pole. He raised the light into the darkness above their heads, looking for the bottom of the world. But all he found was the same smothering night that had covered them for most of their journey.

Ferris pulled at his sleeve. "What are we looking for?" she asked.

"Bryddlough," replied the Dwarf.

"Are we lost?" asked Avender.

"No. We know about where we are. It's just a matter of finding the roof again to get our bearings."

The ship throbbed steadily below their feet. A few light drops of rain fell against their cheeks. Nolo looked upward in surprise. Redburr twitched in his sleep and brushed at his nose.

"Did I just feel—," began Ferris.

Nolo cut her off with a shout. "Get below!" Thrusting the lamp back into the ship, he pulled Grimble down into the cockpit beside him. Then he grabbed the children, who were not moving fast enough to suit him, and pushed them roughly ahead into the narrow passage astern. The stiff canvas scraped against their faces and the backs of their hands.

"Redburr!"

Nolo held the children down with one hand as he looked back over his shoulder for the Shaper. "Get—!" But the Dwarf's voice was drowned out by a sudden hollow drumming, as if an enormous thunderstorm were bursting over a tent. The airship lurched suddenly down and to the left. Half-awake, Redburr stumbled to his feet, then rolled over the side of the cockpit and disappeared into the dark.

Ferris screamed.

There was no chance to save him. She tried to rush back outside, but Nolo's grip was hard as stone. He held her tight against the canvas, and Avender as well, not wanting to lose them also. Ferris sobbed as the *Nightfish* continued to tip slowly forward. Redburr was gone! The drumming grew louder, louder even than the sound of the gorge below the Tear. Then a wave of icy water washed over them, seeming to have sprung from nowhere, and the *Nightfish* rolled forward on its nose. The ship began to fall.

Wind and water raced around them. Ferris choked and spluttered as the cold river tried to drag her back outside. Her stomach lurched as the sensation of falling grew. Desperately she clung to the rough canvas to keep some sense of direction. Both she and Avender would have followed Redburr overboard had Nolo not kept tight hold of them. As it was, she thought she was going to drown anyway. The great wave seemed to never end, and was bitter cold. She felt the ache of it in her bones.

And then it was over, or at least the drowning cold. But the awful feeling of not having any weight remained. Ferris coughed the last of the water out of her mouth and clung to the side of the taut balloon. The wind roared past, as if they were flying through a blasting gale.

"Nolo!" she shouted, as soon as she could speak.

"I'm here, lass." His heavy voice sounded close beside her ear. "I've still got you."

She felt his breath upon her shivering cheek and gave a sob of relief. His stony arms still held her tightly against the ship. Avender was still beside her, too. She clung to both of them in the darkness, not wanting to let them go. Avender hugged her back just as hard. Hot tears warmed her cheeks and nose as she remembered the sight of Redburr toppling over the side.

"Remarkable."

Grimble's calm voice sounded oddly normal in the darkness beside them; instead of making her feel better, his composure made Ferris want to scream. Was Grimble completely mad? Didn't he understand what had happened?

Nolo's steadiness was much more reassuring. "Don't worry, lass," he said. "We'll be all right. I think that was the Cammas."

"T-the C-Cammas?" Her fear ebbed under Nolo's reassurance, until her teeth chattered from cold as much as fear. Her clothes were heavy and wet. Avender hiccoughed in the dark.

"The river Cammas," Nolo assured her. "It drains the lake beside the city."

"We flew into a r-river?"

"More like a waterfall," said the Dwarf. "A big one. Like one of the Veils, only larger."

"And we're out of it now?"

"No." Nolo's voice sounded thoughtful. Ferris got ready to be completely scared once more. "I think we're still in the middle of it. Do you feel strangely light? You do? Well, that means we're still falling. It's the same sensation I had that time I was carried over the falls in Valing."

"A very interesting sensation," added Grimble as he crawled up beside them in the dark.

"But what about Redburr?" asked Avender.

"Yes," echoed Ferris, with even more despair. "What about Redburr?"

"I wouldn't worry about him," said Nolo. "He can always turn into a bird, no matter how far he falls. It's not like there's a bottom to worry about smashing into. He'll turn up."

"Then what about us?" Ferris clung tightly to the cold canvas. "We can't turn into birds. What're we going to do?"

"Gammit'll know. It's not as if this sort of thing hasn't happened before. But we ought to go up to the cranklough. That's where Gammit'll be. We still have the ship, even if it's half-full of water. I don't think any of the balloons have burst. We went down too slowly for that."

He tousled Avender's wet hair and gave Ferris another hug. For once the Dwarf's rough hands felt warmer than Ferris's own skin. Being reminded that a long fall was not such a disaster for someone who could turn into a bird had boosted her spirits considerably.

Nolo led them up through the balloons to the stern. The bags changed quickly from wet to dry as the children slithered between them. The warm glow from the lamp in the cranklough emerged like a beacon above their heads. They hurried the last few feet and clambered up into the chamber; the crank hung motionless from the roof. Grimble followed, his hair and beard plastered wetly across his chest and shoulders like the wool on a bedraggled sheep. Everyone clung to some solid part of the ship around them; otherwise their slightest move would send them floating off into the middle of the room.

"I told you the humans wouldn't weigh so much!" accused Gammit as soon as he saw Grimble. "We've been traveling far too fast! And look what happened—we ended up blundering right into the Cammas! One of these days we'll find ourselves in a fix we can't get out of. If you'd listen to someone just once—"

Grimble blinked blankly at his partner, having long since forgotten the issue of how much the humans weighed. He was much more interested in the loose wrenches and other tools floating weightlessly in the air beside him.

Gammit scowled and turned to Nolo. "Do you see what I have to work with?" he demanded. He seemed far less concerned with their predicament than with the fact that Grimble wasn't listening to him. "It's worse than teaching humans."

"I don't think any lasting damage has been done," answered Nolo. "If we can drain the water from the ship we should be able to float back up to Bryddlough."

"I'm not worried about getting back." Gammit glowered again at Grimble, who was completely absorbed with watching one of the wrenches float across the room after he had given it a gentle push. "This isn't half so bad as the time we blew up. But I am starting to get fed up. A nice, quiet firestone mine is starting to look mighty attractive." He grabbed Grimble's floating wrench from the air, which caused the white-haired Bryddin to blink owlishly and look about for something else to do.

"You can look into that after we get flying again," said Nolo. "In the meantime, let's figure out how to get rid of this water."

"Oh, that's easy." Gammit waved the problem aside. "The river'll thin to mist pretty soon. Then all we have to do is lighten the ship and we'll float right back up again. Once we get a little weight back, the water'll empty right out any hole we cut in the bottom."

The Bryddin went back to work with a will, even Grimble. He

and Nolo set to lightening the vessel by tossing overboard some of the stone bags from the cockpit, while Gammit went outside to cut a hole in the bow to let the water drain out. Ferris and Avender were told to stay put in the cranklough and keep out of trouble.

"But what about Redburr?" asked Ferris.

"What about him?" replied Nolo.

"Shouldn't someone go outside and watch for him?"

"He'll find us a lot easier than we'll ever find him. You just stay here where I know you'll be safe in case anything else happens. You can't fall overboard from the inside."

To tell the truth, Ferris was perfectly happy where she was. The Bryddin might be certain about getting back to Bryddlough, but she would feel safer on the inside of the ship until they did. Gradually she and Avender felt their weight return. The floating tools sank softly to the deck; the dark surface of the water began to recede. Loose junk floated in and out of sight as the water swirled away. Gammit came back to the cranklough and followed the cold water downward to check the status of the ship. More and more struts and balloons emerged dripping from the damp: the vessel straightened. The water emptied from the bow, until at last they were rising once more. Other than a couple of spots where the canvas had been torn from the framing, the *Nightfish* was in good shape. As Nolo had thought, none of the balloons or struts had been harmed at all.

When Ferris and Avender were finally allowed back on deck, they found Nolo and Grimble peering upward. There was still no sign of the Shaper. A light mist fell gently around them: the waterfall had thinned considerably from the thick torrent into which they had blundered. Nolo retrieved the lamp he had stashed beneath the hull and mounted it at the front of the cockpit. A good many of the stone bags were gone, which made the space far roomier than it had been before.

"What about Redburr?" asked Ferris. "Have you found him?"

Nolo shook his head. "Not a sign. But don't worry. He'll turn up soon enough."

They were a lot longer floating up than they had been tumbling down. Gammit made Grimble work the crank with him while Nolo directed their ascent from above. The first thing he did was take the ship out of the mist and order the children in among the gasbags to relay his instructions to the stern. In great circles the *Nightfish* climbed upward around the thickening column of water. Now and again they caught sight of the stream in the light of the bow lamp. So clear and fine was the flow, nearly invisible in the darkness, that it was no wonder they had missed it before.

Finally the ship's light caught the rock of the world above. Nolo called down for Gammit and Grimble to stop cranking and level off their flight. Soon they were cruising slowly along the bottom of the world. Not far away the Cammas gushed mightily from the rock like rain from the bottom of a waterspout. Carefully Nolo marked their position from the falls, then shouted directions to those below until the vessel was finally stopped a stone's throw from the edge of the river.

They floated the last few fathoms upward to the rock. Shadows skittered across the bottom of the world as they rose. One of the darker spots separated from the others: the *Nightfish* approached a low ledge that hung like a balcony from a raised portion of the rock. Gammit and Nolo caught the roof with their hands, their fingers digging into the hard stone. Grimble, as usual, had found something in the rock to distract him, and had completely forgotten he was supposed to help out. The airship swayed slightly, then settled to a stop. The two Bryddin stood with their legs and arms flexed on the top of the hull, keeping the craft from rising all the way up against the rock.

"All right, Nolo," grumbled Gammit. "I don't want to stand here all day. Get your gear together and move on."

"Thanks for the lift."

"Very funny," replied Gammit with a scowl.

"What about Redburr?" asked Ferris as she and Avender shouldered their packs. "We can't just leave him behind."

"He knows where we're going," said Nolo. "But you're right. He should have been here by now. I thought the ship's light would be easy for him to find."

"Well, I'm not going looking for him, if that's what you want," said Gammit.

Nolo tugged thoughtfully at his beard. "You go on," he said. "We'll wait up here on the ledge. He should be able to see our lamps." But Ferris didn't think Nolo was as confident as he tried to sound, and was worried that something might have happened to cause the Shaper to get lost in the darkness. She began to worry herself. What if Redburr had hit his head on something as he fell and never seen the light from the ship?

She peered down into the deep black night as Nolo helped her scramble up onto the dark ledge, but there was no sign of anything but the *Nightfish* in the darkness. Avender followed, catching Nolo's pack as the Dwarf tossed it up after them. Worried though she was about Redburr, Ferris still let out a long sigh as she felt rough rock beneath her feet once more. Flying was not something she was eager to try again, even if it had come out all right in the end.

Nolo climbed up beside them. They called down their thanks to Gammit and Grimble. Grimble wasn't paying attention, and Gammit only snorted in return. Then he called out to the inventor to take his place fending the ship off the stone, and crawled back down to the cranklough.

"Make sure you come visit us in Valing sometime," called Ferris. "Maybe we can build a balloon up there."

But Grimble had already focused on something in the stone and ignored her invitation.

The ship had started to thrum once more and was just beginning to move away from the ledge when a large black shadow flew out of the darkness to cling to the ceiling of the cave. Avender and Ferris both started in surprise, but Nolo only sighed with relief.

"What took you so long?" he asked the large, fat bat that hung from the roof in front of him. "The children were getting worried."

"I was eating," squeaked the bat. His pink tongue flicked out across his ugly nose. "The moths are fat and juicy down here, and they like that light in front of the ship. I got hungry waiting for you, so I thought I'd have a little snack."

"You might at least have told us you were all right," said Ferris.

"I'm here, aren't I? If I'd wanted, I could have flown all the way to Cammas and had myself a proper meal. Consider yourselves lucky I stayed."

Redburr made a very large bat, and seemed even less capable of flight than he did as a bird. But his wings were wide and even the soft glow of the children's lamps showed ghostly through the thin skin as the Shaper flapped them.

"Pretty good, eh?" he said. "I've never been a bat before. It's not bad."

"I see you lost your pack," said Nolo.

"I did. Lucky there wasn't any food in it."

"Being a bat's perfect for the Stoneways," said Avender.

"It is, isn't it?" agreed the Shaper. "Next time, I'm traveling as a bat all the way. No more balloons for me."

He settled himself upside down on Nolo's pack and, with a slight belch or two, fell asleep. Ferris wanted to smack him. After all the worry he had given her, the least he could do was say he was sorry. She consoled herself by thinking of all the things she would say to him when he woke and followed Nolo up the tunnel toward Cammas. Somewhere, leagues ahead in the stony darkness, Reiffen was waiting.

15

The Northway

hy aren't there any lamps?" began Ferris as soon as they had left the Abyss behind. They were in wild cave now, the first the children had ever seen.

"How's that, lass?" Nolo climbed over a lip of stone, the Shaper swaying from the back of his knapsack like a fat pendulum.

"Lamps." Ferris stopped talking for a moment and clambered up after the Dwarf. Avender followed, the darkness swallowing the tunnel behind them as they passed on. "There were lamps all along the Sun Road. Why aren't there any here?"

"Bryddin carry their own lamps." Nolo tapped his forehead, where he had fastened his light to the front of his iron headband. "Makes things a lot easier. And it would take more lamps than we could ever make to light all the roads in Bryddlough. Lamps are for the Bryddenaia—the Dwarf Roads—not wild cave."

Redburr opened an eye. "Beacons," he squeaked. "That's what you need. Ferris is right, only not about the Stoneways. Next time you see Grimble, you tell him to take some of those fancy lamps of yours and mark out the bad spots on the bottom of the world. Then maybe flying around in the dark will make some sense."

"I already suggested it," said Nolo. The Shaper's small bat head bounced as the Dwarf hitched his pack higher on his shoulders. "Now, unless you want to be useful and scout the tunnels ahead, I'd suggest you go back to sleep."

"That's right," said Ferris. "We're mad at you."

"A sloth couldn't sleep hanging from your back," said Redburr.

"I'm sure that won't stop you," Nolo replied.

"What's a sloth?" asked Avender.

"Don't encourage him," said Ferris. "He shouldn't be allowed to talk until he says he's sorry for making us worry."

"Hmph." With a shrug to show he didn't care whether he was allowed to talk or not, Redburr wrapped his wings around his shoulders and closed his eyes once more.

His three companions ignored him in turn and continued on through the tunnel. The pale light from Nolo's lamp played across the cavern around them, casting restless shadows on the stone. Even in the short time the children had spent in the Stoneways, they could see that what Nolo called wild cave was as different from the cleanly chiseled stone of Issinlough as the depths of the forest were from the palaces of Malmoret. Water had flowed through these pipes and chimneys once, but the Bryddin had moved the stream to make its course their own road. It led them wiggling through narrow tubes that looped and curled like balls of snakes, or out into large rooms where the original stream had probably once clattered along the stony floor. In some places, the company had to scramble on all fours to duck below the low roof; in others, the way was so steep they might almost have been scaling a rock face in the Bavadars.

It wasn't a long march. For an hour they climbed up the dry streambed before coming to an obviously carved tunnel. "Not far, now," said Nolo. He quickened his pace, Redburr bumping along on his back. Ferris and Avender hurried after him down the low passage. Ahead of them the road cut straight through the rock, a faint glow showing at the end.

Sooner than they expected, the tunnel ended. They entered an immense, dimly lit cavern, far larger than anything either child had ever seen underground, except, of course, the Abyss. Even Vonn Kurr was tiny in comparison. Below their feet the ground tumbled away like the side of a high hill, above their heads the roof disappeared into a broad vault of stone, and on either side the cave opened into a wide valley filled mostly with the dark waters of a quiet lake.

But they weren't looking at the lake. Above them, the far-off ceiling glowed. Its light wasn't like that from Bryddin lamps, which was always sharp and distinct, like stars dropped out of the sky. Nor was it like the sun, strong and bright. The radiance from the roof in Cammas lay like a dim cloud between the ceiling and the darkness below, as if the air itself was shining. Here and there long arms of luminosity stretched down the walls on either side, like meadows climbing the gentler slopes of mountains. Only, as was the case with so much in Bryddlough, the meadows and the mountains were upside down.

Even Redburr, who had never been to Cammas on any of his previous trips to the Stoneways, was amazed. "What is it?" he squeaked, before Ferris could ask the same question. "It doesn't look like Bryddin work."

"It's not," said Nolo. "It's Cammas. There's a fungus growing up there on the roof. Dimniss, we call it."

"A fungus?" Redburr craned his neck upward. "Why don't you have the stuff growing everywhere? It'd be a lot easier than lamps."

"Because it won't grow everywhere, that's why," said the Dwarf. "Not even in the loughs right here. As soon as we cut it, it dies."

Ferris strained to see some part of the fungus other than the light, but it was all too far away. A pang of homesickness caught her throat. The scene before her was not that different from the view of the lake in Valing, when seen from the hills behind Eastbay on a cloudy dawn. But the longer she looked, the more she noticed the differences. The lake was too dark, and the cottages clustered at the water's edge were stone, not wood. No trees filled the ridges on the shore; no waves washed the stony beach. No birds sang and there wasn't a breath of wind.

They followed the road down the hillside to the village. Mushrooms rose above their heads, thriving in the humid air. Some were capped like toadstools in a forest; others stood tall and slightly curved, like thin hair on a giant's head. Cammas itself was a homey village after the somber beauty of Issinlough. Men and women hurried along the single street with baskets of fish, and strung their nets to dry on long poles along the shore. Boats plied the still water. From the bottom of the village a stone dock ran out into the dark lake, a small round tower at its end.

Ferris and Avender thought there was something curious about the boats, but it wasn't until they saw one up close that they realized what it was that bothered them. The craft were all flat-bottomed skiffs, but they were made of metal, not wood. A large fish dropped in the bottom of one made a hollow clang, as if Hern were in the Manor garden banging cooking pots to scare away the crows. All the same, the iron boats skimmed lightly across the lake, as if they were made of reeds.

They saw no Bryddin. "Not with humans to do the work," said Nolo as he returned the respectful bows of everyone they passed. "There isn't much to interest Bryddin in Cammas. But they need the extra food in Issinlough, so most folks put in a spell of fishing here to lay in a store for the time they spend in the city."

Much to Redburr's dismay, there was no inn. But having a Bryddin as part of their company entitled the travelers to the best hospitality the town could muster. They were honored guests at a hastily arranged banquet, where the several courses consisted of mushrooms with fish, or fish with mushrooms. Everyone was interested in why Nolo was headed north, away from the more important parts of Bryddlough, especially with two children and a talking bat in tow. Redburr assured them he was really a talking bear, just to make them wonder all the more, and explained that Ferris and Avender were a prince and princess from Firron sent by their parents to learn as much as they might about the Stoneways, even its farthest reaches, in preparation for their future reign.

"You didn't have to tell them Avender and I are betrothed," complained Ferris as she laid out her blanket by the fire in the empty house they had been given to spend the night.

"What else could I say?" Redburr chuckled, a very odd sound in a bat. "You don't look anything alike. I couldn't say you're brother and sister."

"You could've said we were cousins," said Avender.

The Shaper wriggled his ugly nose. "Never occurred to me."

They bedded down around the hearth, except Redburr, who hung by his feet from the chimney. The firestone burned red and black, driving the damp chill from the room. Nolo told them it might be their last fire for a while. "There's no wood in Bryddlough. And firestone doesn't just lie around on the ground waiting to be picked up."

Bone weary, they snuggled into their blankets on the hard stone floor. Even Nolo, after all the cranking he had done in the airship, fell asleep at once. The children dreamed of mountain meadows and the small, bright flowers of spring, despite the deep snores of the weary Dwarf and the soft peeping of the sleeping bat.

They woke to a breakfast of cold fish and more mushrooms. Ferris was beginning to wonder if she would still like mushrooms by the time their trip through the Stoneways was done.

The longest stage of the journey lay ahead, and Redburr and Nolo were anxious to be off. Nolo led them up the steep side of the cavern to a tunnel on the north side of the rocky shore, where the road plunged back into darkness halfway up the wall. The soft radiance of Cammas dimmed behind them.

They returned to wild cave, where not even Nolo had been before. Mostly they traveled beside streams and through occasional soaring caverns whose ceilings were lost in the darkness above.

Judging from the road, it seemed to the children that most of the underearth was hollow, a great mass of caverns laced together by underground waterways, but Nolo assured them the world was solid enough. "The Inach holds everything together," he said. "And it's easier to follow road that's already there than carve new ones. Even for Bryddin."

They passed all sorts of wonders. There were caverns where the rock roped the walls in frozen robes of flowing color; caverns covered in fine white crystals that looked like snow and melted at their touch; and caverns thick as any pinewood with branching limbs of stone. Always their road led upward, away from the Abyss. From time to time they found themselves climbing steep stairs cut from the rock; but rarely did the stairs go down. And so they traveled on into the heart of the world, seeing many marvels in the darkness, though undoubtedly missing many others in the deeper glooms that lay beyond the glow of Nolo's lamp.

Their first campsite was a low cavern scattered about with stone columns beside a rushing stream. With no day or night to tell them how long they had been walking, they had to rely on Nolo's judgment about when it was time to rest. Wearily they settled on the hard stone, the stream so clear it could only be seen where the current rippled along the pebbled bed, and so cold that drinking from it gave them headaches.

As Nolo had warned, there was no fuel for a fire, which forced them to eat their traveling porridge cold. "I can't say it's tasty," Mother Norra had told them when she packed their bags in Issinlough, and she had been right. "But it's filling, and light to carry." Cooked, it would at least have been warm. Cold, it had little to offer. Still, it was better than dried fish. No one, not even Redburr, wanted to soak the paleys they had brought with them from Cammas in that icy water, and eat them uncooked the next morning.

"A little milk to drench the fish would be nice," said the Shaper from his perch on a nearby ledge of rock.

"Be happy we have plenty of water," Nolo replied. He picked a pebble up off the ground and cupped it in his hand. "I'm sure we'll have worse campsites than this. Cold and thirsty is worse than just plain cold."

"Do you think we'll see a mander?" asked Ferris, hugging her knees to try and get warm again despite the cold lump filling her stomach.

"How's that, lass?" The Dwarf frowned. "A mander? Where'd you hear about manders?" He gave the Shaper a sharp look. "I don't suppose whoever told you happened to mention that manders are about as rare as black gems. You won't find them wandering around cold cave much. Manders like fire."

"Have you ever seen one?" asked Avender.

"I have."

"Did you fight it?"

Nolo tossed his pebble into the stream. There was a soft plop that echoed quickly through the cavern before the sound was carried away by the hurrying water. "There's always fighting with manders," he said. "They're not like other creatures. But no one's seen a mander for a long time. We used to find them whenever we found nirrin, one mander to every fire. They always attacked us, even when we left them and their fires alone. But we've found no new fires for some time, and no new manders, either."

Ferris rubbed her fingers along the worn ridges of the rock. "Is there anything else besides manders to worry about in Bryddlough?"

Nolo pulled at his beard. "There are some big fish in Cammas," he admitted. "Not so big as your leviathan, I suppose, but pretty big all the same. They live on the bottom of the lake and eat whatever comes their way."

"I'm not worried about fish," said Ferris. "There're pike in Valing eight or nine feet long. We're not in Cammas anymore, anyway."

"Ahhh, pike," squeaked Redburr, no doubt dreaming of broiled fish, with lemon and butter on the side. Then he caught sight of his half-eaten bowl of gruel again, and frowned.

"Well, there are rock eels," said Nolo. "They're more dangerous than fish. They're like big snakes, only much thicker. They like to hide in deep crevices in the rock, their tails anchored onto some outcrop of stone behind them. But you don't see rock eels very often."

"What about spiders?" Ferris remembered all the nightmares she had ever heard about nasty things that filled the Under Ground. "Is it true there are giant spiders in the Stoneways?"

"That's just a story humans tell to scare one another," scoffed the Dwarf. "I've never seen a spider bigger than I am. I wouldn't worry about them. Mostly they just catch bats. Bats who tell too many stories."

"Thanks," piped the Shaper in his little bat voice. "I'll remember that the next time you ask me to do some scouting."

The journey fell quickly into a regular pattern. They would travel for what felt like hours through the cave, rest for a while, then get up and push on. Every third stop they slept, while Redburr or Nolo stood guard. With nothing to eat but cold mushroom porridge, everyone's thoughts soon turned to food. For a while they contented themselves with describing the extravagant feasts they would have as soon as they returned to civilization, but they gave that up after the constant reminder of what they couldn't have quickly became too depressing. They did find fresh mushrooms occasionally in some of the wetter caverns, or fish and crabs in the pools; but no one ever tried to catch anything, because only Redburr would have eaten it raw. And Redburr, as a bat, was too small to catch anything but bugs himself. He was always flitting off after some juicy morsel or other, especially in the larger caves, where they could hear his high-pitched squeaking echo through the darkness.

"Berries," he said one time after he had returned from one of his short hunts. "Fresh berries. Beetles just don't do the trick. Next time I'm in Valing I'm going to the best blueberry patch I know and eat for a week." He scratched his stomach sadly, his wing folded across his shrinking belly. "I think I'm losing weight, and that's just not right."

"Reiffen's probably losing weight, too," Avender reminded him.

Ferris bit her lip, and even the Shaper stopped complaining, at least for a little while.

They rested; they hurried on through the rock. After a while, the wonders of the Stoneways all began to look the same. For all they knew Nolo was completely lost and leading them round and round in rocky circles. Not even Redburr had any idea how far they had traveled, or how long. Nolo told them that only a single week had passed at the top of the world, but even that knowledge was no use to his companions. A week might just as well have been a month for all they felt the passage of time around them. There were never any mornings, and never any change.

But Nolo knew where he was going. Bryddin don't get lost underground, even in the dark. Their passage through wild cave finally came to an end and they found themselves at the entrance to a long, dark tunnel. Ferris thought it looked like it would never have an end. The ceiling was low, and Avender had to stoop often to keep from bumping his head.

"Everyone's water bottle full?" asked Nolo, though he had made sure of that at the last stream. Avender and Ferris nodded. The Dwarf led them into the narrow passage. "No telling how far Delven built this way between water," he said.

"I can find that out soon enough."

Redburr winged off, once Nolo had assured him that fresh-carved tunnel would hardly suit the needs of spiders, large or small. Half an hour later he returned, the others having spent the time tramping through the cramped gloom. There was water well within traveling distance, he said, at a place where the tunnel came out into natural cavern for a time. After that it became their regular practice for Redburr to fly on ahead from every campsite to inspect the coming march, while the rest of them toiled along behind. Rarely was he gone for long. Apparently Delven had dug his Northway with a mind for any humans who might someday want to follow his path, and they were never much more than three or four marches without water.

Straight to the north ran their road, ever on a slight incline, into the tight blackness. Once every other march or so the passage opened out into some larger cavern, or crossed an icy stream; but those were the exceptions. Mostly they made their way mile after dreary mile through a corridor of rough-hewn stone. Except for the Northway's straightness, it didn't seem like Dwarven work at all.

On and on it went. Avender thought his neck and back would never recover from the constant bending to keep his head from scraping on the ceiling. In the small bubble of light cast by Nolo's lamp they shuffled on, never seeing much more than a few paces in front of the Dwarf, or a few more in back of Avender. The occasional caves they happened upon were forgotten as soon as they were left behind. They slogged along, always in the same order, and the weight above their heads seemed to deepen as they went on, despite the slow rising of the road.

They were coming close to Ussene. And the closer they came, the more Ferris and Avender found themselves thinking of Reiffen. They didn't talk about it, because talking about it only made them feel worse, but both children feared what they might find at the end of their long road, in the Wizards' lair.

A t last they came out of the long tunnel and emerged into wild cave again, having all but forgotten there was anything else in the world besides rough stone and cramped darkness. Nolo paused to consider which passage to take among the several that branched before them. Thin shadows flitted back and forth across the humps and hollows of the cavern every time he turned his head.

"About time we got out of that tunnel," he said, pulling at his beard.

"You mean you were tired of it, too?" Ferris looked at Nolo in surprise, never having imagined he might have minded the long tunnel as much as the rest of them.

"Why do you think we built Issinlough in the first place?" he replied. "Narrow cave is narrow cave, no matter how much you like rock and stone. Uhle didn't dream of Abben because of his love of darkness and tight spaces."

He turned back to the choice of paths before them, finally settling on the one he said continued most directly north. They came to a small, swift river, which they followed to a wall of solid rock, where the stream burst from a crack in the stone to race away down the passage behind them. Steps had been cut into the rock beside the gushing channel; above the stair another short, steep tunnel led upward to a second set of caverns. Plainly Delven had been this way already.

They came to a chamber with a small, clear pool at the center, its bottom gleaming in Nolo's lamplight. The Dwarf called a halt and pointed to the roof. "We're past the end of the plains now," he said, dropping his pack to the ground. Redburr hung from the nearest knob of rock. All their packs were lighter now: they had eaten more than half of what Mother Norra had prepared for them in Issinlough. As a result Nolo, who told them they had been some nine days on the Northway, had put them on half rations. Even Redburr thought that was almost a good thing, given what they had to eat.

"I wish we were on the plains right now," grumbled Ferris as she sat down beside the pool. "It's not the same camping out without stars or a fire."

"We'd never have gotten this far if we were up there," squeaked Redburr. He dropped suddenly from his perch and swooped low over the water to snatch an insect from the air.

Nolo began filling his bottle from the pool. "Another day's march will take us under the northern mountains," he said. "We should find Delven soon."

"How do you know where we are?" asked Ferris. "I'd be lost even if we were still on the surface."

Redburr gave a high-pitched belch as he finished off his juicy snack. "Bryddin measure everything," he said. "You can be sure Nolo's counted every step he's taken since Cammas somewhere in the back of his head. He doesn't even know he's doing it. But whenever he needs the information, it's there."

"So how far are we from Ussene?" asked Avender.

"Five or six leagues," said Nolo, stroking his beard modestly.

"Are we close to the surface?"

The Dwarf nodded. "Very close. If we had a stair we could probably see the face of Abben before lunch. But we won't be seeing Abben on this trip. Not unless our plans go very wrong."

"I wouldn't mind seeing the sun again even if it was winter." Despite herself, Ferris couldn't help but dream about basking in warm grass. "I've had enough of caves and tunnels. Even a rainy day would be nice as long as it was a day."

"It never hurts to remember the good in the world," said Nolo kindly.

"Just so long as we don't forget the job at hand," replied the Shaper.

"Not much chance of that down here, is there, lass?"

Ferris nodded. There would be plenty of time for naps in the sun, once Reiffen was safe.

On their very next march, they finally met up with the other Dwarves. Or at least one of them. For some time Nolo had been paying close attention to the rock around them. At each new passage he stopped to run his fingers along the stone and examine it closely. No one else saw anything special about the caves they passed, but Nolo was plainly aware of much more.

"Bryddin have been here," he said. Then he added with a frown, "And others, too."

"Others?" asked Redburr, coming quickly awake on the back of Nolo's pack.

"Manders?" asked Ferris timidly. Behind her, Avender peered cautiously into the dark beyond the lamplight. Both stepped closer to the safety of the Dwarf.

Nolo shook his head. "Not manders. Something that digs in stone, like Bryddin and humans. I can see the signs in the rock. And I can feel the pain in the stone."

"Are they close by?" Redburr shook out his wings and made ready to take to the air.

"Your ears are better than mine," said the Dwarf. "What do you think?"

Redburr stopped his flapping and went very still. Everyone else stood quietly, so the bat might hear whatever lay in the darkness beyond the glow of Nolo's lamp. The children held their breath and felt their hearts thumping in their chests.

"Well, there is something," squeaked Redburr at last. Ferris's fear tightened. "Some kind of knocking sound. Maybe a hammer on stone."

"That's Nurren," said Nolo. "I can feel his stroke in the rock." He laid the palm of his hand flat against the cavern wall. "We should find him soon."

Ferris let go her fright with a long sigh.

As Nolo had suspected, they found the glow of the other Bryddin's lamp shining in the darkness not much later. He was putting the finishing touches on a set of stairs that led up through the ceiling of the next cave. His hammer flashed in the brightness of the lamp at his forehead, and rang out through the chamber as he struck the stone.

"Ho, Nurren!" called Nolo.

Nurren paused and looked down, then nearly dropped his hammer in surprise. Retrieving the tool, he tucked it into his belt, and quickly descended to meet the new arrivals. "Nolo!" he exclaimed when he stood beside them. "What brings you back to Bryddlough? With humans, and so far from Issinlough, too!"

"It's a long story," answered Nolo with a bow. Nurren returned the greeting, his tools clattering at his waist. "But there's no time to explain, now. How close is Ussene?"

Nurren's bushy eyebrows rose. "Another league or two," he replied. "Not far."

"And Delven?"

"He and the others are exploring the nearer caves. But there are others besides Bryddin in this lough."

Nolo nodded. "We know," he said. "I've felt them in the stone. Have you found them?"

Nurren shrugged. "They run off every time we come near. But we don't think they're humans. They've dug too deep for humans, and they're sloppier miners, too. There's a great deal of anguish in the stone."

"Are they watching us right now?" Ferris looked at the darkest parts of the cave around them with some concern.

"I doubt it. They're very cautious. Most of the time they keep as far away from us as they can."

"Do you think they've warned the Three you're here?" asked Nolo.

Nurren pushed his lamp higher up on his head and scratched his brow with a sound like fingernails on a blackboard. Ferris and Avender winced. "Not that we can tell," said the Dwarf. "But I'm a rock-reader, not a soldier. All this watching and being watched is just plain nuisance, far as I'm concerned. Whoever they are, they don't seem to want to go towards Ussene any more than we do. The farther north we get, the less we see of them."

"They don't have to be enemies," suggested Redburr. He had settled on a perch on the side of the cave just above Nurren's head, his squashed nose close to the level of everyone else's face. "They could be escaped slaves. Even down here in the darkness their lives would be better than anything in Ussene."

Nurren looked up at the talking bat with fresh surprise.

"Don't mind him," explained Nolo. "He's with us."

Nurren rubbed his chin, finding it odd to be talking to a bat; but he was inclined to agree that the strangers were not enemies. "Whoever's out there," he said, "they haven't bothered us. But there are many caves and passages, and they could easily have gotten to the fortress without our knowing."

"Friend or foe," advised Nolo, "the quicker we join Delven, the better." Redburr nodded his small head in agreement.

Without another word Nurren turned and led them up the stairs. Nolo waved for Avender and Ferris to go on ahead. Now that there was someone else to lead, Nolo could guard the rear. As they hurried forward, Redburr flitted back and forth above their heads, patrolling the passages both before and behind for any sign of the strangers Nurren had described. Even though the creatures didn't seem inclined to bother them, neither Nolo nor Redburr liked the idea that someone else was out there. They wanted to join up with Delven as soon as possible, and feared what might happen if they were suddenly attacked in the middle of one of the larger caves.

It was their hurry that got them into trouble. They came to a place where the road crossed the side of a steep slope. Loose stone lay all about, both left and right, as well as across the path. Nurren stepped carefully around the jumbled rocks. Ferris, who was right behind him, cautiously followed. But Avender was peering into the darkness below, searching for manders or whatever else might be watching them, instead of keeping his eye on the path. He stepped onto a large flat stone that slipped immediately beneath his weight. As he lost his balance, he threw his arms out to try to keep from falling. The stone beneath him slipped again, and the whole slope broke loose in a curtain of billowing dust and noise. Nurren snatched Ferris away before the slide could grab her, but Nolo had stopped for a moment to study the top of the incline, and was too far away to keep Avender from being swept off with the rock. The boy vanished into the roaring darkness. Then the slide ceased as suddenly as it had begun, with only a few cracks and pops to mark the hopping of the last stray rocks down the new slope. Dust rose in thick clouds, glinting in the pale lamplight.

Nolo and Nurren darted down, leaving Ferris in darkness behind them. She stood anxiously at the edge of the path as they teetered from rock to rock, the stone flattening under the impact of their heavy feet; but no new slide pursued them. Even in their haste the Bryddin knew exactly how the stone lay across the sloping ground. Their lamps glowed in the dust as they descended, until at last they arrived at the bottom of the chasm. A flat wall rose above their heads, their shadows dancing wildly against it as they dug swiftly through the scrambled stone.

Something touched Ferris on the cheek and she nearly jumped out of her skin. But it was only the tip of Redburr's wing as he settled on the ceiling above her head.

"Oh, Redburr! What if—" She couldn't bear to finish her thought.

The Shaper made no reply. Nor, as long as he was a bat, could he comfort her in any way. Ferris pressed her balled fists miserably against her chin and wished she had never left Valing. Even her mother's kitchen was better than this. Reiffen was gone and Avender buried. She coughed as the dust settled around her shoulders, and watched anxiously as the pile of stone grew taller around the Dwarves. She couldn't imagine that even the strength of the Bryddin would get them to Avender in time.

16

Durk

vender woke in darkness, his head aching terribly. Lying on his back in a pile of sharp stones, he found he could move neither his hands nor arms when he tried to rub his temples. His legs were trapped as well. His first thought was he was back with Skimmer, squashed beneath a dozen slumbering nokken. Then he realized it was far too quiet for the rookery. Not a single whiskery snort disturbed the darkness. The air was filled with dry dust rather than the pungent wetness of the nokken grotto.

He sneezed and, with a sudden breathless panic, remembered his fall. For a moment he had thought he might catch himself, until the whole slope slipped out from under him with a jagged roar. Dust had swallowed him up as he rattled downward; stone splinters bit at his face and hands. Something hard had struck his head and knocked him senseless. He had no idea where he was.

He closed his eyes and forced himself to stay calm. Somehow the darkness seemed less threatening when he couldn't see it. He told himself that Nolo and Redburr would save him; they had to be close by. He didn't think he had fallen very far. Though he hurt everywhere, nothing felt broken. He tried not to think what it would have meant had his head not been left free. The rest of him was buried and bruised: his shins ached; his knees were skinned. His ribs complained every time he took a breath and his lips tasted of blood and dust. He could wiggle the fingers of his left hand and twist his head about, but that was all. A layer of rock covered him from neck to toe.

In the darkness he couldn't tell whether he had fallen into a vast cavern or been wedged into a narrow crevice where the roof was half an inch from his nose. Fresh panic seized him as he imagined miles of rock pressing close against his face. Then he noticed that, even though he was breathing heavily, he didn't feel his breath on his cheek the way he would have had there been a wall of stone just beyond his chin. His fear eased once more and he reminded himself again that Nolo, Redburr, and Nurren had to be somewhere near. Probably both Dwarves were already digging for him through the jumbled stone.

He called out, hoping they might be close enough to hear. But his voice sounded tightly muffled, as if he were shouting from beneath a thick blanket. There was no echo. Wherever he was, he didn't think it was a large cave. He wished he could get his lamp out of his pack and at least see where he had fallen.

Struggling to hold back his gnawing fright, Avender set about trying to wriggle free. His knapsack and the stones on the floor beneath him made his position very uncomfortable. His feet seemed higher than his head and his body was twisted slightly. One arm lay beneath him, the other on top of his leg. He shifted his shoulders and heard several of the small rocks on top of him shift as well, but not enough to free either of his hands. When he tried to sit up, more small stones skittered down around him. One bounced off the tip of his nose. He had no idea how much rubble lay on top of him, whether there was just a thin layer of rock he should be able to shake off easily or whether it was an immense pile just waiting to crash down and smother him should he try too hard to slip free.

"Help!" he called again. "Redburr! Nolo! Help! I'm here, under the stones!"

His alarm grew when no one answered. If Nolo and the others were as close as he thought, surely they would have heard him by now. The roof and floor of the cave felt as if they were conspiring to squeeze him flat between them.

"Help, help! Redburr! Nolo! Help!"

"Really!" said a voice from somewhere close by. "You're making far too much noise! You're liable to start the rocks sliding again at any moment!"

Avender lay still, his heart in his throat. It wasn't Redburr's voice that had answered him from the darkness. Nor was it Nolo's, or Nurren's, or Ferris's. It had come from somewhere close by, and sounded half-buried. He wondered if one of the mysterious creatures lurking in the tunnels around them had been trapped in the slide beside him. It wasn't as if anyone had ever suggested that manders knew how to talk.

"Who—who are you?" he asked fearfully.

"Who am I?" came the indignant reply. "I already know who I am. Better I should ask who you are. I suppose you're the one who started the rock slide. Mangy pasty. I hope you broke every bone in your miserable carcass. Now I'll never get out of here."

Avender had no idea what a pasty was. He guessed he was supposed to feel insulted. The fact that the unknown voice seemed more interested in insulting rather than hurting him was something of a relief. "I'm not a pasty," he said. "I'm Avender."

"Avender?" The voice sounded surprised. "That's not a pasty name. Or sissit, either." Its tone changed, narrowing with suspicion. "Are you sure you haven't just made it up to hoodwink me?"

"Why would I want to hoodwink you?" replied Avender. "I don't even know who you are. I can't even see you."

"Of course you can't see me," snapped the voice, still sharply suspicious. "It's, uh, too dark to, um, see anything. It's a good thing, too. If you could see me I'd probably scare you to death."

There was a boastful quality to the voice that made Avender wonder if what it said was really true. Bullies usually took the same tone. But the speaker hurried on, pestering Avender with questions before he had a chance to really think.

"Where are you from?" it demanded.

"Valing," replied Avender.

"Valing? Where in Valing?"

Avender didn't understand the question at first. Valing was Valing. There were towns along the side of the lake, but only the Manor was called Valing.

"From the Manor House," he finally answered. "I'm not from Bracken or Eastbay, if that's what you mean. I'm just from Valing."

"Hmph." The voice didn't sound convinced. "Who's king in Valing?" it asked.

"There is no king in Valing. Everybody knows that."

"Oh, right. I was just testing you." The voice paused for a moment, considering its next question. "All right, then," it asked, "who's the lord of the Manor?"

"There's no lord, either. But if you mean who's steward, it's Berrel and Hern," said Avender.

"Hmm." The voice considered this piece of news. "Those aren't names I recognize. But I've been away a long time, so I probably shouldn't recognize them, I suppose. Oser was steward in my day. I think. I never visited Valing, myself."

"Oser? Oser and Enner were stewards a long time ago."

"Is that so?" said the voice thoughtfully. "I guess I have been down here awhile. It would be hard to keep track of all that time, even if I could."

Avender thought this an odd remark but let it pass. He was still too busy trying to figure out where the speaker was, how dangerous it might be, and whether or not it was trapped close enough beside him in the rock to hurt him even if it couldn't move.

"Maybe you could tell me who you are," said the boy, "since I've already told you about myself."

"I don't suppose it would do any harm." The voice spoke with a certain condescension, as if it had enjoyed asking about Valing more for the sake of hearing itself speak than for any truth about Avender it was trying to discover. "I'm Durk," it said. "Or at least I used to be."

"Used to be?" Avender felt a renewed fear tingle along his spine. They were close to Ussene after all, and he had heard more than enough about the Wizards' experiments to make him start to worry.

"That's right." The voice sounded bitter now. "You don't think I'd remain here if I didn't have to, do you? I'm not some warty toad or belly-crawling snake. I don't like it down here, you know, any more than you."

Neither snakes nor toads had been on Avender's mind, but, now that the voice had brought them up, they leapt straight out of the darkness and into his imagination, poison dripping from their jaws. Maybe Durk was a mander. A small one. There was something in the way Durk spoke that made him seem not very large.

"What are you then?" the boy asked, trying his best not to sound concerned. He thought that, if he at least sounded brave, whatever he was talking to would think twice about attacking him.

"You'd like to know that, wouldn't you, lad?" The voice sounded suddenly sly, as if it had found a new game to play. "You are a lad, aren't you? You don't sound like a warrior, nor a woman, either."

"If you're not going to tell me what you are, then I don't see any reason why I should tell you anything more about me." Avender remembered that he and his friends were trying to sneak secretly into the Wizards' fortress. Perhaps it would be better if he was a bit more cautious about what he said.

"You're a lad, all right," said the voice. "You can't hide that from me. If I can't trust my own hearing, then there's not much left for me to trust. You can pretend to be something else all you want, but I'll hear right through you. The real question is, what's a lad doing down here all by himself? It's not like any of Them up there to let anyone escape. Not unless that's what They want you to do."

Avender began to think the speaker really was a spy for the Wizards. "I have my reasons for being down here," he said cautiously.

"You can't expect me to tell you what they are when you won't tell me anything about yourself."

"You want to know what I'm doing down here?" said the speaker, its bitterness returning. "Down here beneath the deepest dungeon in the world? I'd think you'd know that story as well as I. It's not like it's ever any different for any of us. Pasties and talkers, mooncows and belly rubbers, we're all down here for the same reason. Some of us don't remember, but I do. I was a—a prince, once. But He took all that away from me. Just like He takes something away from all of us."

"He?" asked Avender, though he had a good idea of whom the speaker was talking.

"Oh, no, you don't," said the voice. Avender pictured him shaking his head cagily. "You won't get me saying His name so easily. This is His domain. He'd be down on us faster than groundlings on a muffer if He heard me speak His name. You know who I'm talking about, lad. You'll forgive me if I don't say it right out loud for you."

"But," said Avender, "if you'll pardon my asking, how is it you're still alive if you were once, um, His prisoner? You just said yourself no one ever escapes from Ussene."

"Shhh!" the voice hissed at him from somewhere under the pile of stone. "Don't ever speak even of His fortress! He's always listening. You can't be too careful. But you should know as well as I that no one escapes from Him. You may think you escaped—that's right, I know why you're down here, even if you didn't tell me yourself. But don't think you escaped. Not for a second. You're down here because He's finished with you. That's why we're all down here. You may not remember—you may have forgotten, like most do. But no one ever escapes. When He's done with you He just lets you go." The voice ceased for a moment, but Avender felt the speaker was going to say something more, and waited for it to go on.

"I suppose I'll have to explain it to you, since it appears you've forgotten." Durk's voice changed again and he began to speak formally, as if he were making a speech. "You see, lad, when you fall into His hands He doesn't use all of you. That would be too easy. Instead He just takes what He wants and throws the rest away. If you're lucky, you end up like the pasties, or yourself. You don't remember a thing. But if you're unlucky, you end up like me. He takes what's best from you and you remember it all the same. I was a very handsome fellow once. A pleasing face and figure, to man and maid alike. You may not remember what it was, but I'm sure he's taken the best from you as well. Your youth perhaps, since you're a lad. Or maybe your hardiness and strength. Since you're from Valing, you probably spent most of your life out in the fields with the cows. I don't imagine there could be much else He might have wanted you for."

Avender scowled. He knew there was much more the Three might want from him than his ability as a cowherd. But he held his tongue, suspecting that Durk's insults might be a trap to get him to say more about why he was on his way to Ussene. He asked what a pasty was, to change the subject.

"A pasty?" the voice answered. "A pasty's what you become when He takes out what you have on the inside. Then there's nothing left of you but the cold clay. Pasty white you get, and about as interesting. Pasties know enough to remember to eat when they're hungry, but not much more. Even talking to them is difficult. Though I do think the sissit use them occasionally for spies and such. Learned scholars and wise kings they were, for the most part. Until He got hold of them."

"What about you?" asked Avender. "What happened to you?"

Durk made no answer. Avender saw at once this was something about which Durk, whatever he was, was very sensitive. Maybe he wasn't a spy, after all, but precisely the poor lost prisoner he claimed to be.

"I'm sorry," apologized the boy.

"Thank you," said Durk. "Just think of me as being the opposite of a pasty. It wasn't my insides that were wanted—"

Durk stopped speaking as they both heard a sudden scraping

from the rocks at Avender's feet. Although he felt nothing and none of the rocks around him seemed to move, it did sound as if the stones were being worked on at the other side of the pile. Then the scraping stopped, and the darkness was quiet again.

"What was that?" asked Durk uneasily.

"I think it's my friends," replied Avender, hoping he was right.

"Friends? You didn't tell me you had friends!" Panic edged round the sides of Durk's voice.

"Didn't you see them? They were right there with me when I started the rock slide."

"I didn't see the rock slide, farm boy! Haven't you been listening to what I've said? I can't see—"

The rest of Durk's angry outburst was cut off as the sound of rocks being pushed about was renewed. Avender could hear it clearly now; someone was digging about in the loose stone beyond his feet. He shouted out, "Redburr! Nolo! I'm in here!" but it was some time before they answered. Small dots of light appeared between the gaps in the stones as the moonbeam glow of the diggers' lamps shone into Avender's cave.

"We hear you, lad!" called Nolo at last. "Hold on a little longer!" His voice clashed with the knocking of the stones as he tossed them back behind him. "Nurren and I are almost there."

"Here's a foot," Redburr's bat voice squeaked in through the gaps in the stone with the lamplight. "You see it there? Good. Don't pull it, rockhead! He's not made out of stone!"

Avender found he could wiggle his left foot. After that it was only a matter of time before enough rubble was cleared away for him to be able to see again. He was wedged just past the narrow part of a crevice that widened into deeper darkness behind him. There had been barely enough room for him to roll through the opening, a few stones following behind, but not enough room for the rock slide to cover him completely. He had been very lucky not to have been buried against the stone on either side. Redburr flitted in through the narrow entrance and darted about the cave.

"Be careful," warned Avender. "There's someone else in here."

"Someone else?" asked the Shaper. "I don't see anyone else." He gave a few shrill squeaks and shot a short way up the tunnel. "I don't hear anyone else, either," he said when he returned.

"But there is. I've been talking to him while I was waiting for you to dig me out. Durk! Where are you!"

Avender's voice echoed much more solidly off the walls around him now that there was somewhere for the sound to go. But Durk made no answer.

"Durk!" called the boy again. "Come on out! These are my friends. They won't hurt you."

Nolo pushed his head through the widening gap. The light at his forehead gleamed as it opened up the dark around them. "Who's Durk?" he asked.

"The person I was talking to."

Nolo shone his lamp around the cave. His eyes were better than anyone else's in the dark. But loose stones and further darkness were all that he could see. "There's no one else here," he said.

"He must have run away back up that tunnel behind me," said Avender. "Maybe we should try and follow him."

"I don't think we want to be chasing shadows this close to Ussene," replied the Dwarf.

"Durk!" called Avender once more. But still there was no answer.

Redburr hung from a ridge of rock close by. "That's a nasty-looking cut on your forehead," he said, his face cocked to one side as he eyed the boy.

"I know what you're thinking," said Avender. "But I didn't make it up. I know Durk is around here somewhere. Maybe he's invisible."

"If he were invisible I'd still hear him."

"I'm not making it up," Avender insisted.

"Nobody says you are."

"Where's Ferris? She'll believe me."

"We left her up on the road," said Nolo. Avender was almost free of the stones now and the Dwarf had widened the entrance enough to crawl into the chamber beside him. The three of them, packed tightly together within the narrow cave, left no room for anyone else. "If she tried to come down here she'd just start another slide."

Nurren and Nolo pulled the last of the rock off Avender and helped him back to his feet just beyond the tunnel opening. The boy staggered at first, and would have fallen again had Nolo not held him upright. One of his feet had fallen asleep and the other shin was almost too painful to stand on. But nothing was broken.

"Don't bother trying to walk," said Nolo as Avender took a couple of limping steps. "I'm going to have to carry you back up to the road anyway. The footing's not safe for any but Bryddin feet."

"But what about Durk?"

"If he wanted to meet us he wouldn't have run off."

Before Avender knew what was happening, Nolo lifted him onto his back. The Dwarf had already given Nurren both his pack and the boy's, so Avender was able to hold securely onto the Dwarf's stony shoulders. It was not a particularly comfortable ride and Avender soon discovered that sitting piggyback on Nolo was not much different from riding a rock slide. Both were equally hard and unforgiving of anything softer than they.

"For all we know this Durk is one of the things that have been watching the Bryddin," said Redburr. "Without Nolo and Nurren to come to your rescue you might have been sitting in their stew pot right now."

"He didn't seem bad," said Avender as he tried to hold himself away from Nolo's rock-hard shoulder blades. "At first I thought he was a spy. But all he seemed to want to do was talk."

The boy took one last look down the dark tunnel behind them, but there was nothing to be seen. Redburr winged off towards Ferris in the darkness above. "Good-bye, Durk!" Avender called. "We really won't hurt you if you come out. We could take you back to the surface with us, you know."

They had already started up the slope when a small voice from the scattered stones behind them said finally, "Would you really take me to the surface?"

Nolo and Nurren stopped short and looked suspiciously about.

"Who's that?" asked Nurren.

"That's Durk," said Avender.

Nolo moved cautiously back towards the low, dark passage they had just left.

"There's no one in there," he insisted.

"I'm here," said Durk. But there was no sign of him anywhere.

Avender loosed his grip on Nolo's shoulders and hopped painfully to the ground. The feeling had still not completely returned to his foot. "Where are you?" he asked.

"I don't really know." The voice came from somewhere at their feet, prompting them all to start nosing around the loose stone for some sign of another cave or hollow in the ground.

"How can you not know where you are?" asked Avender. "Are you hurt?"

"What do you look like?" asked Nolo as he picked through the rocks underfoot with his toes.

"A far cry from my original appearance," said the voice sadly. "I'm much smaller than I used to be."

"What are you?" asked Nolo, coming at last to the most pertinent question.

"I believe I'm a stone."

"A stone?"

"How can you be a stone? Stones don't talk."

"It's a very long story. Do you care to hear it?" It seemed to Avender that the rock, or whatever he turned out to be, was never so happy as when he was talking.

"What's going on down there!" Ferris's voice floated toward them from the road above. "How long are you people going to leave me alone!"

"We'll just be a little longer!" called Nolo.

"At least Redburr was nice enough to tell me Avender's okay! Do you have any idea how mean you're being! I see your lights, but I don't have any idea what's going on at all!"

Nurren stooped, and spread the rocks apart with his hands. "This is the one," he said. He stood back up, holding aloft a small gray stone.

"You've got me," said Durk. "I can feel your fingers."

His voice came plainly from the stone. Nurren gaped in surprise. The rock appeared to be completely ordinary, though it was round and pale and not much like the others on the slope around it. It looked more like the sort of smooth stone found at the bottom of a stream than the rough, jagged rocks of the cave. When it spoke it quivered slightly but otherwise looked no different. Nothing moved, and its surface didn't change at all.

Nurren handed the stone to Avender, who clutched Durk closely as he climbed back onto Nolo's back. The stone chattered away as they scrambled up the slope. He wanted to know who they were and where they were from and what they were doing and how many of them there were, but Avender stopped paying much attention once he realized the strange rock was hardly listening to his answers.

Ferris helped him down when they rejoined her on the road. She frowned at the cuts on his face and dabbed at the worst of them with her handkerchief. "You're so clumsy," she scolded, relieved the worst of her fears were past.

"It's my leg that hurts," he told her.

"You could have been killed."

"He almost buried both of us," offered Durk. "I might have been lost at the bottom of that pile of stones forever."

Ferris started abruptly at the sound of the strange voice. "Who's that?"

"It's Durk." Avender showed her the rock in his hand. "He's a talking rock."

"A talking rock? How can a rock talk?"

"A question probably best left unanswered," squeaked Redburr.

"It's a long story," said the garrulous stone. "Filled with pathos and tears."

"And one we don't have time for now." Nolo retrieved his pack from Nurren and regarded Avender with a critical eye. "There's no telling what else might be lurking around here. We need to get on to Delven's camp. Are you able to walk, lad?"

"I think so." Avender took a step and winced. Painful as it was, his bruised shin already felt better than when he first tried to stand. And he could feel all the toes on his other foot again, though their tingling was enough to make him almost wish he couldn't.

"We should move on," counseled Nurren. "The camp is still some way off."

"Camp?" Durk spoke up in surprise. "What's this about a camp? You told me you were taking me to the surface."

"We have something important to take care of first," said Avender.

"I would think the only important thing to take care of down here would be getting as far away from Them as quickly as possible."

"Avender," said Redburr, who had resettled on Nolo's pack now that there was room for him again. "You'd better tell Durk to be quiet."

"Be quiet? Allow me to remind you that I'm accompanying you only as a result of your repeated invitation. No one said anything about my not being able to participate in any group discussions. Had I known I was going to be abducted I would never—"

Durk's protests were cut off as Avender pushed the stone deep into his knapsack. A blanket and his second shirt silenced the rock almost completely, except for the occasional muffled shout that sounded faintly from somewhere behind Avender's shoulders. In relative quiet he limped along behind everyone but Nolo, who brought up the rear. Gradually his aches and pains faded into numbness.

The rock around them became more deformed as Nurren led them closer to Ussene. Sometimes they found themselves climbing slopes of smooth and slippery nirrin that seemed to have frozen in mid-wave. At others they picked their way across broken rock floors where great blocks of olath had fallen from the unseen ceilings above. They crossed few streams, and those they did were so choked with dark sand that Avender couldn't see his boots through the shallow, swirling water.

"There's pain here," said Nolo with a frown. The wall beside him was swollen with knobs and ridges of twisted rock as he squeezed sideways through a narrow gap in the passage. Even Ferris and Avender could see that the stone was misshapen, like overripe fruit close to bursting.

"Cruelty, I'd call it." Nurren brushed his fingertips along the rough rock. "Such hands as did this shouldn't be let near proper stone."

"And there's almost no Inach."

"It gets less and less the further north you go."

Most of the path they followed was natural, but here and there the way was noticeably carved. The narrowest spots had been widened enough to allow one person to slip through the opening at a time, and short doorways had been cut between caverns that would otherwise have slept on unconnected. The lamps of the Dwarves shone upon walls and floors of cracked stone, the fractures running like jagged black spiderwebs across the fissured rock.

They came at last to a cavern that had obviously been worked by Bryddin. A firestone fire glowed from a hearth near a pool the Dwarves had deepened with a low dam. Red and black shadows lurked about the stone columns that ran from floor to ceiling, their polished sides gleaming in the brighter light of Nolo's and Nurren's lamps. A small stream tinkled softly as it spilled across the cavern. Smoke curled thinly toward the roof.

"Ah!" cried Redburr as he darted quickly above the hearth. "Fresh fish! And mushrooms!"

Avender's mouth watered. He couldn't remember when he had last had a hot meal, even if it was the same fish and mushrooms they had eaten ever since first arriving in the Under Ground.

"It's not much of a lough," said Nurren as he led them to the fire. "But there's a little of everything we need close by. Nolo, why don't you get some more firestone while I make us something to eat."

"And Delven and the others?" With his bare hands, Nolo began to break off small pieces from a slab of black rock a few paces from the fire.

"Out surveying." Nurren pulled a string of fish from the pool. "They should be back soon."

Avender removed Durk from his pack and set the stone down on the edge of the hearth. "Ahh, that's nice," sighed the rock. "Close, but not too close. I was a firebrick for the pasties once, and it's not an experience I wish to repeat."

Avender wanted to hear more about the pasties, but Nolo returned with fresh firestone and asked a question of Nurren before the boy could speak. "Have you found the way to Ussene?"

The whole cave echoed with Durk's quick cry of terror before Nurren could even think of replying. For a small stone, Durk's voice was very loud. "Never say that word!" he warned. "Never!"

Nolo and Nurren turned toward the stone in mild surprise. Avender looked back over his shoulder to make sure a flood of pasties wasn't rushing into the cave in answer to Durk's shout.

"Why not?" asked Nolo.

"Because He is always listening!" Durk's voice hissed along with the crackling of the new coal catching fire in the hearth. "He hears everything anyone says about Him! Or His fortress!"

Nolo picked up a handful of mushrooms from a bag beside the fire and dropped them into a large iron skillet. "Well, you'd better get used to hearing it, then, because that's where we're going."

Avender cringed beneath the barrage of oaths and invective launched from the small stone. Once Durk knew Nolo intended to enter Ussene, he wanted nothing further to do with Avender and the rest of the company. "Heave me as far as you can," he demanded grandly, after his first fury had passed. "Off a cliff, or into that stream I hear over there. Any place will do. Just as long as you don't take me back Upstairs."

"You're stuck with us now," said Redburr, munching an insect he had found crawling near his perch. "But you can be sure we'll take you back to Issinlough with us when this is over."

"When!" The stone's terror echoed across the cavern. "It's over now! Or it might as well be. You'll never get home again if you take another step closer to Them. Flee now, while there's still a chance! I beg you!"

While the rock continued to plead with them, Nurren scaled and gutted the fish. Avender and Ferris watched from seats beside the hearth, their eyes as wide as saucers. Avender had never thought he could be so hungry. The fish, sizzling in a bed of mushrooms, looked and smelled far more delicious than anything Hern or Mother Norra had ever prepared. Even when they were finished, the memory of the meal lingered in everyone's mouths like the taste of snow in summer mountains. For the first time in weeks Avender felt warm, both inside and out.

They rested while they waited for Delven and the other Bryddin to return. From his perch on the column closest to the hearth, Redburr made more than a few remarks about what "They" were like, always careful not to mention the Three by name. It was not long before Durk's conceit overcame his caution and he began once more to make cryptic comments about his life before becoming a stone.

"Maybe if you told us a little more about Them," suggested Redburr with a sly wink to his companions, "we'd learn enough to change our minds."

Durk's mood improved at once. "Why, I should have thought of that myself," he said. "What do you want to know?"

"Why don't you start from the beginning," squeaked the bat.

If a rock could preen, Durk would have preened. "That will make for a long story," he pointed out.

"So you've said." Nolo tossed the bones of his fish back into the pool. "If you start to get boring we'll let you know."

"Well then." The rock gathered his voice to tell his tale. "A long time ago, before I was captured by Him, I was a prince of Malmoret."

"Really?" wondered the Shaper. "I don't recall a Prince Durk in Malmoret. Who was your father?"

"Count Lender was my father," answered the rock grandly. "I would not expect you to remember me. It's hard to know how much time has passed when you're imprisoned in a stone, but I believe I was abducted a considerable time ago. Probably long before you were born."

"I don't know about that," said Ferris. "Redburr's lived a long time."

"I was quite young when I was taken," insisted Durk. "I hadn't had much time to make a name for myself before I was snatched away in the bloom of youth."

"That is a sad story," said Nurren.

"It gets worse," warned the stone.

"Especially since I happen to know that Count Lender had only one child," said Redburr. "A daughter."

Durk's voice stiffened. "I don't mean to correct you, sir. But I believe your genealogy is mistaken. After all, I was there."

"So was Redburr," said Avender.

"Haven't you ever heard of Redburr the Shaper?" asked Ferris.

"I've heard of Shapers," Durk admitted. "But it has never been my pleasure to meet one. How do you do, sir."

"It's my pleasure entirely, Count Durk," replied Redburr, matching the courtesy of the stone.

"You do me great honor, sir. Still, Shaper or not, I don't believe you could have known my father quite so well as I."

"Is that so?" Redburr folded his wings across his chest and gave a look that was quite lost on the unseeing stone. "Then perhaps you can tell me how many sisters your father had, and what were their names?"

"Really, sir. This is preposterous. After all the misfortune I've been subjected to!"

"You're right, it is preposterous," Redburr agreed. His ugly nose twitched impatiently. "It's also a waste of time. As I recall, there was a troupe of traveling players who used to frequent Banking about the time Count Lender was alive. I saw them once in Ipside. The lead actor was a handsome fellow with an especially prominent chin, and his leading lady was a charming woman who didn't appreciate the way he threw his cloak across her face in the middle of his speeches. And there was something about a tonic the lady's father used to sell while the plays were being performed—"

"Enough, sir. Please. I see that you were, indeed, there. Spare me the remainder of the episode, if you have any conscience at all. The memory is heavy enough upon my own heart. My fair Elinora, that her fate should have been so cruel!"

"And your own, no doubt," observed the Shaper.

"Why did you tell us you were a prince?" asked Avender.

"Alas, I feared you would find me more interesting as a prince than as a player."

"We don't care what you were," said Ferris. "We're from Valing."

"Just don't try to sell us any tonics," added Redburr. "And you also might try telling us your real story. What happened to your troupe? I remember you and the lady, but I don't recall the name of your company."

"We were the Border Boarders. Do you see? We spent most of our time on the Banking Border, at the edge of the Waste—"

"We get it," said Redburr impatiently.

"Ah, yes. It is somewhat obvious, isn't it." The rock made a noise that sounded suspiciously like he was clearing the throat he no longer had. "But there's no room for subtlety in some parts of the world. The finer poets are completely lost on those who possess rougher sensibilities. At any rate, we were taken by a large band of Keeadini while on our way from Wetbill to Wending. Dorrin—he was Elinora's father and the leader of our company—decided we had to avoid Broadmead, for reasons you can readily imagine, so we crossed to the other side of the river. There had not been any raids for some time, and we thought we would be safe. But stage fighting doesn't work when the savages of Keeadin set upon you and, despite a tremendous effort on my part, we were all carried off.

"For weeks they transported us across the steppe. On more than one occasion I had the opportunity to escape. But I could not leave my companions behind, especially not dear Elinora, who was devoted to me. The savages, knowing how dangerous I might be, kept me trussed hand and foot, day and night. Four burly guards watched my every move. Even so, I almost gained my freedom on more than one occasion. There was a thunderstorm once, and I almost escaped while my captors were cowering in fear. And another time I attempted to burn off my bonds in the campfire, at great personal risk."

It was at this point in Durk's narrative that Nolo caught Avender's eye and gave him a wink. Even the Shaper, who clearly wished the tragedian would come more quickly to the point, rolled his eyes at the more outrageous parts. But Durk, who could only touch and hear, had no idea his audience was taking him less than seriously. Only Nurren, who had never been to the surface and knew very little even of those humans who had come to the Stoneways, took the rock's story at face value.

"Of course we knew all along where they were taking us," Durk continued. "Where do Keeadini ever take their prisoners? After long weeks of horrible suffering we arrived finally at the gates of the fortress. It was a terrible place, and one I shall never forget. The mountains there are black and cruel, and so steep I was unable to see the sky. Through great iron doors they took us into His Great Hall. Filth and brazen beasts were everywhere, snarling at us with slavering jaws. His soldiers beat us with their spears, and laid heavy chains upon us. Poor Elinora! Without my aid she would have been unable to take a single step. They led us to His throne—"

"You actually met Uss—I mean, Him?"

Redburr dropped down from his perch to hang by his claws from the front of Avender's cloak, where he could look closely at the stone. His flat nose twitched with interest, not unlike the way it would have had he been a bear. Avender found himself bowed forward by the Shaper's weight.

"Tell us everything you can remember about that time," Redburr went on intently. "I've never met anyone who's faced Him before."

"I was one of the few present strong enough to face him," boasted Durk. "He looked down at us from an immense stone throne, and very large and terrible He was. I remember especially that His eyes blazed like the sun. I had expected to see a frail and wizened Wizard, much like the scholars in Malmoret, but He's neither of those things. He's twice as big as you or I, with hands large enough to squeeze your head like a melon. He laughed when He saw us, and told us we should be happy to have volunteered for His service. Dorrin begged for mercy. I counseled him to silence, but he wouldn't listen. Then our captor raised a hand and fastened his terrible eyes on Dorrin, and my old friend was never able to make a sound again.

"He spent some time gazing upon us. Elinora and a few others were taken away there and then. He set His guards and wolves upon the rest of us, and they herded us back to the dungeons like so many cattle. For a long time they put us to work digging in the tunnels and breaking rocks. I never saw Elinora again, and Dorrin and the rest of my companions were taken away one by one until at last I was the only one left. Finally, my turn came as well, and I was summoned before Him a second time."

For a long time Durk said nothing more. The memory of what had happened during his second audience with Usseis appeared to have overwhelmed even his love of rhetoric. His smooth sides flickered in the hearth's short tongues of dancing flame. Then, just when his listeners thought he was finished with his tale, the stone went on once more.

"I won't say anything about what was done to me. You don't even want to imagine it." Durk spoke softly, almost whispering. "All I'll say is that He took what He wanted and left me with nothing. Or at least that was what I thought at first. But gradually I came to realize I was still alive. I felt the stone beneath me. I heard things in the dark. Once in a while I even felt the sticky feet of an insect or two crawl over me. It was a long time before I understood what I had become."

"But how'd you get down here?" interrupted Avender. "How'd you get into that cave with me?"

"How do you get anywhere?" asked Ferris. "You're only a rock, after all. It's not like you can move around on your own."

"Oh, I get around," said Durk. "Sometimes I'm kicked. Sometimes I'm thrown. I've been in many fights. For a long time I lived with the pasties. Unlike the sissit, they weren't scared of me at all. Too dim-witted, I suppose. Unfortunately, they're completely undependable. It was because of one of them that I found myself languishing in that cave. Luckily you came along. Or at least it was lucky before you started talking this nonsense about finding a way to get Upstairs."

"These pasties must be what keep hiding from us," said Nurren. "Are they spies?"

"They might be," answered the stone. "They aren't very good ones, though. Their memories are quite poor."

"Are there others like you?" asked Redburr.

"Well," said Durk after a moment's pause. "There might be. I don't really know. I have heard stories."

"What kinds of stories?"

"I've heard the sissit talk about voices in the dark. Voices that try to trick them into doing things. Luring them into bottomless pits, that sort of thing."

"Have you spent as much time with the sissit as you have with the pasties?" asked Redburr.

"Oh, no." Durk sounded honestly scared. "I try to keep away from the sissit. If they knew what I was they'd take me back to Him, I'm sure."

"Then how do you know what they talk about?" persisted the Shaper.

"The sissit come looking for the pasties sometimes. Sometimes they just want to talk to them. Sometimes it's for other, um, things."

"Like what?"

"If they're hungry. The sissit are always hungry."

"Yes," Redburr agreed. "He made them that way."

"All the more reason not to venture any closer Upstairs," urged the stone. "No doubt, now that I've explained the dangers, you'll no longer think of going any further in that direction."

"On the contrary." Redburr looked around at his companions. "We're as firmly resolved as ever."

Avender shivered at the thought of what lay ahead, but Durk's story had made Reiffen's fate seem all the more real. Even if he failed, he had, at least, to try.

"We have a friend to rescue," said Ferris stoutly.

"Then I insist you leave me behind! There's no reason I should have to share in your foolishness!"

"I don't think we can leave you behind now, Durk," said Redburr. "We can't take the chance someone else might find you and learn we're here. I'm sorry, but you'll have to come with us. Besides, I think you might turn out to be useful."

"This is an outrage! Not only do you abduct me, but you impugn my honor as well! Who says I would breathe a word that you were here! Unless, of course, I decide to turn spy just to pay you back for the ill-usage you've shown me!"

The rock continued to protest, but all he got for his trouble was to be put back into Avender's pack. He was still there when Delven and the rest of the Bryddin returned.

17

Bugs, Burns, and Bones

our Dwarves accompanied Delven when he arrived, making seven in all. Not exactly an army, but they were Bryddin, which made all the difference in the world. They wore lamps on their foreheads, but unlike Nolo and Nurren, whose shining stones were pale and white, these new gems gleamed in soft colors: topaz and ruby, turquoise and aquamarine.

Nolo introduced them. Avender and Ferris watched enthralled as rainbows creased the cavern in time with their nodding and bowing. Along with Delven were the brothers Dale and Dell, who had passed through the Abyss together, one with a green lamp and the other red; Snurr, whose light shone with a gentle yellow cast; and Gorr, whose lamp was blue. Among them only Nurren and Delven had learned human speech, but the rest were quick at picking it up as soon it was spoken around them. Language was just another interesting puzzle, as far as Bryddin were concerned.

Before anything else, Nurren insisted his comrades meet Durk. Their heavy eyebrows rose at the vociferous flint's shouts of protest as Avender removed him from his pack, but they paid less mind to his outbursts as they passed him back and forth among themselves.

Each Bryddin held the stone up before his lamp and examined him carefully. They rubbed him with their fingers, sniffed at him, and shook him like an empty rattle close beside their ears. Snurr even bit him, which caused Durk to yelp in outrage.

"Enough!" he cried as Snurr returned him carefully to Avender. The boy checked to see that the stone was still unmarked. "I knew it would come to this! Eaten! Consumed by ignorance in the darkness by an underground goat! That my end should be so low!"

Avender buffed the stone gently on his sleeve. "Nobody's going to eat you," he said. "But if you don't keep quiet, Redburr's going to make me put you back in my pack."

"Oh, we wouldn't want that now, would we," replied Durk. "I might miss the end of the world." Still, he did stop shouting. The long spell in Avender's knapsack, where Durk could tell nothing of what was going on around him, had checked the worst of his petulance.

They held a short council before setting out on the last stage of their journey. Delven wanted to know exactly what Nolo and Redburr proposed to do. There were some snide remarks from the stone as the Shaper explained they were looking for a way into the Wizards' fortress, but none of the Dwarves seemed to think there was anything exceptionally difficult about the idea. Delven pulled a set of maps from his pack and laid them on the floor. The golden lamp at his forehead cast a yellow glow on the parchment, making the maps look older than they actually were as he sorted among them. Finding the one he wanted, he unfolded it and spread it out on top of the others. The rest of the Dwarves drew close around him; the light from their lamps blended softly together to whiten the topmost map once more.

It was an odd sort of map. Its surface was a mass of impossible squiggles, as if a child had dribbled different colors of ink in idle patterns across the paper. Here and there the lines thickened and bulged, and there were occasional symbols the children recognized as Dwarven letters. But neither of them could make any sense of the writing, or of the map in general.

"Here's where we are." Delven pointed to one of the bulges. "And this is where the fortress is." He moved his finger to a spot where the squiggles came to an end. A single rune was written in the space beyond. "The road isn't pleasant, but it isn't dangerous, either. And it's the likeliest way to Ussene."

Durk's voice rang out sharply, "Don't say that name!"

Delven looked critically at the rock, whom Avender had placed on a corner of the map to hold the parchment down. "I don't think we need fear Wizards down here as much as you think," he said. "We're in our world now, not theirs."

"Never mention Them by name, or anything to do with Them!" The rock's voice trembled in agitation. "You don't know what They can do!"

"We're Bryddin," said Delven. "We don't have to know what they can do. Their arts have no effect on us."

"I wouldn't be so sure of that," warned Nolo. "If there's one thing I've learned in the time I've spent with humans, it's never underestimate an enemy. There's more than Wizards' magic in the world."

"Listen to him," urged the stone. "He knows what he says."

"It always makes sense to be careful when dealing with the Three, but we must keep to our purpose all the same." Redburr peered at the map with his weak bat eyes, seeming to find it every bit as hard to read as Ferris or Avender. "How far away do you think we are, anyway?" he asked.

"A single march, perhaps." Delven turned his attention back to the parchment and traced out a path along one of the squiggles with the tip of his thick finger. "This tunnel here leads most quickly toward the greatest pain in the stone."

"Pain in the stone?" asked Durk. "I thought my sensitivity to the vicissitudes of life was unique among the sedentary strata."

Nurren gazed at the talking rock with wonder and admiration. "Break me, but I can't understand a word he says!"

Nolo ignored Nurren's astonishment. "We Bryddin can feel the ways of the stone, Durk. It's one of the things that helps us excel at masonry and mining."

"This close to the fortress I'm surprised you can't feel it yourself," added Delven. "It's plain as a copper vein."

"The only thing obvious to me," said Durk, "is that you're all mad."

"Mad or not," answered Redburr, who, with his squeaky bat voice, did perhaps sound a touch unhinged, "we're here to finish what we came to do."

Beyond deciding the best route to the fortress, there was nothing more to discuss until they reached Ussene. They couldn't put together any sort of real plan without a better idea of the obstacles they would find. Ferris wondered if they would find small, forgotten tunnels winding their way in secret into the dungeon's long-lost foundation. Or maybe a gate, with a portcullis and perhaps a drawbridge over a fiery moat guarded by manders. The only way to find out was to come close enough to the citadel to see its defenses with their own eyes.

Dale led the way. He had explored the closest to Ussene, and had scouted the beginnings of that terrible place. From the start, the stone felt different from what the children had traveled through before. There was a lot more to worry about: pasties and spiders and Wizards' spells, and everything was much more damp. The moist rock felt unclean when Ferris brushed against it, and the air was ripe with nasty smells, as if they were passing beneath the dreary drippings of some drowned dungeon just above their heads. But Dale kept them marching forward, and none of the Dwarves paid the least attention to the growing foulness. Steadily they climbed through the warren of twisting tunnels toward the fortress of the Three.

They had slipped through the slimy caverns for several hours when Redburr let go his perch on Nolo's cloak and flew on ahead. Ferris felt something crunch beneath her boot. Lifting her foot, she saw the remains of a large beetle squashed flat on the bottom. Other insects squirmed luminously across the path in front of her.

Redburr came darting back to the party. He settled on Ferris's cloak and said, "I think I should warn you. There's a cave full of bugs ahead."

"I don't mind bugs," said the girl, offended that Redburr should think she might, and trying hard not to bend beneath his weight. "I didn't grow up in Malmoret, you know."

The bat's black eyes glittered. "We'll see. It's pretty bad up there. You and Avender had better both cover your heads with your hoods."

The Dwarves were already following his suggestion. Lacking cloaks, they took blankets from their packs and wrapped them around their heads and beards until only their long noses poked out. Ferris and Avender quickly pulled up their hoods and held them tight around their faces. In front of them the lines of pale centipedes and crickets increased across the path. A fat bat that wasn't Redburr flew out of the darkness to snatch a winged something from the air.

They hurried on. The carpet of creeping creatures thickened. Something squished with every step, until they could no longer hear the squashings because the chittering and churring around them had grown too loud. The floor seethed with pale bubbles of scurrying bugs, all made the more ghastly by the thin green and yellow lights that played across the teeming pile from the lamps of Snurr and Dale.

But it was much, much worse once they rounded the next turn and entered the cave beyond. Here the slithering and scraping of the insects was joined by a cacophony of bats swooping and diving through the air. Ferris and Avender clutched their hoods closer and hardly dared breathe as they followed the Dwarves into the noisome fog. All about them the walls and floor of the cavern heaved with heaps of pale, clicking creatures. Though the cavern was plainly much larger, their way seemed to pass through a low tunnel of waving wings and jiggling legs, large bats plunging back and forth between the wriggling walls. Small bodies thudded into their shoulders as they hurried on, hunched forward against the chitinous rain. Beneath their feet the ground grew more and more slippery as a residue of all the things they had crushed began to thicken on the soles of their boots—or on the bottoms of the Dwarves' bare feet and in between their toes.

Halfway across the cavern Redburr, who had been hanging from the front of Ferris's cloak, could restrain himself no longer. The sound of this flying feast overcame him completely. He swooped off into the fluttering dark beyond the weak gleam of the lamps and joined the other bats. Ferris felt him go but lost sight of him immediately as he disappeared into the swirling swarm. A heavy beetle thumped against her cheek. She gritted her teeth and pressed on.

Sooner than they expected, but far later than they wished, they came out on the other side. A narrow tunnel led up a steep track away from the infested cavern. For a moment the way was even worse than it had been below. All sorts of slimy crawling things clung closely to the walls of the narrow passage: as the travelers brushed past, the bugs fell off onto their necks and shoulders. A few found their way up sleeves and down collars. Ferris felt tiny legs tickling her neck and arms. Then the worst was past and they were back out into the clearer corridor beyond, where a relatively few beetles still skittered across the floor. The Dwarves threw off their towels and everyone began to dance about as they tried to shake the creatures out from inside their shirts. Small, pale things dropped to the floor in dozens.

The Shaper was still chewing when he came shooting out of the dark tunnel and settled back on Nolo's chest. "I hope everyone enjoyed that as much as I did," he said, swallowing his last mouthful.

His thin red tongue licked the last trace of his meal off the tip of his flat nose.

"That's disgusting," said Ferris, pulling a weevil out of her ear.

The next cave they came to didn't seem so bad as the first. After a few minutes, they left the narrow tunnel and emerged onto a short beach of dark sand that ran down to an equally dark lake. Only the lamplight reflecting on the still surface revealed where the sand ended and the water began. Smooth as the bottom of a deep well, the lake gleamed with an icy blackness. But Dale's first footsteps proved the water wasn't ice. There was a small splash, and a set of shallow ripples widened slowly out across the stillness beyond the shore. A sharp, sweet smell rose up from the bubbles at his feet.

They gathered on the sand. "This is as far as we've explored," said Delven. "I don't think the water's too deep, but there might be a hole or two out there. Be careful where you step. I'd guess the fortress is close by the other side. If we can't find a direct connection, I'm sure we'll find a place to tunnel."

"I'll fly on ahead and see how far it is," said Redburr.

They waited at the edge of the dark lake for his return. His steady squeaking trailed behind him through the air. Their breath fogged slightly in the damp, creating small clouds of color as the different lights of the Dwarves were turned upon them. Ferris shivered, and pulled three more beetles from her sleeve.

Redburr winged back out of the darkness. "There's a second passage on the other side that goes on the way we want," he said. "I didn't find anything else."

Delven took the lead now that they were beyond the paths that Dale had followed. His golden lamp brought no more life to the surface of the still lake than had Dale's green one. They entered the water in single file, the children following Dale and Nolo while Nurren and the others brought up the rear. The lake was shallow at first, barely covering the tops of the Dwarves' feet or the children's boots. But it deepened steadily, and before they had gone far had risen close to everyone's knees. The cold stung both Ferris and Avender as the wetness climbed their legs. Beneath their feet the water clouded as they stirred the light mud on the bottom, and with the eddies came a quickening of the sweet stench they had noticed on the beach. Nolo sniffed carefully at the smell, then ordered the children to cover their faces. They wet their handkerchiefs with clean water from their bottles before pressing them across their mouths and noses. Then they pushed on farther into the lake, moving their legs stiffly so as to disturb the muddy bottom as little as possible. Sometimes, though, the brown silt still swirled up to the surface, and the stench became overpowering, a piercing odor that passed straight from the nose to the back of the eyes like an iron nail. And it was icy cold, if a smell could be called cold. A smell of coldness and crumbled stone and death. Redburr, who had no mask, finally let go his hold on Nolo's shirt and flew up into the hovering darkness to escape the odor. Even the Dwarves complained.

They waded on through the tugging water and, though the sound of their wading echoed in that close space, the cavern still seemed strangely silent, as if no sound could waken the lake's deadness. Avender's and Ferris's legs had never stopped stinging once the water had risen above their boots; now they began to burn where their wet trousers rubbed against them.

"My legs are really starting to hurt," said Ferris. She had tried not to complain as long as she could, but now it was all she could do to keep from reaching down to rub at the burning itch.

Redburr took a deep breath and dove back down to skim close above the surface of the water. He dipped a foot as he passed and pulled it back quickly, as if he had touched something hot. "There's something wrong with this water besides the smell," he called as he passed close above their heads.

Nolo tasted a drop with his hand and grimaced. "Quick," he said, turning to Ferris. "Climb up onto my shoulders. Nurren! You carry Avender. Hurry!"

The children climbed onto the Dwarves, but the burning in their legs didn't lessen even when they were out of the water. "We'll have to run," said Nolo. "It's still in their clothes."

"This way!" Redburr darted overhead to show them the way to the other side. "It's not far!"

They splashed on through the foul lake, no longer caring how much they churned up the poisoned bottom in their haste to reach dry ground. Avender and Ferris clung to Nurren and Nolo with one hand apiece, the others tightly clutching their handkerchiefs over their mouths and noses.

At last the floor began to rise. The Dwarves rushed up the muddy beach on the other side and dropped the children to the sand as soon as they had cleared the water. Drops splashed against the children's hands and faces, stinging where they landed. Quickly they cut away their wet trousers and flung them aside. Their legs glowed pink in the thin light of the lamps, but the burning stopped as soon as they had removed their sopping clothes and rubbed their legs dry with the blankets pulled from their packs.

"I should have realized what was happening sooner," said Nolo as he followed the blankets with dry clothing. He shook his head at the children's raw, blotchy legs, then went back to the dark lake and examined it again with his hand. "It's such a thin solution I didn't recognize the smell."

"What is it?" asked Avender, shivering as he and Ferris pulled their only other change of clothing over their tender legs.

"Acid," said Delven.

"More of Their experiments," said Redburr in disgust.

Durk, who had tumbled out of Avender's pack with his blanket, couldn't refrain from chipping in. "I hope this has gotten all the foolishness out of your system. If getting close to His place is this hard when He doesn't even know you're here, just imagine what it's going to be like when He does."

"You should know by now that nothing you say is going to change our minds," said Ferris.

"We all have to be careful," warned the Shaper. "Uss—I mean He corrupts without caring, and is even more careless with what he throws away. There's a lot here that's dangerous."

Even as he spoke, Ferris stumbled over a rock she hadn't noticed in the shadows while fastening her skirt. She fell backward into a small patch of pale puffballs growing from the slimy stone wall. As soon as she touched them, they exploded into a cloud of fine brown dust that burned her face and hands even more painfully than the water in the lake. She cried out, swatting uselessly at the clouded air as she tried to keep it away from her skin. Redburr was beside her in a moment, his leathery wings fanning the powder away. But the sting lingered anyway, and she could feel her cheek grow hot and begin to swell. Two large tears dripped from her tightly closed eyes to draw small lines down her dirty face.

"As I just mentioned," said Redburr, waving the last of the powder away, "we have to be very careful."

Avender dabbed at the reddening sores on Ferris's face with her damp handkerchief, but there was little anyone could do to ease the soreness or the swelling. Gently he cleaned around her eyes until it was safe for her to open them.

"Don't scratch," he said as she reached to rub her cheek. Ferris gritted her teeth but kept her hands away from her face.

They shouldered their packs and pushed on into the next tunnel. The pale growths thickened along the walls on either side, swelling out against one another like compound bruises. The light from Nolo's lamp caught a small lizard as it darted in between two of the puffballs, leaving a small spray of fine powder hanging in the air behind it. Above their heads the tight passage disappeared into the darkness, as if they were traveling along a narrow gorge that snaked back and forth between twin cliffs. Avender and Ferris couldn't help but feel that something was about to drop down on them from above at any moment: giant spiders, or pasties with cold, grabbing hands. Beneath their feet the rock showed completely black no matter which Dwarven lamp shined upon it, red or yellow, blue or green.

"Do you think it's going to get much worse?" whispered Ferris anxiously. The burns on her face were already bleeding thinly, but it was all she could do to keep herself from scratching them.

Avender nodded and trudged doggedly on.

They hadn't gone far before the passage widened out on either side. Fine black sand covered the floor. They had entered a third cave and, though they could see neither the roof above nor the wall on the far side, it felt far larger than either of the two before. A few pale stones lay scattered on the black ground before them.

Delven led them on. The dark sand crunched softly underfoot. They came to the first of the white stones and found it wasn't a stone at all but rather a small skull pillowed on the sand. Beyond it they came quickly to other bones: skulls and ribs and thighbones, and others not so easily identified. All gleamed white against the black sand in the light of Nolo's lamp, but their pallor was more ghastly beneath the green and gold of Dale and Delven.

Soon the floor was covered with them. There was no place to step except upon a wrist or shin. The Dwarves made a great racket as the bony path snapped and broke beneath their weight. Higher and higher rose the skeletal pile, until they finally found themselves climbing a small hill of broken and fleshless bone. Most of the whitened sticks were unrecognizable, but now and again there was one the children knew: the skull of a wolf; two fingers and a human hand. Shadows flickered like live things behind the jumbled thighs and spines, caged by ribs and arm bones. Huge skulls of creatures not even Redburr could name stared out at them from deep within the piles. Some had huge, flat foreheads and empty eyes; others, great long jaws with rows of sharp and broken teeth. The children shuddered at the sight of them. Once they had been creatures out of nightmare or the darkest woods, but even in death they lost none of their power to provoke terror.

The slope grew steeper as they climbed; they had to pull themselves up the last few yards with hands and feet. Loose bones knocked free by their passing slid down the mound beside them, and the Dwarves had to be careful to put their weight on only the heaviest and strongest pieces. But the children had little difficulty. The bones felt smooth and cold beneath their hands, like dead branches stripped of all their bark.

Redburr flew on ahead but said nothing of what he found when he returned. He clung to the back of Nolo's knapsack as the rest of the company climbed onto the rounded top of the brittle pile. Just out of reach above their heads was the cavern ceiling. In the middle, centered above the hill of bones, a dark hole opened in the rock. The Dwarven lamps showed nothing of what lay beyond.

"We can't go any farther this way," said the Shaper. His voice was muffled by the closeness of the rock overhead.

"Have you already explored the passage?" asked Nolo.

"No," answered Redburr tersely. "And I'm not going to, either. There are watchers up there, without a doubt. We may already have come too close."

"Then why didn't you stop us from climbing up?" asked Delven.

"If they can hear us here, they'd have heard us down below," answered the Shaper. "As long as we don't try to go any further I think they'll believe we're just a few pasties come to pick among the bones."

"What kind of watchers are they?" asked Ferris in a whisper.

Redburr shrugged his folded wings. "Who knows?" he said. "It could be the stone itself. Now that I've met Durk I'm not sure what the limits are to what They can do. But this way will not be unguarded."

"There must be other tunnels in the rock," said Nolo. "And we can always dig our way in."

"I think it's time we go look for them."

Carefully they descended the far side of the pile. The Dwarves were of the opinion that the fissure they had followed into the cavern most likely continued on in that direction. Sure enough, once they had crossed a second stretch of black sand and left the last of the bones behind, they came to another split in the side of the cave wall. Only this time the path was narrower and the sand continued beneath their feet. The pale puffballs grew closely here, and quivered as the lizards among them scattered back to the wall at the approach of the Dwarven lamps.

Nolo took Delven's place at the front of the company. His white lamp lit the narrowing passage. They came to a place where the path became no more than a narrow crevice between the walls, their further progress blocked by the swollen fungi.

Nolo took his short knife from his belt. "Nurren," he said. "Take Ferris and Avender back behind that last turn. The rest of us will clear the passage so we can go on."

Nurren led the children back around the bend. Redburr joined them, hanging from Avender's cloak. They listened as the other Dwarves hacked a way through the bulging growths. The hollow *thump! thump!* of the bursting puffballs sounded a lot like Hern cleaning rugs on the back porch of the Manor. For a moment the children found the darkness unbearable, as memories of green grass and blue skies welled up for both of them. Avender wished he could be up front with Nolo flailing away at something; Ferris just wished she were home. Then the sound was over and quiet fell back over the passage once more.

Nolo summoned them after the stinging dust had settled. His face and beard were shrouded in pale brown powder, as if he had spent a long day carving dirty marble, like Dwvon among his blocks of stone. Beyond the mushrooms the passage narrowed to a fissure in the rock, tighter and darker than any hole they had yet crawled into in the Stoneways. Even the children had to turn sideways to enter, and they were not nearly as broad as Snurr, who was the thinnest of the Dwarves. The passage was too narrow for Redburr to fly, which meant they would have to wait until they got there to find out what lay at the other end. The Shaper crawled inside Avender's knapsack alongside Durk and did his best to keep from being crushed against the rock as the boy squeezed his way along.

They inched like worms through the stone. Beneath their feet a layer of fine sand filled the space between the walls, but overhead the empty blackness rose beyond the gleam of the lamps. They shuffled forward for a while one step at a time, their hands resting on the rough wall close beside their cheeks. Then they began to climb. The fissure continued on into the darkness as they pulled themselves upwards by fingers and toes. Behind them the other wall pressed closely upon their backs. Small stones rattled down around their heads: the Dwarves were working to widen the path above. They clambered up through the crevice like spiders on a wall; more than once Avender and Ferris wished they had a web to cling to, or anything that was easier than the hard and biting stone.

They had been climbing for some time when they met Nolo waiting for them along the way. Their fingers ached from clinging to the tiny ledges and they were glad of the chance to rest, wedged tightly between the crevice walls.

"We're almost there," said Nolo. His lamp seemed to gleam more brightly in the cramped darkness. "Delven and the others are widening the rest of the way."

The sound of steady digging scratched above their heads. A constant shower of rock rattled down into the depths beside them. Redburr poked his head out of Avender's knapsack and frowned when he saw there was still no place for him to fly.

"It's one thing for Durk to ride in here," he complained. "He can't smother. Are we there yet? I think you've broken two of my ribs."

"The fissure's too narrow for any of us just above," said Nolo. He pointed up past his head as he spoke. "But there's an artificial passage close beyond. It won't be hard to carve out the rest of the way."

The word soon came back that Delven had broken through to the other passage. Nolo climbed on ahead but returned at once with the news that they had reached the fortress at last. Ussene, remote and terrible for so long, lay open in the darkness ahead. Its distant dangers were now close and real. Ferris and Avender exchanged glances, wondering at their foolishness in journeying so far on so impossible an errand, even with Redburr and the Dwarves to guide them. Evil and wretchedness awaited them in Ussene, especially in its deepest parts.

Redburr, his head still poking out the top of Avender's knapsack, sensed their dismay. "Don't worry," he said. "We're not expected. With any luck we'll be gone before they even know we're here."

They passed the Shaper up from hand to hand until he was able to fly off into the new passage. He returned in a moment with the news that they had discovered a deserted section of the dungeons. The passage was quite empty. The Dwarves quickly widened their opening; then everyone climbed the last few short feet into the fortress. The way was so narrow they had to remove their packs and hand them along ahead before they were able to squeeze up through the hole in the floor. Avender's throat tightened when it was his turn as he remembered being buried beneath the rock slide. Then his head came clear on the other side, and Nolo's strong hands pulled him out and onto his feet.

The lamps swung in nervous arcs around the soot-blackened walls. The Dwarves had cut their opening in the floor close to one side, where it might easily be hidden behind the loose rubble that lined the passage. Clearly it was a passage, though not one dug by Dwarves. Bryddin tunnels were always smooth underfoot, but this one was rough and uneven, a place anyone might trip were they not careful about where they put their feet. The walls were also rough, and pale growths clung to the cracks. But at least there were no puffballs. Avender sniffed the air. It was different from the smell of the caves below, but no better. Soot and rottenness combined here as if something dead had been rubbed around in cold cinders before being left to decay nearby.

"Where are we?" asked Ferris as she followed Avender up out of the hole.

Redburr shrugged his leathery wings. "Some wretched pit. I

think we're still a long way from the light of day. If it is day up there."

"It's day," Nolo assured them. Nothing ever seemed to shake his sense of time.

"Which way do we go?"

At Ferris's question Avender looked left and right. The corridor extended in both directions, and the boy could see no difference either way. The rough black walls swallowed the lamplight no matter which way he looked. It was impossible to see what might lie even a few strides off.

"The stone groans in both directions," said Delven. He looked doubtfully at Redburr and Nolo. The Bryddin had gotten them as far as the dungeons and now it was their part to lead the party farther.

"Maybe I should do a little more exploring," suggested the Shaper. "There's probably a guardroom or something nearby."

Nolo nodded. Bits of rock and brown dust dropped from his beard. "That's a good idea. This tunnel doesn't seem to be used much. We'll wait here till you come back."

"Maybe you'll find Reiffen," suggested Ferris, voicing a hope shared by the entire company. It made sense that the Three would keep their prisoner in their deepest, safest dungeon. Safest, that is, except for burglars from below.

"It's what I've hoped from the start," confessed the bat. "We'll be gone before they even know it, if I do."

So everyone waited once again while Redburr flew off to sound out the dungeon around them. Nolo sent Gorr and Snurr cautiously down the passage after him to stand guard. But he made everyone else remain where they were, so they would be close to their only path of escape if they were discovered. The Dwarves passed the time waiting for Redburr's return in fashioning a stone door to cover their opening in the wall. Avender took Durk out of his knapsack, then he and Ferris sat together with their backs to the other wall and watched the Bryddin at their work. Durk, once he realized he was back in the fortress, went into a deep sulk and refused to say a word.

When Redburr did return he came in a rush, his small chest heaving. He clung to Nolo's cloak and caught his breath. Gorr and Snurr followed behind as fast as they could, not understanding they were supposed to remain on guard. Nolo had to ask them to return to their posts in case anyone was following behind them. For a few moments more Redburr huffed and puffed, while the rest of the company gathered impatiently to hear his tale.

"It's okay," he finally managed to gasp. "No one's following me. . . . I flew as fast as I could . . . to make sure the guards couldn't keep up with me. U—" The Shaper caught himself as he noticed Avender holding Durk. "I mean the Three must keep Their soldiers on pretty close rations, or they'd never have been so quick to try and make a meal out of a bat."

"What did you find?" asked Nolo.

"We're definitely in the dungeons, at the end of a warren of cells. The corridor turns up ahead. There are a few more branchings, then it comes to a central guardroom. I found a few cells along the way, but not many. Some are occupied, but Reiffen's not in any of them. There's a stair leading up out of the guardroom, and two other tunnels I'd guess are a lot like this one. But I didn't have a chance to explore them because the guards were after me as soon as I entered the room. I was wondering why I didn't hear any other bats down here."

"How many guards?" asked Nolo.

"Three. At least three that I saw. Armed to the teeth, too. They fired crossbows at me."

"Were they alarmed to see you?"

"No. They just wanted to eat me." Redburr scratched his belly comfortably with one of his claws. "That was quite clear from their disappointment when I escaped. The last I heard they were kicking each other for getting in each other's way. Cave chicken, that's what they called me."

"Maybe Durk can tell us where we are," suggested Ferris. But

Durk continued to ignore all attempts at persuading him to speak. Finally Nolo picked him up and threatened to dash him to pieces against the ground and use what was left to line the inside of his forge. The stone wisely decided his present danger was worse than anything yet threatening him from the Three, and broke his silence.

"Fine," he said glumly. "I'll tell you what I can. It might help if you told me what you're looking for."

"We're looking for our friend," said Ferris.

"What sort of friend? If he's as mad as you, They've probably got him breaking rocks with his teeth, or some equally impossible task."

"He's a child, like these two," explained Redburr. "And he's the heir to the thrones of both Malmoret and Rimwich."

"The heir to both? My, your friend is important." The more Durk talked, the more it seemed to Avender and Ferris that he forgot his fear of the Three. "All the more reason for us to leave now, while we still can. Anyone that important is bound to be closely guarded. They won't leave him down here. He's probably Upstairs, where They can keep an eye on him Themselves. And since when did Rimwich and Malmoret get so chummy as to share an heir?"

"It's a long story," said Ferris. "But Reiffen is the real heir, even if his uncle pretends he isn't."

"Royal uncles are a lot like that. You see it all the time in the best tragedies:

> 'Oh cursed fool! That I should live to see
> A brother's son in gifts of state raised o'er me!'

As you can probably tell, I've played many noble kings in my long career. People say I have a natural air of command. That's from Durber's *The Bloody Regent*."

"I've seen it," said Redburr. "We don't need to hear any more of it now."

"Really," sniffed the rock. "You continue to show me no consideration at all, even after asking my help."

"When we rescue Reiffen," said Avender, "you can recite all the poetry you want."

"Thank you, Avender. I knew there was something special about you the first time I heard you speak."

Nolo frowned. "None of this is much help," he said. "I had hoped the boy might be hidden some place where we might be able to dig him out easily. And that Durk might help us narrow down the possibilities."

"That is cruel," said Durk. "I've told you everything I know. It's not as if I had the run of the place, even when I had legs."

"We should be able to find your friend, all the same," said Delven. "I don't think three guards will give us much trouble. When we're through with them we can search all the levels until we find him."

"No fighting," said Redburr. "Not as long as we can help it. Even with seven Bryddin there are only ten of us, against who knows how many of them. This is their fortress. That's one of the reasons we chose to sneak in through Bryddlough in the first place."

"There's nothing for it but to stick to our original plan," agreed Nolo. "Make as little fuss as possible, both on the way in and out. Redburr will just have to get past the guards and explore the rest of the dungeon. It might take a while, but he'll find where Reiffen's being held eventually."

"It might take me a long time," said Redburr. "And the longer it takes me, the more chance the rest of you'll be discovered. Then there'd be almost no possibility of rescuing the boy."

"That's the first bit of sense I've heard from any of you yet," said Durk.

"I don't see what other choice we have." Nolo rubbed his chin unhappily. "I was really counting on them keeping him down here in the dungeons where it would be one, two, three and we'd have him right out."

"Well, there is another way," said the Shaper. "I haven't wanted to bring it up before, because it's dangerous. Especially for the children. But I thought all along there was going to be another reason to bring them with us besides recognizing Reiffen."

Everyone turned to Redburr. He had flown up from Nolo's chest to hang from a small ledge on the wall, his eyes on a level with the circle of Dwarves around him. But Redburr wasn't looking at the Dwarves. He was looking at Ferris and Avender, who were still crouched out of sight along the base of the wall. They didn't know what to think: what his plan might be or what it was the Shaper was about to ask of them. Ferris had been certain this would happen, and that in the end there would be a bigger part for her to play; but Avender felt only a hollow wariness in the pit of his stomach. He gathered himself to accept whatever he was asked to do.

"I've always found," said the Shaper, "that when trying to sneak past Hern into the kitchens for a little something to eat, it's a lot easier to get around if you look like you're supposed to be there."

Delven frowned and tugged his beard. "Why would anyone have to sneak into kitchens for food? Isn't that what kitchens are for?"

Nolo patted him on the shoulder. "Redburr," he said, "is completely outside the experience of Bryddin, and requires a whole new set of rules."

They listened as the Shaper outlined his plan. When he was done Nolo shook his head and gave a wry smile.

"I like it," he said.

"You would," said Delven. "Now that I've learned something about humans, I think you're half a human yourself."

18

Carrot and Stick

ou're not eating enough."

Reiffen didn't bother to look up. Fornoch appeared in the Library the way he always did, without a sound and without using the door. Not for the first time the boy wondered how the Wizard could move from place to place ignoring doors and walls. No matter how hard Reiffen tried to silence it, part of him wished he could do the same. Ossdonc had needed the henge to bring him back to the fortress, but Fornoch seemed to require no such device.

"Do you wish a new servant?" the Wizard asked. Though nothing cast a shadow in that oddly lit room, Reiffen could tell Fornoch was standing right behind him. The Wizard was as conspicuous as a thunderstorm. "I know Molio used to bring you food to spare you the embarrassment of dining with the slaves."

"Molio wasn't my servant. He was my friend."

"In Ussene a servant is more useful than a friend. I suggest you find a servant. If you persist in not eating, Ossdonc might decide to amuse himself by trying to see what sort of food repels you most."

Reiffen kept his face in his book, though he had given up trying to read the moment Fornoch arrived. Since Molio's death, the Wizard had visited him much more often than before. Reiffen was sure that meant the Wizard believed he was weakening. He knew it himself, but somehow the knowledge that Fornoch thought the same bolstered the boy's stubbornness. The idea that the Wizard might have been right all along was too terrible to bear.

Fornoch crossed the room to the spider. Reiffen guessed the creature had been waiting eagerly for Fornoch's touch from the moment the Wizard arrived. At least, thought Reiffen to himself, he still had enough self-respect to keep from greeting his master like an excited dog.

"Do you truly believe you and the spider are the same?"

Reiffen flinched, as he always did when he thought Fornoch was reading his mind.

"The spider has no choice. Your lot is different. You can choose to be master or slave. The spider, unfortunately, has no understanding of such distinctions. In the face of greater power it can only submit. Or be crushed."

In the silence that followed, Reiffen found himself wondering if Fornoch had actually crushed his pet. It would be just the sort of random cruelty he expected from the Wizards, though Fornoch had always seemed better than his brothers. The boy turned to look, but the creature was still plucking happily at the web strings with all eight feet.

Fornoch ceased his petting. The spider stopped quivering, as if stunned by its master's disregard. The Wizard spoke again.

"Perhaps you need a demonstration of the sort of power that might be yours."

He held out his hand. It was the most neatly groomed hand Reiffen had ever seen, nails trimmed evenly without a speck of dirt. The boy hesitated. The memory of Ossdonc's cruel grip came too easily to his mind.

"I am not my brother," Fornoch reminded him. "I believe in the carrot as well as the stick. Come. I will show you many things."

Still struggling within himself, Reiffen accepted the Wizard's clasp. The hand was dry and strong. A feeling of security washed over the boy for the first time since leaving Valing. The tension in his shoulders eased.

Setting his jaw firmly, he forced himself not to trust the Wizard.

Fornoch didn't bother to notice his stubbornness. "The spell is not difficult," he explained. "You would learn it easily, given the proper instruction. I need not even speak a word."

The world changed. Reiffen couldn't tell if he actually felt anything or if the sensation was only the suddenness of the transition. One moment he was in the Library; the next he was at the top of a mountain. Dead brown hills stretched around him; a slab of smooth stone supported his feet. Gray clouds made a low ceiling of the sky. Then, before he could get his bearings, the scene shifted again. Reiffen recognized the enormous room where he had first met the Three. This time he stood on the dais beside Usseis's throne. The vast chamber stretched empty everywhere he looked, the circling pillars silent guards against the outer world.

Another shift, and another. The scenes spun on and on. From room to room they whirled through the fortress, from dungeon to garret again and again. In the kitchen they were gone before the busy slaves noticed their arrival; in a barracks the lounging soldiers leapt to their feet at once. Often the Wizard took them from light to dark and back to light again; in the unlit rooms Reiffen's eyes couldn't adjust quickly enough to see.

He guessed that was just as well. Some of what he saw in the lit rooms would have been better left unseen. But in other places the Wizard showed him chambers filled with gold and jewels, or marvelous creatures with necks or noses longer than a man, or objects as curious as those in the Library. The rooms flashed regularly before him like sheep to a pen, none receiving more time than any other. Each visit lasted long enough for a quick glimpse, a hint and nothing more, before the Wizard moved them on. Reiffen realized, as unimagined caves and passages paraded past his view, that until now he had seen only a very small part of the fortress.

They finished at the Library. Reiffen was glad the Wizard hadn't brought them to the Front Window. They stood as they left, near the spider, which had retreated to a corner of its web. At the Wizard's return it hurried forward again, all eight legs waving frantically.

Fornoch dropped Reiffen's hand. "Do you see how easy it can be?" he said. "Not quite so easy for you, perhaps. The magic is hidden deeper in your blood than it is in mine. You might have to leave a part of yourself behind to travel long distances quickly, but I am certain you will be able to master the necessary skill. The choice is yours."

Reiffen made no reply. He had no wish to tell the Wizard how the tour had thrilled him, how he wished he, too, could dance across the world. But the Wizard recognized his fascination.

"Do not take too long to make your decision," Fornoch advised.

"I've already made my decision," said Reiffen stubbornly.

"Have you?"

A thin smile curled up one side of Fornoch's face like the last wisp of smoke from a burnt-out fire. Reiffen wished he could jump up and shout that he had, that nothing the Wizards might do would ever make him change his mind, but he knew that wasn't true. Every day he felt weaker, in spirit as well as body. If he wasn't eating, it was because some part of him was hoping he would waste away before the last of his resistance finally folded in the face of his bleak despair. He couldn't close his eyes without seeing Molio's face spinning through the sky; he couldn't see a candle drip wax without remembering the smallest splash on the little man's spattered coat. Not once had he been back to visit the Front Window since he had lain crying on the cold stone floor. His cell and the Library were the only places he could stand to be for any amount of time, and even in his cell he could hardly sleep. Instead he waited out the long hours with the door closed to the corridor outside, not knowing whether it was night or day on the surface of the world, or whether he cared.

"My brothers are beginning to lose patience," said Fornoch after a time. "You have already held out longer than I expected. Great kings have shown less fortitude. But strength of mind does not impress my brothers, unless they can use it for their own purposes. You must choose, and quickly, or they will make your choice for you."

When Reiffen still made no reply, Fornoch's face grew cold. The fire of his interest appeared to die away. "Very well. Perhaps you have made up your mind. I had thought the first lesson you received from my brother would have taught you the error of obstinacy, but it appears that has not been the case. I should have expected stubbornness from a child. Perhaps another treatment will have more effect."

The Wizard turned, his gray robe brushing the floor. For the first time he actually used the door, which sprang open at a gesture from his hand. Reiffen followed, knowing that was what was wanted of him. He didn't even think about remaining behind.

Down they went through the dim tunnels. With Ossdonc, Reiffen had been dragged like a small child, his wrist caught in the Wizard's grip. Fornoch, however, had no need for force. For the first time it occurred to him that the Gray Wizard, long thought by the world to be the weakest of the Three, was actually more powerful than Ossdonc. And maybe more powerful than Usseis, too. Usseis would have compelled Reiffen to follow him, the way he had forced him to murder his friend. Fornoch had not even asked.

They passed the guardroom where Reiffen had been jeered when he had gone to help Rib. This time there were no jests, only respect and bows. The tunnel beyond was dark as night. Fornoch spoke a spell and a light appeared in the air behind him. A light to guide Reiffen, not the Wizard. They descended through an open space so huge the boy couldn't see walls or ceiling, then passed across a wide stone floor to a tunnel beneath a low gallery. Reiffen wasn't sure, but he thought he saw the mouths of other tunnels on either side.

The way curved back and forth. The light behind the Wizard's back was barely enough to show the dirty rock at Reiffen's feet. Slowly the boy became aware of a heavy odor filling the thick air, a smell of filthy boots roasting on a smoking fire. The passage wound on without a break, neither ascending nor descending, until at last it came out in another large room. The Wizard's light went out.

Whether it was larger or smaller than the first Reiffen couldn't tell, but the edges of this room were clearly marked by dull red fires that glowed in large hearths around the walls. A band of darkness circled the space between the outer fires and the only other light in the room, a pool of pale white radiance that fell in a widening circle from a small point in the ceiling far above. As Fornoch led Reiffen closer, he saw that the light was like that from the moon at its brightest, casting the faintest of shadows. But, if it was moonlight, the moon that cast it was long dead. In the center, seated on a stone bench like the one he had sat upon when Reiffen first met him, loomed Usseis, bathed in the empty glow. His dark eyes were lost in shadow; his nose protruded from his hidden face like the beak of a pallid bird.

Fornoch halted outside the circle of sickly moonlight. Reiffen stopped beside him. A large hand fell heavily on the boy's shoulder and pushed him forward. Reiffen flinched as he came into the light, but it didn't seem to harm him. Inside, however, he found he could see Usseis more clearly. The Wizard's dark eyes glittered, like a greedy monarch's with something fine and rare finally within his grasp.

"Still unconvinced?" Usseis's voice seemed to drip from his fingers as he brought his hands out from the folds of his robe. Something large moved restlessly at the back of the room. "It is as I have expected."

With his left hand, the Wizard beckoned Reiffen forward. Given his last experience with Usseis, Reiffen wasn't as inclined to obey as he was with Fornoch. Usseis's face tightened; he repeated the motion. Reiffen leapt forward as if kicked from behind. The Wizard's large hand closed around his throat.

"You will obey," he admonished. "Or this foolishness will end."

Reiffen felt as if he were suspended in an iron collar. He had no trouble breathing, and could even swallow. But beyond the confines of his own skin he couldn't move a muscle.

"Give me your hand."

This time Reiffen did as he was told. Usseis released his hold. In the large palm of the White Wizard, Reiffen's hand looked smaller than a child's. Taking the boy's wrist between his fingers like a twig, Usseis examined the hand closely. More than once Reiffen was certain he felt the Wizard's probing glance as a wave of heat washing across his fingers, or an unseen thread rubbing against his thumb.

The Wizard dropped the boy's arm. "Go to the table," he said.

Reiffen looked in the direction Usseis indicated but saw nothing. Nonetheless, Reiffen walked in that direction. Passing out of the pale circle, he found himself beside a stone table. In the dim light beyond the moonshine he couldn't be sure, but he thought the table was made of the same stuff as the henge in the High Bavadars. As he waited for whatever came next, he felt himself almost missing that high meadow, and the pool below where Mindrell had let them rest. His fear then was nothing to what he felt now. And yet, in his weariness, he was almost glad his time had come. Usseis might do what he would, but at least Reiffen would have the satisfaction of knowing he hadn't given in, no matter how tempting the carrot, or cruel the stick.

The light brightened once again. Usseis had joined him at the table, bringing his magic moonbeam with him.

"Put your right hand on the stone."

Again, Reiffen did as he was told. The table was cold as night beneath his palm. Usseis produced a small silver-bladed knife, a knife that would have looked normal sized in Reiffen's hand. A shiver slipped across the boy's shoulders; it took all his remaining nerve to keep from pulling back his arm. The knife gleamed as if it had never been used before. The Wizard turned to his victim, his black eyes drinking up every last drop of Reiffen's fright. With his right hand he clamped Reiffen's arm to the table. With his left holding the silver knife, Usseis bent close above the stone, his shoulder blocking Reiffen's view.

But Reiffen didn't have to wait long to learn what the Wizard was doing. Not that he couldn't have guessed anyway. As cold sweat began to break out on his forehead, a high scream broke from his throat, piercing the moonlight and vanishing in the vast darkness above. Searing pain shot upward from his hand. By the time it reached his chest the shock almost stopped his heart. Nor did the pain ease but went on and on, as if the Wizard wasn't actually cutting anything with his silver blade but only inflicting hurt. Indeed, that was what Reiffen thought as his mind finally forced its way through his agony in an attempt to understand why the agony wasn't going away. Rather it increased, and with such intensity that Reiffen eventually had no other sensation but pain. The moonlight vanished; he didn't hear his screams. In a blaze of sobbing torment, he suffered alone.

It ended.

Reiffen found himself on his knees, his arm twisted painfully at elbow and shoulder as his hand was still held upon the table. Usseis's white robe swayed close beside his face, the fabric soft as a pillow as it brushed his gasping cheek. Reiffen's hair was plastered to his forehead as if he had been playing in the rain.

Usseis released his arm.

"Now for the other hand," he said.

When they were done, Reiffen slumped exhausted on the ground, his back against a table leg. Shadowy shapes moved against the flickering red fires along the far walls. Usseis's arc of moonlight was gone; Reiffen couldn't recall whether the Wizard had left or merely moved to another part of the room. Tired to death though he was, Reiffen floated in a blissful haze, free of pain. Something was different, though he couldn't remember what.

"Can you rise?"

Reiffen blinked, trying to refocus his eyes to the dark. An enormous shadow loomed above him. Usseis? No. Usseis's voice was thicker. Reiffen didn't feel like he'd fallen into a barrel of slops—it couldn't be Usseis. Ossdonc didn't wear robes, so it had to be Fornoch.

"You do not want to remain here, Reiffen." Fornoch's voice was almost comforting. "You are not yet ready. And when Usseis returns he might decide to remove your thumbs as well."

With a start, Reiffen's head began to clear. He rose to one knee and put out a hand to steady himself. A sharp click sounded as his fingers touched the stone. He brought his hands to his face, but the light was too dim to see what had made the clicking sound. Both his little fingers throbbed, the pain replaced by the dull feel of blood rushing round the edges of a wound.

"I will not carry you." Fornoch spoke a third time, his voice patient even when his intent was to hurry the boy along. "I will guide you, but you must walk yourself. This is not a safe part of my brother's fortress and it is best not to use magic here unless forced to do so."

With effort, Reiffen pulled himself erect. His little fingers clicked again as they touched the table. Whatever was on his fingers, it didn't feel like rings. As Fornoch turned and strode off across the hall, the boy felt along his hands. Cold metal met his touch. He recalled the thimbles his mother and Anella wore on the ends of their fingers when they worked their embroidery or stitched his torn trousers. Something similar capped each of his little fingers, though the metal felt like cold iron rather than the warm gold his mother used. Still wondering what had been done to him, he hurried after the tall figure of the Wizard before Fornoch's long strides carried him out of sight.

Not until they were back Upstairs did the Wizard speak to him again. Reiffen was almost too tired to listen. For once his rough bed looked as inviting as a down mattress in winter. The long climb back to the upper reaches of the fortress had exhausted the last of his strength. He fell heavily onto the hard mattress and lay on his stomach with his palms up along his sides. Fornoch's long shadow filled the room as the Wizard stooped in the doorway.

"Remember what I have said about leaving part of yourself behind." The Wizard's voice filled the room like a whisper of wind. "Should you ever wish to return, all you must do is say the word."

Wondering why he would ever wish to return, but lacking the strength to continue defying the Wizard, Reiffen fell into a sleep as deep as drowning.

He dreamed he was deep beneath the waters of the lake. Nokken, rolling silently through the black water, watched him from a distance. Above his head a shimmer of light showed the surface. He reached as high as he could, but the light was slipping away. He felt himself sinking slowly, like a pea in a glass of oil. Desperately he tried to swim, but nothing he did brought him closer to the light. The sky grew farther and farther away.

Something glimmered just beyond the line between lake and air. A face. Avender's face. Reiffen reached for his friend, but his friend did nothing. The water between them stilled. Reiffen found himself wondering how they had come to be switched. Avender was the one who had drowned. Reiffen reached for his friend again, but still the other failed to return the gesture. Avender stared impassively, as if content to watch Reiffen slip away. His fear growing, Reiffen called out, but all he got for his trouble was a mouthful of lake water. He began to cough: deep, racking coughs that coursed through his throat and chest. Avender did nothing. Frantically Reiffen tried to claw his way back to the surface. The water turned to crumbling earth, and the sky above shrank to a single crown of blue above Avender's head. Then it disappeared.

He woke coughing. Spasms shook his chest as he gasped for breath. His wounded fingers throbbed, and he almost chipped a tooth on one of the thimbles when he put his hand too quickly to his mouth. Too tired to attempt anything else, he fell back once more upon the bed as soon as his fit had passed. His choices, like his strength, were quickly fading.

He wondered if he should give in. He was never going to escape, never be rescued. The walls of Ussene were too thick and too well guarded for even Redburr to get through. If he didn't submit, Usseis would compel him to obey anyway, and then who knew whom he'd be forced to kill? At least if he did what the Wizards asked, Usseis had told him he might save his friends.

He tried to persuade himself that life with the Wizards wouldn't be so bad. Ferris, he was sure, would love learning magic as much as he. They could fly across the world together, from Malmoret to Valing.

Avender would never have understood, but then what Avender thought didn't much matter anymore.

He wished he were back home, with nothing to decide but whether to go for a swim or a sail. A week's worth of sleep was what he wanted most now. And maybe an afternoon in a boat running before a southern breeze, with Skimmer plunging through the lake beside him and Ferris singing into the teeth of the wind:

"Wind and lake!
Sky and peak!
The breezes blow! The mast goes creak!"

A small sob escaped his throat. Valing was as far away as Malmoret. Farther, even, when he remembered that it was to Malmoret the Wizards wanted to take him, to make him king. Valing he might never see again at all.

Weariness pulled at his heart the way fear and anger had before. There was nothing left to be afraid of; his anger had long since worn away. Now all he wanted was a few minutes of peace, a full night's sleep, and no dreams to plague him.

Had he thought the Wizards could give him that, he would have yielded to them in a moment.

19

Redburr's Reason

efore Redburr winged off alone into the dungeon for the last time, he took Ferris and Avender with him into one of the cells. The room was small and cramped, with barely enough space for either of the children to stand, and smelled horribly even though it didn't appear to have been used in a long time.

"I'll meet you here when I come back," he said from his perch upside-down on the heavy, barred door. He turned to Nolo, who was waiting outside. "You'd better take their knapsacks."

"Why can't we have our knapsacks?" asked Ferris.

"You're supposed to be prisoners, not casual travelers, that's why." Redburr scowled at her for not figuring the reason out herself.

"At least they're good and pale." Nolo peered closely at their faces. His lamp shone weakly in their eyes. "Good and grubby, too. If Hern saw either of them now, you and I'd sure catch it, Redburr. Do you think their clothes should be a little more torn?"

"We can take care of that." Ferris started ripping the hem of her cloak, glad to have something to do other than be nervous. Reluctantly Avender reached for his own.

Redburr stopped them. "You're dirty enough already. And the swelling in your face helps, too, Ferris. Don't overdo it."

He went back outside to the Dwarf. The two spoke together for a time; then the Shaper finally flew off. The last light leaking in through the open door from Nolo's lamp disappeared; the deep night of the Under Ground settled over the children completely. Ferris and Avender sat down close together on the floor at the back of their filthy cell.

They left the doorway open. Through it they heard occasional muffled sounds of the Dwarves working farther back down the passage, carving new tunnels and secret ways between the cells. "No telling when we might be back," Nolo explained once when he popped his head in to check on them. "Might as well add some touches of our own before we go."

Ferris and Avender wore away the hours waiting for Redburr by filling Durk in on everything that had happened in the many years since he had been taken by Ussene. He was amazed to learn that the Three had actually been defeated just before the children were born, and took heart when told that Dwarves were impervious to magic. "Fascinating," he said. "I don't suppose you could persuade Nolo to be the one to carry me, could you?"

Ferris frowned. "You are the most selfish person I've ever met," she said. "Avender's the one who found you. He's your friend. Don't you have any loyalty at all?"

Somehow the rock made a sniffing sound, as if to suggest he could care less about Ferris's suspicions. But Avender said, "Leave him alone, Ferris. I'm scared, too. Aren't you?"

"Of course I am. But being scared doesn't keep me from doing what I'm supposed to."

"Madam, you wrong me," said the stone stiffly. "To aid the heir of Malmoret and Rimwich is a task no loyal subject could possibly shirk. Were there anything I could do, rest assured I would do my duty. But I am a mere chip. A pebble. Did you wish to build a dam or lay the foundation of a mighty fortress, then perhaps I might be of some small service. But as for invading Their innermost keep, I fear there is nothing I can do to help you."

"If I could think of something, I'd make you do it," said Ferris.

"And I should happily comply. But as there is not, I think it best for all concerned I take my place with Nolo, or that Nurren fellow. He seems a steady chap."

Nolo would hear of no changes to the plan when they asked him. "Redburr said for Durk to stay with you, lad. We don't need him down here, and he's the only one who's been Upstairs. He might end up being useful. I'm sorry, stone, but that's the way it has to be."

Durk fussed and fumed, but there was nothing he could say to change Nolo's mind. In the end Avender wrapped the stone in his handkerchief and stuffed him in his pocket to keep him quiet. They could still hear his muffled complaints but fooled him into complete silence by pretending that Redburr was about to return. When enough time had passed for that to be obviously not true, the stone just sulked.

Snurr and Delven were on guard when Redburr finally did come back Downstairs. The two Dwarves sensed the Shaper in the corridor almost as soon as he left the guardroom and hurried back to tell the others. Nolo took one last look at the children before he shut them into their cell and barred the door behind him.

For a time everything was silent. Fear and excitement sparked the children's hearts. The darkness wrapped around them. They felt empty and alone, as if the whole world had been drained away, though they knew the Dwarves had left off their work and were waiting to rescue them instantly if anything unplanned should happen. Ferris reached for Avender's hand, to make certain he was there. He was glad she did.

At last they heard voices approaching along the corridor. A thin crack of light appeared at the bottom of the door. The voices were followed by the sound of footsteps, and the rough squeak of leather and rusty chain.

"Here's the one," said a nasty voice from beyond the door. "But there's nothin' in there, I tell you. There ain't nobody in this section."

Then Redburr spoke. "I don't know nothin' about it," he said in a voice much rougher than normal. Ferris squeezed Avender's hand anxiously. "The Bosses sent me to pick up a couple prisoners, so that's what I'm doin'. If there's nobody here, it ain't my problem. You know the Boss. Nothin' he likes more than blamin' somebody for somethin' they ain't done."

"There never was nobody in this cell," grumbled the unseen jailer. "See for yourself. It ain't right, puttin' the trouble on me."

The door rattled in its frame as the guard removed the bar. Then he opened it with a swift kick, banging the heavy portal into Avender before the boy could crawl out of the way. Avender yelped despite himself and rubbed his shin. The jailer jumped back out of the doorway in surprise.

"It's ghosts!" he shouted.

"No," said Redburr. "It's the Boss's prisoners, just like I said."

Grabbing the jailer's torch from his hand, the Shaper pushed inside. He had changed back to human form and his red beard gleamed in the blazing torchlight as he winked at the children. The light was much stronger than that from the Dwarven lamps. They felt its heat and smelled the heavy stench of burning pitch.

"Have a look yourself," said Redburr.

He pulled back out of the doorway as suddenly as he had pushed in and handed the torch to the astonished jailer. Planting his broad hand on the other's back, Redburr shoved him inside.

"What in the name o' Darkness?—"

The jailer pulled up at the sight of the two children cowering against the back wall. He was a big sissit, the first the children had ever seen. Shorter than Redburr but almost as wide, he completely filled the doorway.

"Don't ever ask questions, that's what I say," Redburr's voice boomed over the sissit's shoulder. "There's no tellin' what the Boss can do with that magic o' his. Better t' keep your trap shut and be ready for anything, if y'ask me."

The sissit leaned farther into the cell, leaving barely any room for the children. His skin was pale white and his face seemed to have hardly any nose. Drops of sweat on his hairless head glistened in the torchlight. He wore greasy trousers and a leather vest that left his fat white arms bare to the shoulders, except for a pair of iron bands wound tight around his wrists. His breath smelled of onions and spoiled meat. It washed over them when he spoke, like heat surging from an open oven door.

"Where'd you two come from?" he snapped out at them. Bits of his last meal streaked his rotten teeth. "Speak up now." He poked at them with his torch.

"I-I don't know what you mean," Avender stammered as he turned to avoid the torch's flame.

"Here now, you can't 'spect a couple o' scraggly kids like them to have any idea what the Boss did to 'em." Redburr pulled the sissit out of the cell and elbowed him aside. "Come on out o' there, you."

Avender and Ferris stumbled out from their temporary prison into the harsh light, looking for all the world as if they had been locked away for weeks.

"Probably magicked 'em down here, he did," said Redburr. Now that they were all out in the corridor together the Shaper gave no sign that he was anything other than a human jailer. "Like as not they don't even know what happened to 'em. Do you, scum?"

"I'm—I'm scared," said Ferris, following Redburr's lead. She grabbed Avender's arm with both hands and drew him beside her. He could tell she wasn't particularly alarmed; it was hard to be really scared with the Shaper there to help them if the plan went wrong.

Still, Avender wrapped his other arm protectively around her. He, at least, had sense enough to know they should be frightened.

The sissit scratched his head. "You're prob'ly right, I guess. But it's not like the Boss. He likes everything neat an' tidy down here in the dungeons. Falls into all kinds o' bloody fits when it ain't. Think o' what happened to Scrum that time he let that lot over on the ninth level starve to death. Jus' when the Chief wanted 'em shipped off to Number Three, too."

"Stick t' your orders, that's what I always say," said Redburr. "An' right now my orders are t' bring these two Upstairs. So that's what I'm gonna do. Come on, you."

He pulled Avender roughly forward. Ferris followed, her hands still locked tightly to the boy's arm.

"What about chains?" protested the guard. "How you gonna take 'em Upstairs without chains?" He reached for a set of heavy links looped about his thick waist.

"I got my own chains," said Redburr. He shook a hand menacingly in Avender's face. So real did the gesture seem, Avender thought for a moment that his old friend had been caught by Usseis while he was gone and twisted round to the Wizard's own ends.

"Suit yourself." The sissit shook his head to indicate he wasn't one to question matters he didn't understand. "Once you take 'em, it's on your head, not mine."

"A couple o' kids?" Redburr laughed at the idea. "You been down here too long if you're afraid of a couple kids. I brought a rope to truss 'em up, but Upstairs we eat kids."

"Then you're luckier'n we are." The sissit licked his lips. "The Boss ain't let us eat nobody since that little farm girl. There's a nice, plump bat flyin' aroun', though. Other shift told us they seen it twice. It's only a matter o' time 'fore we catch it and get some nice eats, too."

Redburr tied the children together with a loop of cord around their wrists and pushed them heavily on ahead of him down the corridor. Immediately they discovered a second, fatter sissit leaning against the rough wall and picking his teeth with the point of his knife. Their hearts jumped despite Redburr's presence, as the new guard eyed them carefully before taking his spot at the front of the party.

He led the way back to the guardroom. Redburr followed with the prisoners, while the first sissit brought up the rear. There was no sign of the Dwarves, or their tunneling. Now and again the children heard the cry of some poor unfortunate locked within the cells on either side as they proceeded through the dingy tunnel. They shuddered at the thought of the miserable wretches stuck down here in the depths of the fortress, and wondered if they would have a chance to free them when they returned. If they returned.

There were two more sissit in the guardroom. When the prisoners entered, one grinned toothlessly at the other and claimed the ragged purse that lay on the table between them. A small fire burned in a large metal grate at the center of the room; several potatoes roasted in their skins among the coals. The fire's thin smoke curled blackly along the ceiling in search of the chimney that wasn't there. A carpet of trampled soot and cinders covered the floor. Other tunnels ran off from the four corners of the room, except the opposite passage, where a set of rough stone steps followed the smoke up and out of the guardroom to whatever levels lay above.

The sissit behind them turned to Redburr and asked uncomfortably what he was going to report to the Boss.

"I tell 'em whatever They ask me," Redburr replied. "That's the best way."

"You gonna tell Him we didn't know they was here?" The jailer scratched his armpit nervously.

Redburr shrugged. "Chances are the Boss'll want t' know his little trick worked," he said. "If he asks, I got to tell. He gives orders an' we all jump, right?"

The jailer rubbed his greasy hands against his vest. "You think maybe he's checkin' on us?" he asked. "You think maybe we should take a look-see in the other cells? Maybe there's a few more down here he ain't told us about."

"If there are, I 'spect you're better off not knowin' about 'em. The Boss may not like you sneakin' round, tryin' t' learn his secrets. You check out the rest of the cells if you want, but it ain't somethin' I'd be eager to be doin'. If you know what I mean."

"We know whatcha mean," said the fat sissit. With a smooth motion he pared a layer of filth out from under a thumbnail and flicked it onto the floor. "An' we don't need you tellin' us how t' do our jobs, neither. So why don't you just take your grabbin's Upstairs and we'll all go on about our business?"

Redburr stared hard at the fat sissit. For a moment the children were afraid there was going to be a fight despite the Shaper's precautions. The sissit pretended to pay Redburr no mind, but it was plain he was watching the Shaper closely from the corner of his eye. Then Redburr drew himself together and turned away. Without speaking, he took the torch from the first sissit's hand and pushed his prisoners across the room and up the stair. In a moment they had climbed high enough to leave the sight of the dirty guardroom behind them, if not the smell.

Ferris turned at once to say something to the Shaper; he hushed her with a finger and led them on. The stair ran straight upward, each step as crooked as the one before. The tunnel, like most of the dungeon, was indifferently carved. The thin smoke from the brazier below made them sneeze as they hurried along. When Redburr finally thought they were far enough away for the air to be more bearable and the sissit more distant, he allowed them to stop and ask their questions.

Ferris poked at him immediately. "Where'd you get those clothes?" He was dressed much the same as their jailers, with the addition of a short sword in a leather scabbard at his side. With his great masses of red hair sticking out from every part of his body, he looked more fearsome than the real minions of the Three.

"Found them in an empty barracks," he replied as he loosened the ropes around their wrists. "If I'm going to pretend to be a guard I have to look the part, don't I? There," he added as he finished with the ropes. "Now they won't chafe so much."

"Can't you loosen them some more?" asked Avender. "Then we can slip them right off if there's a fight."

"No fighting," replied the Shaper sternly. "If there's any fighting the end will be the same whether your hands are tied or not."

"Then why'd you almost get into a fight with that sissit back there?"

"Him?" Redburr grunted scornfully. "I was never going to fight him. But I had to look like I was or he might have had a try at sticking me in the back. It's not a pretty place, Ussene."

"Have you found out where they're keeping Reiffen?" asked Ferris.

"No more than Durk already told us." The Shaper looked up the tunnel ahead. "We're still going to need more information when we get Upstairs. He's in the upper levels somewhere, I'm sure, and that's still a long way away. Say, you didn't by chance happen to bring along a bite or two of something to eat?"

Ferris and Avender both rolled their eyes. Even in the darkness beneath Ussene some things never changed.

"You made us leave our knapsacks behind," said Ferris. "Remember?"

"You could at least have put a little something in your pockets," said the Shaper mournfully. "It's what I would have done. I haven't eaten since those bugs back there in the cave. Oh, well. I guess it can't be helped. You brought the stone, though. Right?"

Avender patted his pocket. "Durk's right here."

"Good. Let's hope we don't get so lost we have to bring him out."

He pushed the children ahead of him up the stair, warning them that another guard post was close ahead. Ferris and Avender prepared themselves to look like miserable prisoners once again, but so far it had all gone so well they found it hard to keep up the proper attitude of cowering fear. Until they encountered more sissit and passed through a second round of nasty jeering.

After the second guardroom, the nature of the dungeon changed. The uneven stairs ended in a long corridor that disappeared into the darkness. Redburr paused for a moment on the last step, as if steeling himself for what lay ahead. His eyes narrowed with fierce concentration. Then he plunged forward, pulling the children roughly behind him. Nearly running, Ferris and Avender followed. They wondered what buried horrors could make the Shaper so nervous.

They found themselves in a tunnel wide enough for all of them to walk abreast and high enough that Redburr could carry his torch above his head without worrying about knocking it against the ceiling. But, no matter how high he held the crackling flame, the tunnel remained dark and menacing around them. Except for the rare branching corridor that loomed suddenly to left or right as a blacker darkness against the inky walls, nothing showed within their scrap of light. Even the floor was empty of the waste and rubbish that had littered the levels below.

And there was something wrong about the branching tunnels. Each felt different, though all looked the same. Some were cold and lifeless, as if nothing alive had ever ventured past their empty mouths. Others seethed with malevolence and fear. All seemed to reach out with hidden hands to clutch and throttle as the company passed by. Though the openings were few and far between, their malice oozed far out into the main passage. The children kept as close to Redburr as they could. Just brushing up against him made them both feel better.

"It's like the feeling we got on top of those bones." Ferris shivered as she turned away from another one of the empty portals, its magic seeping. "I keep thinking something's watching us."

"Don't fool yourself," growled the Shaper, his breathing ragged.

"Something is. But whatever it is, it's sleeping now. As long as we don't do anything to wake it we'll be all right." He quickened his pace and pushed them on, his face twisted with effort.

During all the time they were in that long, dreary corridor, they saw no sign of a single living creature other than themselves. Bats, rats, insects, all knew to keep out of the way of anything carrying a light in that famished realm. Redburr hurried them relentlessly on. The dark scurried close behind, ready to pounce at the slightest flagging of their spirit.

The corridor ended at the side of a vaulted gallery. Redburr stopped to take a deep, cleansing breath. The air felt fresher on the children's cheeks. A pair of thick stone pillars rose a few steps before them, and beyond those the cavern disappeared in vastness. More pillars circled around on either side behind them, and the children caught glimpses of other tunnels leading away from the back of the gallery as well. The fortress of Usseis was far larger than Ferris and Avender had ever imagined; it stretched long fingers of fear deep into the heart of the world. They wondered what poor creatures lay at the bottom of that lightless grip, the debris of power and evil, broken and tossed away.

Redburr stepped out beyond the gallery and shook his head. His dirty beard seemed fuller as it swayed across his chest.

"Are you all right?" asked Ferris. She took a step toward the Shaper and touched his arm.

"I'll be fine," he answered. "There's a lot of magic in that last tunnel, even if it is asleep." He gathered himself and took a deep breath. "I've been through it three times now, and each time it pulls on me a little more. But I'll be fine."

Holding the torch high, he led them on across the enormous hall. Carefully they picked their way past pools of oily water that gleamed blackly in the light. Mindful of the burning the dark lake had given them, the children avoided the puddles entirely.

A wide ramp led upward from the middle of the room. "We'll reach the upper levels, soon," warned Redburr. His eyes glittered fiercely, flickering from more than the torch's flame. "The guards there are human, not sissit, so you'll have to be more careful of how you look and what you say."

"How do you know which way to go?" whispered Ferris as the Shaper started them up this new path.

"I followed the changing of the guard. But hush now, girl. We're coming to places where the things that listen can understand as well as hear."

The ramp ascended steeply, without a single twist or turn. Both edges of the way fell straight down to the stone floor below; only the path was visible in the torchlight once they climbed above the bottom of the chamber. Ferris and Avender felt as if they were following a bridge through nothingness, until the road plunged suddenly back into heavy rock. A speck of light appeared in the darkness ahead, the first they had seen other than Redburr's torch since leaving the last guardroom. It came just in time as well, as their own light was finally sputtering out. Their last few steps were passed creeping upward along the dark tunnel to the mouth of light above.

The guards were up and waiting for them when they arrived: before it had died, Redburr's torchlight had heralded their approach as loudly as any fanfare. These guards were all human, rogues and renegades from the southern lands or the forest. The chamber was lit with torches on the walls and another brazier burning in the center of the room. A single wide tunnel led farther into the fortress on the other side.

"So, you're back." The sergeant stepped forward as Redburr pushed his prisoners beyond the fire. The other guards barely looked up from their stone benches along the walls. All wore leather armor studded with iron, their crossbows and swords close at hand. The sergeant regarded Redburr and his prisoners carefully.

"I see you found what you were looking for," he said. Ferris and Avender did their best to cower behind Redburr.

"They're the ones," answered the Shaper. He pulled them closer to him with the rope. "I'm already runnin' late. Those frightened mice Downstairs didn't believe me when I told 'em the Master himself wants to see this lot."

The sergeant gave a short bark of laughter. "They'll catch it, if He doesn't get what He wants just when He wants it. And you'll catch it, too, good excuse or no."

"That's the truth." Redburr pushed his charges closer toward the opening on the other side of the room. "So, if you don't mind, I'd like t' get going. It'll be my back catches it if there's a problem."

"Fine by me. But you've got to give the password, first."

" 'Shadows,' " answered Redburr. "I s'pose you thought I'd forget it while I was Downstairs. But I got a question for you, too. My orders is t' take these two up t' the other one, only I don't know where the other one is."

"What other one?" The sergeant's eyes narrowed suspiciously.

"You know. The other one like them. The other kid."

"What other kid?"

"I dunno. They didn't tell me. I'm jus' supposed to get these two an' bring 'em t' the other one. You mean you don't know where the other one is, either?"

"If I did, I sure wouldn' tell you. You should o' figgered that out 'fore you left." The sergeant laughed again, more softly this time. Ferris didn't like the way he looked at her, or Avender.

Redburr drew his arm back, half-threatening to strike the other man. The look in the Sharper's eyes reminded Avender of the time the bear had charged him in the meadow by the henge. In response the sergeant sneered hopefully and rested his hand on the hilt of his sword. Behind him, his fellow guards were suddenly paying more attention to Redburr and his charges.

"Just try it," dared the sergeant.

For a moment Avender and Ferris were certain Redburr had forgotten everything he had said about not fighting. The muscles tightened in his neck and shoulders; the thick hair on his arms began to bristle. The sergeant edged his blade free from its sheath. The

Shaper snarled. The two stared at one another; the children and the other guards watched with wariness and alarm. Then, as suddenly as his savagery had begun, the fire faded in Redburr's eyes. His shoulders relaxed; he seemed to remember once more what and where he was. He pulled sharply on the children's tether, then pushed them on ahead of him out of the room. Behind them the sergeant put his hands on his hips, and led his fellows in a chorus of loud jeers.

The guards' laughter followed the children and the Shaper down the tunnel. Redburr panted heavily, still struggling to control himself. At first the road was dark as pitch; then a small glow began to grow in the gloom ahead. They continued on cautiously until they came to a sputtering candle mounted high on the wall. Other lights followed sporadically, but the darkness between each light was almost complete. The candles were very thick and looked as if they might last a long while; ages of wax dripped below them like thickened sap from a riven tree.

"What are we—," began Ferris.

Redburr cut her off with a hard pull on the rope. "Shut up, you," he growled. "None o' your lip now."

She understood Redburr was still playing his part but rubbed her sore wrists all the same. He could have pulled a little less hard. Avender gave her a warning look as they trotted down the tunnel. Finally she was as scared as he. They would all have to play their parts completely, now they had reached the upper levels of the fortress.

They passed several branching passages before Redburr abruptly led them off the main way. He was still breathing heavily, straining forward as if to escape some pursuit that only he could see. Left, right, and left again: he took them quickly through a short maze of unlit tunnels until they finally stumbled through a doorway and into a small closet. They tripped over several smashed barrels in the darkness before finally settling down amid the rubbish. The room itself smelled of sour ale several seasons old.

"We should be safe here," growled the Shaper in a ragged voice. Several pieces of broken barrel rattled as he settled heavily to the floor.

"That time I really thought you were going to get into a fight," said Avender, his own heart still pounding.

Redburr's panting was loud in the small room. "It was . . . close."

"Are you sure you're all right?" Ferris scrambled across the floor to the bear's side, growing more concerned when Redburr didn't answer. Avender crept forward as well. If something happened to Redburr they knew they would never find their way out of Ussene, let alone rescue Reiffen.

"Redburr!" Ferris's voice hissed fearfully through the dark. "What's happening to you?"

"Can't . . . stop . . . have to . . ." Redburr strained to speak, as if something was constricting his throat.

Avender reached hesitantly for his friend in the darkness, dreading whatever foulness had seized the Shaper.

"He's changing!" Ferris whispered. "Feel his hands!"

The boy felt along Redburr's hairy arm. The Shaper's skin trembled beneath his touch. When he found it, the hand seemed much too large, and the fingers much too short. And, as Avender had feared, the nails were already sharp and long.

"Changing . . . ," Redburr agreed, his choked voice nearly unintelligible.

"Why?" Ferris's voice turned soft with fear.

Avender stroked the Shaper's arm with his own bound hands. Already Redburr seemed much more hairy than before. At the boy's touch he sighed, a long, low gasp like wind at the edge of a forest. The children's hearts jumped in fright.

"What did you do?" asked Ferris sharply, still whispering.

"All I did was rub his arm. Do you think he's dying?"

"Do it again—quick!"

Timidly, Avender rubbed the Shaper's arm again. Redburr groaned but sounded less pained than before. Encouraged, the boy combed his fingers tenderly through the bear's thin fur. This time the children hardly heard the Shaper's tranquil moan.

"We have to keep him from changing," Ferris whispered. "If he turns into a bear they'll know who he is at once!"

"Maybe if we keep rubbing him—"

"Of course we have to keep rubbing him. It's like grooming him back home. You know how much he likes that."

"But that's when he's a bear. How do you know grooming him won't just make him turn into a bear even faster?"

"Do you have any better ideas? I just wish I had my brush, but he wouldn't let us bring our packs, would he?"

Avender decided not to mention what had happened the last time he had seen the Shaper wake after changing. Instead he concentrated on trying to make his fingers feel as much like a brush as possible. Together the two children rubbed stubbornly at the Shaper's hands and arms, neck and shoulders. Gradually Redburr's breathing softened. The darkness grew quiet. The bear claws turned back to fingers, though he didn't seem any less hairy.

"I think it's working," said Ferris.

Avender kept grooming. A memory of the bear's den rose up through his fear, the blue lake gleaming in the bright sunshine through the window. A lump came into the boy's throat and threatened to overwhelm him in tears. He had been underground too long; his heart cried out for sun and sky. And now Redburr had been hurt by the magic of this place, and Avender and Ferris might be left alone in the midst of darkness and evil.

"I think I'm all right, now. . . . Thank you, children."

The Shaper reached out a human hand to each of them. Ferris and Avender buried their faces in his chest. He smelled of leather and sweat. "We were so frightened," Ferris sobbed. The tension rolled out of Avender along with the dampness in his eyes.

In a minute they all felt much better.

"What happened?" asked Ferris.

"I almost lost control," he said. "The Wizards' magic nearly overpowered me. Whenever something makes me really angry, all I want to be is bear. And nothing makes me angrier than the Three. The two together, magic and anger, were almost too much. If you hadn't been here to bring me back to reason, I'd probably have lost myself entirely. It's always hardest when I'm human. But you were here, weren't you." He snuffled and gave a little sneeze. "The smell of old beer in here isn't helping any, either."

They rested awhile in the darkness, gathering strength for the task ahead. The shabby cave was less frightening now that Redburr had regained his self-control.

"What are we going to do now?" Despite her best efforts to contain it, Ferris's voice showed a tiny quiver of fear. "How will we find Reiffen?"

"This is a pickle," Redburr agreed.

"Maybe we should wait and follow those guards when they get off duty," suggested Avender. "I'll bet they know where Reiffen is even if they say they didn't."

"Even if they do, they'll go back to their barracks, and not go visit prisoners. You still have a lot to learn about the world, boy. We're going to have to find Reiffen on our own."

"That means we're right back where we started." Avender cupped his chin gloomily in his hands. "We might as well have stayed in the dungeon and let you keep on exploring up here."

"I wouldn't say that. As long as I have the two of you with me, I can still hunt openly and ask directions. Believe me, it'll be a lot quicker this way than if I had to flit around on my own."

"It'll still take forever," grumbled Ferris.

"Maybe Durk has an idea."

Avender pulled the stone from his pocket and unwrapped him. But the petrified rock, who had heard the human guards and knew they were all the way Upstairs, had nothing to add. "Just keep away from Him," was all he would whisper. "He'll see through you in an instant, if you cross His path. He's no sissit."

There was nothing else to do but leave. Redburr checked their ropes to make sure they were still secure. Avender slipped Durk back into his pocket. Then the Shaper led them out into the pitch-black corridor once more, where they felt their way through the solid darkness to the dimly lit main road.

For some time they searched cautiously through the tunnels, working their way upwards. Occasionally they passed small companies of soldiers, who paid them no mind after Redburr kicked Avender and Ferris roughly each time to hurry them along. Less often they saw slaves in tattered rags scurrying back and forth on the errands of their masters. At the sight of Redburr the slaves fell to the ground at once, and cowered against the wall until he and his prisoners had passed.

But mostly they wandered through dimly lit and deserted passages. Redburr had learned something of the fortress on his earlier visit and managed to keep them clear of the more traveled paths. All the corridors seemed much too large, until Avender remembered Nolo had said that Ossdonc was very tall.

The filth in the tunnels decreased the higher they went, replaced by the general dustiness of less-traveled ways. Twice they ran into soldiers who were plainly standing guard. Both times Redburr pulled the children up tight on the end of their tether and asked about the other prisoner. The first time the soldiers had no idea what he was talking about, but on the second attempt one of the guards suggested he go up to Level Seven and talk to Captain Kender.

They had been searching for Level Seven for perhaps half an hour when they came to yet another guardroom well away from the main passages of the fortress. A single officer was the only person in the room.

Redburr took a deep breath and led his prisoners forward. "Captain Kender?" he guessed, saluting briskly.

The officer looked up. "The kitchens are back that way," he said tersely, pointing in the direction they had come.

"Excuse me, sir." Redburr snapped his charges roughly forward. "I was told t' bring these two in t' the other one."

The officer regarded Redburr briefly, then studied the prisoners for a longer time. Redburr waited patiently for the man to turn to him again.

"I've heard nothing about this," the captain said at last. "Who was it gave you your orders?"

"The Master, sir."

"The Master Himself?" The officer frowned. "And what exactly were His instructions?"

"He told me t' fetch these two from the dungeons and bring 'em up t' the other prisoner."

"That's all?" asked the officer.

Redburr nodded. "Yes, sir."

"No orders about guarding them, or what I should do with them after they're here?"

"No, sir."

Captain Kender's frown deepened. Clearly he didn't like the annoyance of more prisoners to guard. Avender thought it odd the officer should be guarding so important a prisoner as Reiffen all by himself; but perhaps there were other guards at Reiffen's cell.

"Go ahead." The captain finally made his decision and waved his arm back toward the door. "Orders are orders. I suppose They'll tell me what They want when They're good and ready."

Redburr hesitated a moment, as if unsure of himself before so awesome a figure as the captain. "'Scuse me, sir?" he asked. "Which way do I go?"

The captain waved his arm towards the door a second time. "Down the corridor. First right. The boy's in the cell on the left."

"Thank you, sir."

Redburr saluted stiffly once more, his belly jiggling, then led the children out the door. They were elated, their fears forgotten in their excitement. Reiffen was just around the corner—they had nearly found him! They tried hard not to rush down the passage in their excitement, for fear of giving their true interest away. But, when they saw the second corridor was empty and there were no more guards, Redburr dropped the children's rope and they raced forward as quickly as they could. They had found their friend at last.

20

Redburr's Rage

t wasn't a long corridor. At the far end a smoky candle threw a dirty light across two doors. The one on the left stood ajar. Within, a withered figure lay beneath a rough blanket upon a wooden bed. The candle outside cast a thin trickle of light across his sleeping face.

With a cry Ferris pushed open the door. Redburr held the children back with one thick arm while he searched the room carefully for traps, then followed them inside.

"Reiffen!" called Ferris in a soft, fearful voice. His eyes opened slowly as she knelt at his side.

"Hello, boy," said Redburr, looming above her.

"Is it him?" asked Avender.

"Of course it's him!" cried Ferris. "How can you think it isn't?"

Avender looked closely at the thin figure on the narrow cot. He did look like Reiffen, a Reiffen with almost all the life twisted out of him. The shadows of his friends fell across his pale face. His eyes, which seemed to have grown larger above his painfully hollow cheeks, regarded them blankly.

"Reiffen," Ferris pleaded. "Don't you recognize us? Please say you do. It's me: Ferris. And Avender, and Redburr. And Nolo's with us, too, only we left him Downstairs."

Reiffen's eyes narrowed. His mouth formed a word, but no sound came out. He frowned at the effort and tried again.

"Ferris?" he whispered. His friends held their breath to hear him. "Avender? I thought you died."

"Skimmer saved him." Ferris placed her bound hands gently on the blanket. A sad smile limped across her face. Reiffen's chest felt thin and cold beneath the ragged cloth. "What have they done to you?" she asked.

The pale face shook feebly. His tongue worked dryly between his lips before he spoke again. "It's nothing," he whispered fiercely. "They've been trying to make me do what they want. But I haven't let them."

He smiled faintly and closed his eyes. His head dropped back upon the mattress.

"Don't let him talk anymore," said Redburr. "He'll need all his strength if we're going to get him out of here."

"He can't possibly walk," said Ferris. "Look at him. It looks like they've been starving him."

She reached under the meager blanket to press his hand and a horrified look came over her face. Gently she lifted the side of the blanket and gasped.

"Look what they've done to him."

The little finger on Reiffen's left hand was missing the first joint beyond the knuckle. A thimble of black iron capped the rest. Avender clenched his own hands into fists. His anger at the Three was beginning to overcome his fear.

"We have to get him out of here."

The Shaper pushed Ferris and Avender aside and bent to pick up the stricken boy. As Redburr lifted him, Ferris tucked in the corners of the blanket where they dropped like shrouds around the Shaper's arms.

"I can walk," croaked Reiffen.

Redburr shook his head. "It'll be faster this way. You can walk when we're not in such a hurry."

"What about Captain Kender?" asked Avender.

A savage look crossed the Shaper's face. "I'll take care of Captain Kender."

He set off with the boy in his arms. Ferris and Avender followed at the end of the rope, their hands still loosely tied. At the end of the short corridor back to the main passage Redburr stopped and turned to Avender.

"Think you can hold him for a bit?" asked the Shaper. "He's light as a feather. I'll signal for you to follow when I'm done."

Avender nodded anxiously.

"I can stand," insisted Reiffen. His voice seemed stronger than it had been before and the old fire had begun to burn in his eyes.

Redburr regarded him closely. "All right," he said. "It might do you good to stand for a minute or two. We might as well find out what'll happen if I have to put you down."

With Ferris and Avender lending support at either side, the Shaper set Reiffen on his feet. The boy's blanket slipped to the floor, but the boy himself, with both hands on the shoulders of his friends, was able to stand. That was when they noticed that both his little fingers had been lopped short and capped with the strange thimbles. Cold and dark as only iron can be, they looked as if they had been soldered to his skin. It didn't appear that either would come off easily.

Reiffen noticed their stares. "It's not as bad as it looks," he said, holding up his hands and wiggling his fingers. "They only just started trying to persuade me."

Ferris set her jaw but said nothing. Redburr stepped out into the main corridor. The Shaper made no attempt at stealth as he walked down the passage, trusting that Captain Kender would be expecting his return. At the entrance to the guardroom he disappeared. Ferris and Avender strained to hear some sound of what was happening inside. But the stone was thick around them and the silence of Ussene remained absolute. Sooner than they expected, Redburr reappeared, waving the children forward to join him.

"That's done," he said, breathing heavily as he met them at the door. His bulk blocked their view inside, but there was blood on his beard and hands. His eyes gleamed. "The alarm will be up soon, but with any luck they'll never expect us to escape by going down. They'll seal off the outlets to the open air." He picked Reiffen up as he spoke, as easily as if he were lifting only the ragged blanket. "But it might take them a while to think to seal off the ways to the underearth as well."

"Can't I walk?" pleaded Reiffen. "I'm feeling a lot better."

"Can you run?" asked Redburr. "No? Then you'll still be carried."

"What about torches?" asked Ferris. "Won't we need torches when we go back into the dungeons? Nolo made us leave our lamps in our knapsacks."

"We can get torches down below. They'll have plenty at that first guardroom. Now, come on."

The Shaper stepped out of the doorway and strode down the hall with Reiffen in his arms. Ferris and Avender peeked into the room behind him, then quickly turned away. There was no sign of Captain Kender, but blood and torn clothing were scattered all about the room. An empty boot lay beside a sheathed sword. Something sodden slipped off the wall and plopped thickly on the floor. They hurried off after the Shaper, Ferris with her hand to her mouth and Avender trying to blink away what he had seen.

They descended much more rapidly than they had gone up. Once Reiffen realized where they were headed, he directed them along the safest way. "They let me go just about anywhere," he explained as he was carried along in the Shaper's arms. "Except the dungeons."

"We already know our way through those," said Ferris.

They met no one on the less-traveled paths. But they had hardly set foot in the main passage leading to the dungeons before they heard coarse shouts and tramping feet in the distance behind them.

"They know we've taken him, now," growled the Shaper. He slowed their pace to a fast walk. "But from the sound of it, they haven't figured out which way we're going. All that ruckus is back at the main gate. Hopefully the dungeon guard won't know about our escape yet and we'll be allowed to pass. Don't run, though. Anyone sees us running, they'll know what's up at once. The longer we keep up the bluff you're my prisoners, the better."

At the fastest walk possible they hastened down the tunnel. Behind them the tumult faded. The search appeared to be concentrated above and behind them, closer to the day. All the same, Avender expected a company of sissit to burst out from one of the side passages at any moment. Remarkably, by the time they passed the last of the branching corridors, they were still alone. Behind them the noise of pursuit started to rise again. Mixed in with the distant shouts and trampling feet, they heard the harsh cries of hunting wolves.

The guardroom appeared ahead, dim and red with fire. As they drew closer the figures of the guards were outlined as dark shadows against the murky light. The commotion at the far end of the tunnel had caught the soldiers' attention, and they were all up and waiting to see what was coming their way. Redburr slowed the children to a more moderate pace and put Reiffen back on his own feet.

"Now we can fight," he said, a hint of satisfaction in his voice. "But if we do, I want the three of you to keep out of the way. If I can't handle the four of them myself I'll know the reason why."

He started to tie Reiffen's hands with the same rope that bound Ferris and Avender, but Reiffen shook his head. "That'll make them more suspicious," he said. "I haven't been tied up since I got here."

Redburr gave the boy a searching look, then gathered the rope and pulled the other two children on down the passage. Reiffen hobbled after them as best he could.

The guards were waiting for them when they arrived. They had stepped back into the low chamber, their backs to the fire. Avender assumed they were more concerned with keeping people in the dungeons, not out. So, when Redburr entered with Reiffen and his string of prisoners, he wasn't surprised to find the soldiers more curious than quarrelsome.

"Back so soon?" asked the sergeant. "What's all the fuss at the Front Gate about?"

Redburr pulled his charges in close behind him. "Some prisoner got away or somethin'," he said. "I been ordered t' take this lot back Downstairs for safekeepin'."

"Prisoner? Escaped?" The sergeant scratched the back of his head in confusion. "No one's come up this way. An' that boy's the only one They're keepin' Upstairs." He nodded toward Reiffen.

"Well, I guess they must o' brought in another, 'cause you can see for yourself this one ain't gone nowhere." Redburr took a step forward, still keeping a tight leash on Ferris and Avender. "Now, how 'bout getting' out o' my way so I can finish my job. They'll keep 'em cozy enough Downstairs."

The sergeant straightened and put his hands challengingly on his hips. "What's the password?" he demanded.

"Still 'Shadows,' far as I know," said Redburr. "Ain't nobody told me any different."

The sergeant stepped aside. Redburr led the children around the fire to the tunnel on the far side. It looked for a moment as if they were going to get clean away, without a fight at all. But, as Reiffen passed, with Ferris and Avender behind him, the sergeant seized the first boy by the shoulder and pulled him aside.

"Not this one," he sneered. "We got orders never to let him Downstairs without one of the Three."

"But he was told to come with us!" cried Ferris.

As soon as she spoke, Ferris knew she had made a mistake. She had forgotten she was still supposed to be a meek and pliant prisoner. She reached for Reiffen as she called out, but the sergeant knocked her down as soon as she stepped forward. Avender, tied to

Ferris as he was, couldn't help but fall, too. He stumbled heavily into the brazier, catching his trousers on the iron grate, his pocket ripping as he tumbled after Ferris to the ground.

"Try that again, girl," snarled the sergeant, "and I'll give you a lot worse." He looked back at Redburr with sudden suspicion. "The boy stays here."

"I got my orders," Redburr growled. "The Boss told me t' take 'em Downstairs, an' that's what I'm gonna do!"

The sergeant drew his sword in reply. Behind him his fellow guards brought their crossbows to bear, all bolts pointed at Redburr. Ferris and Avender scuttled backward across the floor, freeing themselves of the rope along the way when they saw no one was paying attention to them. But the sergeant still gripped Reiffen tightly in his free hand so Reiffen couldn't follow. From the tunnel behind them came the sudden howl of one of the hunting wolves, closer now than before.

"If it's a fight you want . . . ," warned Redburr. He didn't reach for his sword. At his most dangerous he generally forgot about human weapons. Besides, to reach for his sword would give the other guards enough warning to loose their bolts at him. They would never expect him to charge them bare-handed.

Then, just as the Shaper was about to spring, a commanding voice cried out:

"CEASE THIS QUARRELING! AT ONCE! HOW DARE YOU DISOBEY MY COMMAND!"

Everyone, guards and prisoners, looked around. But there was no sign of where the voice had come from.

"FOOLS!" it went on. **"LET THE PRISONER PASS! NOW! THAT IS MY WILL! THEN REPORT TO THE FRONT GATE! THE TROUBLE LIES IN THE CORRIDORS ABOVE, NOT BELOW! GO! AND INSTRUCT THOSE WHO ARE FOLLOWING TO TURN THEIR ATTENTION TO THE SEVENTH LEVEL, NOT THE DUNGEONS!**

"GO!"

With that final harsh command the guards, frightened to death by what they couldn't see, as well as the regular wrath of their Master, turned and raced off into the main tunnel. Reiffen was thrown to the floor. He lay dazed in the filth, the last of his meager strength exhausted.

"What . . . ?" Ferris looked mutely around the room.

"Durk." Avender, who had been surprised by that particular voice before, felt for the stone in his pocket. His fingers slipped through the empty tear in his pants instead.

"Quick!" ordered the Shaper, who had also realized what had happened. "There's no time to talk! They'll figure out their mistake soon enough!" He grabbed a torch from the wall with one hand and scooped up Reiffen with the other. The wild light was beginning to shine from his black eyes once more. "Follow me!"

"I have to find Durk!" Avender scrambled wildly across the floor, searching the refuse for the stone. "We can't leave him behind now!"

"I think I'm near the door." Durk's voice had returned to his usual, and much more worried, tone.

In a shot Avender was across the room, grabbing the rock in his hands. Redburr had already disappeared down the sloping tunnel to the dungeon. There was no thought for caution now. Ferris and Avender followed as fast as they could, the boy clutching the stone as he ran.

"How'd you know you could fool them?" he gasped before he was completely out of breath.

"I didn't," answered Durk, who had no breath to lose. "But I had to try. When I fell from your pocket and heard the guard seize your friend, I knew I had to do something. I didn't think you'd leave him there after all the trouble you'd already gone to, and I knew you'd all be slaughtered if you tried to stay and fight. So I remembered Act Four, Scene Three, from *The Knight of Deepwood Forest*, where the knight hides in a hollow tree and pretends to be the bandit leader. And it worked, just as it does in the play."

They came out of the tunnel and onto the ramp that crossed the vast chamber beyond. Redburr had pulled well ahead of them despite carrying Reiffen; for a moment Ferris and Avender lost him as he vanished beyond the columns. They continued as best they could, splashing through the darkened puddles until he reappeared, his torchlight flaming upward in the arch above his head.

"This way," he called quietly. "I've tried to set a false trail to throw off the wolves."

He led them around the outside of the gallery. Their shadows raced through the arches beside them, dodging from pillar to pillar like wisps of smoke against the back of an empty hearth. At the long passage back to the dungeons they paused, remembering the fear that had gripped them before. All of them felt the grasping magic that waited for them on the far side of the dark threshold.

"This is the hardest part." Redburr's chest heaved as he took great, shuddering breaths. The torchlight faltered a few weak steps beyond the first rough stones before them. "This time the watchers will be awake. I'll have to go as quickly as I can, because I'm not sure how much magic Reiffen and I can take. If you fall behind, remember to stay straight on to the stair. Don't follow any of the side passages! And don't lose sight of my torch!"

He stepped into the tunnel and began to run. Ferris and Avender followed as quickly as they could, but the strain of their long ordeal was starting to tell. Their footsteps sounded muffled now after the high, splashing echoes of the hall. Redburr's light drew steadily farther and farther ahead. Fat he was, but his fatness was a bear's fatness and only made him stronger.

Behind him, Ferris and Avender felt the cold gloom nipping at their flying heels. They were both sure that if they stopped, the darkness would certainly catch them. Almost they felt its hot breath on the backs of their necks, even though they knew nothing was there. And somehow they also knew if they ever let their fear get the better of them and looked back, then nothing would turn into something, and they would be lost.

Strange thoughts and visions came over them as Redburr's torch bobbed far ahead in the darkness. No longer were they racing deep beneath the ground. Now the tunnel lay just a short way beneath the earth. Close above their heads, the sun was shining in a bright blue sky. Why was it, they asked themselves, that they chose not to go to the surface? The surface was where they would be safe. No clutching shadow would touch them there. Green grass and warm sun were much better than filthy darkness.

"Quick, Avender!" called Ferris suddenly. The empty mouth of one of the side tunnels loomed close beside her. "This way! This is the way out!"

She grabbed Avender by the hand and began to pull him towards the tunnel. He was puzzled for a moment, and didn't want to follow. Why, he wondered, did she want them to go down that particular passage? Didn't she remember the way to the surface was farther on? Unsure of the way himself, he was about to follow her into the deeper darkness when he noticed a small sparkle of brightness mirrored in both her eyes. He turned as she was still trying to pull him forward, and caught sight of Redburr's torch winking in the distance. No, that was where the light was. It wasn't up above. If the light was safety, then they should head toward that.

He shook his head to clear his thoughts and remembered they didn't want to go to the surface at all. And, even if they did, the dark passage before them was hardly the way to get there. Hadn't Redburr warned them to stay on the main path? He pulled hard on Ferris's arm and hissed urgently, "Don't you remember! Redburr said we have to follow his torch! This way!"

It was Ferris's turn to be confused. She stared at him, even as the far-off light of Redburr's torch continued to flicker in her frightened eyes. Avender saw he was close to losing her. Not knowing what else to do, he pulled her with him down the passage after Redburr's light, now very faint in the distance. Avender was much stronger, and Ferris was forced to follow or else be dragged along the rough rock floor. Soon he had pulled her far enough away from the side tunnel that she was free of that particular passage's grip. Then she clung willingly to his hand and fled swiftly beside him.

They kept their eyes on the warmth of the torch ahead. Almost at once the light began to grow. They had passed the last of the side passages; the clutching darkness could now reach out for them only from behind. They hurried on without looking backward, and caught up at last with Redburr where he was waiting for them at the top of the dungeon stair.

"Are you all right?" the Shaper asked as they crashed, gasping, into his side. His belly heaved as he caught his breath; Reiffen swayed up and down in his arms like a cork bobbing in the open sea. Ferris gave them both an enormous hug. Redburr's clothes smelled, and he smelled, but Ferris couldn't even begin to say how glad she was to be close to him once more.

"I'm sorry I had to leave you alone back there," he went on. "But it was the only way. The worst is over. A few sissit to deal with in the guardrooms, then we'll be back with the Dwarves."

At that moment Reiffen stiffened and tried to stand. His eyes wild, he reached out over the Shaper's shoulder toward the passage behind them, his fingers twisted like claws. In a loud voice he cried out something they couldn't understand and struggled briefly to escape the Shaper's grip. But the Shaper held him tight. The boy's fit ended as quickly as it began. Exhausted, he collapsed back into Redburr's arms and fell into a deep sleep.

The Shaper shivered. The hair on his arms was bristling again. Then, as if in answer to Reiffen's call, from far off down the passage they heard a distant stirring. The rock trembled beneath their feet.

"Quick!" cried Redburr, his eyes yellow as a beast's in the torchlight. "Down the stairs! There's no time to lose!"

Ferris and Avender stumbled forward through the gloom, fear forcing them on. A second, closer rumbling followed the first. It washed over them from above, almost as thick as a wave of water. Once again the black tunnel thrummed around them.

Wearily they staggered down the uneven steps, but Redburr

brought them to a sudden halt much sooner than they expected. He raised a warning hand and growled, "The first guardroom is just below. Remember what I said about fighting. Just follow me through. I'll stop on the other side in case they try to come after us, but you keep right on going. I'll catch up to you before you reach the next level."

"What about that?" asked Avender, glancing nervously up the stair.

"We'll deal with it when we have to. Here, girl. Take this."

Redburr nearly dropped the torch as he handed it to Ferris. Both she and Avender could see the Shaper's fingers had become almost entirely nail. But there was no question of stopping to groom him now.

As if it had heard them, a third and louder rumble blew down from above. The walls continued to shake after the low thunder had passed. Without waiting another moment, Redburr turned and rushed down the stairwell, his arm cradling Reiffen's sleeping head as best he could against the danger below.

Two of the guards were peering up into the darkness when he appeared. They drew their swords, but Redburr was much too quick and strong for them. Leaping down the last few steps, he lowered his shoulder and knocked them both aside with a roar. Ferris and Avender came flying behind him, shrieking and shouting as loudly as they could: The other two sissit threw down their weapons and fled.

"That way!" The shaper pushed the children toward the passage that continued on downstairs. "Avender! You carry Reiffen."

Avender slipped Durk into his pocket and accepted his limp friend. Redburr's harness and clothing hung from him in tatters; when he was rid of Reiffen his belt burst and his sword rattled to the floor. He seemed twice the size he had been; his beard and hair were much thicker. For a moment he waited to see if any of the guards might try to follow, but those that could still move were already far away. With a last look back for whatever was chasing them, he drove the children before him and bounded down the stair.

They never reached the second guardroom. The rumbling behind them increased until there was a regular pounding in the walls. Small stones crumbled from the roof. Something very large was pursuing them through the tunnel, gaining with every stride.

A light appeared ahead, pale and white. A feeling of relief swept over them; Nolo's short, stocky shape stood outlined in the soft glow. Behind them the noise had grown so loud they couldn't hear a word of what the Dwarf was shouting, but his gestures were plain enough. He stood beside a narrow doorway in the wall, his lamp gleaming at his forehead, and caught them as they came hurtling down the stair. Ferris first, then Avender with Reiffen in his arms. The Dwarf pushed them through the door, where Dale and Dell held them fast at the edge of another fissure that opened in the rock at their feet. Dale took Reiffen. Avender stumbled, but Dell caught him at the edge of the narrow chasm. A shower of small rocks disappeared into the darkness beneath his feet.

Another great roar sounded from the passage above. A second roar, nearly as loud, answered.

"Where's Redburr?" asked Avender, peering into the passage.

Nolo nodded mutely back up the stair. A thunderous crash set the whole passage trembling. A large rock tumbled from the ceiling and rolled away. Shouldering his axe, the Dwarf charged back the way the children had come.

His jaw set in determination, Avender followed.

"Avender!"

Ferris's cry was cut short behind him by another pair of monstrous roars. Avender plunged after Nolo through the darkness, the Dwarf's pale light half-hidden behind a curtain of falling stone. With every thud and crash a fresh shower of rock filled the passage. Something struck Avender on the side of the head and he fell to the steps, briefly stunned. The broken stone scraped his hands and knees. By the time he scrambled back to his feet, the Dwarf was far ahead. Avender kept on, hardly knowing why. He didn't even have a knife. But if he stopped now he would never forgive himself.

Another crash scattered a fresh storm of stones across his back as Avender burst into the guardroom he had left just minutes before. A great black lizard, its scales the size of pie plates, had the bear wrapped in its thick tail and was snapping at him with its jaws. The Shaper clawed and roared in return, his long fangs bared. Nolo, axe at the ready, hopped back and forth beside them, looking for a chance to strike. Scattered across the cracked floor, the coals from the fallen brazier glowed like a crevice of red fire. Something glittered darkly: one of the guards' cast-off swords.

Avender scurried across the cracked floor for the weapon. It felt awkward and oddly weighted in his hand. A booming crash echoed through the room: the mander had smashed the bear against the nearest wall. The Shaper roared and raked his claws across the monster's back with a horrible metallic screech, like something out of Grimble's workshop. Nolo swung his axe. The mander squealed as the weapon bit deep into its tail.

With both hands raised, Avender rushed forward and gave the monster a mighty stroke. The sword shattered and the creature swept him aside. Banged and bruised, the boy landed heavily on the far side of the room.

"Get out, lad!" Nolo called over his shoulder. He didn't dare take his eyes off the mander for a second. Another opening came and his axe cut deeply again. The mander snapped at the Dwarf with its rows of gleaming teeth. Specks of yellow spittle sprayed across the room, sizzling where they struck the floor. Nolo caught the creature a glancing blow on the side of the head. Faster than Avender would have thought possible for so large a beast, the mander caught Nolo's arm between his teeth and shook him like a dog with a rat. With his free hand, Nolo whacked it twice on top of the head with the flat side of his axe. The mander shook its head again; Nolo flew bouncing across the room.

Avender looked around for another sword. Maybe he'd have more luck going for the mander's eyes. The bear continued to claw futilely at the creature's back. His rage grew with every useless blow, his muzzle stretched in rabid fury. The mander concentrated on the Dwarf, wary of what the axe had already done to its wounded tail.

The battle slowed. The creature ceased pounding the Shaper against the walls. Deep cracks and fissures ran across the ceiling, but no more stone was falling.

Avender found a jagged shard of rock. Stone in hand, he saw his chance. The creature was turned almost entirely away from him. If he was fast enough, he might be able to catch it off guard. Quickly he raced along the creature's side and jabbed the stone into its right eye. The mander howled. Blindly, it knocked Avender to the ground. Its drool burned like fire. As it searched for the boy with its one good eye, Nolo stepped forward with another ferocious blow to its tail. The mander bellowed again. Gouts of black blood pooled across the floor. Avender rolled toward the wall, away from the blood and burning slaver.

Horribly wounded, the mander released the bear. The Shaper attacked again instantly, flailing madly with his claws. The mander rocked beneath the blows but took no fresh wounds. Nolo swung his axe. With a fresh cry of pain, the mander turned quickly for the stair. Fast as a leaping fish it was gone. A dark trail glistened behind it.

In as much a rage as ever, the bear surged forward in pursuit. Avender leapt painfully to his feet. "Redburr! We've won!"

The Shaper turned and snarled. Avender gasped. The beloved friend of his childhood was gone, replaced by a thing of madness and wrath. Worse even than the poisoned jaws of the mander were Redburr's gaping teeth and throat. His fangs gleamed like knives in the light of Nolo's lamp; his scarlet eyes had shrunk to the size of peas. Nolo pulled Avender out of the way just as the great muzzle snapped shut where the boy's head had been.

Dwarf and boy fell back across the room. The bear, in his haste to come at them again, slipped in the mander's blood and skidded into the far tunnel. As he scrambled to his feet the black wetness matted his fur and began to burn. With one last howl of pain and fury, the Shaper raced off up the stair along the mander's trail, back to the heart of Ussene.

Avender, spattered with burns and bruises, fell to his knees and wept.

21

Losses in the Dark

Ferris's fear only increased when everything grew quiet. A falling stone had knocked the torch from her hand, but Dell had brought out his lamp to keep away the dark. Caught in the swirling dust, the red light made the narrow chamber seem to float like a ruby in the rock around it. Ferris coughed and rubbed her nose. Reiffen stirred uneasily but didn't wake; Dale had sheltered him from most of the tumbling rubble.

The two Dwarves spoke to each other in the thick accents of their own speech. The heavy words clunked and thudded like shifting stone. Ferris was desperate to know what was going on outside, but neither Dale nor Dell knew enough of the human tongue to tell her. To keep from thinking of all the terrible things that might have happened to her friends, she tried to make Reiffen more comfortable by fanning the dust from his face. Despite her efforts, she shivered at the thought of Redburr and Avender clawed apart, or Nolo smashed to pieces. She felt terrible doing nothing while her friends risked their lives.

As if he felt the same way, Dell moved to the front of the cave. Carefully he pulled the door open. A dark crack appeared from the passage beyond, but the silence remained. Dell slipped out, his lamplight flickering across the steps like embers glowing in a dying hearth. Behind him Dale and Ferris dropped back into deeper shadow.

Ferris strained to listen. Were those footsteps she heard? Dell darted away at the sound, leaving the others without any light at all. But soon the passage was washed in illumination again as Dell, Nolo, and Avender emerged upon the stair.

Ferris pushed forward, angry and relieved. Avender's clothes were torn, and dark bruises showed through every rent, but at least he was alive. "How could you do that?" she cried. "How could you run off and leave me behind!"

She stopped suddenly. Leaning around Avender, she peered back up the stairs. "Where's Redburr?"

Avender dropped his eyes to the ground.

Nolo laid a heavy hand on her shoulder. "Not here, lass. We still have to escape."

Ferris stood her ground. Sighing, Nolo pushed her into the cave. "Where is he?" she repeated.

"We couldn't stop him, lass. He chased after the beast as soon as we drove it away."

"Why would he do that?"

"It's who he is."

"Is he coming back?"

"If he doesn't get himself killed."

"Killed! Why would he be killed?"

Gently, Nolo took the girl's hand. In the narrow cave there was barely room to breathe. Behind them, Dell sealed the entrance. All trace of the door disappeared beneath his fingers.

"Because he doesn't have the sense to stop fighting, lass." Nolo shook his head tiredly. "Once he gets his anger up, nothing can bring him back to reason till there's nothing left to fight. Especially when he's a bear."

"We kept him from changing before," Ferris insisted hopefully. "When we first got to the fortress."

"You did?" Nolo's bushy brows rose above the weary hollows of his eyes. "Well then. Maybe there's more hope than I thought. I've never known him to be satisfied short of somebody's killing when the blood rage comes over him. And I don't think he'll be killing the mander."

Ferris gasped. "It was a mander?"

"Aye. A great mander. Three times the size of any I ever saw."

The Dwarf turned to Reiffen, who still slept in Dale's stony arms. "How's the boy?"

Ferris pushed deeper into the narrow crevice and laid a hand on her friend's thin face. "I don't think he's doing well at all," she said. "He's very weak."

Dale said something in his own tongue; Nolo nodded agreement. "Dale's right. We need to get moving. We can't rest here. The Three have other servants. And they'll be after us themselves soon."

"But what about Redburr?" In the pale light of Nolo's lamp, Ferris's face turned ashen with dismay. "We can't just leave him!"

"I'm afraid Redburr's on his own now, lass. I've already told you there's nothing we can do. And there's Reiffen still to rescue. We're not free yet. Redburr won't want us to come all this way for nothing, no matter what happens to him."

Ferris's shoulders slumped. Even she knew Nolo was right. All the same, the joy of Reiffen's rescue would ring hollow if it came at the cost of Redburr's life.

Nolo nodded to Dale and Dell, who maneuvered Reiffen down into the narrow cleft beneath their feet. The Dwarves' fingers and toes grabbed the rock like it was so much soft mud. When the crevice grew too narrow to descend farther, they followed the new tunnel they had carved through the wall. Avender and Ferris crawled behind, the stone scraping their backs and knees.

Nurren and Gorr met them with their packs in another small cell like the one Redburr had fetched them from, what felt like a month before. In the passage beyond, they found Delven and Snurr watching the corridor that led to the guardroom. The two Dwarves had heard something of the fight with the mander on the stairs above but had seen no sign of the bear. Nolo nodded grimly, and led them all back to the tunnel in the floor.

Reiffen stirred briefly when Dale and Dell laid him down on the rough stone. Ferris was beside him at once, brushing his hair back from his face and holding his hand. Avender reached for Durk, to show his friend who it was had saved them from the guards, but found his pocket torn and empty. The rock was gone.

"We have to go back!" he cried.

"Hush, lad." Nolo raised his hands to calm the boy. "There might be other things listening down here besides guards."

"You don't understand! We have to go back! I've lost Durk!"

"You lost the stone?"

Avender nodded. Tears welled in his eyes. First Redburr, and now Durk. And he had been the one in charge of Durk.

The Dwarf looked back the way they had come. "Do you know where?"

"I think it was in the cave by the stair. I tripped, and Dale took Reiffen. Or maybe it was during the fight." His words trailed off miserably as he tried to remember what had happened. But there had been so much noise and confusion. And he had been so scared.

Nolo thought for a moment, then shook his head. "We can't go back. The Wizards will be all over the place by now. We need to get as much stone between us and the fortress as we can."

"But we'd never have escaped without Durk's help! We can't just leave him!"

"We have no choice, lad. Going back would be foolish. We didn't go back for the bear, and we can't go back for the stone, either. Reiffen's our first concern."

Avender bit his lip. He knew the Dwarf was right. But knowing that did nothing to soften the feeling that he had betrayed the stone. If only he had noticed Durk was missing earlier. For a wild moment he thought he might run off and look for the rock by himself, but that idea passed as quickly as it came. A trick like that would only make everything worse. He hung his head, thinking that anyone who forgot his friends was no hero, no matter how many people he rescued.

"Go on, lad." Nolo tapped him on the shoulder. Avender looked up to see Ferris disappear into the fissure in the floor. He took a deep breath and followed, but his cheeks burned and his eyes were wet as he groped his way through the tunnel. The rest of the Dwarves came behind to guard the rear. At the very end, Nolo swung shut a pair of cleverly constructed doors that made the crack in the floor seem natural. It might not fool a Wizard, but it would certainly trick the sissit guards.

The different colors of the Dwarven lamps swept back and forth across the crevice as they descended, spotting the rough stone. Dale and Dell helped Reiffen, while Ferris and Avender slid from ledge to ledge on their own, too tired to try holding on by fingers and toes. By the time they reached the bottom Ferris was almost as bruised as Avender. But there was no rest at all when they finally set foot on the black sand; Nolo hurried them quickly on to the edge of the bone cave.

"We'll have to run here," he warned, taking Reiffen from Dale and hoisting him on his back. He peered anxiously ahead at the white mound in the middle of the cavern. "If the Three have learned where we went, this is the best place for them to cut us off. Let's hope Redburr thinks to meet us further on."

He set off quickly, Reiffen bouncing on his back. Somehow Ferris and Avender managed to stumble tiredly after him. The heavy feet of the other Dwarves plodded behind, their shadows rushing ahead in the thin lamplight. At the bone pile Nolo led them around the outer edge. Avender, though he couldn't see it in the gloom at the top of the cavern, felt the hollow watchfulness of the dark hole above his head. Despite himself, he remembered the long passage where Ferris had almost led them the wrong way, when the watchers had woken and the mander had soon followed. His sense of dread only grew after they passed the bones; then the danger loomed unseen behind. Only when he had left the cavern and reached the relative safety of the first turn in the tunnel beyond was he finally rid of the notion that another mander was about to crash out of the ceiling and smash down across the splintering bones to seize them in its jaws.

Even then Nolo wouldn't let them rest. They no longer had to run, but he hurried them along the road all the same. When they reached the edge of the dark lake in the next cave, Reiffen wrinkled his nose at the sour smell and looked uncertainly at the walls around them.

"Where are we?" he asked.

"In the . . . in the Stoneways," panted Ferris. "Below Ussene."

"The Stoneways?"

"It's . . . it's a long story."

Nolo called out to the Dwarves in their own tongue. Dale and Dell nodded. He turned to the children. "Avender, Ferris. You go with Dale and Dell. No sense getting burned twice."

The children climbed onto the Dwarves' shoulders, glad to rest their weary legs despite the uncomfortable perch. Carefully Nolo led them into the dead lake.

Reiffen looked back at his friends. "At least tell me what happened in the guardroom," he asked as the Dwarves sloshed deeper into the water. "Where'd that voice come from?"

"That was Durk." Avender looked down at the thick blackness swirling around Dell's knees.

"Who's Durk?"

"A talking stone," said Ferris.

"A talking stone?" Reiffen was more confused than ever.

"It's a long story."

Reiffen began to cough before he could ask another question. Ferris and Avender brought out their handkerchiefs to cover their faces, remembering how piercing the stench had been the last time they crossed the lake. Reiffen, who had no handkerchief, had to make do with his rough blanket.

There was still no time for conversation when they reached the other shore. Nolo and Delven quickly fashioned a sling from Reiffen's blanket. Each of them lifted one end and started off at a trot down the next tunnel, the boy dangling between them. Ferris and Avender staggered along behind. They swatted their way past the bugs in the next cavern without a thought; they had more serious dangers to frighten them now. Then they were off again at a steady pace. As Nolo had said, they wanted to put as much stone between them and Ussene as possible. Reiffen, exhausted by the fumes from the lake, fell back to sleep in his makeshift litter.

It was a long march through cold tunnels to the Dwarves' camp. Occasionally Nolo called a halt and the Dwarves all stood perfectly still, their bare feet feeling the rock for any ruffle of pursuit. But there was none. Nor did they find any sign of pasties or talking stones. Avender slogged miserably at the back of the company, his mind set glumly on Durk and Redburr. Ferris walked beside Reiffen, hoping he would feel better when he woke. Both children collapsed beside their friend when they finally reached the Dwarves' old campsite. It had been two long days, Nolo told them, since they last had any rest. "That fool bear will find his way back whether you're awake or not. Now both of you, go to sleep."

Nolo turned away, but not before Avender had seen a look of worry cross his heavy brow.

They slept a long time. Even the Dwarves slept, though at least one of them watched the caves around them the whole time for any sign of pursuit. When Ferris and Avender finally woke, they found Nolo and Nurren frying fish in a pan at the fire. Miserable and sore, Avender stretched and looked around the cave. There was still no sign of the bear.

Aching all over, he followed Ferris to the stream. Judging from the faces she made as she began to wash, she felt no better than he. Her cheek wasn't as swollen as before, but thin lines of red scab marked the edges of her burns. She shuddered at the sight of her own face in the clear mirror of the pool. Not even a hot meal, or Reiffen sleeping soundly beside them, was enough to make them feel better about the missing bear. Or Durk.

Reiffen woke while they ate. Ferris hurried to fetch him a plate of food.

"Feel better today?" Nolo looked closely at the boy.

"A little."

"Good. You're going to need your strength. It's a long walk home. Even I can't carry you all the way back to Issinlough."

"We're going to Issinlough?" Reiffen's weary eyes sparked with the first interest anyone had seen in him since his rescue.

"Aye." The Dwarf nodded. "It's only fair. Ferris and Avender have already been."

Ferris handed Reiffen his bowl of mushroom gruel. "It's beautiful," she told him. "The most beautiful thing you'll ever see. You won't believe the way it hangs in the darkness, all lit up. Just like the chandeliers in the Great Hall."

Reiffen nodded and accepted the offered food. He was much more interested in his first meal outside Ussene than in descriptions of Issinlough, no matter how much he wanted to go there. He gobbled his bowl of mush, topped with freshly fried fish, as if it were tastier than the finest mussel stew.

"Ease up there, lad," cautioned Nolo. "You'll make yourself sick."

The boy slowed his pace slightly, just enough for everyone to notice the clicking of his thimble on his spoon. The black iron reflected nothing of the golden flames dancing in the fire. His companions regarded him with a mixture of pity and sadness. All wondered if he would say something about his time in the fortress, but he still wasn't ready to speak.

"You rescued me just in time," was all he said, mumbling self-consciously between bites. "They were going to take my thumbs off next."

Avender thought darkly of what Durk had left unsaid when he had told them about his last meeting with the Three. Ferris frowned and laid aside the last of her breakfast.

"Where's Redburr?" asked Reiffen when the first edge of his hunger was filled. "It's not like him to miss a meal."

Ferris and Avender exchanged a look. "Don't you remember?" asked the girl.

"I remember the three of you rescuing me. And something about a talking rock, and a lot of narrow caves." Reiffen winced as he rubbed his elbow with one of his thin hands. "But nothing more about Redburr."

"We haven't seen him," said Avender.

"Not since the fight with the mander," added Ferris.

Reiffen's face tightened. "You mean Redburr's still back there?"

Ferris nodded, blinking through her tears.

"There's no knowing what's happened to him, lad." Nolo laid a stony hand on Reiffen's shoulder. "For all we know the great fool's lost somewhere in the Stoneways. Chances are there's more than one way out of that fortress. Delven and the others are off looking for some sign of him right now."

Ferris wiped her eyes with her sleeve and looked up hopefully. "Do you really think he's safe? Shouldn't we stay and help find him?"

Nolo shook his head. His scraggly beard wagged across his chest. "None of that, lass. I'm taking the three of you straight home, now that I've got you. Bears running around loose in Bryddlough are bad enough. Don't think I'm going to let you do it, too."

Avender didn't have the heart to tell Ferris that Redburr had almost killed him before he ran away. That part of the tale he would leave for another time, when the Shaper's loss wasn't so fresh. But later, when Ferris was at the pool helping Reiffen wash off some of the filth from the fortress, he asked the Dwarf what he really thought had happened to Redburr, and whether any of them would be safe if the Shaper did return.

"It's all one and the same, lad." The Dwarf stared hard at the boy with his deep-set eyes. "If he comes back, he'll be fine. If he doesn't, he's either dead or the Shaper in him is gone forever. Not all the other Oeinnen died. Some are still out there. You just can't tell they're anything but wild animals anymore.

"As for seeing him again, I'm not giving up hope. You shouldn't, either. There'll be plenty of time for mourning if we get back to the surface and find out for sure. Don't think the Three will leave it a secret if they've slain Redburr. In the meantime you need to think more like Ferris." Nolo nodded toward the pool, where the girl was worrying at Reiffen's torn and dirty clothes. "All I did was give her a little hope, and she perked right back up."

The Dwarf grinned suddenly, the thick lines of his face cracking wide in amusement. "You didn't think we'd ever rescue Reiffen, did you, lad? But Ferris did, and she was right. Maybe she'll be right again."

Avender tried hard to be hopeful after that, but somehow it just wasn't in him. Even with Reiffen back, he couldn't convince himself that anything had changed. As far as he could tell, all they had done was swap Redburr for Reiffen. Reiffen was his friend, but Avender knew there were a lot of people who wouldn't think Redburr for Reiffen was such a great exchange. And there were those thimbles to think about, too.

After breakfast, Nurren bowed to each of them in turn before they set off.

"You'll keep an eye out for Durk, won't you, while you're looking for Redburr?" asked Avender as he said good-bye.

"I'll do that." Nurren's tools jangled as he hooked his thumbs on his belt. "We all will. I know I'd like to hear that rock talk again. A regular geode, he is."

They left Nurren kicking the fire apart; a few coals sizzled as they fell into the pool. Then Nolo led the children back toward the Northway and the mansions of the Dwarves. They had barely left the cave before Ferris insisted Nolo tell them everything that happened after she and Avender left with the Shaper. "Maybe there's a clue about Redburr you missed. And how is it you built that tunnel just where we needed it, anyway?"

"That's easy. You didn't think we'd sit around on our hands while you were off looking for Reiffen, did you?"

"But how did you dig it so fast?"

"You know better than that, lass." The Dwarf frowned as he stumped along the rocky floor. Beside him Reiffen concentrated on his walking, with little extra breath to waste on talking. "Bryddin always dig fast. And we weren't paying any attention to how it looked. That's why the way was so rough. Dale and Dell wanted to fix it up while we were waiting, but I knew keeping a lookout for you was the better idea."

"We'd have been in a lot of trouble if you hadn't been there," said Avender.

"Well, there wasn't supposed to be any fighting." Nolo stroked his beard. "Delven and I figured it might be easier to go round the guards on your way back, in case there was any trouble. We found a fissure we liked in the stone and went to work. Cutting tunnel isn't hard if you let the stone give you a good start."

"But how could you be sure the sissit wouldn't find you first?" asked Ferris.

"Bad luck for them if they did." Then he told her about the fight with the mander, and how Avender's blow to the creature's eye was what saved them.

Avender blushed and said that wasn't really the case, that Nolo was the only one the mander had feared. "I couldn't have done anything if it hadn't been watching you so closely. Even Redburr couldn't hurt it."

"I think you're a hero," said Ferris.

Avender looked down at the stony ground as his ears began to tingle.

"It scares me, though," she continued, "to think that Redburr can lose control like that."

"He went after that mander like iron shavings after a lodestone," said Nolo. "Just because he looks human sometimes doesn't mean he ever is. You humans always think anything that can talk is just like you. But we aren't." He ducked his head to pass beneath a particularly low section of cave, and scrambled on.

Avender followed. He gritted his teeth and, wishing he had one of those Inach swords that Nolo said he was going to make, added Redburr's murder to the list of what the Wizards had to pay for.

They passed back down the Northway, their mood somber. Gradually they gave up looking for Redburr to return. With every march their spirits dropped, even Ferris's. She stopped looking up every time a bat flew overhead in the darkness. If Redburr hadn't found them yet, it was getting less and less likely he ever would.

They traveled slowly at the beginning but, as Reiffen grew stronger, gradually extended their marches. Every day he looked a little better, even cold porridge helped him regain his strength. His eyes began to shine and his cheeks filled out, though it would take a warm sun to put some color back into the ashy pallor of his face.

Avender and Ferris told him about their own adventures: the race down the Sun Road in the rickety wagon; how Skimmer had rescued Avender; how they had all nearly drowned in Grimble's airship. But Reiffen remained silent about his time in Ussene. His friends gave each other knowing glances. No matter how much better Reiffen looked on the outside, he never seemed to get any better on the inside. It became more and more obvious to all of them that he had been changed by his stay with the Wizards. Maybe not in the way they had anticipated when they set out to rescue him, but changed just the same. He seldom spoke and never smiled. More than once Avender found himself wondering if the change was to more than just his friend's mood.

Ferris insisted there was nothing wrong with Reiffen that going home wouldn't cure. "We can't even imagine what the Wizards did to him," she told Avender and Nolo. "How do you think you'd feel?"

Neither Dwarf nor boy argued with her, but they kept their watch on Reiffen all the same, just as Redburr had told them to.

Eventually they reached Cammas. Though his friends had prepared him for the sight, Reiffen was still astonished. He even perked up a bit again when he saw the vast cave filled with dim, hazy light and the boats fishing on the windless sea. Twin lumps came to Ferris's and Avender's throats when their friend told them how much he thought the lake looked like Valing at daybreak on a gloomy day, when the white peaks of the Bavadars were hidden above the clouds. Both wondered if Valing would ever be the same without Redburr to share it with.

A Dwarf named Rolk met them at the first hut. He had sailed with Gammit from Issinlough as soon as Delven's mistrin had brought Dwvon the news of their success. The *Nightfish* was waiting for them at the mouth of the Cammas loway. But the humans in the village had seen two children go off into the Stoneways and three come back, and they all wanted to know where the extra boy had come from. And what had happened to the bat? Nolo had already decided he had to tell them some version of the truth. When everyone heard it was Reiffen who had been added to the party, and that he had been rescued from Ussene, there was no stopping them from having another feast to celebrate the company's safe return.

Redburr, they were told, was returning to Issinlough by a different route.

Eagerly everyone gathered round to get a good look at the young prince. Most of them were from Wayland or Banking, but all knew the story of Reiffen's parentage. Legitimate or not, they wanted a glimpse of the nephew of the king. They murmured among themselves and shook their heads at the marks of misuse on his hands, but they were glad to see the proof of his escape all the same. One stepped forward, delegated by the others to make a speech of welcome for them all. A rough miner he was, with hands and fingers as knobby as the rock he carved. "It's good to see you safe and well, my lord," he said, ducking his head respectfully. "I saw your mother once. Riding in a carriage past the Old Palace in Malmoret, she was. A real princess. She'll be glad to see you home, I'll guess."

Reiffen thanked him for his kindness, and the others for their concern. He was not used to such attention—few folk in Valing had ever cared much about that part of him—yet he was gracious all the same. Giserre had taught him well for the future she was certain he would have. Everyone in Cammas agreed he was a fine example of his house.

"Quality shows," said one woman to her friend after both had done their curtsies. "And after what he's been through, too."

"It's such a pity the princess is promised to the other one," her friend replied. Both tried hard not to stare at the thimbles.

But the crowd in Cammas wasn't large, and all were respectful of the boy's condition. They let him and his companions enjoy the feast as they wished. Only occasionally did they interrupt for a speech or two, especially after the ale had begun to flow. Even then, when the travelers expressed their desire to rest before the revelry was finished, there was only a little bowing, and one final, brief good-bye, before they were allowed to go.

They retired to the same small cabin they had slept in before. Only this time there were four of them crowded into the little room, where before they had only been three plus a bat hanging from the chimney. Avender grew quiet as he remembered the way Redburr had liked to open one of his small, beady eyes to check that he and Ferris were all right, before he wrapped his wings tightly across his stomach and went to sleep himself. Nolo was a much better guardian, and had certainly always been the more responsible of the two in every way; but losing his gluttonous friend was nearly as bad as losing his mother. At least when Reiffen had been taken, there had been the hope of rescue. For Redburr, there was no going back at all.

Reiffen, for the first time since he had been taken from Valing, actually felt comfortable. He lay pressed tightly between his friends, the fire warming his feet as the food warmed his belly. If he closed his eyes he could almost imagine he was home. The bed might be a bit harder than what he slept in at the Manor, but Avender was beside him and his other friends close by. He rubbed his chin comfortably along the edge of his blanket and wiggled his toes by the fire.

"He told me I could learn magic," he said.

"Eh? What's that, lad?" Nolo stirred sleepily from somewhere near the door.

"Magic?" Ferris sat up at once. She sounded much more interested than the Dwarf.

"You know," said Reiffen. "What Wizards do."

"I know what magic is," said Ferris. "I was just surprised. Why would the Three want to teach you magic?"

"It wasn't the Three. It was Fornoch. And he did it to try and get me to do what they wanted. I think they thought if they gave me some sort of present, I'd do what they asked."

"What did they ask?" said Nolo. He had sat up beside the doorway and was paying closer attention now.

Reiffen looked up at the roof of the hut. The stone ceiling was slanted as steeply as it was in his and Avender's room back home. He didn't like thinking about the Three even now, though they were far away. But since he had begun to speak, he knew he must keep on or never tell the tale.

"They wanted me to claim my crown. They told me there were a lot of people who wanted me to be king instead of my uncle. They said they'd help me."

"That's just what Redburr said they'd do," said Ferris.

Then Reiffen told them most of what had happened to him while he had been with the Wizards. For a long time no one interrupted: even Ferris understood that the flow of his words, if ever stopped, might not pick up again. The shadows of the dying fire grew still. He told them almost everything: his meeting with the Three; how they had allowed him to run freely through the upper levels of the fortress; of the Library that Fornoch had said was summoned specially for him.

"That was when he said he'd teach me magic," the boy explained. "You should have seen the books there. Hundreds of them. You'd have loved it, Ferris. History and poetry. The lives of kings and queens. But mostly they were books of magic. And the ways of Areft and the world. And there was a spider, and a skeleton, and a green stone that throbbed whenever I came close to it."

"A green stone?" asked Avender.

Reiffen nodded. "Fornoch told me I'd never die if I took it. When he held it close I could feel it beating in time with my heart. It was like it was alive."

"Now that I'd have liked to see," said the Dwarf. "A living stone."

"Durk was alive," said Avender. He picked up a pebble from the floor and tossed it into the fire. A shower of sparks bolted up the chimney when it struck.

"Durk didn't throb," said Ferris.

"He throbbed when he talked," said Avender. "You could feel it in your hand."

"Maybe the green stone was like Durk." Ferris turned to Reiffen. "Did your stone talk?"

"Not that I heard." Reiffen thought for a moment. "But it didn't seem to be alive like that. It was more like a snake. Or a tree. A tree's alive, but you can't talk to it."

"Maybe Durk was that kind of stone," suggested Avender. "Only he got away and Fornoch couldn't use him for what he wanted. I hope Nurren's found him."

Ferris turned back to Reiffen, her eyes gleaming in the firelight. "Were you tempted?"

"Not really. Mostly I was scared."

"I'd have been tempted. Imagine being able to use magic! Think of what you could do! And never dying, either!" Ferris hugged her knees close beneath her blanket, cozy in the warmth of the little cabin, far from dungeons or Wizards bearing gifts.

"Did they tell you why they wanted you to live forever?" asked Nolo from his place by the door.

Reiffen shook his head. "I think it was just another gift to get me to help them. I don't even know if they really meant it, or if it would work. How would a stone let you live forever? They were always telling me what they would do for me if I did what they asked."

"And if you didn't?" the Dwarf went on. "Did they tell you what would happen if you didn't do what they wanted?"

Reiffen frowned. "They said it really didn't matter what I decided. They said they could make me do whatever they wanted and no one would ever know the difference."

"That's not true." Avender looked carefully at his friend. "You'd know. If you gave in to them, you'd have to live with being a traitor the rest of your life."

"I think the other would be worse," said Ferris. "Knowing they were making you do something, and everyone thinking you were a traitor just the same."

Reiffen said nothing. He remembered a tall window and a little man, and the gloomy afternoon light on the narrow valley beyond. He had said all he wanted to say about his time in Ussene. But now his memory had been stirred, and the cozy comfort of the cabin was gone. His darker mood returned, he said nothing more of what had happened to him. His friends, once they saw he had finished, rolled themselves back in their blankets and went to sleep. But Reiffen lay still and sleepless while everyone else snored around him. His heart ached at what he had done, though he knew he had been compelled by a will much stronger than his own. A coldness lingered inside him that no hearth could warm. He curled up closer to the fire and held his hands out to the flames. The iron thimbles remained dark and cold. Quickly he put his hands back beneath his blanket and tried once more to sleep. But it was hard to close his eyes for a long, long time, for fear of what he might see.

22

Thimbles

When they woke they breakfasted in Cammas, then followed the loway back to the bottom of the world. Gammit and the *Nightfish* were moored in the same spot they had left them in on their outward voyage, this time by a short cable to the underside of the stone. Ferris looked up at the bare rock, half-expecting to find Redburr hanging by his claws from some narrow crevice overhead. Though she tried to hide her disappointment, Avender noticed her worried frown when she saw the Shaper wasn't there. He wished he could think of something to say to make her feel better. At least she still had hope.

Gammit glared at them when they arrived. "Back again, I see. Well, the sooner you get aboard, the sooner I'll get back to important work. Come on."

One by one they clambered onto the airship. Nolo introduced Reiffen, and Gammit gave him a look that suggested they had all gone to a great deal of trouble for very little return. When everyone was crowded onto the deck, Rolk untied the cable from the mooring and jumped on board beside them.

Slowly the ship settled downward, away from the great stone roof. Gammit muttered something about extra weight: Rolk tossed several bags of rock overboard. The *Nightfish* bobbed back toward the ceiling, but not before they had dropped far enough to see a large lamp shining brightly around the corner of an outcrop in the stone above.

"That's a good idea," said Ferris, shading her eyes as she looked around the ship. "Where's Grimble?"

"Back in the workshop." Gammit frowned as he coiled the cable and stowed it below the hull. "Some Bryddin have all the luck."

Other lamps shone overhead as they left Cammas and flew on through the empty night. Each light stood out like a sentinel star against the darkness, the next emerging just as the last disappeared astern.

Nothing else about the trip was new. The Dwarves spent most of the journey tinkering with the ship, which left the children to themselves. They passed the time in napping and talking as the darkness slid by. Ferris did most of the talking, though Avender did his best to help. Reiffen still had little to say, though he did brighten noticeably when Nolo took him for a tour belowdecks. The boy's interest pleased Gammit, who went on to show him everything from the gearing in the stern to the blazing lamp in the bow. "He might not be strong enough to work the crank," declared the Dwarf, "but at least he knows the difference between a sprocket and a spanner. There may be some hope for you Abbeninni after all."

At length one of the lamps overhead grew brighter as they approached, instead of fading back into the darkness behind them. Reiffen looked on in awe as he gazed at Issinlough for the first time. The thin curtains of the Veils shimmered in the light of the lamps; the unnerets and gossamer paths gleamed like spider silk.

Beside him, Ferris softly repeated the words Nolo had sung when they first came to the city many weeks before.

"*Falling waters break the night;*
Silver's shine slips into sight.
In the darkness, deep below,
Lies the light of Issinlough."

"You're right," Reiffen answered. "It is the most beautiful thing I've ever seen."

Willing hands were there to help them guide the *Nightfish* back into its berth when they arrived at Grimble's workshop, but none of their old friends had come to greet them. Grimble was distracted with other projects, and Dwvon and Uhle were busy in Vonn Kurr. The company made their good-byes to Gammit and Rolk, then followed Nolo wearily through the maze of passages back to the city and the Rupiniah. But even the beauty of Issinlough wasn't enough to make up for losing Redburr. Dwvon's barren unneret echoed their mood; the empty halls and passages thudded dully beneath the sad tramp of their booted feet. Even the lovely smell of Mother Norra's kitchen, spreading thick through the upside-down tower like the leaves of a hidden tree, left the children cold.

"Beans and bacon!" she exclaimed when she saw them. "And to think how worried I was I might never see you youngsters again! So this is Reiffen! He looks like he could use a peck or two of stew! And you could all of you use a good washing. Those clothes look like they haven't been changed in weeks!"

She rushed across the room to envelop Ferris and Avender in a white-aproned hug. For a moment they caught a glimpse of a large man seated at the table with his back to them, but they didn't see him again until the happy cook had set them free. The sound of a large slurp filled the kitchen as the other guest finished his soup; with a rattle of spoon on stone, he dropped his arm back and turned around.

"Redburr!"

Ferris rushed forward, in time with her leaping heart. Avender and Reiffen weren't far behind. The Shaper, smelling of soup and beer, wrapped all three of them in his enormous arms. For a long moment his three friends were children again, everything that had happened to them since leaving Valing forgotten.

"What took you so long?" he asked, leaning back for a view of something more than the tops of their heads.

"Us!" Ferris looked up, tears shining in her eyes. "We're not the ones who disappeared! Where have you been?"

"I had to come back the long way." Despite himself, the Shaper beamed. "While the rest of you were lolling around on that flying sack Gammit calls an airship, I was winging across the surface as hard as I could on my weak little wings."

Nolo's eyes narrowed suspiciously as the children disentangled themselves from Redburr's arms. "Did Gammit know you were here? I'll cook him in my own furnace if he did."

"None of that now, Mr. Nolo." Mother Norra fluttered forward, waving her apron with her hands. "Mr. Redburr didn't arrive until after Mr. Gammit left. And he only just got up. He's been having a nice, long nap since he flew in. A fat pigeon, he was. Scared me half to death when he landed on my window there and started to talk. I had to climb half the stairs in Issinlough to find clothes big enough for him when he woke."

Nolo relented with a wide smile and banged the Shaper happily on the shoulder. Redburr winced at the blow. "Careful," he warned. "Or I'll leave again and let you deal with these three all the rest of the way home."

Nolo's smile only broadened, his face opening wide as fresh-plowed earth.

Reiffen stepped forward and bowed, his face as solemn as stone. "I have not yet thanked you, sir, for saving me. You risked grave danger for my sake. We all thought you dead. My debt can never—"

"That's enough, boy." Redburr waved Reiffen's thanks away. "I had to come get you, or never hear the end of it from your mother. As for my getting away, let's just say I had to find a different exit."

"What about the mander?" asked Avender, remembering too vividly the fight in the guardroom.

Redburr shrugged. "I don't know what happened to the mander. While I was chasing it I ran into a company of sissit instead. Unfortunate for them, but fortunate for me. When we were finished, my head finally cleared. The whole fortress was after me and I had no idea where I was. So I did a couple more shifts, and led everyone a merry chase up and down Ussene until I finally found my way to the roof and flew away."

"What about those flying creatures you met before?" asked Ferris. "The ones who chased you last spring."

"I suppose they were all out combing the mountains for you. I never saw them."

"No, I don't suppose you did." Nolo studied the Shaper thoughtfully. "And I guess our easy escape had nothing to do with everyone chasing you instead of us."

Redburr threw up his large hands. "Never occurred to me."

The children's mood was completely changed by the time Mother Norra led them upstairs for a wash before dinner. With Redburr returned, their triumph was complete. Avender forgot about Durk for a while, and even Reiffen looked happy. The water clattered merrily as the baths filled. Thick steam dampened the stone walls. They laughed and sang in their tubs, Ferris and the boys calling back and forth to one another through the open windows of their rooms. Their voices raced across the darkness like larks above a summer meadow.

> "Crash and boom!
> Thump and roar!
> The falls ahead will crab your oar!
> But we can race away to shore
> With sails that bring us home once more!"

"How's that?" Mother Norra asked after Ferris had told her she and Avender had lost their spare clothing. "Rotted away in a burning lake! Only in the Stoneways, I suppose. But never you mind. I've got some things of Mr. Dwvon's I can take in for you. Mustard and mutton, I've half a mind to burn what you've been wearing all this time!"

When they came back down to the kitchen they stuffed themselves to bursting on another of Mother Norra's famous stews. But they had slept so much on the *Nightfish* that, even with their bellies full, no one was tired when they were done. So Nolo led them down to the bottom of Dwvon's unneret, where the lowest chamber had a floor of clear glass. One could stand in the center of the room and look into the Abyss below, deepening darkness the only thing visible beneath one's shoes. Mullioned windows circled the room; a stone bench ran below. On one side the windows looked out onto the silver dish of the Bryddsmet. On the other, four of the Veils sparkled and wove like rainwater dripping from the eaves of far-off houses.

"It looks a lot like the Tear," said Ferris. "Except for the floor." She slid one foot carefully forward just to make sure there was no sudden end to the glass.

"Actually, it's the Tear that looks like this," answered Nolo. He seated himself on the bench beside the door with a contented sigh. "We call it the Bryddis B'wee. Sometimes we come here to look for Brydds' return."

Reiffen stood in the middle of the floor, staring down at the emptiness beneath his feet, but Avender and Ferris preferred to sit near Nolo. Redburr crossed unconcernedly to the other side of the room, where he flopped down on the bench and pulled from his pocket a jar of jellied minnows he had snuck out of Mother Norra's cupboard. "Now then, boy," he said to Reiffen as he opened the lid and drew out the first of the small fish, "there are some things we have to discuss. I've been talking to Nolo, and we need to make a few decisions before we go back to Valing. First off, what do you think those things are Usseis put on your fingers?"

Reiffen shrugged. "I don't know," he said.

"Have you tried to take them off?"

"I've tried. But I can't."

He took a deep breath, then grasped the thimble on his left hand firmly with the fingers of his right. He grimaced for a moment, partly from effort and partly from pain. When he stopped, his face was flushed and red.

"Maybe I should try," said Nolo.

Redburr gulped down another fish and shook his head. "You're too strong. You might pull the finger off entirely. I think I'd better be the one to try."

He put down his jar and crossed the glass floor to the boy. Reiffen offered him his hands. Gently the Shaper took the left in both his own, and examined thimble and finger. He twisted them this way and that, and even bent over to sniff at the cold metal. When he was satisfied there was nothing more to learn, he stiffened his grip and tried to pull the thimble off. Reiffen clenched his other hand until the knuckles went white but said no word. Redburr changed his grip and tried again. Once more nothing happened.

"That's not coming off," he said as he stepped away. Reiffen tried to massage the feeling back into his hand. "Not unless we cut off the finger."

"You can't do that!" cried Ferris.

"We might have to, girl." Redburr retrieved his jar from the bench and sat back down. "It's definitely magic. And we have no idea what it's for." He pulled another fish from the jar and swallowed it down.

"They were just torturing him," said Ferris. "That's all it is. Reiffen said so himself."

The Shaper wiped his greasy fingers on his beard. "The Three have no need for torture," he said. "It's an uncommon person whose will won't bend to theirs at the first try. No, I'm inclined to believe there's a purpose to what's on the boy's fingers."

Reiffen said nothing. He continued to stare down through the floor into the Abyss, but his thoughts were far away to the north, in an enormous room with a stone table and a beam of false moonlight.

"But what can a pair of thimbles do?" asked Ferris.

"Maybe they keep him in the Wizards' power while he's so far away," suggested Nolo.

"We don't have any idea what they do," said the Shaper. "And it's no use trying to guess. It's not like we have any great experience with magic."

"Do you think you're different?" asked Avender suddenly of his friend.

Reiffen considered the question. "Well," he replied after a moment, "I'm not the same. You wouldn't be, either, if you'd spent as much time as I did in that place. But I don't feel like anyone's controlling me, if that's what you mean. I don't feel like they've done anything to me. But I guess Usseis could have done just about anything he wanted and I probably wouldn't even remember."

"I think they put those things on you just to make us suspicious," said Ferris. She looked about at her companions one by one, almost challenging anyone to disagree with her. "We know how much they like to make us fight among ourselves."

"That's true." Redburr lifted his nearly empty jar and tilted it forward to see what was left inside. A few gobs of jelly spilled onto his beard. After eating those, he cleaned out the inside of the glass with his finger, smacked his lips, and went on. "All the same, you and Avender need to remember why I brought you along. You need to keep an eye on Reiffen. If he does anything strange, you let me know right away."

Reiffen lifted his eyes from the floor. "What do you think I might do?" he asked, looking at the Shaper.

Redburr combed the last of the jelly from his beard, then licked his fingers clean. "It's hard to say, boy. For all we know Usseis wanted us to rescue you. Then, if you ever challenge your uncle for the throne, it will look like the Wizards had nothing to do with it. We, on the other hand, will never know the real truth one way or the other. But if those thimbles really do anything to you, it's most likely to be some sort of control. What Usseis likes best is to bend things to his own will. He's never happy unless he's twisting something to his own purpose. We'll just have to keep our eyes and noses open for anything suspicious. After all, it's just as likely we really did rescue you, and those caps on your fingers don't do anything at all."

"But you don't really think that, do you."

"No, boy. I don't."

Reiffen and Redburr regarded one another steadily, as if there were no one else with them in the B'wee. Behind the Shaper the lights of the city gleamed like colored lanterns on a summer night. On the boy's side of the room there was only dark. He looked very much alone. If Redburr was right, then Reiffen's would be the real burden. Others might watch for some sign he was no longer himself; but, if their worst fears proved true, they would still be the same in the end. Only Reiffen would be lost.

"I still think cutting off his fingers is the best idea," said Nolo. This time Ferris leaned over and swatted him angrily on the arm. Redburr chuckled as she wrung her stinging hand, and even Reiffen had to smile.

"Well, it is a horrible idea," said Ferris.

"Yes, it is," agreed the Shaper, still smiling. "Which is why I think we should let him keep his thimbles for the time being. And his fingers. Until we're sure what those caps are for, it'd be dangerous to fool with them. For all we know, cutting them off might even kill the boy." He turned to Reiffen and his tone turned more serious. "But if you show any sign at all of not being yourself, then we'll have to take more drastic action. For our sake, as well as yours."

So it was that Ferris and Avender spent the rest of the journey watching their friend closely. If he minded their scrutiny, he never gave a sign. And though they never thought for a moment that he was under the influence of any spell or glamour, they were also certain he wasn't the same old Reiffen, either. He had said so himself. His mood was too often darker and more distant than it had been, and frequently he seemed to be looking at things no one else could see. Rarely did he speak unless Ferris or Avender spoke first, which meant that Ferris had to work especially hard to keep any conversation going among the three of them. But at the same time, he was still definitely Reiffen. Avender couldn't explain why they thought so, but Ferris could. "It's his eyes," she told Redburr when he asked. "Those are Reiffen's eyes. I'm sure there's no one else inside."

The next day, after another filling breakfast, Ferris argued with Mother Norra about whether their filthy clothes should be burned or washed.

"I'm not going back outside with nothing to wear but cut-down Dwarf breeches! I need my own clothes."

"But think of where they've been, dearie! Better to burn them than carry around even the smallest pinch of that nasty magic!"

"I already told you, we never saw the Wizards!"

"Yes, but you were in their halls! There's spells in the dust and dirt, I'm sure!"

"I want my clothes!"

It was some time before Avender had put enough stone between him and the kitchen to lose the sound of their arguing. He was feeling sorry for himself again, and wanted to think of all the things he might have done to keep from losing Durk. For a while he wandered among the unneret's empty rooms. When Redburr finally found him, he was leaning on the railing of one of the balconies, his eyes locked on the shimmer of the Veils.

"Nolo told me what happened to Durk," said the Shaper as he came up beside the boy. "It wasn't your fault."

"It was." Avender frowned stubbornly. "I was the one who asked him to come with us. He'd never have gone back to the fortress otherwise."

"That was his choice, not yours, boy. You did what you thought best."

"I was wrong."

"No, you weren't. You offered Durk the best chance he was ever going to have of getting out of Ussene. He knew that. It's why he came with us."

"We made him come with us. He could've stayed behind with Nurren. That's what he wanted to do."

"I made him come with us, not you." A hint of Redburr's bearish growl lingered across the night. "Blame me if you want, boy, but don't blame yourself."

"You put me in charge." Avender bit his lip and stared into the darkness so Redburr couldn't see his eyes. "I was the one who lost him."

The Shaper leaned on the rail beside him and stared at the dark as well. "Soldiers fall in battle all the time, boy. Don't think you'll ever get used to it. You didn't suppose we were going to tangle with the Three and come away without a scratch, did you? We've been lucky enough as it is. I'm alive, and you have no idea how lucky that was. And Reiffen's alive, and so's Ferris. I hope you have wit enough to understand that. Don't ever think you have to eat all the berries on the bush."

Redburr straightened and turned his face from the darkness to the city. "Now come on. It's time to go back to the others. Nolo wants to show you the Dinnach a Dwvon and Uhle's Forge. And Ferris is in a hurry because she wants to get back in time to wash her clothes."

Avender followed the Shaper back inside the upside-down tower. Behind them the Veils and the city gleamed. He knew Redburr was right, and the fact that even the Shaper forgave him was a great comfort. Still, deep in his heart, he wished he had been quick and smart enough to save the stone.

From Issinlough they were four hard days climbing the Sun Road. The last night they spent in the Axe and Ruby, where Redburr made them take dinner in their rooms. "The longer it takes for the

Three to find us again, the better," he confided between tankards. "In the meantime we'll just be five travelers on our way to Valing."

It was high summer when they came out from Uhle's Gate into the daylight once again. The late-afternoon sun had already fallen behind the round shoulders of Aloslomin. All of Grangore lay in early shadow below. But, high up on the slope of Ivismundra, the sun still shone warm upon their faces, and they had to shield their eyes from the brightness. Nothing the Bryddin could build would ever match the strength of the sun. Around them the trees swayed in the breeze; birds and squirrels scolded and sang among the branches. It was the wind the children had missed the most during their long weeks underground: the wind brushing against their faces and whistling past their ears. The wind and the rain and all the small sounds of woodpeckers and bullfrogs, crickets and crows. The Under Ground was a silent place, unless there were Dwarves at work close by.

"It's funny." Ferris took a deep breath of clear, fresh air. "I feel like I'm already home."

"That's because you are," said the Shaper. "The Stoneways aren't for humans, for all the lamps and gold."

They spent one night with Huri and Nurr, then continued on to Upper Crossing. Angun had returned to Bryddlough, Huri told them, after deciding there was nothing worth his interest aboveground. From Upper Crossing they took the river route back to Mremmen, where they had no difficulty hiring another ship to take them north to Lugger. Nolo had brought a few lamps back with him from Bryddlough, enough to hire a royal barge.

Reiffen asked Redburr why they couldn't go back through Malmoret and Rimwich, at which the Shaper cuffed him affectionately. "We go to all the trouble of rescuing you from the Wizards, and you want to risk your neck in your uncle's court? Your mother would have my hide in front of her hearth if I even thought about taking you to Rimwich." But Avender heard him tell Nolo afterward that he was glad to see Reiffen still thinking like a child. "It's the boy that wants to see Malomoret," he said. "Not Wizards. Maybe we've been lucky."

Two weeks from Grangore the party rode over the top of the pass on horses purchased in Lugger and came home finally to Valing. The lake glistened before them; beyond rose the sharp peaks of the High Bavadars. To the north, the long plume of spray from the falls swirled like chimney smoke high into the cloud-dotted sky. Rainbows crossed the cliffs. Last spring's lambs, now nearly as large as their mothers, looked up from the meadows as the travelers rode by, and the orchards past Easting were thick with half-sized fruit. The smell of fresh-mown hay filled the air.

No one noticed them until they had almost reached the Manor. Then a pair of woodcutters spotted the travelers as they rode out of Goston's Wood toward the Neck. "Why, tick me if it isn't Nolo and Redburr come home," said one.

"Who's that with 'em?" asked the other. "The first two's Ferris and Avender, but I don't recognize the third."

They tossed their caps in the air and gave a cheer when Ferris told them it was Reiffen. Then nothing would do but the travelers had to stop and shake hands all around. The woodcutters wanted them to dismount and tell their tale right there, but Redburr pointed out they were hoping to see some supper before nightfall, and that someone was no doubt waiting for the loads of wood the woodsmen had dropped by the side of the road. So the woodcutters hurried them on with loud cheers that had everyone rushing out from the nearer farms to see what was up. It wasn't long before the party had picked up a train of children and dogs willing to risk missing supper for the greater fun of accompanying Reiffen on the last short leg of his journey home.

They were quite the small crowd by the time they crossed the Pinch to the front gate of the Manor. Dennol Longbay had already come halfway out from the gatehouse to see what was causing all the uproar. When he recognized Nolo and Redburr riding at the front of the little party, he relaxed and leaned easily on his pike.

"What's all this noise you've brought with you, Redburr?" he asked, grabbing the bridle of the Shaper's horse and winking at the children behind him.

"We've brought back the boy."

"The boy? And what boy might—! You mean you've got Reiffen?" Dennol took another look at the three children in the rear. "I see Ferris and Avender, but I don't—"

Then they all realized how much Reiffen had changed if an old friend like Dennol didn't recognize him as soon as he saw him. A closer inspection, however, caused the forester's jaw to drop in surprise. He shook his spear and grinned fiercely. A smile lit his face just like those on the leaping children, and he danced a little jig of his own.

"Welcome home, boy!" he crowed. "Welcome home!"

"Yes, it is welcome, isn't it," said Reiffen. He seemed suddenly older, as if he had been gone for long years instead of months, and sadder, too. A quiet smile ghosted across his face as they passed through the gate and back into the old, familiar courtyard. The high gables and side porches of the big house threw long shadows across the dusty ground.

Gleeful children surged into the yard around them. Stable boys raced from the barns to see what all the commotion was about, and kitchen maids gathered at the scullery door. "It's Reiffen! It's Reiffen!" came the cry, and the news sped quickly back through the halls of the Manor. An argument broke out between the stable boys and some of the older children over who had the better right to hold the travelers' horses while they dismounted, which opened the way for Atty Peeks and his friends to do the job instead.

Reiffen was just sliding off his horse when Berrel and Hern came wondering out onto the front porch to stare in astonishment at the returning travelers. Nolo had only taken Ferris and Avender with him to visit Issinlough, yet here he was returning with Reiffen and Redburr as well. There had never been any talk of rescue from that direction. Clearly a great deal of explaining needed to be done, none of which was anywhere near as important as the joy at seeing Reiffen safely home. The stewards hurried down the steps and into the courtyard, great smiles beaming on their faces. Everyone tried to talk at once and no one understood a word. Dogs chased one another through the dirt. The courtyard rang with barking and cheers.

Then all fell silent. The dry summer dust spun in the evening light. Giserre had appeared on the front step of the Manor. She waited for her son to see her, knowing he would find her on the porch long before she found him in the swirling crowd. In a moment he had pushed across the yard and was kneeling on the step before her. She looked down upon his face, tears glittering in her eyes. Then she held out her hand and drew Reiffen up onto the step beside her. Together they looked out upon their friends standing quietly in the courtyard.

"My son is returned." Giserre spoke simply, but in such a voice that everyone could hear. "Great is our debt to you all."

Her face shone with gladness. Looking away from the crowd, she offered her son her arm. Together they went back inside. Another great cheer followed them, and all the dogs joined in once more.

There were many tales to be told and explanations to be made, but for the moment Redburr and the rest of the company were happy just to follow Hern to the kitchen. She sent Tinnet off to the Tear with a tray filled with Reiffen's favorite food, then turned her attention to the rest of them. By the time they had eaten their fill of fresh bread and pickled graylings most of the story had already been told. Hern was especially unhappy when she learned the details of how she had been deceived. She half-threatened to banish the Shaper from Valing forever for his part in the plot, but everyone knew she didn't mean it, especially after she had Atty bring out a fresh jar of honey while she was still in the middle of her scold.

Then Dennol, who had forgotten to return to his post, asked to hear about the *Nightfish* again; and of course the tale took twice as long in the second telling and had grown to include a description of how it had been the ghost of Brydds who woke Redburr before he fell too far to ever fly back up to Bryddlough. Berrel puffed his pipe and nodded along, and even Hern's eyes shone as Ferris described the Seven Veils, and Issinlough gleaming like a jewel in the night.

It was late in the long summer evening before anyone saw Reiffen and Giserre again. Anella came to bid Ferris and Avender to the Tear, and the children followed her back along the path at the top of the high cliff, past the orchard to the stone stair that descended to the gorge. A soft wind whistled through the windows of the passage; the roar of the falls increased as they approached the Tear. There wasn't much mist, though the noise was tremendous. The lake was low and the water at its summer ebb as it burst through the notch in boiling white sheets, and plumes and gouts of spray. Above the rush and roar, the Tear hung half-hidden amid the wisps of whirling cloud.

Inside, Giserre and Reiffen stood together beside the fire. Wood smoke curled up to the chimney in the roof. Even at the height of summer there was always a fire in that room, to thin the damp of the constant cloud.

"Welcome, my heroes," said Giserre. She glided up the steps to greet them. Anella slipped silently to a place at the side of the room. Giserre held out a hand to each of her guests as she led them to seats by the fire. "I have been thoughtless in not thanking you before," she said graciously, "but I know you understand how precious the hours have been since you brought me back my son."

"We're not heroes," said Avender. "Redburr and Nolo did all the work."

"Speak for yourself," said Ferris.

Giserre laughed, a beautiful, musical laugh that made them all as happy as she. She had never seemed more content. "Ferris," she said, "I fear sometimes your ambition appears to surpass even mine.

But yes, in this you are right. Avender speaks with false modesty. You are heroes. You have succeeded where many others failed."

"Redburr and Nolo did most of it," Avender insisted. "And Delven and Dale, and the other Dwarves. We hardly did anything at all."

"You risked your lives for your friend," said Giserre. "That is more than enough for heroes." She sat down beside Reiffen on the cushioned bench near the fire and took his hand in hers.

Reiffen echoed his mother's feeling. "I owe you my life," he said. "I shall never be able to repay you."

"You'd do the same for us," said Ferris.

"I thank you for the compliment." Reiffen dipped his head in a little bow. He spoke in the formal manner his mother had taught him, far different from any other way of speaking he had ever learned in Valing. "Let us hope the opportunity shall never arise."

"There's not much chance we'll ever be that lucky," said Avender.

"No," agreed Reiffen. "It is unlikely. Not while the Wizards live still."

Ferris turned to Giserre. "What about you, milady?" she asked, picking up the thread of Reiffen's formality. "Will you tell us what happened when you went to Malmoret?"

Giserre smiled at the girl and the whole room brightened. "Luckily, I never came to Malmoret," she said. "Had I, I might not have returned quickly enough to be in Valing for your homecoming. I met Brannis in Rimwichside, and though he pretended sympathy for my tale, he refused to allow me passage to Banking. He feigned I was his guest and would not hear of my departing, at least not so long as I intended to cross to the southern side of the river. 'Yours is not the only loss,' he said, preaching false wisdom. 'There are other mothers whose children have been taken by the Three. Someday the Wizards' grasp will stretch farther than their strength, and then they shall feel the thrust of Wayland and Banking vengeance.' Then, as if mere words might be enough to satisfy me, he turned away to feed his dogs."

"Mother was going to find some way to go on to Malmoret

anyway," said Reiffen. "But Prince Gerrit came to her in Rimwich instead."

"I have not seen my brother in many years." Giserre looked into the fire as she spoke, her memory far away. "He came as soon as he received the news I was in Brannis's court. Even so, he understood there was nothing to be done. To ride alone with a few others across the northern wastes would have achieved nothing. But we did not expect to raise an army in Rimwich, did we?" she added with a fresh smile, and the room brightened again with her cheer. "It was Redburr's plan that was the right choice all along. My son is returned to me."

"Am I?" he asked.

He gave them all a strange look. His eyes had widened until they were as deep and black as the Abyss, though he still stared intently at the fire. No light reflected from them, nor from the caps upon his fingers. Giserre looked upon him in alarm.

"We all know we cannot be certain nothing was done to me in Ussene," he continued bitterly. "I must watch myself as carefully as you. Who knows what I might do?"

"You won't do anything," said Ferris fiercely. "It'll be the Wizards, if something happens, not you. You haven't changed."

Reiffen shook his head. "You don't know what it's like," he said, "not knowing who you really are. I've had to live with that all my life. I am the proper king of Wayland and Banking both, but I will never sit on either throne."

Giserre stiffened. "You must never give up hope," she cautioned. "You may yet gain what is rightfully yours."

"It has already been mine for the taking once, Mother," Reiffen replied, coldness in his eyes. "Usseis offered it to me himself. Do you think I would ever accept it now, knowing that is precisely what he wants me to do?"

He stared hard at her, trying to make her understand. She pursed her lips and made no reply, but the happiness that had flushed her face began to fade.

"Maybe that's why Redburr's always telling you not to think about it," suggested Avender. "Maybe he knew something like this was coming all the time. Usseis using you, I mean."

"If not Usseis, then someone else." Reiffen's anger ebbed. Wearily, he leaned against the bench. "There's always a pretender to the throne in every history I've ever read." He raised his hands to the fire and spread his fingers wide, ignoring the iron caps.

"We'll make sure you don't do anything that isn't right," said Avender stoutly.

"We'll even rescue you again, if we have to," added Ferris.

Reiffen smiled, despite himself. "You would do that, wouldn't you."

But Giserre, who had never been rescued from her own misfortune, turned towards the windows beyond the fire. She had seen her son's determination, so opposite her own. The steady rain from the mist outside traced thin fingers along the glass. Sensing her sorrow, Ferris and Avender left mother and son alone once again.

"I knew he'd never be king," said Ferris, as they climbed with Anella back up beside the gorge. "He always knew better, except when he was small."

Avender made no reply. He wasn't so sure. It had always been exciting to dream about riding at a king's right hand, even if he and Reiffen had both stopped talking about it long ago. He supposed that was all over now. If Reiffen had really given the idea up, it was only right that he should, too.

Alone in his room that night, Avender went to the window and looked out across the lake. The bowl of the sky was filled with stars; the cloudless night ran free before the rising of the moon. He remembered the same stars set in the dark roof in the lough in Grangore, where the Dwarves had sung their song for Brydds. But these stars were different. These stars moved as the night swept round the world, and below them a soft wind brushed the mountains and the lake.

The curtains in the window touched his cheek. He remembered

his first sight of Issinlough, when the world had seemed for a moment to turn upside down. He remembered the dark mouth above the hill of bones. He remembered Durk, the mander chasing them down the stair, and the Shaper's gaping jaws, and knew he was lucky to be alive. There was nothing heroic about it. With a last shiver he crawled into bed; the sheets were soft and cool. For a moment, in the brief time between wakefulness and sleep, he remembered his mother beside him, kissing him on the forehead as she tucked him beneath the covers. It was good to be home, even if there were some things still missing. There was much that he and Reiffen had to do. The trip to Malmoret would still be planned, and the swords the Dwarves would fashion from the heartstone in the henges would need strong arms to wield them. He fell asleep with the stars still out and the wind whispering softly across the mountains from lake to sky.

A t the other end of the Neck, Reiffen lay at his old place by the fire and listened to the rumble of the gorge and the murmur of his mother's soft breathing. Try as he might, he couldn't sleep. Once, the thunder in the flume would have soothed him as much as his mother's voice, but neither had the power to comfort him now. The nightmare he had hoped to leave behind in Ussene had followed him all the way home.

He had been so relieved when he woke in his cell and found his friends standing over him. After all the misery and despair, he had thought he might really be rescued at last. Redburr was taking him home. Even when his black mood returned, and the memory of Usseis and Molio choked his sleep like ice on the lake in winter, he had hoped it was just the Stoneways. Maybe when he reached the surface his nightmares would fade.

For a while the beauty of Issinlough, and Mother Norra's homely cooking, had comforted him, but even those delights had lasted no longer than a day. Through each stage of the journey he had hoped the next would be different: the Vale of Grangore; the bustle of Mremmen; the bright, clear wind of the open sea. But each, in turn, had faded from delight. Each had washed him clean for only a short while. More and more he had come to pin his hopes on Valing, where his mother would brush his hair back from his face, and kiss him and tell him everything was all right. And she had.

But it hadn't been enough. Now Reiffen knew it would never be enough. The Wizards had stolen his life as thoroughly as he had stolen Molio's.

He would have to take it back.

Hope flashed through him at the thought. His eyes brightened; he stopped feeling sorry for himself. No longer wanting to even try to sleep, he tiptoed up the benches to the door. Softly he crept out to the narrow balcony that circled the Tear. The summer mist bathed his forehead; his bare feet gripped the wet rock without slipping. It was a wonderful feeling. Nothing so clean and fresh could ever be imagined in Ussene. Below him the water frothed and churned.

He wondered why he had never thought of this before. Perhaps he had to come home to understand. The fact that he had finally made up his mind made him feel immeasurably better. He would fight the Wizards on their own terms. He would return to Ussene and learn everything Fornoch offered to teach him and then, when the time was right, serve the Wizards back for what they had done to him. He wouldn't be able to tell anyone what he planned to do; they would have to think the Wizards had truly turned him. Avender would hate him, Ferris would despise him, but either was better than the sad, watchful pity they showed him now. Their wonder at his sacrifice when he triumphed in the end would make it all worthwhile. Yes, the Wizards had turned him. What they didn't know was that he planned to turn again.

The only question now was to find the quickest way back to Ussene. His thimbles clicked as he shifted his hands on the balcony railing. In an instant he remembered what Fornoch had told him about leaving part of himself behind. Perhaps there was a purpose to the thimbles after all.

He reached for the one on his left hand. Gently he tugged at the cold iron. The mist had made the surface slick, but the metal was rough enough that he could still get a good grip. Nothing happened. Frowning, he tried again more firmly. A second failure made him think, and then he recalled the Wizard adding a last command to his instructions. " 'All you must do is say the word,' " Fornoch had said.

What the word might be came to Reiffen almost as soon as he began to think about it. Fornoch wouldn't want to tax him on this particular test. Not if he didn't want Reiffen to change his mind.

There was no chance of that now. The word would be the same Ossdonc had spoken at the henge. Reiffen was sure of it. He took a deep breath and reached for his finger a third time.

"Reiffen? What are you doing out in the wet? Come in before you catch cold."

Giserre stood in the doorway, one hand clutching her robe. The warmth inside the Tear swirled past the open door and out into the night. Reiffen took a step forward to see his mother's face more clearly in the mist. Sharp sorrow rose within his chest as he remembered how terribly lonely he had been in Ussene.

He came to a sudden decision. "Mother," he said. "Take my hand."

With a smile Giserre reached for both of his with hers. His right remained curled around the little finger of his left. Drops of mist beaded like pearls in his mother's hair.

"Return," Reiffen whispered.

The thimble fell to the ground as he slipped it off his finger. The night winked clean away.

In the morning Avender woke to the warm sun peeping through the window and a pigeon cooing on the sill. He rushed into his clothes and down the stair. There were so many things he and Ferris and Reiffen planned to do on their first day home.

Ferris was already in the kitchen with her mother. "I've been down to the lower dock," she said excitedly. "Skimmer's already been by. Old Mortin says he told him he'll meet us at the Rock as soon as we get there."

"I've packed a lunch." Hern, her smile almost as wide as her daughter's, patted the top of a basket bursting with bread and jam and muffins and pie. "Why don't the two of you go rouse Reiffen while I make sure there's nothing I've left out."

Ferris and Avender raced through the scullery yard to the orchard. The pigs grunted as they passed. From the top of the Neck all Valing stretched south in ribbons of blue and green. At the top of the stair Ferris elbowed Avender aside with a laugh and darted on ahead. He finally caught her again at the second set of doors. She stood with her arms extended, holding the heavy oak panels apart, staring into the empty room.

"Where are they?"

A breath of mist tickled Avender's ear. "Look," he said. "The door to the balcony's open. Maybe they're out there."

"What's that on the ground?"

Avender looked down. Something small and dark wedged the door open against the jamb.

Ferris screamed.

Avender pounced on the thimble and pushed open the balcony door. The mist lifted its white fingers past the empty terrace toward the sky. Avender hardly dared look down. As quickly as he could on the slippery stone, he circled the outside of the Tear. The balcony was empty. He had almost convinced himself Reiffen and Giserre had made the circuit ahead of him by the time he reached the door at the other end; but, when he went back inside, Ferris was still alone.

She clutched her throat. Avender unfolded his hand; the iron thimble lay heavy and cold on his palm. It had to be one of Reiffen's. But whether Reiffen had fallen to his death in the gorge or been taken once more by the Wizards there was no way to tell.

Avender didn't know which possibility he dreaded more.